# Tornado Hill

a Novel
by

## Arley Owens, Jr.

Tornado Hill
Copyright © 2016 Arley Owens, Jr.

Bible quotations from the
Authorized King James version

Cover Art: CL Owens

Editor: Pitman Sanders

First Printing October 2016
Printed in the U.S.A.

Soft Cover Edition
ISBN: 978-0-9896273-4-4

SHORTY MAE PRODUCTIONS
P.O. BOX 81102
MIDLAND, TEXAS 79708

Other books by Arley Owens, Jr.
A Tale of the Mojave
The Cyrus Syndrome
A Texas Ghost Story
Incident in Baltimore
Death Ranch
20 Miles to Justified
The Genocide Directive

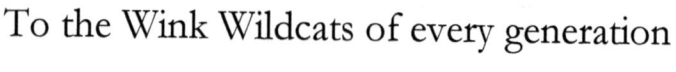

To the Wink Wildcats of every generation

# Preface

Though its central theme is high school football, *Tornado Hill* is not a sports story—it's more of a coming of age saga and is, most likely, the closest I'll ever come to writing a mainstream novel. You'll find no travelers lost in another dimension, no beautiful women pretending to be ghosts, no love-struck college student reliving sections of time, no out of body experiences, no sex cults or hardcore erotic scenes—no demons, angels, invisible towns, or any science fiction element.

This is a tale of what takes place in a small town in the Texas panhandle from the beginning of the Class 2A Division I High School Playoffs until the State Championship. I owe a debt of gratitude to my lifelong friend Jerry Don Payne for informing me that small towns like Wink, where we grew up and played football, are no longer classified as 1A but 2A (I'd used the former designation in the original manuscript).

*Tornado Hill* is my 8th published book but I actually wrote the first draft before *Death Ranch, 20 Miles to Justified,* and *The Genocide Directive* were conceived. When I finished that draft in 2010 I felt compelled to put it on a shelf, planning to leave it there indefinitely—feeling it was just one of those yarns I had to get written out of my system, like several other novels I've inked over the years that will never see the light of day.

Then, in July of 2014, during a creative quagmire where I was juggling several rough manuscripts around, I stumbled across *Tornado Hill* and decided to read it for a distraction—hoping to come away with at least an inkling about which of the other stories I should sink my teeth into for polishing. To my surprise the story moved me, and the passing of time had given me enough objectivity to clearly see it wasn't the characters or plot that caused me to bail on it before, but a rather weak homogeneity that could be remedied by some backdrop and expanding several scenes I'd moved through too quickly.

And so I decided to quit worrying about those other manuscripts for the time being and remain in Sleeping Bear, the imaginary town wherein this tale unfolds, and not a day went by since without me slaving on *Tornado Hill* until I felt honing the manuscript any further would only tend to sharpen it dull.

Now I humbly present the fruits of that labor. I hope you enjoy it and please spread the word if you do.

–Arley Owens, Jr.  December, 2015

"Football is not a contact sport, it's a collision sport—dancing is a contact sport." –Vince Lombardi

"I've learned that something constructive comes from every defeat." –Tom Landry

# CAST OF CHARACTERS:

Eli Adams: Computer Programming Genius.

Noah Adams: Resigned Seminary President, Reclusive Farmer, Eli's Uncle.

Will Amarod: Used Car Dealer in Langton.

Bud: The Budweiser Man.

Coach Rainey: Head Coach of the Sleeping Bear Kodiaks Varsity Football Team.

Jimmy Cocker: Kodiak Right Tackle on Offense and Defense, Sophomore.

Darlene Fox: Kodiak Head Cheerleader, Senior at Sleeping Bear High.

Anita Fury: Hooker.

Jetti Fury: Ward of Rutherford and Gwendolyn Simmons, Abandoned Daughter of Anita Fury, Senior at Sleeping Bear High.

Myles Grange: Sheriff of Kodiak County.

Wayne Harding: Kodiak Offensive Left Tackle, Right Defensive End, Senior.

Lucy Higgins: Amarillo Paramedic.

Kenny Higgins: Langton Lions Strong Side Linebacker, Lucy's Nephew.

Rick Holt: Kodiak Quarterback, Senior.

Steve Holt: Kodiak Equipment Manager, Sophomore.

Delbert Hutch: Kodiak Fullback and Weak Side Linebacker, Senior.

Truman Jette: Head Coach of the State Champion Langton Lions Football Team.

| | |
|---|---|
| Heckle Johns: | Yagerville Yellow Jackets Free Safety. |
| Seth Jones: | Kodiak Backup Quarterback, Sophomore. |
| Delores Kaye: | Kodiak Cheerleader, Junior. |
| Jerry Lane: | Langton Lions Quarterback. |
| Luther: | Al Pond's Valet and Chef. |
| Martin Lawrence: | Yagerville Yellow Jackets Wide Receiver. |
| Joie McClain: | Kodiak Cheerleader, Junior. |
| D. J. Morgan: | Winthrop Cougars Defensive End. |
| Bart Newly: | Saloon Proprietor and Deputy. |
| Kelly Newly: | Forman of the Pond Ranch, Bart's Nephew. |
| Abel Norris: | Kodiak Middle Linebacker and Offensive Left Guard, Junior. |
| Marybeth Overton: | Kodiak Cheerleader, Senior. |
| Dick Parsons: | Langton Lions Defensive Coordinator. |
| Allen Pierce: | Langton Lions Running Back. |
| Al Pond: | Owner of the Pond Ranch, Richest Man in Kodiak County. |
| Cooper Pond: | Kodiak Tight End and Strong Safety, Al's Son, Senior. |
| Cooper Forrest Pond: | Patriarch and Founder of the Pond Ranch in 1838. |
| Claudia Queen: | Registered Nurse in Abilene. |
| Pat Queen: | Kodiak Cheerleader, Claudia's Younger Sister, Sophomore. |
| Annabel Rainey: | Coach Rainey's Wife. |
| Emma Riley: | Irish Widow, Newspaper Woman. |

| | |
|---|---|
| Cindy Shane: | Junior at Sleeping Bear High. |
| Gwendolyn Simmons: | Rutherford's Wife. |
| Rutherford Simmons: | Second Richest Man in Kodiak County. |
| Bibi Smith: | Kodiak Cheerleader, Senior. |
| Gilbert Smith: | Kodiak Center and Defensive Left Tackle, Bibi's Fraternal Twin, Senior. |
| Burl Swain: | Deceased Entrepreneur. |
| Burly Swain: | Owner of The Kodiak Cave Restaurant, Burl's Son. |
| Ruthie Swain: | Burly's Sister. |
| Dearl Tipps: | Kodiak Tailback and Strong Side Linebacker, Senior. |
| Maureen Tipps: | Disowned Daughter of Rutherford and Gwendolyn Simmons, Dearl's Mother. |
| Mike Vaughn: | Kodiak Left Wide Receiver and Left Cornerback, Junior. |
| Lyle Whitney: | Kodiak Right Wide Receiver and Free Safety, Junior. |
| Hugo Wildemont: | Langton Lions Wide Receiver. |
| Rex Winters: | Owner and Editor of The Hibernator Newspaper. |
| Mark York: | Kodiak Kicker, Senior. |
| Zechariah: | Mysterious Tramp with no Last Name. |

# Prologue I

40 years ago: a small farm south of Little Rock, Arkansas

Noah Adams heard a baby crying.

He killed the engine and dismounted his tractor, stepping into withered corn stalks over six feet high.

*Waaaaaaaaaaaaaah!!!*

Following the sound, Noah threaded his way through the dead remains of this season's harvest—thanking God for alerting him to the infant's presence. He could easily have turned the poor child to mulch otherwise. Ten, twenty, thirty, at least forty paces he shoved through the lifeless forest before halting in his tracks. Centered on a circle of soft grass he'd never seen before, lay a newborn baby boy, forehead and eyes covered by a thin film of afterbirth.

His mind reeled as he gawked at the scene before him. There were no trails through the brittle stalks save that which he'd formed getting here. Either someone managed to clear a two-foot diameter circle from a helicopter before lowering the patch of grass and infant from it, or they'd been deposited by the hand of God.

*Waaaaaaaaaaaaaah!!!*

Leaning over, he brushed away the gooey caul and pulled the baby gently to his chest. The tot stopped crying but Noah was hyperventilating.

The grass had vanished.

He looked up at the clear sky and prayed for guidance. A small cloud blew over, holding just enough moisture to color it gray, then the wind kicked up—thirty miles an hour at least. Not bothering with his hat, probably a half acre away by now, he fought the stiff draft all the way to his house. When he reached for the doorknob the wind stopped.

Noah gave the sky one last glance. Three separate cloud streams, each resembling a giant frayed rope, were stretched across the blueness, perfectly parallel. Then the strands spiraled around each other, forming an uncannily tidy braid that grew tighter and tighter. Chills bubbled through his insides as the cloudy plait formed an equilateral triangle before dispersing into a faint mist that soon disappeared.

Noah hurried into the house, laid the baby on the center of his bed, and while surrounding him with pillows so he couldn't roll off, the tiny penis caught his eye: it didn't have foreskin.

*Waaaaaaaaaaaaaah!!!*

He started to pick him back up but just the touch of his hands immediately quieted the boy. Noah pulled away, the infant wailed until feeling his palms again. Twice more he did it and got the same result. "A sign from God, has to be!"

*Waaaaaaaaaaaaaah!!!* he heard the whole time milk warmed on the stove.

Once more the baby stopped wailing the instant he touched him. Noah cradled the child in his left arm and fed him from a bottle whose nipple had only been sucked by orphaned sheep and piglets until now.

"That's right, little fella, siphon it all down, then I'll put you back on the bed for a nap. While you sleep I'll make a run to town for diapers, pajamas, human nursing formula, and a crib."

Any sane man would take him to an orphanage, thought Noah, but he couldn't shake the notion God had sent the boy for him to raise. The disappearing grass, strange wind and cloud formation, had to be signs from heaven. What other reason could there be for sending him here?

Noah felt the same spiritual compulsion that had caused him to resign from the seminary, where he'd served for years as president. Yes, he concluded, the child was sent for him, and him alone, to care for and teach. The Lord wanted the boy sequestered from the world until the time came to send the lad into it to perform His will.

"I don't know what The Almighty has planned for you," he said to the miraculously circumcised infant, "but you're

bound to have a very special call on your life. Sorry you
won't have a mother's love, but I'm committed to a life of
celibacy."


## COUNTY OF LOS ANGELES

Coroner's report – Jane Doe #**3
Race: Caucasian
Immediate Cause of Death: Maternal, post partum bleeding.
Fate of infant unknown.

# Prologue II

19 years ago: Kodiak County Fairgrounds, Texas Panhandle

She'd been two grades behind him in school. Now he was a sophomore at Texas and she was a senior at Sleeping Bear High, working the kissing booth at the Easter Bunny Fair, held every third Saturday in March. He had his back to her, ordering something at the concession stand.

Kelly Newly, a junior, paid his dollar and got his smooch with her still looking at *him*.

"It's an honor to kiss the Kodiaks' best player."

"That mean I get another'n for free?"

"No, Kelly, it doesn't," she answered, still gazing past the fullback, watching the guy she'd been mad for since seventh grade slip away from view.

Rex Winters, Kelly's best friend, laid his dollar down and grinned. "Pucker up."

After Rex collected his smack she hollered at Anita Fury, walking by with a fresh ball of cotton candy.

"Yes?" said Anita.

"Would you mind taking my place for awhile? I need a break."

Shocked by the request, but obviously flattered, Anita said, "Me?"

"If you don't mind."

"I better not. I'm sure it would offend some people if you know what I mean." The eleventh-grader moved to Sleeping Bear from El Paso last year and word soon got around that Anita was a prostitute.

"Oh, never mind, Anita!" *He* was heading for the booth. "I'll take a break later."

Anita strolled away and he walked up.

"Where's your wife?"

He heaved a sigh and glanced away for a moment. "Left

her in Austin . . . We seemed to have come to an impasse."

Heart pounding, knees weak, she could barely hide her excitement. *Act sympathetic!* "Um, care to talk about it?"

His eyes wandered to the strawberry blonde ponytail covering the front of her left shoulder and upper arm as he appeared to think it over.

Pretending she had an itch on her spine, she reached back to scratch it, which forced her boobs to really stick out.

It worked. He shifted his gaze to them—then, slowly, to her face.

"Well," he said with a nervous smile, "if you're willing to listen I'd like to discuss it . . . but I sure can't do it here."

"Hang around until a girl passes by that I can talk into replacing me, then you can take me somewhere."

He waited patiently as she took care of ten more customers before a fellow senior agreed to work the booth, collecting dollars for the First Baptist Church, and they were soon in his pickup.

"So you came back to Sleeping Bear by yourself, huh?" she asked as he drove north on the Amarillo Highway.

"Yeah. You know what, it just dawned on me I forgot to buy a kiss."

"I'll see that your dollar makes it to the coffer. Of course you'll have to kiss me before I'll take it."

On his face—*The Look*—he wanted her too. He didn't want to want her but couldn't help it, she could tell. It made her feel guilty, but she couldn't pass up this chance to finally be intimate with him—she'd probably never get another. "We seemed to have come to an impasse," he'd said. He and that beautiful Austin blonde had come to an *IMPASSE.*

"I might not be able to make him leave her," she said to herself, "but he's mine right now."

# The Next Morning

She woke up in her own bed with brutal regret over being in his yesterday, the one he'd slept in before leaving his childhood home.

Reality could be such an ugly thing at times, so cruelly infringing on idyllic dreams—but a dream was all it had been. His status, his handsomeness, his charismatic charm had convinced her she *should* see him as that special one, but she'd fallen in love with a mirage. At some point between their first kiss and his sexual climax, she'd been devastated to find the powerful love she felt for him held no true carnal aspect—it was merely strong affection, not much unlike that shared by close siblings. And since she did feel that way about him, she couldn't bear for anyone to know he'd been unfaithful to his wife.

He'd been in an extremely vulnerable state and she'd taken advantage of it, therefore the guilt lay squarely on her. That sweet, sensitive man was innocent and she'd hurt him. But she'd never do it again. His marriage might be over and it might not, but either way no one would ever hear about his adultery from her lips. She'd take that secret to her grave.

# PART 1

# Strangers ain't welcome here

# 1

## *The Present*

ZECHARIAH HAD BEEN WALKING ALONG the same highway for days, sleeping in fields, eating whatever he could kill or catch—usually a rabbit, dove, or rattlesnake—but sometimes he had to settle for insects. According to a road sign his destination lay three miles ahead: Sleeping Bear, a small Texas town located southwest of Amarillo.

He paused to adjust a leather belt cinched like a holster around the waist of his faded jeans. Upon one side hung a sheathed hunting knife and a pouch containing a slingshot, tooth brush, and baking soda. A canteen and canvas bag—holding toilet paper, hand sanitizer, coffee, shortening, salt, and pepper—dangled from the other. The travel-thinned soles of his shapeless boots wouldn't hold out much longer. Zechariah suspended one foot in the air for several seconds, then the other to cool them a mite. Loosening the straps of a knapsack stuffed with pup tent, sleeping bag, coffee pot, cast iron skillet, basic cooking utensils, and a hatchet, he eased it off his sweaty back and lowered it to the ground for a few minutes' relief.

It was late autumn but the temperature had to be in the nineties. He unsnapped his threadbare denim shirt to air out his chest—sticky with perspiration, rancid with body odor—and flapped the tails a few times to fan his sides. While refastening it, he gazed down the sweltering asphalt of the two lane highway.

The dank stench of crude oil had been assaulting his nostrils for the last few miles, stinking like rotten eggs in the arid breeze. It'd grown stronger the closer he got to a battery of storage tanks up ahead. Off to the north, a spiraling composition of red rock projected skyward from the flat horizon, ending in a plateau that seemed to balance itself atop the tower as if it was a separate configuration altogether. The formation looked like a wide tornado composed of reddish rock. He'd never seen a stranger natural phenomenon in his life.

Judging by the position of the sun, he made the time to be around three o'clock, but checked his pocket watch to be sure. Three-fifteen. A panel van whizzed by, stopped, and reversed towards him. Zechariah motioned for the driver to go on ahead. He'd walked almost six hundred miles and had been forced to turn down over a dozen drivers who'd offered a ride.

♦♦♦

Chewing on the eraser of his number 2 pencil as Coach Rainey rambled about an algebraic equation—punctuating his remarks on the blackboard with a stick of chalk—Dearl Tipps couldn't keep his mind on the hodgepodge of numbers, letters, dashes, equal signs, and parenthesis. Tomorrow's playoff game in Plainview preoccupied him.

2A schools didn't have enough players for the good ones to play only on offense or defense. First string on both, Dearl also played on special teams. He was the tailback and strong side linebacker on a varsity football team that had just completed an undefeated regular season for the fourth year in a row. That feat had never been done before in Sleeping

Bear.

He glanced at his best bud, Cooper Pond, and saw he was pretending to find the blackboard interesting as well. Coo played tight end and strong safety. Dearl shifted his gaze to a window. Tornado Hill stood like a sentinel, two miles past the western edge of town. The remarkable edifice rose six hundred feet, twisting upward before mushrooming into a level expanse of rock that seemed to defy gravity. Even from as far away as his algebra two class he could see the pock marks and winding scars of erosion on the red funnel which gave it an animated appearance, making it appear to actually be spinning like a real cyclone. It always seemed to be inching towards town, even though it hadn't moved at all since some odd geologic aberration formed it back in prehistoric times.

"Pearl, you with us?" Coach Rainey spouted.

"Uh, yes sir, Coach!" Dearl snapped to attention, focusing his eyes on the blackboard, knowing he was about to be made an example of because Rainey called him Pearl. He only used the term when either excited about something Dearl had done, such as scamper ninety yards for a touchdown, or upset with him, like now.

"Glad to hear it. Tell us what the C-Two variable represents."

Dearl thought about guessing but knew he'd only be in deeper water if he missed, so he opted for total honesty. "Don't know, Coach."

Giggles arose from just about every girl in the room but there were a few males cackling as well, and Coo was one of them. Dearl wanted to shoot him a go-to-hell look and give him the finger but he'd be dead meat if Coach Rainey saw it.

"All right, settle down," Coach commanded. A hush fell over the classroom and a slow grin formed on Rainey's square-jawed face. "I know it's hard to concentrate on math with a big game tomorrow, Tipps, but you keep your brains on algebra till that bell rings. And once it does I don't want you thinking about anything except annihilating Winthrop. Got me?"

"Yes, sir." Dearl sighed with relief over receiving such light chastisement.

As soon as Coach turned back to the board, Dearl gave Cooper that look, but Coo donned a disarming grin and he found himself grinning back in spite of himself. Then, to his horror, he saw Jetti Fury thought he was grinning at her. Taking full advantage of the situation, she cast him one of her flirty smiles. Dearl jerked his head forward, facing the blackboard. Like a laser beam burning into the side of his face, he could feel her staring. It made him painfully nervous.

His problem with Jetti Fury wasn't because she didn't meet his standards—she had gorgeous brown hair, so dark it was almost black, that hung to the middle of her back, sometimes in braids. Her killer gray eyes, straight-edged nose, and pouting lips were the sexiest he'd ever seen. Besides having a fantastic build on a five-eight frame, she was also brainy, and belonged to a rich family.

Jetti made him uncomfortable because she intimidated him. No other girl in sleeping Bear did, only her, because nobody else could shatter his insides like she could if he let himself fall for her. Jetti attracted him more than Delilah could possibly have enticed Samson, but her draw to him was propelled only by what he did on the football field. Before size began to catch up to his talent four years ago, she didn't know he existed.

He wanted to check, hoping his instincts were wrong and she wasn't looking anymore, but fearing she'd catch him, he focused on the blackboard as Coach Rainey edified and pointed—answering his own questions for the benefit of the class. Something hit the side of his neck. Dearl turned to see Cooper, who'd thrown a spit wad, silently laughing while pointing back and forth between him and Jetti, thankfully now looking at the blackboard. He shot Cooper the bird and turned towards Coach Rainey, scribbling more notations on the blackboard. A large analog clock on the wall showed the time to be three twenty-five. The bell would ring in five minutes.

It was Dearl's last class of the day and the only one he shared with Jetti Fury. From there he'd go to the Kodiak locker room—located in the new gym, constructed a hundred yards away from the stadium—to change into his game uniform for the short pre-game workout. They took place on Thursdays during the regular season, but playoff games were played on Saturdays, so dress rehearsal got moved forward a day.

When the bell rang he waited until Jetti left before rising from his desk.

Cooper punched him on the shoulder. "Buuuck buck-buck-buck."

Dearl sneered at him. "Cut it out, Coo, I ain't no chicken!"

"Oh yeah? The prettiest girl you and I will probably ever see in person has the hots for you and you're too chicken-shit to take advantage of it. Buuuuuuuuuck buck-buck-buck—"

"Cut it out, man." He headed for the door with Cooper right behind him. "She doesn't really like me, she's just trying to snag me because I'm a football star, and I ain't got no use for fair weather chicks."

Coo, now beside him, said, "I'm a football star too, and she doesn't like me."

"Yeah, but you're ugly."

"Well hell, so are you."

Both laughing, they ambled down a hallway bustling with students hurrying from the building. The school day had just concluded for most of them. They made their way outdoors and headed for the gymnasium.

A couple of giggly sophomores walked past, gaping at them with admiration. Dearl gave the girls a nod of appreciation.

Cooper pulled a comb from his hip pocket and ran it through his thick dark-blonde hair, remarkably similar to Dearl's in both color and texture. "Want me to move things along between you and Jetti?"

He glared at him. "You keep your fucking nose out of this, Stupor-Cooper!"

"Nothing stupid about it, dickhead. C'mon, let me talk to her and—"

"No!"

"All right, chicken shit, but you're making a mistake."

"You tend to your own business and let me worry about mine, rich boy."

Cooper heaved a frustrated sigh. "Okay, poor boy, whatever you say."

Dearl tried not to show the remark wounded him. He *was* a poor boy, though he never felt like it until someone reminded him. When it got put into words the reality of it bit into him, turning his whole world gray until the emotion ebbed. When anyone even hinted about it, he seemed to lose a piece of himself. Cooper never used the term maliciously—it was just a retaliatory nickname Coo had come up with after he'd started referring to him as 'rich boy' back in grade school—and it usually didn't hurt at all. He didn't know why it impacted him so hard this time.

The heavy air in the locker room reeked of salt tablets, sweat, and liniment. Steve Holt, the equipment manager, was laying out the game uniforms. Born with club feet, Steve had been denied the athletic prowess of his older brother Rick, the quarterback. He deposited a deep blue jersey with a white 89 on front and back at Cooper's stall.

Coo offered a high five. "What say, Holt?"

Dearl did likewise.

"What say?" Steve echoed while returning their gestures.

Dearl's locker lay a ways down from Cooper's because they were delegated by jersey numbers. He stopped at 20 and undressed as fullback Delbert Hutch, 21, kicked off his shoes. Blacker than the ace of spades, Hutch had a huge mouth showcasing dazzling white teeth that looked like they belonged on a horse. Though only five-eight, Hutch was one big two-thirty pound muscle who'd yet to meet the dude he couldn't lay out with one punch. On defense he took care of the weak side as linebacker while Dearl manned the strong side. Abel Norris, a husky junior with a ton of talent, played middle linebacker.

Hutch slapped him on the ass and said, "You better fetch us some touchdowns tomorrow, Tipps, or I'll know the reason why. Hear?"

Dearl covered his heart with both hands. "Hutch, would I ever let you down?"

The fullback donned his horse smile. "You da man!"

"Just don't fumble." The voice came from the other side of Dearl and belonged to number nineteen, Rick Holt. Six-four, sculpted like a Greek god, the quarterback had the features of a movie star. Dearl wondered why Rick and Jetti Fury had never hooked up. They were made for each other, each a perfect specimen of their gender. For whatever reason they hadn't, and Rick's girl of the moment—no female in Sleeping Bear with the possible exception of Jetti could say no to him it seemed—was Darlene Fox, a luscious blonde who'd broken Cooper's heart in eighth grade.

Dearl always felt short when he stood next to Rick, two inches taller than Cooper. They perfectly stair-stepped in height: him 6-0, Coo 6-2, Rick 6-4.

"I predict you'll make at least four rushing touchdowns tomorrow, Tipps." Rick spoke it with utter confidence while putting on his shoulder pads. He seemed intent on smoothing over the jab about the fumble.

"What makes you say that?"

"Because Rainey informed me D. J. Morgan got his knee blown out in practice yesterday."

D. J. Morgan was Winthrop's All State defensive end.

"Let's hope you're right." Dearl stuck his head through the hole of his shoulder pads. "But Morgan's not the only reason Winthrop ranked so high in rushing defense, their linebackers are awesome. I'll be lucky to cross the goal line on a run even once, but hopefully we'll win anyway."

*"Hopefully* we'll win? C'mon, Tipps, you gotta believe, man. It's gonna be a one-sided blowout all the way. Give me a hand."

Dearl pulled the quarterback's jersey over his shoulder pads.

"Thanks. Turn around and I'll do you."

Cooper walked up, fully dressed, carrying a blue helmet with a single white stripe down the middle and a menacing bear's head on one side, a bear's paw print on the other. "Sounds like a personal thing."

Holt hung him the bird. "Get a life, Pond."

Delbert Hutch backed up to them. "Hey, somebody do me."

"No problem, bro." Cooper grabbed the tail of Hutch's jersey and yanked it down.

The four of them were seniors, and being recruited by major colleges. After losing all but one game in the seventh grade, they vowed to never have another losing season and to win State in high school. They won only two games more than they lost in eighth grade, but after making the varsity as freshmen they became the All Stars of a team that never experienced a regular season loss in four years of high school play. However, they'd yet to win a playoff game, and the same team ended their season three years in a row.

That team, the Langton Lions, had four stars of their own that had grown up together like Cooper, Rick, Delbert, and him. In three consecutive battles for the Bi-District title the Sleeping Bear Kodiaks had fallen to the Langton Lions 42-20, 35-21, and 31-28. The last defeat was the most painful to Dearl because they would have won if he hadn't fumbled the ball on the Langton one yard line during a run which should have gone for the winning touchdown with no time left on the clock.

One of the Langton Four, a linebacker named Kenny Higgins, made the mistake of trying to tackle him high from behind after penetrating the line on a blitz. Dearl carried him on his back for three yards and would have made it to the end zone, but Higgins managed to strip the ball at the one and it sailed out of bounds, ending the game and the Kodiak season. The Lions went on to become state champs for the third consecutive time. Everyone had been sympathetic, but Dearl never forgave himself.

The imaginary line marking the eastern boundary of the district area next to Amarillo's, within which lay Sleeping Bear, ran right through Langton. This year the Lions had been designated part of the district to the east of that line instead of the one west of it, so the Kodiaks would be facing the Winthrop Cougars for Bi-District this time.

Coach Rainey and his three assistant coaches had everyone's attention on the field. "Okay, girls, we didn't draw the Lions this year but don't get overconfident. The Cougars are full of talent and they want to advance as much as we do. As most of you already know, D. J. Morgan won't be on that field tomorrow, but his backup would be starting on another team so don't think the going will be any easier because of

Morgan's injury. In the end it'll be the team that makes the fewest mistakes that'll win. Say it with me, girls—*no mistakes!*"

"No mistakes!" shouted the whole team.

"Okay, let's do a walk through . . . ."

♦♦♦

Bibi was proud as peaches of her brother Gilbert. No longer uncoordinated because of his mammoth size, he'd been outstanding at football this year, playing center and left defensive tackle, first string on both. Like their daddy before them, and Grandpa Smith before him, they were born and raised in Sleeping Bear. They actually came into the world thirty minutes apart in an Amarillo hospital, but only because Sleeping Bear didn't have one. Thankfully, blonde hair and blue eyes were the only genetic traits she shared with the goliath besides a high smile. Gilbert had love handles and a double chin, she was very svelte—weighing a mere 105—and had learned how to grin without exposing her upper gums during the sixth grade.

The 70 on the back of Gilbert's jersey disappeared from her view and most of the white stripe running the length of his blue pants turned almost perfectly horizontal as he got set to hike the ball. She sat in the stands with her fellow cheerleaders awaiting the first snap of this pre-game practice.

Dearl Tipps took a handoff from Rick Holt and ran half speed behind Gilbert, pushing back an imaginary lineman to give 20 a running lane.

♦♦♦

Cindy Shane didn't sit on the first row in the home stands to watch the Kodiaks practice every time they went through their dress rehearsals—she hated Sleeping Bear—yet never missed the ritual because of a particular senior. He always stood near the bench when the coach spent the first ten minutes or so talking to the players before the action started.

She never bothered with any of the full workouts. They took place on the practice field, the players wore boring dull-white uniforms, and there was no place for spectators to sit.

Her parents drug her to this fucked up town from Lubbock nine months ago, promising she'd get used to living here. Nothing had changed, and she'd relish hearing about its revered football team blowing Bi-District for a fourth straight time. She never went to any of their games, home or away. However, she secretly rooted for 89, Cooper Pond, and loved seeing him in his game uniform. A grade ahead of her, they didn't share any classes but she often saw him in between, and always during lunch, where she'd sit as close to him as possible in the cafeteria.

Cooper only dated popular girls so she hadn't been able to catch his eye so far. She never passed up an opportunity to say hi and he always returned the greeting with that sexy smile of his, appraising her boobs each time.

Hopefully someday he'd also notice she had a pretty face and ask her out.

Darlene Fox, the head cheerleader, and several of the other girls in the 'popular' clique were also in the stands. She savored the fact that Jetti Fury, hands down the most beautiful girl in Sleeping Bear, didn't hang with them. Snotty Darlene wouldn't be the leader then, she'd be in second place by a large margin. Jetti was very special and she'd love to make friends with her, but the girl kept to herself. Cindy hadn't gotten close to anyone, but other than the cheerleaders most of the girls were friendly with her, and all the boys. In her opinion only Jetti topped her in looks but she didn't care to be outgoing like she'd been in Lubbock because she fucking *loathed* Hicksville, her term of disdain for Sleeping Bear.

There was nothing to do here—no mall or bowling alley, no Chuck E. Cheese or pizza places of any kind, no Chinese food restaurants. The Kodiak Cave offered the only place to eat out, and the one movie theater had been out of business for years. Being underage she couldn't go in the bar to shoot pool, something she loved to do even though she wasn't very good at it.

Sleeping Bear didn't even have a jewelry store, just a small assortment of rings, bracelets, earrings, and necklaces at Overton's Drug & Variety and a dress shop that sold men's clothing as well. The nearest Walmart was in Amarillo and the only place to buy music of any kind was at Overton's, which also served made to order ice cream treats.

No wonder all the kids that grew up here had such strong school spirits: their only entertainment away from home was sports and school dances.

◆◆◆

Her clothes were strewn across his desk chair. In the dark closet he mauled her breasts and groin with his soft, puffy hands while slobbering kisses on her mouth and throat with drooling lips, before forcing her to kneel down and take his limp penis into her mouth. He thrust back a forth a few times—grunted—and his putrid semen dribbled onto the back of her tongue. It was all she could do to keep from puking as she leaned forward to keep that shit from going down her throat. He huffed and coughed while regaining his composure.

He stepped outside to get dressed, closing the door behind him. She hastily wiped her tongue dry on an inside corner of his smoking jacket and waited until he summoned her before coming out. That was the way the living nightmare always went. Though the pervert had never said it, she knew he'd instituted that command because he couldn't bear for her to see him naked. She, on the other hand, would have to dress in front of him just as she had to let him watch as she took her clothes off. Sometimes he undressed her before sending her into the closet to await his nude arrival.

"Okay, you can come out now." His voice sounded weak, drained, old.

She opened the door and stepped into the light, body glistening with mild sweat caused from lack of ventilation rather than any form of arousal. As his sunken eyes, filled with unhinged lust, ogled her nakedness, she barely managed to hide how repulsed she felt.

"Better get dressed quick, hon. Grandma'll be home any minute."

"Yes, Grandpa." She reached for her bra he'd slung over the chair while eagerly undressing her a few minutes ago.

◆◆◆

When the Kodiaks' short pre-game workout ended, Marybeth Overton left the stands with the rest of the cheerleaders: Darlene Fox, Bibi Smith, Joie McClain, Delores

Kaye, and Pat Queen. The lone black-haired member of the squad, Marybeth was also the shortest at five-two. Joie had dark brown hair, Pat's was medium-brown, the other three were natural blondes.

She had the dubious distinction of being the only one who'd ever lived anywhere but Sleeping Bear. Her family had moved here from Clovis, New Mexico after her brother graduated and she'd advanced to seventh grade. Her pharmacist dad leased the ancient drug store that had been around since the 1920's. Other owners had refurbished parts of the huge building but her favorite area, unused for years before the Overton name got painted on a new sign, had been renovated by a construction crew hired by her daddy.

Like Darlene and Bibi, she'd made cheerleader as a seventh grader and every year since. Now they were seniors and would once again be cheering for the mighty Kodiaks to win Bi-District tomorrow. She hoped to God it wouldn't be the last time the three of them would don their cute blue-and-white outfits for a high school football game.

The seventh grade Kodiaks had been a disaster and barely managed a winning season in the eighth, but ever since then they'd only tasted defeat at the hands of the Langton Lions. When she'd heard there'd be no chance of playing Langton for Bi-District this year two opposing emotions had battled within her: relief there'd be no rematch, anger there wouldn't. At the moment relief led the race, but her wrath could also be satisfied, for she'd just been informed by Darlene that if neither the Kodiaks nor Lions got knocked out of the playoffs they'd be squaring off again, but this time for the 2A Division-I State Championship.

# 2

REX WINTERS RAN THE HIBERNATOR, the only newspaper in Sleeping Bear. He bought it sixteen years ago from the last living relative of the original owner—who published the first edition in 1897—and still hadn't upgraded to offset print, using the old linotypes and Ludlow instead. Hot metal typesetting was in his blood, he guessed. He was working on tomorrow's game, filling in as many slots as he could without knowing the outcome. The next edition would hit the streets the day after so he had to make sure only the unknown details remained to complete it.

His only employee was Emma Riley, a fiery-eyed redhead who'd immigrated to America at the age of twenty to marry a Fort Worth businessman fifteen years older. He'd come to her native Ireland to work out a complicated import deal, happened to pick the pub she worked in to unwind each evening, and they wound up falling in love. But tragedy struck. A skiing accident put him in a coma and Emma became a widow before their first anniversary. For nine years she'd remained in their beautiful Fort Worth home, occupying her time with charity work and social events, turning down several marriage proposals along the way.

Four years ago she'd driven through Sleeping Bear on her way to visit a friend who'd moved to Goodwell, Oklahoma. She stopped at The Kodiak Cave for lunch and sat down at a table next to his, where he'd been working on a cheeseburger. Emma struck up a conversation and they wound up trading life stories. After a three day visit with her friend in Oklahoma, she returned to Sleeping Bear and never left.

Financially independent due to inheriting her husband's estate, she hadn't been looking for a job, but hearing about what it took to get each edition of The Hibernator out on time every Wednesday and Sunday had prompted her to say, "Have you no one to help you then?"

"An occasional teenager," he'd replied. "There aren't any adults around here willing to work for minimum wage. Small town newspapers aren't exactly gold mines. I do all right but can't afford to pay more than that without cutting into my monthly retirement fund."

She'd donned a faint smile and said, "There's something I haven't told you, Rex—I'm looking for a new start in life, and this friendly small town seems the ideal place to find it. So laidback, no traffic jams, nobody to badger me for a bloody donation. Your newspaper sounds like a challenge I'd enjoy. I'll work for you if you'd be willing to teach me."

He'd hired her on the spot but didn't start training Emma until she returned after visiting her friend.

Unable to find a house she liked, he'd invited her to stay with him in his rambling two storey. They enjoyed a totally platonic relationship, a fact every Sleeping Bear resident well knew. However, they sometimes quibbled and chided each other like an old married couple.

"We'll win State this year," he muttered over his plates.

Emma looked up from her print tray. "Hope so, but we've gotten knocked out early in the playoffs every year since I've been here. Why should this one be any different?"

"Simple, we're not playing Langton for Bi-District this time."

"It amazes me how seriously you Texans take your football."

"Oh, it's not just us Texans, Emma. All sports replicate

combat, and football is the ultimate. It's the closest thing to war you can get without the real thing."

"Closest thing to war, me arse—it *is* war." She placed a section of stamped-out lead on her tray. "Those kids try to kill each other, I swear."

Rex ran a hand over his thinning brown hair and realigned a segment of linotype. "Nah, it just looks that way. There's a real strategy for everything that's being done on the field."

"So did you play football when you were a kid, Rex?"

"With my slight build, are you kidding me? No way I wanted any part of that bone-breaking fray."

Emma laughed. "So, it's not war but you were scared to get into the bone-breaking fray—right?"

"Right," he answered with a grin.

"Right. Thanks for clearing that up for me."

"Pretty hypocritical sounding, I guess."

"Just a titch."

"Football really is, I dunno, spiritual for lack of a better term. Even those of us too chicken to play the game enjoy it every bit as much as those who do. When they win we win, when they lose we lose. It's some sort of emotional connection that can't be explained by mere words."

"So it's a religion then, is it?" she giggled. "In Ireland football is taken very seriously as well, but it's not what you Yanks would call football."

"So I've heard."

"I do hope they can pull it off this time. That poor Tipps kid. When he fumbled last year I just wanted to cry, my heart broke for him so."

Rex adjusted a metal paragraph beneath the headline. "That was a tough break all right, but he didn't drop the ball, it got stripped. He's being recruited by every major college in the state. Oklahoma, Kansas, and Nebraska have sent scouts down here to look at him as well. Dearl Tipps is the best high school football player I've ever seen. He'll play professionally, no doubt about it."

"He needs to. That poor mum of his needs the financial relief."

"Yeah, poor Maureen. That's a real sad situation."

Emma wiped her hands on her apron, fished a cigarette from one of the side pockets, and lit up. "Exactly what happened there, anyway?"

He eyed her exhalation with longing. "Dearl's mother got pregnant with him shortly before she graduated high school. Her father disowned her and she moved to Lubbock. Nobody knew where she'd gone until she came back with a new last name when Dearl was five. Maureen worked at Piggly Wiggly before she got afflicted with multiple sclerosis. Ever since then she's been on disability."

An indignant frown swooped across Emma's face. "How could her father be so cruel?"

"I don't know. Anyway, no one ever knew who sired the baby, or if they did, they kept it to themselves."

"Who was her father?"

"Is, you mean. Rutherford Simmons."

"That rich old fart, you've got to be kidding me!"

"Nope. Why he never gave in and took her back into the fold, I don't know, but they act like total strangers."

Emma took a drag and exhaled while saying, "Where was the lad born?"

"Don't know."

"What a cold hearted bastard Simmons is—disowning his own daughter and not taking her back even when she gets stricken with such a horrible disease."

"Yeah, pretty cruel dude." He watched her take another drag. Cigarettes had to be the most addicting thing on Earth, and he wished he'd never touched one. He'd smoked his last one years ago but still craved them as bad as ever. "Wonder what he'll do when his grandson turns pro and becomes a millionaire."

"Humph! Bet he'll change his tune then, all right. I certainly hope Dearl doesn't give him a bloody cent. It'll serve the old wanker right."

An idea struck him. "You know what, Emma? I think we should do some digging, find out if Maureen married a guy named Tipps or just acquired the name on her own—and if she did really get married, get the background on her husband, all that good stuff. Dearl is destined to become a sports celebrity, and his hometown newspaper might as well have the scoop on him. Don't you agree?"

She grinned. "Where do we start?"

"Right at the source. Dearl's mother Maureen."

"Think she'll tell you anything then?"

"Won't know till I try, will I?"

♦♦♦

Business was slower than hell, Will Amarod hadn't sold a used car in almost two weeks. He'd bought the dealership in Langton for a song three years ago and soon found out why the guy had been so eager to unload it. Just about everybody in this town went to Wichita Falls to buy vehicles. Good thing there were plenty of pot smokers around or he'd be in the red.

Dick Parsons, defensive coordinator for the Langton Lions, purchased a new set of tires from him ten days ago. That was the last honest dollar he'd made. They'd discussed the upcoming playoff game and Dick had said he was relieved to be in a new district.

"Why's that?" he'd asked the assistant coach.

"So we won't have to play Sleeping Bear for Bi-District again."

"Hell, Dick," he'd replied, "seems to me you'd love to have the Kodiaks—they've never beaten you guys."

"The players *are* disappointed over it but not me. We barely scraped by them last year. If Kenny Higgins hadn't stripped the ball from Dearl Tipps Sleeping Bear would be the defending State Champs. We were the only team that came near matching them, and it suits me fine not to have them on our slate this year . . . at least not yet."

# 3

THE GAME HAD BEEN A blowout as Rick Holt predicted. Sleeping Bear beat the Cougars 42-0 to advance to the Area playoffs where they'd face the Hitchcock Hogs in Wichita Falls. Dearl had scored five rushing touchdowns and Cooper caught a nice pass from Holt for the other. The bus ride back from Plainview had been bedlam, with all the guys running on pure adrenalin and testosterone. They pulled into Sleeping Bear at four-thirty that afternoon.

Cooper's dad had promised to throw a keg party for the whole team if they were finally able to advance past round one. The big shebang was slated to kick off at eight o'clock on the Pond Ranch. Dearl begged Cooper not to invite Jetti Fury but Coo had said, "I wouldn't dream of not inviting her, my man—for whether you know it or not, this is the woman of your destiny. Besides, all the high school kids are invited. Dad had Luther put up posters all around town."

So while everyone else whooped and hollered as they left the locker room, Dearl felt sick to his stomach and quietly slipped away for home after promising he'd be ready when Cooper came to pick him up.

Coo had offered him a ride but Dearl—who only drove his mom's ancient Subaru to get groceries in order to save money on gas—had opted to walk, even though his legs were rubbery and spent. Most of the energy that usually fueled them had dissipated on the Plainview football field. He plodded along trying to think of some excuse Cooper would buy for him not coming to the party. Being a big

Saturday night event in a town that rolled up the sidewalks at sundown, there was no way Jetti wouldn't be there. Dearl finally gave up trying to find a way out. He'd just have to grin and bear it—stay away from her as best he could, and talk one of the kids who hadn't drank any booze into taking him home early.

The brick duplex he lived in was one of several government housing projects constructed in an area everyone considered the poor side of town. When he got near his house he noticed Rex Winters driving away. He couldn't recall ever seeing the editor in this part of Sleeping Bear before.

He stepped inside to find his mother leaning forward in her electric wheelchair crying, face buried in her hands. Panicked because she rarely gave in to tears no matter how upset she was, he hurried to her side. "What's the matter, Mom?!"

Obviously not expecting him to catch her weeping, the proud, stubborn woman quickly wiped her eyes and forced a smile. "Nothing, sweetie. I'm just sorry I didn't get to see you play."

That was a bald-faced lie—she hated that he'd continued playing football after entering high school, and had repeatedly begged him to quit during his freshman season, fearing he'd get hurt playing against young men instead of little boys. He'd never bucked her over anything else when his actions made her unhappy, but he couldn't give up the sport. Coach Rainey had talked to her, explaining it would be a horrible waste of God-given talent if he didn't pursue a professional football career. She'd told Rainey sharply she felt he didn't give a damn about anything but using him to accomplish his own personal goals. Dearl had been horribly embarrassed by her dressing down his coach, and told her he'd never be happy doing anything else. She'd glared at him for a small eternity before responding to his angry declaration. "Okay," she'd conceded, "if it means that much to you then I give up. Go ahead, but I'm still afraid you might get hurt, so don't expect me to watch you."

The awkward scenario still bothered him, and he figured it always would.

"What was Rex Winters doing here?"

"Rex? Oh he was just checking on me, wanting to see how I was doing."

He sucked in an impatient breath. When she didn't want him to know something she'd lie like a dog if he persisted in quizzing her about it. She'd even refused to admit anything was wrong with her until the cursed multiple sclerosis eating away at her nervous system forced her to quit work.

"Mama, what was Rex Winters doing here? What's going on?"

"I told you, he was just—"

"Rex Winters has never been here before, and right after he leaves I find you bawling! Now what is going on?!"

She raised her head and glared at him. Her threatening eyes looked out of place amidst her emaciating features. "Don't you raise your voice to me, Dearl Virgil! I said he was checking on me, now let it go at that."

His heart broke. Since she obviously didn't want to discuss it he'd never get her to tell him, and he had no right to upset the poor woman—not when she was so weak from that horrid disease slowly destroying her. "Sorry, Mom."

A smile gradually surfaced. "Rex told me you made five touchdowns."

"Sure did." She actually seemed excited about it, and that thrilled him. Normally when he told her what he'd accomplished in a game she'd say, "Well I hope you'll think it was worth it if you wind up paralyzed."

"Rex also told me he thinks you're the best high school

athlete he's ever seen. Isn't that something? I am so proud of you."

That infused him with elation. Rex Winters was a big wheel in Sleeping Bear. "He really said that?"

She nodded. "When is that nice man from Oklahoma coming to see you again?"

"I don't know. Told him I was leaning towards Texas, so he may not be back."

"Oh he'll be back," she said with a sigh of resignation. "All those recruiters will be, Rex told me so."

"He did?"

"Mm hmm."

Knowing she couldn't have been crying over self pity because his mom never felt sorry for herself, and got super pissed when anyone offered sympathy over her physical condition, he resisted the urge to again ask what had brought on the tears, choosing instead to stay with the topic she'd chosen. "OU would be a lot closer than Austin. So would Tech for that matter. Maybe I shouldn't go to Texas. I was leaning towards Austin because that's where Coo wants to go. His dad went there you know."

She donned a reminiscent smile. "Of course I know. Don't forget I grew up with Al Pond and his two younger brothers, God rest their souls."

Cooper never met his uncles, they'd died in their teens. "How come you never talk about your school days, Mom?"

The question turned her somber. "Because they were the most horrible times of my life. This was always a real gossipy little place, everybody always sticking their noses in everyone else's business. Honestly, I don't know what possessed me to move back here. We should have stayed in Lubbock."

He'd heard rumors that Rutherford Simmons was really his grandfather, but his mother had told him that was nonsense, just frivolous gossip started by some old bitties with nothing better to do than dream up negative things about people when they didn't know the facts.

A haunting memory of the old man still lingered in the back of his mind. Even as a child of ten he'd been aware of Simmons being the second richest man in Kodiak County, and the most eccentric. His babysitter had a date and dropped him off at the Piggly Wiggly supermarket. He was helping his mother set out tomatoes when Simmons walked by. She grabbed him by the arm and spun him away from Rutherford's view, and firmly held him in that position until the guy got out of sight. She'd worn her *say-a-word-and-I'll-blister-your-butt* look which he'd learned the hard way never to defy, so he hadn't dared ask what that was about. He still vividly recalled the odd glare that jumped on Simmons' face upon seeing his mother.

A strong intuition told him Rex Winters' visit had something to do with old man Simmons. Dearl didn't know why he thought that, but knew better than to say anything. It would upset her again. Besides, she would never back off from the smokescreen thrown up to keep him from knowing the real reason she'd broke down.

He sometimes just knew things, and on the occasions he'd been able to test the intuitions they'd always been valid. One he'd silently carried for several months was that his grandparents had never lived in Lubbock, and weren't dead like his mother claimed.

Dearl had never seen his dad or any member of his paternal family. He'd heard rumors that his mother conceived him out of wedlock when she was in high school and her father disowned her over it. She'd called it malicious gossip. According to her, the Simmons line she stemmed from wasn't related to Rutherford Simmons.

Supposedly she'd moved with her parents to Lubbock

after graduating from Sleeping Bear High and married a soldier named Earl Tipps, who got killed before he was born. After his death she moved back in with her parents and one day while she was at work, still pregnant with him, their house burned down with them in it. Every piece of memorabilia about his father and grandparents from both sides had gone up in flames. Dearl had never seen a picture of any of them, and often wondered if she'd made it all up to keep him from knowing he'd been a love child.

"Why *did* you move us back here, Mom?"

"I don't remember anymore, but aren't you glad I did? You might not be a star in Lubbock, having to compete with so many more boys than here."

He grinned. "Are you kidding me?"

"Of course I am. You must really be something on that football field."

"Why don't you come to the game next Saturday? I've made it this far without getting hurt, and it's the playoffs. Please come watch me play."

"I must confess I'm tempted." Her eyes glistened with pride. "But Wichita Falls is almost a four hour drive from here and I don't think I could handle the long ride even if I had someone to take me, which I don't."

"I'm sure Al would be glad to have you ride with him and Luther."

She seemed to consider it a moment, then heaved a long sigh. "Al probably would, but the truth is I just don't think I could handle seeing you get hit by some big bruiser. You know I never wanted you to play high school ball in the first place."

He felt cheated. His mother wouldn't come watch him, he didn't have a father to tell him how proud he was of his gridiron exploits, and there were no brothers or sisters to share in his glory. His mom being an only child, he didn't even have an aunt, uncle, or cousin to impress either.

Dearl went to the kitchen and cooked their supper. Meals On Wheels brought his mother's lunch on weekdays, but he always fixed their breakfast and supper. He'd been cooking for several years now and had gotten pretty good at it. Following an old dog-eared cookbook to the letter, he'd yet to fail. Tonight's fare consisted of chicken tetrazzini quick style, meaning canned chicken instead of home simmered and de-boned, and cream of mushroom soup instead of cooking the rich sauce from scratch. He'd compliment it with sides of canned green beans and corn. All the items had been purchased with food stamps. He hated having to use them—felt totally humiliated about it—so he tried to do a week's worth of shopping every Wednesday night when most of the town was attending midweek services at one church or another.

His mother wheeled herself into the kitchen. "What time's the party?"

"Eight." Dearl stirred the soup with a large bent spoon.

"Well I hope you have a good time. Stay out as late as you want."

He let out a big yawn. "I'll probably be home pretty early. I'm tired."

She studied him for a moment. He could tell she knew he was lying. "What's wrong, son, don't you want to go to the party?"

"Sure I do," he evaded.

"Is there something you'd like to get off your chest?"

"Like what?" He focused on the steaming mixture.

"You usually beg to stay out as late as possible, even after a football game. And weren't you supposed to spend the night?"

He didn't want to tell her about Jetti Fury, it would only give her something else to worry about. "This was a playoff game, they're different—it's a lot tougher."

"I see." Her frowning face conveyed the lie had been unconvincing.

"There's a frozen breakfast in the freezer, Mom—the kind you like. You can pop it in the microwave in the morning if I do spend the night, which I'm pretty sure I won't."

"That'll be fine. You go to that party and have some fun."

"I'll go, but like I said, I'll probably come home early."

She let the matter drop and after supper they watched TV until Cooper showed up.

Coo gave her that disarming smile of his. "Hi, Maureen."

"Hello, Cooper. How's your dad doing?" Her voice seemed strong and vibrant.

It tickled Dearl how much his mom loved Coo. Just his presence seemed to brighten her day and give her renewed strength.

"Ornery as ever."

"You boys behave yourselves tonight."

"Well, Maureen, if we can't behave we'll—"

"Be careful," Dearl finished for him.

◆◆◆

Zechariah marveled at how fast the temperature dropped after sundown in these parts, turning from hot to cold in only twenty minutes. Yesterday he'd walked all the way around the eastern outskirts of Sleeping Bear and back to the highway without finding a suitable spot to spend the night. From there he'd trekked a few miles north alongside a barbed wire fence. It merged with a rock wall that ran about a thousand feet on either side of a cattle guard with a sign above that read POND RANCH. Stopping where the barbed wire continued again, he'd climbed over the wall, traversed at least half a mile inward, and made camp.

He'd killed a cottontail hiding at the base of a mesquite, whose thorny branches made it look more like an overgrown bush than a tree. The rabbit was roasting on a spit he'd formed with some of them. When the meat got done he'd have to put the fire out. His tent blocked a direct view of the campfire from whomever lived in the opulent ranch house, but they might spot a glow around it—and a driver happening to glance this direction from the highway could possibly see the flames.

Bone-weary, sick and tired of having to kill his food, he couldn't wait to complete this final task of the many assigned to him two years ago. The folks in that beautiful home had soft beds and bathtubs—oh what he'd give for a hot bath—cold milk and no telling how many goodies in a refrigerator. They could watch TV or listen to the radio, stretched out on a couch all nice and relaxed, not a care in the world. His entertainment consisted of looking at the stars for a spell before crawling inside the pup tent and zipping up his sleeping bag to keep crawling bugs out of it.

A gas pocket rose from his bowels and he suddenly had to go. He hated having to defecate without a toilet.

♦♦♦

Rex moaned and waved Emma off when she passed a platter of fried chicken to him. "I couldn't eat another bite. That was dee-lish-us."

She rose from table and took his plate. "Go on in the living room, I'll bring our coffee in there."

He stretched out in his recliner and patted his belly,

wishing he still smoked because a cigarette never tasted so good as it did after a fried chicken dinner. A tempting thought to indulge just this once plagued him, like it did after every meal, but he knew only one puff would hurl him right back to four packs a day. The eagerly awaited caffeine boost would have to suffice.

Emma handed him a steaming cup, seated herself on the couch with her coffee, and lit up. The second hand smoke smelled wonderful and horrible at the same time. He watched her blow a stream into the air, not giving a thought to what affect it might have on him. He'd never mention it bothered him—she'd never smoke in his house again, and therefore would no longer feel comfortable here. Emma took reproof to heart. It was impossible to convince her that a mere suggestion wasn't a severe reprimand.

"So," she said, "now that we've got tomorrow's edition behind us, tell me how it went with Dearl's mum. Did you ask her the big question?"

"No, too soon to do that. I just bragged on Dearl and told her I was thinking of doing a feature article on him. Would you believe she's never seen him play a single high school game?"

"Most certainly. A mother doesn't relish the idea of seeing her boy get smacked about by a bunch of thugs in armor."

That made him chuckle. "Thugs in armor, huh. Never heard it put like that. Anyway, you're right. She doesn't want to see him get 'smacked about' as you said."

"So when are you going to pop the big question?"

"After I manage to win her over. She was pretty suspicious of my visit, I'm afraid."

Emma frowned. "Hmm, maybe I should do it."

"How would you go about it?"

"I'd have you introduce me, then you could sort of fade away, as they say. The way it is with women, we'll either hit it off or we won't."

He sipped coffee and coveted her cigarette while thinking it over. "So you'd know right away whether you'd be able to get anything out of her?"

"Most certainly I would."

"Well, it's worth a try."

◆◆◆

Dick Parsons' eyes were blurry from watching game film, and his ulcer was flaring. Sleeping Bear had steamrolled their way past Bi-District. He hoped like hell the Kodiaks wouldn't make it to State like his team was sure to do for the fourth consecutive time, but knew damn well they were going to. *Forty-two to fucking nothing!* he shouted in his mind while downing a bog dose of Maalox. The Kodiaks shut out the Cougars, a team he'd faced in the regular season. Truman had come up with a great game plan as usual, and Dick hadn't resented the head coach tweaking his defensive scheme a mite—those adjustments were brilliant—yet the Winthrop Cougars scored 21 points against them. Sleeping Bear hadn't played against Winthrop's ace defensive end D. J. Morgan as they had, but all the Cougar's offensive hot shots were on that fucking field, yet the Kodiaks shut them out, the only team to do so all season.

His eyes weren't weary from watching the Lions' next opponent, he'd start preparing for that game tomorrow. Tonight he'd been studying last year's slim victory over Sleeping Bear—Dearl Tipps in particular. Fear motivated him: a deep rooted hunch the Lions would be facing that boy in the state championship game. He had to find some kind of edge because Tipps would have taken them down last year if Kenny Higgins hadn't managed that last second strip. Now the kid was ten pounds heavier, all of it muscle, and the added weight hadn't taken anything away from his speed. A six-foot two hundred pound nightmare awaited Langton at the end of this season's ride. Dick knew it in his gut.

# 4

DEARL WAS ACTUALLY HAVING A good time, and had even called his mother to let her know he'd be spending the night after all. As expected, Jetti came to the party but he'd managed to avoid her as everyone celebrated the Kodiaks' Bi-District win.

Sleeping arrangements had been made for anyone who wanted to spend the night. Those who drank had to surrender their car keys and would be driven home at midnight if they didn't want to crash at the Pond Ranch. Al had purchased two kegs of beer for the party, a ton of wine coolers, and hired an Amarillo caterer to supply massive amounts of barbecued meats, side dishes, sandwiches, and desserts. Chips and dips of every variety had been provided as well.

The Pond mansion had two front entrances: one led to the living room, the other—located next to a four-car garage—emptied into a wide hall, sixty feet long, connecting the garage with the main house. In between lay a 60-by-80 game room designed by Al's late father. A sculptured-log veneer ran two thirds of the way from the garage, but glass composed the last twenty feet of the room's front wall, and contained the door, also transparent. Eight huge ceiling fans with mahogany blades hung in pairs from a high vaulted-ceiling. Oak paneling covered the eighty-foot walls while the back one—sheathed with river rock—had a fireplace in the center. A Budweiser man had set up the kegs near one side of it, an old fashioned jukebox stood on the other. The catered food and wine coolers were in Al's spacious meeting room inside the house. Al doled out the coolers from locked ice chests.

The pool, foosball, and air hockey tables were getting heavy use. Most of the stools, armchairs, and sofas were occupied by high school wallflowers. A hundred folding chairs had been brought in for the party. Very few were empty at the moment but that wouldn't be the case when the jukebox started playing again. A cleared out area serving as tonight's dance floor would be packed.

Luther, Al's valet and chef, served as bartender and guard—filling and refilling the beer cups, refusing anyone who'd obviously had enough. The full blood Cherokee looked it, mostly because of his shoulder length black hair. He wore casual western attire instead of a suit, and had been a fixture on the Pond Ranch since being discharged from the army after a tour of duty in Vietnam. Al's father had saved his life, and Luther had sworn to serve him and his family until his dying day. He'd turned off the jukebox to give his ears a fifteen minute rest.

Cooper stood nearby, laughing it up with a pretty sandy-haired junior as Dearl handed his cup to Luther for a refill. She'd been eyeing Cooper since her arrival and had finally cornered him.

The buxom eleventh grader gave him a smile as Luther serviced his cup. "You were so good today. My name's Cindy Shane."

"Howdy, I'm Dearl Tipps."

"Oh I already knew that."

"Did you already know my name before we met?" Cooper asked, looking a mite concerned, and jealous.

"Of course I did. I heard you made a touchdown today."

"Heard?" said Cooper, frowning. "You didn't come to the game?"

"No, just heard about it in detail, but wish I had now. I bet you were great, making that touchdown."

Dearl grinned at her. "He was just lucky, that's all."

"Lucky? My man, luck had not one damn thing to do with it, and you know it." Cooper signaled with his eyes he wanted to impress her.

"Yeah, I was just popping off, Cindy. We'd be nothing without Cooper here. Think I'll grab a snack."

"You two look like brothers," he heard Cindy say to Cooper as he walked off. Dearl made his way to the big room where all the grub had been laid out, thinking about what Cindy said. She wasn't the first to comment on their similarities, they'd heard it since kindergarten. He ladled a glob of chili-cheese dip near an edge of a paper plate, loaded the rest of it with Fritos, and went back to the game room.

♦♦♦

Jetti sat on a sofa watching Dearl cut up with Delbert Hutch in front of the fire place. Every now and then another football player would join them after replenishing his Budweiser cup, and they'd high-five each other in congratulations over today's victory in Plainview. Then that jock would leave only to be replaced by another, sometimes with a girl in hand. Cooper Pond and Cindy Shane were talking to them now. Rick Holt and Darlene Fox joined them and the boys exchanged hand slaps with the quarterback.

Taking a sip of Dr Pepper, she wondered what beer tasted like. Everyone who drank it sure seemed to enjoy it. Her grandfather would freak if he knew she even contemplated such a thing. The thought of him sickened her, so she put him out of her mind and concentrated on Dearl.

He and Cooper could pass for brothers, but Dearl was the special one. His eyes seemed to embody some hidden insight not available to others, and she sorely lusted after his athletic body. She'd been unable to coax him into approaching her so it looked like she'd have to take matters into her own hands. It wouldn't be wise to try anything tonight, celebrating with his teammates seemed to be the only thing on his mind at the moment. Thank God he wasn't serious about another girl or she'd just die, because that's not what fate intended.

Fate. She and Dearl had been inflicted by it family wise. His father got killed in action and she had no idea who hers was. Her mother was a prostitute and abandoned her to a rich pervert. Dearl's mom suffered from multiple sclerosis and wasn't long for this world.

Abel Norris had Dearl's attention at the moment as Luther refilled the big junior's cup. She'd dated his older brother a few times last year. He'd called from Texas Tech, hoping to spend time with her over the homecoming weekend but she'd turned him down. She'd gone out with several seniors from ninth through eleventh grade, but only because Dearl hadn't been available. With all the stars steadily lining up now and the wheel of love about to start spinning, nobody would be granted that privilege again.

If it was up to her grandfather she wouldn't be allowed to date anybody or attend social functions where he couldn't keep an eye on her, but Grandma encouraged it. Up till now the creep hadn't found a way to stop it without arousing his wife's suspicions. He'd glower at her when she got all gussied up for an evening out, but never said a word about it when they were alone, as that would take time away from his molestations.

One day soon Dearl would put his hands on her and send her straight to the portals of heaven. They'd go away to college together and after that, some NFL City for sure—hopefully Dallas or Houston. She'd build a nest for the two of them in a lovely home, bear his children, and love him like no woman has ever loved a man before. Until then all she could do was watch from afar, like now, and smile with anticipation.

◆◆◆

Cindy had never experienced such thrills—Cooper was a beast in bed. The party was still going full swing and no one knew he'd snuck her to his bedroom.

A couple of wine coolers had given her the courage to walk right up and tell him how she felt. She'd nearly fainted when Cooper had responded with: "This proves there's a God, Cindy, because I'd made up my mind to ask you for a date before the night was through."

Now they were going steady.

Her ex boyfriend in Lubbock, two years older, had been the only guy she'd gone all the way with until now. The fire had gone out on her end by the time she moved—his kisses no longer stoked her passion, his cutups she once thought so cute quit making her laugh, his hands lost the ability to turn her on, and his lovemaking became a burden to bear. She didn't know why, exactly, since he'd been sweet, devoted to her, and a good lover in every respect. Perhaps it was the lack of danger, knowing he'd never leave her or do anything to hurt her. Whatever the reason, she'd grown tired of him and the more he'd sensed the distance growing between them, the more possessive he'd become. He'd cried when she ended it, and that had torn her up inside for hurting him, but she'd refused to take it back when he'd begged her to give their relationship another chance. She didn't have anyone else to compare Cooper's sexual expertise with but couldn't imagine any guy topping it.

He fondled her breasts and said, "Listen, Cindy, I was already exhausted from the game and now I'm totally beat. Mind if I take a short nap?"

"No," she replied, stroking his beautiful hair, "but what if your father comes in?"

"Nah, Dad and Luther have to stay on top of the booze, nobody'll bother us. Wake me up in twenty minutes okay?"

"Sure . . ." she kissed him.

◆◆◆

*Delbert's going to hate himself in the morning,* thought Joie McClain. Marybeth and she had been visiting with him and several other players near the kegs, and he'd downed at least five twelve-ounce cups of beer over the last forty minutes. No telling how many he'd drank before they'd decided to quit dancing and fraternize with some of the heroes they cheered for on the track of every field the Kodiaks played on. Delbert didn't appear to be drunk but all those brewskis were bound to catch up with him before long.

Unattainable Dearl Tipps and unavailable Rick Holt were rehashing today's victory. Delbert was so ugly he was cute, but she didn't date black guys. Fellow juniors Abel Norris and Lyle Whitney were handsome enough to suit her but neither seemed in the mood for romance tonight. The love machine had left the game room with Cindy Shane while she'd been dancing with a tall, handsome, but very conceited senior who only played basketball. It was a shame Cooper wouldn't commit to a relationship. He'd asked her out several times and she'd finally let him go all the way on their last date. Had she known what an incredible lover he was she'd have given in on the first one like Marybeth had. Neither of them could wait for that stud to ask them out again. Neither could Delores or Bibi. Darlene and Pat were the only cheerleaders that hadn't slept with him.

Cindy Shane really worried her because Cooper seemed quite taken with the busty pretty who'd moved here last February. Surely the newcomer from Lubbock wouldn't be the one to finally turn him into a one-woman man.

"Hey, Joie, how 'bout a dance?" solicited Mark York, a skinny senior with a strong right leg. He came off the bench only to kick off or punt for the Kodiaks, and had done so since seventh grade.

◆◆◆

Watching Joie shake her ass to *Twist and Shout* with Mark York, Bibi wished there was something on that damn jukebox worth listening to. She carried her cup to Luther for a refill and checked out the tunes again. Not a single song that wasn't a hit before 1970. Eons ago.

Someone pinched her on the butt and she whirled around to see Delbert Hutch grinning. His big mouth only spread wider after she slapped his face.

"Well worth the price, blondie," he declared.

"I'll kick you in the balls if you ever do that again, Delbert."

"Eew I'm soooo scared."

Dearl came over, put an arm around him, and tactfully turned him away from her.

"We the best damn team in Texas!" Delbert shouted in his

ear.

"Of course we are, let's shoot some pool, what say?" Dearl gave her a wink before guiding Delbert towards one of the pool tables.

"You da man, Tipps, you da man!" Delbert hollered along the way.

She wished that wink had been a flirt but knew Dearl had only done it to let her know he was rescuing her from Delbert.

Jetti Fury stood in her way or she'd have thrown herself at the football star years ago as she had Cooper. The way he squirmed in algebra two each time that beauty smiled at him, and the merciless way Cooper pointed back and forth at him and Jetti afterwards made for good entertainment. The same thing had gone on in every class she'd shared with the three of them since their freshman year. She'd never understand why Jetti had let those seniors he'd gone with keep her from closing in on him. No girl could compete with Jetti Fury, not even when she was a ninth-grader. Now, only Dearl's obvious fear of her blocked Jetti, but this year the smiles had gotten sexier and bolder with each passing day. There was no way Dearl Tipps would make it to graduation without belonging to Jetti.

# 5

JETTI HAD KEPT TO HERSELF last night and went home at eleven, so he'd been able to completely unwind for the remainder of the party. Dearl was lounging on the patio with Cooper after a late breakfast.

"Wanna know something, poor boy?"

"What's that, Coo?"

"I'm in love."

Dearl hacked a laugh and said, "Too bad Cindy only likes you because of your daddy's money."

"Nah, Cindy wouldn't have put out if she didn't really love me. She's only slept with one other guy before."

"Sure she put out, Cooper, what'd you expect? She plans to hoodwink you into marrying her."

"Not true, Dearl, and you know it."

"Oh do I?"

Cooper started thinking it over real hard, a deep frown proved it. "Dearl, you don't really think that do you?"

"Of course not—just having a little fun, that's all."

"Honest and for true," Cooper mimicked with his Betty Boop voice, batting his eyes in the process. He could do great impersonations.

"Nah, I'm lying, *rich* boy."

"Well come on, poor boy, make up your mind."

That one was Jack Nicholson.

"How about I ask her out to test her motives?"

Coo looked real concerned again. "Dearl, you stay away from Cindy. She's mine and you belong to Jetti."

"I don't belong to Jetti."

"Yes you do, and you damn well know it. It's only a matter of time."

That drained the humor out of him. "Enough fooling around. Cindy likes you for you, Cooper, no other reason, I'm dead dog sure of it."

Delbert Hutch came ambling outside cradling his head. "Man, somebody call a doctor . . . I think I'm gonna die."

Coo grinned at the fullback. "Hutch, you only drank about fifteen beers, I can't imagine why you're feeling poorly."

"Yeah," said Dearl, "I believe you floated one keg all by yourself."

Hutch slowly shook his head, rubbing his temples. "I don't never want no more beer—*ever*—I swear. If I even mention booze again, somebody shoot me dead on the spot."

"Have a seat, my man—" Cooper kicked a chair back from the patio table.

Hutch groaned and started to sit, then decided to remain standing.

A sly grin crossed Cooper's face. "Don't forget Dad is going to throw us another bash if we make it to the state championship game, and this time he's going to let us have whiskey and tequila and vodka and rum and raw eggs and monkey brains and—"

"Oh fuck!" Hutch ran to a nearby hedge and vomited.

Dearl felt sorry for him but couldn't help laughing. "You're cold blooded, you know that, Coo?"

Cooper was frowning again, looking at something in the distance.

Dearl turned and saw what troubled him. A column of smoke was rising in the air. "Brush fire?"

"No, somebody's got a campfire going. I better get Dad."

◆◆◆

Riding shotgun in Al's pickup, Dearl gazed across the prairie at the smoke. Cooper sat in the middle.

"Been a while since I've had to string up a poacher," Al chuckled.

Dearl laughed. Everyone knew Al Pond was the most generous inhabitant of Kodiak County if not the entire state of Texas. Unless he was a fugitive from justice, whoever started that fire had nothing to fear.

Luther had told him that when Cooper was a baby Al caught a transient trying to make camp on his land and took him into his home, cleaned him up, bought him some new duds—even offered him a job, but the camper had plans to hitchhike home to Utah. Al gave him three hundred dollars and had Luther drive him to the airport in Amarillo with instructions to buy him a one way ticket to Ogden. Luther said he'd warned Al he was crazy for taking such a chance, bringing a potential thief or even a killer into the ranch house. Al in turn had insisted he could tell that particular soul was an honest man who'd fallen on hard times.

When the transient sent a Christmas card the following December, Luther had to admit Al's instincts were right. Along with the card came a check for five hundred dollars and a letter expressing his gratitude for all Al had done for him. He'd gotten a job landscaping and had such a knack for the craft his employer wound up doubling his salary, so he was saving up for a down payment on a house. Al tore up the check and wrote him back, insisting the man stash the five hundred with his savings. The two stayed in touch through the years and the transient not only managed to buy a house, he'd started his own landscaping company, married an optometrist, and had two kids.

The smoke emanated from a campfire all right. A rough looking character with long filthy hair, and a beard that hung to his upper chest, stuck a coffee pot into a big knapsack and looked their way.

Cooper grinned as they came to a stop. "Look, Dad, it's Moses."

Dearl laughed, but Al warned Coo to behave as he lowered his window.

"Hello there," Al addressed the intruder.

"Howdy," replied the transient in a wary tone. "This your land I'm camped on?"

"Sure is, partner."

"Sorry, meant no harm. I'll move along."

"Where you headed?"

"Sleeping Bear eventually."

Al got out of the pickup. "Well let us give you a hand. We'll load you up and take you there."

That seemed to trouble the guy. He cut his eyes the direction of the highway and nervously stroked his beard. "I appreciate the offer, but I'll just be moving on afoot if you don't mind me walking across your land to the road."

"Not at all, but I'd be glad to take you. If you'd like, you can come up to the house and freshen up a bit, maybe have a bite to eat before you go."

The bum's eyes lit up when Al mentioned food. "No, thank you very much, but I'll just get my stuff together and be on my way if it's all the same to you."

Al frowned at him. "I can't allow you to keep a fire going because the wind might kick up and start a brush fire, so if you won't let me take you to town I'll have to insist on following you to the road."

Wiping his brow with a dirty shirt sleeve, the man said, "I know it must seem strange to you that I can't accept your offer of a ride, but I can't. You're welcome to follow me, but

I'll have to walk."

"Well at least let me help you with that tent."

The man's greasy beard spread with a grin. "I'd be obliged if you would."

"Where you from?" Al grabbed a corner of crumpled tarp.

"Arkansas," the tramp answered, doing likewise.

Al raised the canvas and the foot-traveler did the same, then Al turned loose when the dude latched onto it. Grasping the bottom, Al pulled it up to the man's hands, whereupon the vagrant took it from him, folded it twice more, and stuffed the tent into his knapsack.

"Whereabouts in Arkansas?" said Al, kicking dirt on the fire.

The bum helped him finish the job, relaying while doing so: "A small town south of Little Rock."

"What brings you to Sleeping Bear?"

"You wouldn't believe me if I told you."

"Sorry, didn't mean to offend you. It's none of my business and doesn't concern me anyway."

"Oh, it concerns you all right." The transient pointed at the pickup. "And that boy over there."

"Which boy?" Al asked.

"The one sitting by the door."

Dearl had to scratch away a tingling sensation from the back of his neck, brought on by the scruffy guy's statement.

Al folded his arms across his chest and adjusted his stance. "You're starting to worry me, partner. What business do you have with that boy?"

"Not me . . ." the dude strapped the knapsack to his back and started walking. "I'm just a messenger. It's God that has the business with the boy."

"God? What business, and how does this concern me?"

The tramp didn't answer, just marched along.

Dearl's throat turned dry from a severe case of heebie

jeebies.

"Man, what a weirdo," Cooper muttered.

"Yeah," he quietly agreed.

Al shook his head with disbelief while returning to the pickup. He winked while sliding behind the steering wheel and said, "I'll give Myles a call when we get back to the house, and let the sheriff know Sleeping Bear is about to be invaded by an alien."

◆◆◆

Driving towards the Pond Ranch in his cruiser, Myles Grange ran a finger back and forth across the top of his handlebar moustache, the same burnt-red as Yosemite Sam's, which his ex wife had derisively nicknamed him.

"He seems harmless enough," Al had told him over the phone, "but he said God had some kind of business with Dearl Tipps, and that spooked me a little. Just thought you ought to know he's heading for Sleeping Bear."

Myles spotted the interloper and pulled over. The dude looked like he hadn't been next to a bar of soap in a month, and judging by the length of his hair and beard, he hadn't seen the inside of a barber shop in years. He shifted to neutral and rolled the window down. "Where you headed?"

"Sleeping Bear eventually."

"Hop in, I'll give you a ride."

"I appreciate the offer but I have to walk."

Myles removed his Stetson and wiped a trickle of sweat off his bald head. "What's your name?"

"Zechariah."

"Zechariah what?"

"Just Zechariah."

"What's your business in Sleeping Bear?"

"You wouldn't believe me if I told you."

"Try me."

"God sent me."

He stifled a chuckle. "Sent you to do what?"

"I haven't broken any laws and I'm not a threat to anyone. Please, leave me in peace."

"I'm the sheriff of Kodiak County and we have a vagrancy law. You got any money on you?"

The tramp turned up his palms. "I'm afraid not, Sheriff."

"Well that makes you a vagrant. You've got two choices— either leave the county or I'll have to take you into custody."

"Why?"

"Because a man's gotta eat, and since you don't have the means to buy a hamburger, you'd have to resort to some form of theft."

"You're wrong there, Sheriff. I only eat what I can catch or kill, such as a cottontail. I'd never steal anything, you've got my word."

"I'm afraid that's not good enough. Get in the car, I'll drive you to the county line. If I catch you back across it you'll find yourself in jail."

◆◆◆

Seeing Cooper walk Cindy Shane down the hall between classes, Darlene cringed inside with jealousy. Rick high-fived him as they passed by, and grabbed her hand again. His touch didn't have the same magic anymore.

Cooper had only gone steady with one girl before now— her, back in eighth grade. She'd broke it off, really devastating the poor guy. They were adults now, not fourteen going on fifteen, and she was the only girl on the cheerleading squad besides Pat that hadn't slept with him. Marybeth, Joie, Bibi, and Delores, said they'd marry him without a second thought, and not because he was Al Pond's son. They couldn't all be exaggerating about Cooper's sexual talent, but how was she to know he'd grow up to become such a stud when all they'd ever done was kiss and pet? And not once had their petting gone beneath their clothes. She'd rubbed his pants-covered penis and he'd felt her up with hands on top of fabric and bra.

Rick was a good lover and the handsomest boy in school, but she found herself wishing the hand holding hers belonged to Cooper.

He'd broke down when she told him they were through, and with tears in his eyes had demanded to know why she didn't like him anymore.

"It's not that I don't like you, Cooper," she'd said.

"Then why are you breaking up with me?"

To keep from hurting him even more, she'd lied: "We're too young to only see each other. Who knows how much we'll change in high school?"

The real reason for calling it quits mocked her now, for according to her fellow cheerleaders Cooper had not only overcome the deficiency, he'd *mastered* it.

◆◆◆

"Mister Rainey, may I go to the girls room?" Jetti asked.

Coach nodded without interrupting his reading.

Her fabulous body was covered by a snug-fitting sweater and tight jeans. Dearl ogled it when she returned to her desk five minutes later. Two rows ahead and to the right of him, she eased into it and suddenly one of her flirty smiles sent him reeling. Feeling like a klutz, he turned and gazed stupidly at the blank blackboard. A Cooper-launched spit wad slammed against his right cheek. He couldn't retaliate—she might still be looking. Coo fired a second paper missile and this time Dearl launched a counterattack. When he did, Jetti giggled while boring a hole through him with her laser stare. His stomach lurched, and to make matters worse he'd done it for nothing. Cooper managed to dodge the shot. Several girls were laughing now, Bibi Smith the loudest of them.

Rainey looked up from his desk, the giggling ceased, and everybody looked as if they were working on a set of equations from their textbooks that had to be handed in at the end of class. Dearl quickly solved the first three but the rest were increasingly complex, and he barely finished the last one by the bell. On the way out of class he felt Jetti staring at him from behind. He turned as if to check out Cooper, and confirmed it. Her intimidating eyes appraised him unblinkingly—beckoning him to be as bold as she. Dearl spun around and hurried down the hall with Cooper ragging on him for being such a wimpy weenie.

"What's it gonna take, Dearl, a sign from God? The girl's panties are soaking for you and you're too damned chicken to take advantage of it. I don't get it. You go steady with three different seniors our first three years of high school, yet haven't got the nuts to even *talk* to Jetti."

"Knock it off, Coo."

"Let me talk to her, tell her you'd like to date her. She'll do the rest. What say?"

Just the thought of it made him paranoid. "Cooper, you say anything—*anything at all* about me to Jetti and I'll kick your ass from here to Amarillo!"

"Buuuuck buck-buck-buck-buck."

"Cut it out, Coo . . .!"

Cooper kept it up all the way to the locker room.

The Friday walkthrough went perfect, they were ready for the Hogs. Rick Holt started a chant everyone repeated all the way into the locker room: "Bring on the Hogs, bring on the Hogs, bring on the Hogs . . .!"

♦♦♦

The Hogs were brought, and the Hogs were slaughtered. Dearl snared two touchdowns, Cooper scored on a long bomb from Holt, and Hutch busted one up the middle from the one yard line. Defensively they managed another shutout. The world belonged to the Sleeping Bear Kodiaks, on their way to Regional—three games away from State.

♦♦♦

They were taking a coffee break. Leaning on the linotype, Rex battled an urge to steal a cigarette from Emma, who sat on a nearby stool smoking. "So you didn't hit pay dirt, huh?"

"Not at all," she said while exhaling. "Whatever that lady's hiding, she'd sooner die than have it out in the open—and believe me, she *is* hiding something. I don't think we're going to find the answers through her. We need to find out where the boy was born and start from there, then maybe we can find out who his father is."

He sighed. "Maybe we should leave this alone. If Maureen doesn't want anyone to know about her past, what business is it of ours to uncover it?"

Emma raised her brows. "Some news sleuth you turned out to be."

"I know, I'm a sentimental fool. A mercilessly nosy, sentimental fool."

"We're the press, we're supposed to be mercilessly nosy."

"We're a small town newspaper, Emma, not the New York Times."

# 6

ZECHARIAH DIDN'T WANT TO BREAK the law but he'd have to in order to obey God's command. The sheriff had ordered him a takeout meal over his mobile phone while driving to town, picked it up at the restaurant's drive-through, dropped him off at a roadside park a short distance past the west county line, and sternly warned him not to cross it.

He'd been at the same camping spot thirteen days now. Afraid the sheriff would catch him again, he'd begged God for instructions on how to avoid it. So far the Lord hadn't given him any, and it looked like The Almighty wanted him to act on his on initiative. It was Saturday. When God gave him this mission he'd been told to speak to the woman on the third day of the week. Why, the Lord hadn't said. He decided to sneak into Sleeping Bear this Tuesday, and prayed God wouldn't let him get thrown in jail.

◆◆◆

The stands were packed on both sides of the field, residents of Sleeping Bear and Wilburn comprising less than half the attendance. Besides the college scouts, Dearl had no idea why so many others were interested in today's game. Adrenaline brought on by anticipation numbed his extremities. His throat was bone dry. Shifting from one foot to the other, he vainly tried to summon some spit to the desert in his mouth as Rick Holt called tails.

Sleeping Bear had been dubbed the visiting team. Visitors won the coin toss and would receive. The Wilburn Wildcats chose to defend the goal behind him. Dearl switched sides, shook hands with the opposing captains, and scarcely felt his feet touch the ground as he trotted towards the end zone to await the ball. He was the return man on kickoffs and punts.

Wilburn's kicker sent the football sailing and the stadium became a cauldron of screams . . . but as the ball started downward Dearl no longer heard the cheering fans. Feeling all alone in the universe, he focused on the tumbling oblong of brown, eagerly awaiting its touch. It fell nicely into his hands as he ran full speed to catch the short kick. Within seconds the cheering returned—the world had received him again, and his feet could finally feel the turf. He'd returned the kickoff for a touchdown.

Delbert Hutch pounded his back, Cooper bear-hugged him, the sidelines emptied and all his teammates swarmed him. This promised to be a fine, fine Saturday afternoon . . . .

When the final whistle blew, the scoreboard read:

    HOME: 07          VISITORS: 35

The Sleeping Bear Kodiaks had made it to Quarter Finals.

◆◆◆

Jetti wanted so badly to run onto the field and cover Dearl with kisses. He'd only scored one touchdown but it had put the first points on the board and set the tone for the rest of the game. Amassing almost two hundred yards rushing, he'd intercepted three passes on defense, and made the critical tackles that halted numerous threatening drives by the

Wildcats.

She'd never tried out for cheerleader—it seemed silly to her, all that jumping around and showing off—but at the moment she'd give anything to be one of those girls on the field in their blue-and-white pleated skirts so she could be near him. All she could do was sit beside her grandparents, cheering as those brave Kodiaks, led by her man Dearl Tipps, headed off the field with another playoff victory in tow.

♦♦♦

Hutch, fresh out of the showers and still naked, popped him on the butt with his towel. "You da man!"

"No, this time you da man!" spouted Dearl, likewise wearing his birthday suit. Hutch had garnered three touchdowns on a special pass play Coach had installed only that week. Dearl returned the favor, his wet towel slapping against Hutch's backside with a loud pop.

"I'm the man," belted an impatient masculine voice, "and you girls better quit jacking around and get dressed if you don't want to walk back to Sleeping Bear."

"Yes, sir, Coach!" they hollered in unison.

Coach Rainey left the vicinity and the towel popping recommenced . . . .

♦♦♦

Truman was the last to board the bus as usual, but instead of taking his reserved seat, he lowered his cell phone and called for everyone's attention.

"You guys say you want the Kodiaks? Well, you're liable to get 'em. I just got word that Sleeping Bear dismantled Wilburn thirty-five to seven."

Dick's stomached tightened.

"Hurray!" Kenny Higgins shouted, jumping into the aisle with his beefy arms raised. "Guys, let's hope they make it all the way to championship game like we'll definitely do. They're the best team out there other than us, so just think how sweet it'll be to kick their butts for State instead of just Bi-District."

All the players cheered and repeatedly hollered, "We want the Kodiaks!"

*Stupid kids,* thought Dick, whose electrical excitement over today's victory flatlined with Truman's announcement. Wanting to play against the best opponent possible was an admirable trait, but he had a bad, bad feeling they couldn't beat Sleeping Bear this year. He prayed they wouldn't have to face them.

♦♦♦

Marybeth loved the old malt shop section of the rambling drug store, the area her dad had restored after leasing the building before they moved here from Clovis. Her mom ran it while he took care of the pharmacy and the rest of the store. Before they'd taken over, it'd been roped off. No one had sat at the bar or booths enjoying a malt, milkshake, or soft drink served in an old fashioned soda fountain glass for eleven years prior. Burly Swain, the owner, had stipulated in the contract that no burgers, fries, or any other food that required cooking could be served here, as it would compete with his business at The Kodiak Cave. But every type of ice cream delight was available, along with the fountain drinks.

She'd been in the mood for a chocolate milkshake, Bibi opted for a vanilla malt. They were sitting at the booth farthest from the cash register so her mother wouldn't overhear from the stool she parked on in between customers.

Bibi sucked on her straw while running her fingers through her hair—sunflower blonde, cut in a ruffled pixie. She and Pat were the only cheerleaders with short hair. Pat wore a cute pageboy, cropped just below her chin. Every once in awhile Marybeth thought about getting hers cut for the convenience, but didn't want to lose her natural waves that for some reason didn't start until almost at her shoulders. From there they cascaded in loose black curls to the middle of her back, where she kept it trimmed.

The suction dimples on Bibi's cheeks disappeared. She swallowed and said, "We're actually going to be playing in the Quarter Finals next Saturday, Marybeth. Seems like a dream, doesn't it?"

"Yeah. It'll kill me if we don't make it to State now, my hopes are so high."

"Mine too . . ." Bibi siphoned some more of her malt. "My daddy played on the only other Kodiak team to make it to Regional before now."

"Oh really, what position?"

"Guard and defensive tackle. Kelly Newly was the Dearl Tipps of that team. Dad said he was a great fullback and a good linebacker. They played Seagraves and lost by one point. Today's win is really historic. I tell ya, Marybeth, I'm still pinching myself over it."

"Oh me too, believe me."

Cindy Shane took a stool at the bar and ordered a banana split.

"Don't you just hate her?" she whispered to Bibi.

Bibi nodded and whispered back: "When she moved here last year I knew Cooper would wind up taking her out because of her big boobs, but never thought he'd fall for her."

"Me either. He's never gone steady with anyone other than Darlene."

"Yeah," said Bibi. "She screwed the pooch there, didn't she?"

"Mm hmm, but Cooper was only fourteen. He didn't turn into a love machine until two years later."

"Hey girls!"

Darlene and Joie were heading their way.

The head cheerleader slide into the booth on her side, Joie sat beside Bibi.

Eyeing her milkshake Darlene said, "Now that we're Regional Champs, think I'll splurge and have myself a chocolate sundae. Be back in a jiff."

She sat down on the stool beside Cindy and ordered. Neither acknowledged the other's presence. Darlene returned with her sundae a few minutes later.

"Nothing for you?" Marybeth asked Joie.

"No. Drank a Pepsi on the way over."

Bibi put a hand to Joie's ear and whispered, "Did you notice who's sitting at the bar?"

"Yeah, should we kill her now or later?" Joie giggled under her breath.

"Later. Too many witnesses."

They all laughed.

Cindy glanced their direction, then turned her attention back to the banana split.

"I've dated Cooper lots of times," Marybeth said aloud, watching for Cindy's reaction.

"So have Joie and I," Bibi ragged, doing likewise.

"I went with him in eighth grade but broke up with him,"

Darlene broadcasted to further aggravate Cindy. "I felt so bad that he took it so hard. Cooper's been on the rebound ever since, poor thing."

Without looking their way Cindy left. At least two thirds of her banana split remained untouched.

♦♦♦

Cindy was mad at herself—she shouldn't have let those snotty bitches get to her. Overton's Drug & Variety gave a mild break to the monotony of Sleeping Bear because she liked the old-timey atmosphere of the soda jerk part of the store. Mrs. Overton was a very sweet and engaging lady, nothing like her snooty daughter Marybeth. She'd known before completing her first week at Sleeping Bear High that Bibi, Darlene, Marybeth, Delores, and Joie were insanely jealous of her. Pat Queen, who'd been friendly last year, had started snubbing her after getting elected cheerleader, only due to peer pressure she felt sure.

A large part of the reason she liked Jetti Fury so much was her refusal to be a part of their clique, which included five popular non-cheerleaders, one of whom was the drum major. Jetti didn't put on airs.

Cooper told her she'd been head over heels for Dearl since the three of them started high school.

"How come Dearl doesn't like her?" she'd asked. "I can't imagine any boy rejecting Jetti Fury."

The laugh that shot out of his mouth had startled her. "Oh, don't kid yourself, Dearl's nuts about Jetti, but he's scared of her."

"Why?"

"He thinks she only likes him because he's so great at

football, but I know that's not the case. I've tried my best to convince him of it but the stubborn fuck won't believe me."

"Does Jetti know that?"

"No."

"Well you should tell her. She'll be able to make him see the light I'm sure."

"Dearl would kill me if I did. I've asked him to let me do that very thing at least a thousand times but he always says no."

"How about if I tell her?"

Cooper had rolled his eyes and said, "Promise me you'll never say a word about it to her, Cindy. Dearl's a tough guy but he's real sensitive about that—*real* sensitive—and he'd never believe I didn't put you up to it."

She'd made that promise reluctantly and would've broke it without hesitation had it been anyone but Cooper demanding it. Informing Jetti about Dearl would have provided the perfect opportunity to make friends with her.

Cindy turned onto Tucker Drive from Ribbon Lane and arrived home a few blocks later. Alone in her room, she stretched out on the bed and thought of how wonderful Cooper made her feel—not just physically but emotionally. She'd never been in love before, and the feeling had a magic quality to it that defied reason: it couldn't be explained, at least not adequately.

The sight of her body in the mirror now turned her on because Cooper loved it so. She'd never felt this way about herself—she cherished her breasts, her vagina, her legs and ass because Cooper adored them. As she considered the remarkable transformation of her ego it occurred to her that at least one facet of falling in love *could be* accurately elucidated. Falling in love meant admiring one's self to the point of blatant narcissism, yet without being narcissistic—all obsession stayed focused on the lover.

◆◆◆

His mother was in the living room asleep in her wheelchair when he got home. Dearl tiptoed into the kitchen so as not to wake her, grabbed a Dr Pepper from the fridge, downed half of it in a couple of swallows, put the can on the kitchen table, and went to the bathroom. A few minutes later he was back in the kitchen where he demolished a bag of Fritos, a can of bean dip, and drank another Dr Pepper before starting supper. He chopped onions, browned ground beef, added diced tomatoes, tomato paste, oregano, thyme, crushed red pepper, garlic powder, salt, pepper, and a bay leaf. Popping a lid on the pot, he set a saucepan of water on another burner and turned the stove timer to thirty minutes. When the water began to boil he emptied a bag of macaroni into it, gave the simmering sauce in the other pot a stir, and hollered, "Mom, supper will be ready in about fifteen!"

He frowned when she didn't answer like always when he gave a wake up call.

"Mom?!"

No answer.

Dearl ran to the living room.

◆◆◆

Rex sadly put the large letters in the slot and kicked on the Ludlow to make hot lead squirt out the headline: *MAUREEN TIPPS, MOTHER OF KODIAK STAR DEARL, DEAD AT 37.*

Emma lit a cigarette and exhaled a funnel of smoke. "That poor woman. What's to become of Dearl? Will he just live alone now or what?"

"It's up to him since he just turned eighteen."

"Think old man Simmons will bother attending his daughter's funeral?"

Wanting to snatch the cigarette from her hand and take a deep drag, he shook his head.

"Bloody bastard," Emma cursed, bringing the cigarette to her lips again.

# 7

DEARL DIDN'T HAVE ANY EMOTIONS left for the funeral. He'd bawled out his grief Saturday night, spent Sunday in a sorrowful daze after choosing a casket, skipped classes on Monday but went to practice, and had kept his focus on the game plan since. Practically the whole town attended but he felt little gratitude, knowing it was only because of him. If they weren't here because of his football status, then why hadn't all these *friends* of Maureen Tipps come to visit her before she died?

He'd fully expected to see Jetti Fury, but for some reason she didn't make it. Her grandmother came though, and wept uncontrollably. He couldn't imagine why.

◆◆◆

How she hated the bastard! Of all the sorry things he'd done to her, not letting her go to Dearl's mother's funeral was the most unforgivable. He'd tried to forbid Grandma to go as well but she'd defied him.

This time when he grabbed her boobs from behind and tried to unbutton her blouse, Jetti doubled up her fist, spun around, and hit the old pervert in the face with all her might. Grandpa fell backwards, smacked his head against the desk, and crumpled to the floor. Horrified at first to see he was unconscious, she gathered her wits and ran to the cemetery.

The crowd was thinning out when she arrived, the graveside service had ended. She ran to her bawling grandmother and asked about Dearl.

"He's already gone home, dear . . . ."

♦♦♦

Zechariah made it to the address without being spotted but no one answered the door. He'd have to find a place to hide out and come back later. Before he got to the sidewalk a sleek car pulled into the drive. An old woman drove and a beautiful young lady sat on the passenger side.

The driver rolled down her window. "Are you looking for someone?"

"Yes, ma'am. Maureen Tipps."

An incredulous gasp shot out of the lady's mouth. "Why would you expect to find her here?"

"I was told this is her address."

"Who told you that?!"

"You wouldn't believe me. May I ask who you are, ma'am?"

"I'm her mother."

The girl fainted and fell over on the woman's lap.

"Jetti . . .?!"

♦♦♦

Myles locked Zechariah in a cell and went to his office. Not only did the tramp still claim not to have a last name, he swore he never went inside the house. A punch-bruise on

Rutherford Simmons' jaw said otherwise. The blow knocked him down and the side of his head hit the edge of a desk, snapping Rutherford's neck. It didn't take a forensics expert to put the pieces together. Gwendolyn and Jetti had driven up just as the killer tried to make his escape. He'd found the smelly drifter two blocks away from the scene of the crime. Al Pond verified him as the transient he'd found camping on his ranch.

Zechariah didn't carry any identification so he'd fingerprinted him and was scanning his prints into the computer. With that accomplished he printed them out, fed the paper to the fax machine, and punched in an Austin phone number. It wouldn't be long before he'd get a return fax stating the weirdo's real identity.

He leaned back in his chair, fired up a cigar, and blew smoke at the ceiling. Despite the loss of two Sleeping Bear citizens to the grim reaper within the same week, he couldn't curb his excitement. Since the town's founding in 1890 the Kodiaks had never made it to the quarter finals. He hoped the loss of his mother wouldn't distract Dearl Tipps to the point of losing his gridiron edge. They needed that hoss to stay sharp.

Seagraves had kept Sleeping Bear from advancing the last and only time a Kodiak team had gotten this far in the playoffs before now. Kelly Newly had been the star ball carrier then. One point knocked them out of the running for State. That Regional loss prompted Kelly to swear off football and he'd turned down several college scholarships. Now Kelly resided on the Pond Ranch, working as Al's foreman.

◆◆◆

Pat Queen couldn't believe the changes in Maureen Tipps' appearance. The frail corpse she'd seen lying in a casket several hours ago bore little resemblance to the vivacious strawberry blonde that used to work at Piggly Wiggly. Dearl had opted for only a graveside service and she'd stood at the end of the viewing line with the rest of the cheerleaders. Cindy Shane having Cooper's arm around her the whole time had made the mournful event even sadder, at least for most of her fellow cheerleaders. Sitting in The Kodiak Cave with her parents, waiting for a steak finger basket, she sized the girl up in her mind, trying to determine why Cooper picked Cindy to go steady with over Joie McClain, who looked more like Shane than any of the other girls Cooper had been dating this year.

Cindy's hair was practically identical to Joie's: long, thick, straight, parted in the middle—the only noticeable difference being Joie's was dark brown, Cindy's very light. Neither of them could honestly say they were prettier than the other, and they were the same height. It had to be Cindy's D-cups over Joie's C's that tipped the scales in Shane's favor.

Her parents named her Patricka Anne but she'd always gone by Pat. Claudia, her older sister by six years, called her Rickie. When Claudia finished her freshman year at college she spent the summer in Sleeping Bear and one hot Saturday afternoon at the community swimming pool Cooper, sixteen at the time, had the nerve to ask her nineteen-year-old sister for a date: supper at The Kodiak Cave. Later that night Claudia seduced him and Cooper gave birth to his legend—going from virgin neophyte to grand master in her van. Allegedly, she'd been the only one Claudia told, but word soon spread that nobody could thrill a girl like Cooper Pond.

Now a registered nurse in Abilene, last summer had been the only one Claudia hadn't screwed Cooper since that infamous night. She'd gotten engaged.

Pat planned to remain a virgin until meeting her soul mate, which she figured probably wouldn't happen until she went to college. After telling Cooper that when he'd asked her out, the date never transpired and he hadn't approached her since.

Abel Norris came in with Lyle Whitney. Pat wished she wasn't sitting with her parents so they could join her. She giggled when Abel ordered two double bacon-cheeseburgers and three large orders of fries, his standard meal when eating here. The big linebacker would scarf every bit of it down, yet he was all sexy muscle. It surprised her he didn't tack on a fried pie as he usually did. Lyle chose a steak finger basket.

Before they got seated the waitress brought hers over, then fetched her parents' pot roast dinners.

Abel took a chair at a table near the door and waved her over as Lyle sat down.

"Um, Mom, mind if I eat with Abel and Lyle?"

Her mother glanced at them and grinned. "Sure, go on ahead, honey."

"What, I don't have any say in the matter?" her dad teased.

"You don't want me to, Daddy?" she ribbed in return.

"No. You're my baby girl and I don't want you messing with boys, ever."

She pecked him on the cheek and got up. "See you guys later, I'll get them to drive me home."

Abel swiped several of her fries as soon as she sat down. "Pay you back when my order gets here."

She laughed. "Your stomach's just a bottomless pit, Abel."

"Yeah," said Lyle, "like Dearl Tipps. I've never seen anybody that can put away groceries like those two that wasn't fat."

*Dreamboat Dearl,* she thought. How often she'd wondered

what it would be like to have him on top of her, the both of them naked. She'd never find out of course. That boy was the property of Jetti Fury even though he didn't know it yet.

Her thoughts went depressingly back to his mother's funeral. Lyle and Abel were Maureen's pallbearers, along with Cooper, Rick Holt, Delbert Hutch, and Gilbert Smith.

"What's the matter?" Lyle asked.

"Oh . . . just thinking about the funeral."

The boys turned somber and she regretted answering truthfully.

"I can't imagine how bad it must feel to lose your mama," Abel said, fingering a tiny mole on his right temple. "Maureen was such a great gal. I'll never forget her catching me snitch a candy bar at Piggly Wiggly when I was ten. She made me tell the manager what I'd done, call my mom and confess it to her, then she paid for it and gave it back to me. I haven't even thought about stealing anything since."

"She warmed my britches one day when I was seven," said Lyle, grinning. "Right there in the store."

"What for?" Pat asked.

"Running and sliding down an aisle right after she'd mopped it. 'Boy, that's a good way to get your head busted open,' she said. I told her I was gonna tell my mama, but about that time Mom came around the corner and I wound up getting my hide tanned a second time for sassing Maureen."

Pat laughed again. "She was *so* pretty before that awful disease got hold of her."

"Yeah, she was gorgeous," Abel agreed.

Lyle nodded. "So how does it feel to know you'll be cheering for the Regional Champs next Saturday, rookie?"

"Like a dream come true." She was the youngest of the cheerleaders and the only sophomore on the squad. She'd tried out last year but a senior beat her by three votes, getting the sixth most.

Abel winked and gave her a cute grin. "You'll be cheering for us at AT&T Stadium in Arlington before we're through. We're gonna take State, darlin'."

"I sure hope so, *darlin'.*" Abel and Lyle both called her that. Maybe someday one of them would mean it and she wouldn't have to wait till college to meet her soul mate. They were in a dead heat in her ratings book, second only to Dreamboat Dearl. Rick Holt was too aware of his prettiness to be in it, and Cooper would never be able to stay faithful to only one woman. At least that was the consensus of Bibi, Marybeth, Delores, and Joie.

◆◆◆

Relaxing in his recliner after supper, Rex marveled at what a strange, emotional week it had been. Maureen Tipps lost her battle with multiple sclerosis only hours after her son's team advanced to the next round of the playoffs, then three days later her estranged father got bushwhacked by a burglar. Myles wouldn't let him interview the accused man until the fingerprint experts in Austin found his identity.

He'd been discussing the matter with Emma, stretched out on the couch.

"Serves the old bastard right for not going to his daughter's funeral."

"Emma!"

She heaved a callous sigh. "Well I'm sorry but it bloody well does, Rex. By the way, what's the scoop on Jetti Fury? She's about the loveliest lass."

"Ah, now that's a story." He straightened the recliner and reached for his coffee. "Her mother, Anita Fury, is a prostitute and no one knows who Jetti's father is—probably not even Anita. She left her on old man Simmons' doorstep with a card attached to the basinet explaining who the baby was. He and Gwendolyn took her in and raised her as their granddaughter."

Emma's jaw dropped. "Did I hear you right? The jerk disowns his own flesh and blood for being in the family way, yet takes in a stranger's bastard child?"

He shot her a grin. "Oh it gets better. Anita took Simmons to court and tried to get custody of Jetti four years after dumping her off. The judge appointed Rutherford and Gwendolyn as her guardians when Anita refused to give her up for adoption. They wanted her to have the Simmons name but Texas law forbade it since the natural mother wouldn't agree to it. After the judge warned Anita he'd make Jetti a ward of the state rather than allow her to have custody, she agreed to let the Simmons raise her."

"Gawd what a mess. What happened to Jetti's mum, does she still live here?"

"No. She moved away several years ago."

Rex had never been so shocked in his life as when he'd been informed the pretty tenth-grader who'd moved to Sleeping Bear from El Paso in mid October was a seasoned pro at prostitution. They were the same age and became friends right away, but she'd never even hinted about being a whore around him. Anita possessed some sort of sixth sense about who to solicit and who not to. He and Kelly Newly fit the latter category while Burly Swain and a few other boys belonged to the first one. Kelly had refused to believe it when he'd told him about Anita's profession soon after hearing it from Burly, but Burly and a new kid convinced him.

"Reckon Jetti will inherit the old man's fortune when his wife dies?" said Emma.

"I suppose, since Maureen was their only child. Of course Dearl is her grandson. Gwendolyn never wanted to lose her daughter, that was all Rutherford's doing, so she's liable to include Dearl in her will. I suspect Dearl doesn't know they're related, and if that's true, he won't even realize he's been left out if she doesn't. It won't matter much either way in a few years, since he's bound to be a millionaire as soon as he turns pro."

# 8

TWO WEEKS HAD GONE BY in an emotional blur—even the playoff game that occurred midway through seemed hazy. Dearl scored three TDs, one of them on defense when he'd ripped the ball out of a running back's hands and ran eighty yards to pay dirt as the Kodiaks took the Quarter Finals title. Still coming to grips over losing his mother, he hardly remembered making his other two scores. But Dearl knew any points he managed to get in this battle for Semi Finals would be forever etched in his memory, because if they won he'd be playing in the state championship game.

Everyone had finished suiting up in their white uniforms trimmed in blue, and Coach Rainey addressed the team in Lubbock-Cooper's visitors locker room at Pirate Stadium in Woodrow—a small town connected to Lubbock's south side—the field where they'd lost to Langton three years running as the designated home team. They were about to take on an awesome squad that hadn't given up over ten points a game all year, while scoring at least thirty-eight in each outing, including the playoffs.

"Okay, girls, we're one game away from State. *One game.* Not only is this our chance to advance to the big show, it's also an opportunity for retribution. I just got a text informing me the Lions blew out the Boing Bears, so if we take the Yellow Jackets this afternoon we'll get another shot at those guys.

"Now then, put the Lions out of your mind and focus on the job at hand. A few reminders on what we've worked on all week. Hutch, remember they blitz ninety percent of the time from the nickel so if you're not the primary receiver on any pass play I signal on third and long, ignore whatever route you'd normally run and stay home to block. Tipps, watch for that weak side fake, they love to run Martin strong side on it and he's the fastest wide receiver in the state. Holt, remember their free safety, Heckle Johns, is their most dangerous defensive player. Whatever you do, don't toss the rock his way. Eat it if you have to . . . ."

Last year the ball had bounced out of bounds at the one when Langton's Kenny Higgins stole it from him, so Dearl felt a sense of dread when the Yellow Jacket kicker launched the pigskin into the air on the same field.

A light rain was falling and the ball felt slippery when he snatched it near the sideline where the kicker had aimed it, trying to keep him from catching it on the fly. He charged up field from the five and got gang tackled at the thirty-one for a twenty-six yard return.

Dearl waited beside Cooper, Hutch, and his other offensive teammates who played on kickoff returns, as Rick Holt and the rest of the offense trotted onto the field.

They huddled up.

"Twenty flanker black twenty-four cross on three," barked Holt. The first number of Coach Rainey's offensive system designated the position. Twenty meant backs so Dearl would receive the handoff. Had it been twenty-one, Hutch would have gotten the ball. The Four in Twenty-four referred to the hole he was supposed to run through. Even numbers were left, odd right, each ascending in order from the center, the zero hole. Color designated which side of the offensive line the tight end lined up, making that the strong side. Black meant strong side right, red would have put Cooper beside the left tackle. This particular play called for Dearl to line up at flanker a step behind and to the right of Cooper, who'd cross to the weak side at the snap and surge through the four hole ahead of him.

"Blue eighty-four! Blue eighty-four!" yelled Holt with his hands tucked under Gilbert Smith's rump. "Hut, hut, hut!"

Dearl shot to his left, right arm high, left arm low across his body. Holt jammed the ball against his stomach. He curled over it, ran behind Coo and left tackle Wayne Harding, and didn't hit the turf until fifteen yards of real estate had been chewed up.

Hutch slapped him on the butt. "Great run, Tipps!"

"Huddle up," Holt yelled after getting the signal from the sideline for the next play. "Eighty-nine black hitch-and-go on two."

All pass plays started with Eighty and the second digit dictated the receiver. Cooper's number had just been called.

"Forty-niner green! Forty-niner green! Forty-niner green, hut-hut!"

Dearl took down a blitzing linebacker before the dude could sack Holt, and Hutch cut a cornerback's legs out from under him, shooting in from the other side. From the ground Dearl saw the ball spiral smoothly away from Rick's right hand. Then he heard several of his teammates screaming, "Mayday!"

"Mayday" meant the ball had been intercepted and alerted everyone that the offensive squad had just become defense.

Dearl jumped to his feet in time to see Cooper tackle Yellow Jacket free safety Heckle Johns.

"Shit!" screamed Holt, slapping his helmet with both hands.

Dearl watched him trot off the field, knowing a severe ass-eating from Rainey awaited the quarterback, who'd been warned not to tempt fate by passing towards Johns. Rick Holt only played on offense.

"Hell he came out of nowhere," said Cooper as he trotted past Dearl, leaning forward with hands on knees as linebacker, awaiting the snap of the opponent's ball. Cooper stood a few yards behind him at strong safety.

The Yellow Jacket quarterback lined up behind his center. "Red fifty-five! Red fifty-five, hut!"

Their star running back, who wore the same number as Dearl, took the handoff as sophomore Jimmy Cocker, the right tackle, got double-teamed to open up a huge gap. Dearl lowered his head and filled it, taking 20 to the ground hard for no gain.

"Second and ten!" the ref declared after blowing his whistle to signal the play over.

The opposing offense huddled up and a few seconds later assumed their positions. Dearl watched the ball closely, recognizing the Yellow Jackets' alignment from the week's preparation. Yagerville was planning to fool them by having their All State wide receiver Lawrence Martin take a handoff for an end around after the quarterback pump-faked to another receiver weak side.

Tuning out the QB's cadence, he stormed forward the second the football moved, shooting through a gap his linemen created between a Yellow Jacket guard and tackle. Martin's eyes went wide and he tried to stutter-step, but Dearl launched himself, burying his right shoulder in the receiver's chest, the momentum forcing him backwards to the ground.

"Third and sixteen!" yelled the referee.

Dearl had tackled Martin for a six yard loss, nailing him right after he took the handoff.

Martin caught a pass on the next play, a wide receiver screen. Cooper and free safety Lyle Whitney brought him down, but only after he'd gained eighteen.

"First and ten . . .!"

They tried to get the ball to Martin again on a slant route but Dearl, sniffing out the play, shadowed the receiver and garnered an interception. He'd dove in front of the wide receiver to steal the ball, and landed on his belly. Martin touched his shoulder pads to make double sure he couldn't advance since the whistle hadn't blown. Then it did, and Dearl rose to his feet, awaiting the rest of the offense to take the field.

"You saved my ass, Tipps," laughed Rick Holt from the huddle. "I was planning on walking home if they scored. Okay, everybody listen up. Eighty-one red fake-slant twenty-one on one."

Dearl grinned at Hutch as they broke huddle. That play had been designed especially for the fullback. They'd only ran it three times and he'd scored on each in their victory over Wilburn. It called for Dearl to take a fake handoff as Lyle Whitney, who played right-side wide receiver on offense, ran a slant, both heading strong side. Then Holt would pump-fake towards Lyle before throwing it to Hutch, waiting on the opposite side, a yard behind the line of scrimmage.

Unfortunately the Yellow Jackets had done their homework and limited Hutch to only a nine yard gain.

Coach called his number next and Dearl got a first down after a four yard run off tackle up the three hole. The same play got signaled again and he only managed two yardsticks worth of ground, making it second and eight.

"What the hell is he thinking?" said Holt, looking towards the sideline to get the next play. He let out a big sigh as they huddled up. "For some reason Coach is calling the same thing."

Dearl scowled at the quarterback. "Call something else, Coach must be having a senior moment."

Holt chuckled. "He's only in his forties, Dearl. Let's do it on three."

Before Dearl made it to the line of scrimmage he realized, far from going senile, Coach Rainey was a genius. He'd outfoxed Yagerville's coach, who'd bet the bank on a pass play and called for a maximum blitz.

Dearl hurdled Heckle Johns, diving for his shins, and when Cooper leveled the lone defensive back who hadn't charged the line, nothing but Lubbock-Cooper turf stood between him and the goal line.

The game became a total defensive struggle after that and the Kodiaks earned the right to take on the Langton Lions at AT&T Stadium in Arlington for the Class 2A Division-I State Championship with the humble score of thirteen to seven. Heckle Johns scored the Yagerville touchdown with a pick-six.

♦♦♦

Al kept his word and threw another bash for the team. This time the party started at seven instead of eight. Dearl was working on a pile of hot wings when Jetti walked in, passing Al who was heading for a bathroom. She'd been despondent since her grandfather's murder, and he hadn't seen a flirty smile on her face in algebra two since. Watching her scoop cherry cobbler into a disposable bowl, he wanted to offer his condolences, but didn't know if he should bring up the subject. Despite feeling a certain kinship with her because they'd both lost close loved ones only three days apart, Jetti still intimidated him, and he flinched when she sat next to him.

"You don't mind do you, Dearl?"

The awesome smell of Jetti's perfume only served to

make her more daunting. They were alone in the room so she had plenty of other places to sit, and he wished she'd chosen another spot. Nonetheless he shook his head in reply.

"You guys really had your hands full with Yagerville, huh?"

He nodded and brought the drumstick portion of a chicken wing to his mouth.

She dipped a plastic spoon into her cobbler. "You made the only offensive touchdown for both teams. What a defensive battle that was. I believe the Yellow Jackets' number forty is their best player." The spoon slipped between her pretty lips and came out empty.

Watching her chew turned him on and he relaxed a little. If Jetti didn't try to talk to him about anything but football he could get through this without her discovering how much she terrified him. "Yeah, their number forty is Heckle Johns, and he's the best defensive back we've ever played against. Poor Rick finally got picked off for six after not giving one up all year."

"Not to sound like a know it all, Dearl, but you're mistaken. Rick has thrown several interceptions this year. Have you forgotten he threw two today?"

"No, I didn't mean that. This is the first pick he's thrown this season that got returned for a score. That's what I meant."

An embarrassed smile crossed her beautiful face. "Didn't understand that's what you were saying. How are you doing since your mother passed away?"

"I'm managing. How about you? How are you hanging since losing your grandfather?"

A tear slithered down her cheek but she wasn't crying. "Dearl, I need to talk to somebody about that or I'm going to go crazy."

Her vulnerability emboldened him. "You can talk to me if

you want."

Though they were alone, she cautiously glanced around the room. "Not here. Grandma gave me my grandfather's car, that's how I got to the party. Could we drive somewhere so no one will overhear?"

He'd been looking forward to a fun night of camaraderie with his teammates and didn't want to leave. "Um, maybe some other time. The guys would miss me, you know? This is the first time the Kodiaks have ever made it to the state finals, I can't let the team down. Everybody's planning to spend the night. Even Coach Rainey's gonna drop by for awhile."

She didn't say anything for several seconds, just stared into his eyes, sucking away his bravado. "I understand. Do you mind if I hang with you tonight? You know, be your date and all?"

His stomach tied itself into a panicky knot and it took him a minute to muster up the nerve to answer. Imagining Cooper mocking him if he dared to back out, he tried to sound nonchalant as he muttered, "Sure, that would be cool."

The words sounded beyond hokey to his ears.

Cooper came bounding around the right corner of the double doors of the meeting room, held open with doorstops. His brows shot up with pleasant surprise. "Well now, don't the two of you make a pretty couple! Let me get my digital camera, got to have a picture of this. Don't go anywhere!"

He disappeared before either of them could say anything. Jetti looked at him and giggled. Dearl faked a chuckle which sounded even dorkier to him than his klutzy statement.

When Cooper came back and started snapping photos, Dearl nearly lost his breath when she leaned her head on his shoulder for some of them. Then he totally flipped when she told Coo to take one of them kissing and she wanted copies of all the pictures.

Before he could react to her statement she turned his head towards her and kissed him on the mouth. Dearl was glad a table cloth hid his lap because the magic smooch gave him an instant hard on.

"Now that's what I'm talking about!" shouted Cooper. "Hold that pose, let me get a bunch of takes."

Jetti worked her tongue into his mouth while Coo snapped away. Dearl couldn't help but kiss her back. She grabbed his hand and brought it to her breast.

"Whoa," Cooper gushed, "this is getting *really* good!"

He pulled away from her and shot Cooper the bird. "That oughta be enough pics."

Cooper grinned. "Buuuuuuuuuuuck buck-buck-buck-buck."

Dearl glared at him for a moment, then grabbed Jetti and planted a hard one on her lips. He heard Cooper snapping away like a maniac. Before long she slid her hand under the table and started rubbing his crotch.

"So this is how you unwind after a game, Pearl?"

Shocked, he jumped to his feet, forgetting he had a woody throbbing in his jeans. Cooper saw the bulge and burst out laughing. Coach Rainey, who'd spoken, sported a wide grin.

Face burning with embarrassment, Dearl quickly sat down and scooted to the table to hide his erection. "Uh, hey, Coach . . . so glad you made it."

Cooper winked at Rainey and said, "Looks to me like he's *exceptionally* glad you made it, Coach."

Coach put a hand on Coo's back. "Let's leave these lovebirds alone, Pond."

When the two of them walked out of the room, Dearl heaved a nervous sigh. "I'm sorry, Jetti."

She tossed him a teasing smile. "For what? I thought it was funny."

He cleared his throat, feeling more embarrassed by the minute, which managed to deflate his penis. "Come on, let's go to the game room and get some beer . . . ."

Jetti handed Luther her car keys when the big Cherokee insisted on having them before he'd allow her to drink. "Al or I will drive you home after the party if you don't want to stay the night."

"Not necessary. I'll call my grandmother and let her know I won't be home till tomorrow."

Luther filled a cup and handed it to her. She eyed it thoughtfully, holding it with both hands.

"What's the matter?" Dearl asked.

"I've never tasted beer before."

"You're kidding me."

She shook her head. "This'll be my first."

"Well if you don't like it, Al bought a ton of wine coolers. They taste pretty much like a soft drink. Or have you already tried one?"

"No. I've never drank an alcoholic beverage of any kind."

He held up his cup for a toast. "Here's hoping we return from Arlington as state champs."

"Is that where the championship will be played?"

He nodded and took a swig. "All the state championships will be played at AT&T Stadium this year over four days, from six man football on up to Six-A. We'll be leaving for Arlington after a Wednesday walkthrough to spend the night at a motel. Our game is slated for one o'clock Thursday. It'll be my first time to get to see Jerry World from the inside. Coach said school will be out this Thursday so everybody can make it to the game."

"That doesn't seem fair. You'll lose two days of preparation."

"So will Langton, Jetti. I'm just glad the game won't be played at Pirate Stadium where they took us down last year—and the year before that, and the year before that."

Jetti slowly raised the frothy cup to her lips, took a tiny

sip, and made a face. "Eeeeew, I don't *even* like beer!"

Dearl laughed, now feeling almost totally at ease with her. "I didn't like my first beer either. It takes a while to develop a taste for it."

Cooper entered the room with Cindy Shane instead of his camera, and made his way to Jetti and him. "What say, guys?"

"What say?" Dearl returned.

Eyeing Cindy's drink, Jetti said, "I just had my first sip of beer and it sucks. Could I have a taste of your wine cooler?"

Cindy immediately handed over her bottle with a batch of strawberries pictured on the label. She seemed thrilled over Jetti's request for some reason.

"Now that's more like it." Jetti smiled as she gave it back. "Where can I get one of these, Cooper?"

"You have to go through Dad. He puts all the wine coolers in big ice chests that lock."

Luther winked at Jetti. "I'll fetch you one, gorgeous. Guard the kegs for me, boys, and don't let anyone have beer till I get back."

Dearl raised his cup and grinned at Cooper. "Can you believe we did it, man? We're actually going to play for all the marbles next Thursday."

"Yeah, but it won't mean a damn thing if we don't come out of it with a W."

"That's for sure." Dearl took a big pull.

"Oh I already know we're going to win, guys," Jetti prophesied. "God wouldn't have it any other way. Langton got their three championships at our expense, now it's payback time and this one's ours. Funny though, I'm already nervous about the game."

"Join the party," Cooper laughed. "You nervous about it too, Cindy?"

She shook her head.

"That sure we're gonna win huh?" said Dearl.

"Well," she smilingly replied, "I'm sure my Cooper's going to play great, I know that much. And of course so will you."

"All our mighty Kodiaks are going to play great," Jetti insisted with a touch of anger in her voice.

"Oh, I didn't mean to offend you, Jetti—honestly. I'm just partial to Cooper and Dearl, that's all."

Jetti cocked her head and gave Cindy a hard look. "I realize you weren't raised a Kodiak, but I would think our school spirit would have gotten in your blood by now. And you know? I don't recall ever seeing you at a single game."

"That's because I haven't been to one." Cindy took a swig from her bottle.

Cooper grimaced and threw his head back. "My girlfriend's not a Kodiak fanatic! What evah shall I dew?!"

Dearl cackled. Coo had perfectly imitated Scarlet O'Hara from *Gone With The Wind.*

The look on Jetti's face relayed she didn't find it humorous at all.

Cindy took note of it and said, "All right, I'll go to the game next Saturday if I can ride with you."

"Gotta deal," said Jetti. "But it'll be Thursday I've just learned, and school will be out. And just maybe you'll be a true Kodiak by the time it's over."

Hutch ambled over. "Hey, where's the bartender?"

"I'll fix you up," said Cooper.

"Touch that nozzle and I'll break your hand," Luther warned, holding Jetti's wine cooler. "Nobody operates those kegs but me."

Cindy giggled. "You wouldn't really break Cooper's hand would you?"

Luther gave the bottle to Jetti and crossed his arms across his broad chest. "Why don't you ask Cooper?"

"Yeah, he'd do it," Coo declared, grinning.

Hutch chuckled and held out his cup.

"What's that make? You told me not to let you have more than six."

"It's only my fourth, Luther . . . I think."

After servicing Hutch, Luther reached for Jetti's unwanted beer which she held in one hand while holding the cooler in the other. "I'll dispose of it for you."

Jetti relinquished it and took a sip from the bottle.

Rick Holt guided Darlene Fox to the kegs, and before long the big center and left defensive tackle Gilbert Smith showed up for a refill along with some of his fellow linemen.

Dearl watched Jetti from the corner of his eye to see if he could catch her admiring the quarterback, and was pleased to find she seemed indifferent to the stud.

Holt held up his brew. "Here's to stomping the crap out of Langton this Thursday, gentlemen."

"Here, here," said Coo.

Everyone downed a swallow, including the girls.

Dearl cleared his throat. "And here's to me holding on to the damn ball for four whole quarters."

Jetti punched his shoulder. "You always hold on to the football, Dearl Virgil! You've only fumbled, what—like ten times in four seasons."

That amazed him. The number was exactly right. He thought back to their conversation earlier where she'd commented on today's game being such a defensive struggle. Chicks usually didn't understand football that well. Pride had begun to replace trepidation over Jetti's attraction for him. Maybe Cooper was right, maybe they *were* destined to be together. He found himself hoping so as he gave her a big smile. "I'm flattered you knew that, Jetti. Do you know any of my other stats?"

She grinned, proudly. "Freshman year: fifteen

touchdowns, five two-point conversions, twelve hundred fourteen yards rushing, one-o-nine receiving, four hundred twenty-nine kickoff and punt return yardage combined. Defensively you had four interceptions, three sacks, and while I can't recall your total tackles, at least a dozen of them were for losses. As a sophomore you ran for fifteen hundred forty yards and—"

"Whoa," cried Cooper, "you're a computer, Jetti!"

Dearl could only gape at her with wonderment.

Holt raised his brows. "Very impressive. What were my freshman stats?"

Jetti shrugged. "I don't know."

"How about mine?" Coo asked.

She shrugged again and turned up her cooler.

Hutch squinted at her. "Interesting how you only seem to know Tipps' stats. Do I smell cupid hanging around you two?"

Her pretty lips spread into a sexy grin. "I can't speak for Dearl but I'm obsessed. Have been for a long time."

◆◆◆

After once again praying for deliverance Zechariah rose from the cell bunk with a weary sigh. He'd been falsely accused of killing Rutherford Simmons, the father of the woman he'd walked across Texas to see.

Arraigned the day after the murder, the judge had found sufficient evidence existed to try him for the crime on Monday, December 28, sixteen days away.

A town of only seven hundred residents laying just inside the southern border with a constable keeping the peace was the only community in Kodiak County besides Sleeping

Bear, the county seat. The judge and justice of the peace were the same guy, and the only attorney in the county. Qualifying as an indigent defendant, the public defender's office in Amarillo would've sent someone to represent him free of charge, according to the sheriff.

But he'd declined. A lawyer couldn't help, he was here because of God's will and dared not interfere with it. The circumstances were squarely against him, so if the Lord didn't prompt whoever killed Simmons to come forward, or intervene in some other fashion, he'd surely be convicted.

At least he was alone and the other two cells were empty, so he didn't have to worry about being accosted by a bully or worse yet, a pervert . . . for the time being. That seemed to be the only thing going his way at the moment. He thought of Elijah taking on Ahab and the prophets of Baal, backed by the evil Jezebel, and how blind the wicked king had remained even after God proved Himself by sending fire down from heaven to burn the water-soaked sacrifice in front of the Israelites. Before that, Elijah had been sent to a widow, just as he'd been sent to Maureen Tipps. Then he thought of John the Baptist being beheaded by Herod Antipas at the behest of ruthless Herodias. Did he have his own particular female villainess to face in Simmons' widow, who'd convinced the sheriff he was the only one that could have done it?

The woman's granddaughter fainted upon hearing she was Maureen's mother, and that had really puzzled him. Why had the granddaughter not known? Did the boy not know as well?

◆◆◆

"We're really going to State, Emma, it's not just a dream any longer."

She frowned at him. "I know that, Rex. How many times are you going to keep repeating it?"

"I don't know, probably a million at least." He couldn't help it. It felt like the whole town had finally become a winner, a force to be reckoned with rather than merely a collection of fourteen hundred and seventy-three citizens inhabiting a community whose only previous claim to fame was Tornado Hill. Twenty-five youngsters and a brilliant football coach had infused every Sleeping Bear resident with a taste of glory, and Rex relished it.

"Need I remind you who we're playing against next Thursday?"

"I know, Emma. It's going to be tough, but I can't help believing we'll take them this time. Don't forget, if it wasn't for that linebacker stripping the ball from Dearl at the end, we'd have beaten them last year."

Emma pushed her dessert away and ignited a cigarette. "This has just been too much if you ask me. Maureen Tipps dies of MS, old man Simmons gets murdered by a tramp three days later, and yet no one seems to care about anything but football."

Rex rose from the dining table for more coffee. "Now, Emma, that's just not true. Everyone knew Maureen was living on borrowed time, and no one except Gwendolyn and Jetti had any real feelings for Rutherford. Maureen's suffering is over, and I feel like fate exacted a toll from Simmons for turning his back on her so long ago. You said the same thing yourself."

She blew a gray cloud his direction. "So are we going to Al Pond's to take pictures for the next edition or not? It's eight-thirty, and you said you didn't want to embarrass anyone. Most of those kids are probably well on the way to getting drunk by now."

♦♦♦

They were slow dancing to an ancient tune. Rick had been moving them in slow circles but she subtly resisted when the turn would've taken her view away from Cooper. Cindy Shane had just left the game room and Darlene wished Rick had to take a leak so she could talk to Cooper, hanging with Lyle Whitney by the beer kegs.

By the time the song ended, Cindy still hadn't returned. "Would you mind getting me a wine cooler?"

"Sure," said Rick.

She'd made the request because Al doled them out in the room where the food was, and Rick wouldn't make it back for at least five minutes.

He headed for the door and she made a beeline for the kegs. "How's it going, guys?"

"Party city," Lyle laughed.

"How are things with you, Cooper?"

"Very good."

"Where's Cindy?"

"Answering nature's call."

"Um, are you two pretty serious?"

"Mm hmm. Like you and Rick. Why'd you ask me that?"

Turning so Lyle couldn't see her lips move, she mouthed, *I have my reasons, call me some time,* then vocalized for Lyle's benefit: "I was just curious. Well, better go find my Ricky. Bye."

# 9

COACH RAINEY AND HIS ASSISTANT coaches stood in front of the game room fireplace, and everyone who came to the party—all the players and most of the other high school kids—were waiting to hear him speak.

"First off, I'd like to thank Al Pond for throwing this party to celebrate the Kodiaks' first trip to the state finals in the history of Sleeping Bear."

Al took a bow as applause filled the air.

"Secondly, I want to thank my assistant coaches. All three of them work their butts off week in and week out to give our boys the best chance to win."

Another round of handclaps.

"Thirdly and most importantly, the players—without whose diehard execution the best laid game plans in the world are meaningless. Every one of you guys leave it all on the field, every workout, and every game. You've worked hard and sacrificed to get here. I wish us coaches could party down with you, but we're off to watch film and start game planning. You Kodiaks enjoy this celebration tonight and rest up tomorrow, because come Monday we've got to start preparing to kick some Lion ass."

Everyone hooped and hollered and high-fived the coaches as they made their way out the door.

Jetti slid her arm around his waist and Dearl returned the gesture. When she leaned her head on his shoulder this time, instead of an attack of nerves he felt warm inside and gently cocked his head until it contacted hers. "If you still want to go somewhere to talk, I'm game. I doubt anybody would mind me leaving now."

She looked up at him. "Luther took my car keys, remember?"

"Not a problem, we can take a walk through the countryside. It's a mild night, temperature's in the upper fifties."

"Let's do that. I've got to get something off my chest."

Dearl had Luther refill his beer, Jetti received a fresh wine cooler from Al, they put their coats on, and left the house.

Tornado Hill seemed to smile at them in the distance, faintly visible under the full moon. He held Jetti's hand as they walked. When they'd put about a hundred yards between them and the ranch house he gave it a light squeeze, let go, and sat down on a patch of winter rye, beckoning her to do the same.

"Well, here we are, all alone. What did you want to tell me, Jetti?"

She sat cross-legged in front of him, hands cupped around her wine cooler. Her face seemed to mask some horrid secret, and the expression made him feel nervous again.

"I don't know any way to say this, Dearl, except to just come out with it, so I will. That transient didn't kill my grandfather . . . I did."

"What?!"

Jetti nodded and started crying. "I don't want that poor man to be punished, because he didn't do anything. It was an accident . . . I didn't mean to hurt Grandpa."

Dearl felt dizzy, and not from beer. "Well why didn't you tell Sheriff Grange that? I can't believe this."

"Because if I tell why, I'm afraid no one will believe me, and I know Grandma will disown me like Grandpa disowned your mother when she got pregnant with you."

The beer slipped from his fingers but landed on the ground upright as if an invisible hand had caught it. He gawked at Jetti, so shocked he couldn't speak.

"You didn't know about that, Dearl?"

He shook his head.

"Grandma told me about it when we got back from your mother's funeral after the transient said he was looking for Maureen."

"Looking for my mom?" His voice cracked as he said it.

"Yeah. He asked Grandma who she was and I literally fainted when she told him she was Maureen's mother. Grandpa disowned Maureen when she got pregnant with you and forbade Grandma to have anything to do with her."

A torrent of emotions whirled inside but he refused to let them get the better of him. He was a man now, not a kid, and a man wouldn't bawl. The cup was shaking in his hand as he took a gulp. Recalling the weird statement about God having business with him, Dearl wondered why the bum had sought out his mother, and why he thought he'd find her at old man Simmons' place. "I've heard rumors since first grade that Rutherford was my grandfather but Mom said it wasn't true. I didn't see you at the funeral."

"I got there too late, you'd already left. That's why the accident happened. Grandpa wouldn't let me go, and the reason he wouldn't is why Grandma will disown me. He didn't want her to go either but she went anyway. I . . . I hit him and he fell back against his desk. I knew he was unconscious but I swear, Dearl, I honestly thought he'd come to any second, so I ran to the cemetery."

Dearl tried to digest all he'd just been told. Picturing his mother's emaciated face in her coffin, he rubbed his eyes, fighting back tears. Anger at old man Simmons burned hotter by the second. Her face disappeared as he imagined digging up the bastard's grave, opening the casket, and pissing on the creepy miser's face.

"I know I have to tell Sheriff Grange it was an accident and I did it—but what am I going to do after that, Dearl? Grandma will kick me out and I won't have any place to live."

What kind of people spawned his mother? The thought of Gwendolyn Simmons casting Jetti out the way her sorry husband had done his mom made him burn. He wondered if the stress of living a lie had significantly contributed to his mother being stricken with MS. Thinking she wouldn't have been if her father hadn't been so cruel increased his rage, but he forced himself to let the notion go. It wouldn't change anything. Nothing could change what happened.

Dearl focused on Jetti's worried pout. He'd have to vacate the government duplex when the school year ended but could provide her with food and shelter until then. His mother's disability checks would no longer be coming but her small life insurance would've been enough to support him through May. Al had insisted he put that money in a savings account and let him supply his groceries and other necessities after he'd turned down a gracious offer to move in with Cooper and him.

His mother's death had finalized his decision on which college to attend, and the Texas recruiter assured him the full scholarship he'd been offered would cover his needs once he got to Austin.

"I'm sorry, Dearl." Jetti wiped her eyes and sighed. "I shouldn't have dumped all this on you."

"No, I'm glad you told me. If your grandmother boots you out, you can live with me if you want. At least until I leave for Austin in June."

She leaned forward, kissed him, and settled back with her wine cooler. "If you only knew how much I want that."

His throat tightened up. She'd been giving him the eye since their freshman year, but he still felt like it was only because of his football exploits. "Jetti, would you still like me if I wasn't an athlete?"

"What a stupid thing to say. You *are* an athlete, Dearl."

"But what if I wasn't, would you still like me anyway?"

It took her a moment to respond. "How would I know? It's impossible to say since it's so much of who you are. I know I like you now, so what difference does it make?"

Jetti only keeping up with *his* statistics and not bothering with Holt's lightened his concern a little, but what if she was merely into running backs? If he was behind center and Rick played tailback, would it be Holt's accomplishments she'd memorized? The right girl would love him even if he'd never scored a single touchdown. Why hadn't Jetti ever flirted with him before he became a star? "It makes a lot of difference."

She took a light nip from her bottle and sighed again. "Okay, let me ask you a question. Would you still like me if I wasn't pretty?"

He shot her a wily grin. "So who says you are?"

Her eyes twinkled in the moonlight as she ignored his joke. "Would you, Dearl?"

"No, I reckon not."

"So don't you see? My looks are part of who I am, just as your talent on that field is part of who you are. I mean, I might still like you as much, but we'll never know, will we."

"Suppose I got hurt and couldn't play anymore. Would you still like me then?"

"Oh yes, but I think its time we got something straight, Dearl Tipps. I don't just like you, I'm in love with you—and nothing could make me stop loving you."

That hit him hard and he didn't know how to respond, thrilled though he was to hear it. "I guess we should be getting back."

A knowing smile came to her. "I just scared the shit out of you, didn't I."

"Um . . . yeah, to be honest."

"I'm not leaving this spot until you say you love me too."

Dearl stood up and started for the house. "Don't do this to me, Jetti."

"I mean it—I'll stay here all night if you don't tell me!" she hollered after him.

"Watch out for coyotes . . . ."

His thoughts returned to his mother. Why had she moved them back to Sleeping Bear where she had to know he'd eventually learn the truth? It should have been the last thing she'd have wanted. She had to have a specific reason, and that meant there was something else he didn't know.

Jetti caught up with him before he'd walked fifty feet. "Would you really have left me out here?"

"We'll never know, will we."

# 10

AFTER BREAKFAST AT THE POND Ranch, he rode with Jetti to the jailhouse. They hadn't told anybody at the party about it last night so Bart Newly, who spelled the sheriff as deputy on weekends, would be the first to know.

To Dearl's surprise the husky man with a bushy red moustache sat behind his desk. Myles Grange looked up from his newspaper.

"Well if it ain't Mister Football himself. What brings you and this pretty lady out here on a Sunday morning, Dearl? If you're looking for Bart, I took his shift because he's got a migraine."

"No, sir. We came here because Jetti has something to tell you."

"Oh?"

She nervously cleared her throat. "Um, my grandfather's death was an accident, Myles. The man you arrested had nothing to do with it."

Furrows rippled across the bald sheriff's wide forehead. "Is that so. How do you know that?"

Jetti broke down. "Because . . . b-because I did it."

"Huh?"

"I hit him because he wouldn't let me go to Maureen's funeral. I was only trying to break free because he was physically restraining me."

The sheriff rose from his desk, looking very suspicious. "Where'd you hit him?"

"On the face . . . and when I did he fell back against his

desk. I didn't know it killed him—I promise I had no idea. I ran to the cemetery and rode back with Grandma. That transient thought Maureen was still alive and only came to the house because he thought she lived there. I don't know why he was looking for her but you have to let him go."

"Why'd you wait so long to tell me?"

"Because of Grandma."

His brows shot up. "Because of your grandma?"

Jetti bowed her head and sobbed into her palms.

It reminded Dearl of catching his mother doing that very thing when he'd walked into the house after Rex Winters left. Somehow it made him utterly aware he couldn't live without Jetti, and that his main job in life was to protect her. "She's afraid Gwendolyn will disown her the way Rutherford did my mom."

The red moustache bristled over the sheriff's gaping mouth. "You know about that, Dearl? Maureen would turn over in her grave if she knew you'd found out. She called me shortly before she died, worried about Rex Winters printing it in The Hibernator, and asked if there was any way I could keep him from doing it. She was scared he was trying to warm up to her so she'd give him all the details about your childhood after he told her he wanted to write an article about you. She never wanted you to know, so how'd you find out?"

"I told him last night," said Jetti. "Grandma told me about it after you arrested the transient the day of Maureen's funeral."

Myles stroked his moustache, frowning with surprise. "Well if that don't beat all. The cemetery's eight blocks from your house, that's a long way to run. Why'd you wanna go to Maureen's funeral so bad?"

"Because of Dearl. I'm in love with him. You believe me don't you, Myles? I did it and it was an accident."

The sheriff heaved a sigh and reached for the phone. "Wouldn't be calling the judge if I didn't, Jetti."

♦♦♦

Zechariah sat on a bunk, idly gazing at the area beyond his cell. To the far right stood a door he'd been brought through. The two other cells were still empty but a constant dread tugged at him. He feared that door would open and the sheriff would bring a real criminal in—maybe a big, violent man who couldn't stand hippy types. Of course he only looked like one, but that fact wouldn't help him any. *Lord,* he silently prayed, *if somebody else does get brought here, please make the sheriff put him in the cell farthest from mine.*

He'd learned early in life that the Lord couldn't be outguessed. God had specific reasons for everything that happened to anybody and only He knew what those exact reasons were. Ephesians 1:11 stated it plainly: "In whom also we have obtained an inheritance, being predestinated according to the purpose of him who worketh all things after the counsel of his own will."

What His purpose was for him being falsely accused of murder only The Almighty knew at the moment, and like always, he'd bow his knee to it and not resist. Maybe he was being sent to minister to some poor guy in prison unjustly convicted of a crime, but he sure hoped not. Lord he hoped not!

*CLICK!!!*

A key turned in the lock and it wasn't meal time! Apprehension racing up and down his spine, Zechariah glared at the door. Then heaved a sigh of relief.

The sheriff walked in by himself, holding a ring of keys. The boy whose mother he'd been sent to, and the young lady who'd been with Maureen Tipps' mom the day he'd gotten arrested, stood at the doorway, shyly looking in.

To his amazement, the sheriff stabbed a key into the lock of his cell door and said, "Well, amigo, you're free to go. Seems Rutherford's death was an accident. Now you remember what I told you about the vagrancy law, right?"

Zechariah nodded, trembling with relief and gratitude. *Thank you, Lord God Almighty—who was, who is, who is to come!*

"What's the vagrancy law?" the young lady asked from the doorway.

"A person with no visible means of support and no place to live isn't allowed to hang around Kodiak County. This here feller is about to get escorted to the county line."

"He's got both if he wants them, Myles."

Zechariah turned to see the rancher put his arms around the boy and girl.

"I followed these two young'uns here to see what the heck they were up to. Luther overheard them whispering during breakfast about needing to talk to you."

Looking thoroughly confused, the sheriff scratched behind his ear. "You saying you're offering this dude a job, Al? I still don't know his last name, the Austin boys haven't been able to match his prints. Don't know it'd be wise to take a chance on such a character."

The Good Samaritan released the teens and walked up to his cell. "How about it, Zechariah? You look like a pretty strong hombre, and I'll have my foreman teach you how to be a cowpuncher if you're interested. Instead of having you fill out a W-Two Form I'd pay you in cash and record it as contract labor so I don't mind not knowing your last name since it won't get me in trouble with Uncle Sam."

Maureen Tipps' death prevented his mission from being completed the way it had been assigned to him. With no further instructions from the Lord about what to do now, he took the offer as a sign from heaven. "I'd sure be obliged."

Zechariah glanced at the boy. He could tell he made him nervous.

The sheriff twisted his key and opened the cell door. "Mind telling me why you were looking for Maureen Tipps now? When I asked before, you said I wouldn't believe it if you told me."

"I'm afraid you still wouldn't, Sheriff."

◆◆◆

"Dearl, hold up a minute!" Al hollered as he and Jetti started for her car in the jailhouse parking lot.

Al asked Zechariah to wait in his pickup, and walked over to him. "Um, Dearl, Luther also overheard you and Jetti discussing her telling you about Rutherford being Maureen's dad last night. Your mother made Kelly, Luther, and I promise we'd never tell you. That, of course, meant Cooper couldn't know either, or you'd have found out through him. Hope you won't hold it against us for keeping our word to Maureen."

"No, Al, not at all," he replied, honestly. "Y'all were all friends with her long before I came along. Do you know why she was so determined to keep me from knowing?"

Al shook his head. "Well, guess I'd best tend to my new hired hand . . . ."

◆◆◆

Rex called Myles to see if he could finally talk to the man accused of killing Rutherford Simmons. Stunned to hear what the sheriff had to say, he hung up the phone and waved for Emma's attention. "I won't be doing that interview after all. Myles said old man Simmons' death was an accident. Jetti Fury hit him because he tried to stop her from going to Maureen Tipps' funeral. It wasn't that tramp that made Rutherford fall and break his neck after all."

Emma gaped at him.

"On top of that, Dearl Tipps now knows all about Simmons being his grandfather and kicking his mother out. My suspicions were right about him not knowing before."

She rose from the couch. "And the transient?"

"Myles released him an hour ago. He's going to work for Al Pond."

"What a news story, eh?"

Rex laughed. "This used to be a dull town."

"Aye, now it's a regular Peyton Place."

♦♦♦

"It'll cost you ten big ones," Will Amarod said to the mouthpiece of his home phone.

*"Hundreds?"*

"No, thousands. My cousin won't go any lower than that."

*". . . All right, but it'll take me a few days to raise that kind of cash, and I'll need what I'm paying for right away or no deal."*

Will buffed the fingernails of his free hand on his chest. "I think I can arrange that."

*"If I don't have it by ten tonight, the deal's off, and you fucking better not burn me, Will."*

"Let me give her a call and I'll call you right back."

*"All right . . . ."*

Ten minutes later he called him back.

*"Is it a go?"*

"Yeah, but I have to have the money by Thursday so I can give her half of it on Friday or she'll squeal on us, and believe me it's not a bluff."

*"Okay, you'll have your ten gees no latter than Thursday."*

# 11

THEY WERE ON THE PRACTICE field a block away from the stadium wearing their workout whites with black numbers. Only their helmets identified them as Kodiaks. A lot of the town folk stood outside the chain-link fence surrounding the area to watch Monday's practice.

They'd just completed the first part: calisthenics. Coach Rainey shouted for everyone to take a knee in front of him.

"Okay, girls, we've drummed up a gimmick play designed especially for Langton. I didn't mention it during the film session because I'm not going to bother drawing it out on paper—we're going to practice it until none of you can possibly forget what to do. There's nothing fancy for you linemen to learn, you'll be blocking for a sweep. You think you can throw a pass, Tipps?"

Dearl grinned. "Are you teasing me, Coach?"

"No, I'm serious. Can you toss the rock or not?"

He salivated with excitement, having never gotten to pass the ball in a game before. "Well I can't throw like Holt but I can hold my own against anybody else on the team."

Hutch let out a laugh. "That's bullshit, I throw twice as good as you."

Rainey eyed the fullback. "Glad to hear you say that, Hutch, because you're going to throw on this play too."

Hutch's eyes flared, showing the whites above and below the irises, contrasting sharply with his ink-black skin. "I am?"

"You am. Now everybody listen up. The play starts as a right-side option sweep. Pond, you'll line up on the right. Go in motion when Holt signals you with his knee, and set on the left like you're planning to block. Hutch, at the snap run five yards straight towards the left sideline, then stop and act confused like you forgot the play, but be ready for the ball. Meanwhile Holt and Tipps will be heading for the right corner. When Holt laterals to Tipps all the defensive backs will be flying towards him, thinking run all the way. Dearl will then pass it to you and you'll throw a bomb to Pond running a post route. The play is called 'eighty-nine black motion red sweep double lateral'.

"Pond, you'll have to sell it. Run three or four steps to the right like you're blocking for the sweep before heading downfield. Tipps, if Hutch is covered, toss the rock to Cooper if you can. If not, tuck it away and take what you can get. Let's walk through it a few times . . . ."

The first attempt was such a disaster Rainey said they looked like the Keystone Cops. After explaining who the Keystone Cops were to several bewildered players, Coach had them do it again. Dearl overshot Hutch by a good five yards and everyone razzed him about it. The third try, Holt's foot got tangled up with his and they both went down before Rick could lateral the ball. But on the fourth go-round the play succeeded, albeit without facing any defenders.

Coach then had the defense, supplemented with several second-stringers, play against it at full speed. They ran it a dozen times in a row before resuming regular practice where the defense didn't know what offensive plays were being called. When they slipped the new play in on occasion, Cooper hit pay dirt two out of every three attempts.

He saw Jetti drive up as the emphasis shifted to defense.

"Okay girls," shouted Coach Rainey after they'd concentrated on special teams, the last football phase of every regular practice. "Time for wind sprints."

Dearl hated this part of practice. Fifty yards at full speed, fifty yards back in a trot, and they had to repeat the process until Rainey finally blew the whistle. His lungs were burning by the time they were told to hit the showers.

Cooper drove him home and they found Jetti sitting on his front porch.

"Oh baby!" Coo fired excitedly. "I think you're about to get some, poor boy."

"Not likely. I hope her grandmother didn't disown her like she was afraid of."

"Want me to hang or bail?"

He made a sour face. "Now what the hell do you think?"

Cooper laughed and shifted into first gear. "See you tomorrow."

Jetti rose from the porch with a big smile as he walked up. If her grandma kicked her out she didn't seem too worried about it.

"Hi, Dearl."

"Hey." He looked around, wondering how she got here. "Where's your car?"

"Left it at the practice field."

"Why'd you do that?"

A sexy gleam filled her eyes. "So no one would know I was here."

"Why?"

"Why do you think?"

His nerves lurched into high tension—he wasn't ready for this. Quickly changing the subject, he said, "How'd it go with your grandma? She gonna let you stay?"

She nodded, but the look on her face assured he'd be unable to veer her away from what she'd come for. "Let's go inside, Dearl."

Swallowing hard, he unlocked the front door and motioned for her to enter before him. Jetti sat down on the couch and he made for the kitchen. "Want a Dr Pepper?"

"Sure."

He downed half of his in three nervous gulps before returning to the living room. "Here you go."

Jetti accepted the can and projected one of her flirty smiles. "Where's your bedroom?"

Exhausted from football practice, yet full of nervous energy brought on by fear, he said, "We're not going in there."

"Why not?"

"I'm totally whipped, and besides that I don't have a rubber."

"I don't want you to use a condom, Dearl, and I'll find a way to revive you, trust me."

The look on her face and seductiveness of her voice fiercely turned him on, but not enough to override his anxiety. Nobody knew or even remotely suspected he was still a virgin—not even Cooper. As one of the most popular jocks in school, he'd be a laughingstock if anyone ever found out he'd never even made it to third base. "Coach doesn't want us fooling around during the week."

Boldness accentuated the desire in her eyes. "Coach will never know."

"Look, Jetti, I can't. Sorry."

"You don't have to worry about catching anything, Dearl, I'm a virgin. I've been felt up and fingered and all, but I've never had intercourse."

Jetti appeared to be telling the truth which made him want to confess, but he couldn't bring himself to do it. "Mind if I ask who the lucky guy was?"

"Guys, you mean."

"Oh, more than one got lucky huh?" He began to relax, feeling the ball had now bounced to his court and he'd be able to come out of this unscathed.

She frowned. "Well not all that many. I'm not a whore."

"I didn't think you were."

"So how many chicks have you gotten lucky with?"

Dearl downed some more Dr Pepper and wiped his mouth. "I don't kiss and tell."

"Ever had oral sex?" She raised the can to her lips.

The ball had just bounced back her way. He couldn't tell Jetti he never had, but for some reason he couldn't lie to her either, even though he'd started to. "Want to stay for supper?"

"Dearl Virgil Tipps, you're blushing, how cute! Now quit trying to change the subject. There's nothing wrong with talking about sex—especially between us. I love you, can't you understand that?"

"Jetti, let this go, we're not going to do it tonight and that's final. Now I'm fixing to start supper and I need to know if you're staying so I'll know how much grub to drum up."

"Don't you like me, Dearl?" she asked, eyes brimming with frustration.

"More than you know."

"Then why don't you want to make love to me? I don't understand."

He forced a grin. "Maybe I'm just old fashioned, ever think about that?"

"Are you?"

"No."

She laughed. "Well then why, what are you saving it for?"

Drawing a deep breath, he tried to muster the nerve to tell her—it seemed the only way out. "Jetti, you're not going to believe this, and if you tell anybody I'll deny I ever said it, but . . . ."

"But what?"

"Nothing. So are you staying for supper or not?"

"Oh I'm definitely staying," she firmly asserted, "but

whether I eat anything depends on what you plan to make?"

"Salmon patties, mashed potatoes, and ready-made salad."

"Make enough for me too then, I love salmon croquettes. So how long can I stay?"

"Till ten, that's when I hit the hay on school nights. How many salmon patties will you eat?"

"Two."

"Only two?"

"Yeah, how many do you eat?"

"Eight to ten."

Jetti gawked at him like such a thing was unheard of.

Snickering, he went to the kitchen and started getting things lined out as she took a seat at the table.

"Here, make yourself useful—" he tossed her a potato peeler and pointed. "The taters are in that bin over there."

"How many do you want me to skin?"

"Half a dozen."

"Six?" she laughed. "That's way too many potatoes for just the two of us."

"I'd mash up five if you weren't here."

"How can you eat that many potatoes and not get fat, Dearl?"

"I've got a fast metabolism, plus I'm an athlete." As vegetable oil heated in a twelve-inch cast iron skillet, he tore off a sheet of aluminum foil, stretched it out on the cabinet, and poured cornmeal in a bowl next to one containing two cans worth of pulverized salmon mixed with eggs, store-bought bread crumbs, dehydrated onions, and ground parsley. Then he went to work forming patties and laying them on the foil.

"Wow," said Jetti, grinning, "you're moving as fast as Grandma does when she makes salmon croquettes. She tried to teach me how to do it but I got totally grossed out when I stuck my hands in the fish and raw eggs."

"Sissy," he teased.

Thirty minutes later Jetti took a bite from one of her two patties and beamed as she chewed. "Hey, this taste as good as Grandma's."

"Thanks. I owe it all to an old Betty Crocker cook book of Mom's. Glad you like it."

They ate in silence for awhile, then she leered at him with yet another sexy glare. "So when *are* we going to do it?"

The ball had just sailed back to him. "When the time is right, we'll know. Not just one of us, we'll both know."

Jetti looked down at her plate. "There's something I need to tell you. I've only gone down on one guy, and he forced me to do it."

Rage swam over and through him so severely his belly cramped. His fingers involuntarily locked around his fork, clutching the handle with a death grip as he jerked it in front of his face, teeth aimed at the ceiling. "Who forced you, I'll stomp his fucking ass!"

"Not unless you know how to fight a dead man. It was my grandfather."

His hand went limp and the implement fell into his mashed potatoes.

"Thank God Grandma believed me when I told her yesterday. She said she'd been suspicious something like that was going on but had never been able to catch the old bastard."

"So that's why you were afraid she'd kick you out. You thought she might not believe you."

"Mm hmm."

"I wonder if he molested my mom."

"Probably not since they were blood related. I think he somehow justified mauling me because we weren't."

He groaned. "Why didn't you expose him?"

"I was afraid to. I didn't think anyone would believe me,

and I knew he'd never admit it. He warned me that he'd see to it I wound up in a home for troubled juveniles if I ever did. I totally freaked when Grandma told me she'd been suspicious, but even with that, I doubt she'd have taken my word over his because he could make her believe most anything. He had a real talent for lying."

How he wished that evil, twisted, selfish old man was still alive so he could make that son of a bitch pay for what he'd done to his mother and Jetti. He imagined punching Simmons until his face became a melted mass of bloody flesh, resembling a wax figure's after being assaulted by a blow torch. He smiled inside while picturing the pervert rolling on a prison floor, begging for mercy as a bunch of muscle-bound thugs who relished getting their hands on child molesters kicked him to death. The smile widened at the realization the monster had to be burning in hell.

Trying to clear his mind of Simmons, he blew out a deep breath. "Do you think your grandma knows who my father is?"

She looked surprised by the question. "You mean you don't know?"

He shook his head, slowly. "Since Mom lied to me about Simmons being my grandfather, I figure she invented Earl Tipps just like she made up her fake parents."

"Grandma doesn't know, Maureen wouldn't tell her. By the way, she wants you to know you're welcome in our house anytime. In fact you can move in if you want. She'd also like to help you out financially. Grandma's embarrassed to tell you herself because she's ashamed of giving in to Grandpa when he disowned your mother."

That surprised him almost as much as learning Jetti had been molested by the old lady's husband. Gwendolyn apparently had a heart after all. "Tell her I appreciate that, but I'm doing okay."

"She told me all about what happened with your mom if you're interested."

"*Yeah* I'm interested, tell me."

"Maureen told my grandparents about being pregnant as soon as she found out, but she refused to say who the father was. Grandpa wanted her to get an abortion but she defied him. That's why he turned his back on her. Grandma tried to talk him out of it but he wouldn't budge. Your mother left town and nobody in Sleeping Bear heard from her until she came back when you were five.

"She and Grandma saw each other secretly through the years, meeting up at Tornado Hill, and Grandma helped out all she could without Grandpa getting wise to it. Grandma begged Maureen to tell you the truth, but she never wanted you to know they were your grandparents. She also begged your mom to tell her who your father was, but she still wouldn't. Grandma thinks she was protecting a married man."

Dearl wiped a tear off his jaw. "Someone here in Sleeping Bear?"

Jetti nodded.

"I wonder if my dad's still alive."

"I don't know . . ." she rose from the table. "I'll wash the dishes. If we can't act like man and wife through sex, at least let me spoil you all I can in other ways."

"Oh, spoil away by all means." He loved to cook but hated cleaning up afterwards.

Watching her work, he realized another mystery had been solved. His mom moved them back to Sleeping Bear so she could continue a relationship with her mother in secret. Had wanting to be near the man who'd fathered him also been part of her motivation?

After the dishes were done he walked Jetti to the practice field to get her car. They held hands along the way.

"Weren't you afraid of getting pregnant if I'd given in without a rubber?"

"Mm mm. I'm going to be the mother of your kids, Dearl Tipps, and wouldn't mind getting an early start at all."

A rush of euphoria washed over him, but then he again started worrying she wouldn't love him if he wasn't so good at football. "Um, would you have made those other guys you fooled around with use a rubber if you'd let them go all the way?"

"Of course I would have, silly. You're the only one that'll ever make love to me without protection."

"Wait a minute here, you said you were going to have my kids, so why are you talking like there'll be other guys in the future?"

Jetti giggled. "Sorry, that came out wrong. No one but you will ever make love to me period."

She drove him back to his house and he kissed her goodnight.

# PART 2

# Why didn't you say you were a prophet?

# 12

ZECHARIAH SAT ACROSS FROM LUTHER at Al Pond's dining table. He'd met the big Cherokee Indian and Cooper when his new boss brought him to the ranch from the jailhouse yesterday. Al had driven him to Amarillo after breakfast this morning and they'd spent the day there: a doctor gave him a physical, a girl cleaned his teeth in a dentist's office, then Al took him shopping for clothes, boots, cowboy hat, and toiletries.

Luther offered to cut his hair and trim his beard.

"I'd love for you to—I hate being shaggy, but I'm bound by the Nazarite vow not to have a blade of any kind touch my hair or beard."

Al grinned at him. "Well at least both are clean now. You look and smell much better, and those new duds seem to suit you right well."

"I surely do appreciate it, Al."

Luther winked at him. "It's true you smell better, Zechariah, but you still look like a mangy mutt with all that hair."

Cooper got a kick out of the razz and Zechariah chuckled himself.

"Why'd you take that vow?" Luther asked.

He drug a biscuit along the edge of his beans and bit off the soaked edge. "I didn't. Two years ago God bound me by it until several missions He gave me were complete. The last of those missions brought me to Sleeping Bear. So, Al, what have I got to look forward to my first day as a cowboy tomorrow?"

"My foreman Kelly Newly will decide that, he's who you'll be working under. I warn you right now all the cowhands are a bunch of practical jokers so get ready to get teased a lot about your hair and beard."

"I can handle a ribbing . . ." he took a sip of iced tea. "These beans are mighty good, and this barbecued goat's really tasty."

Luther nodded once to show his appreciation. "The proper term for goat meat is cabrito if it's from a young goat, Zechariah. It's called chevon when it comes from an older animal. What you're eating is chevon. Your first lesson in becoming a cowboy. "

"Thanks for enlightening me."

Al folded his hands on the table and turned serious. "What did you mean when you said God had some business with Dearl Tipps?"

Zechariah swabbed a path across his plate and finished off the biscuit. Al had introduced him to Dearl and Jetti Fury at the jailhouse.

"Well?" said Al, impatiently.

"Not just Dearl, you too. God sent me to Sleeping Bear to speak to the boy's mother. Can't understand why the Lord took her before I could finish the mission."

"What were you planning to tell her?"

He cleared his throat. "Reckon this is a conversation you and I had best have alone."

"You sure you haven't been out in the sun too long, Zechariah?" said Luther, brow wrinkled. "When a man goes around saying God tells him what to do directly, I've got to wonder if he's not a few arrows short of a full quiver."

Zechariah shrugged. "Wonder all you want. I'm a servant of the Lord, and I fear Him, not man. Most folks I come across think I'm crazy, so you're not alone on that."

From the corner of his eye he saw Cooper watching him with more than a little curiosity. He turned to the handsome youth and smiled. "How long have you and Dearl known each other, Cooper?"

"Since kindergarten. That's when Dearl and his mom moved here."

"Back here, don't you mean?" Zechariah took careful note of Al Pond's face. The rancher seemed a mite nervous. The reaction didn't surprise him. "See, I know she was born and raised in Sleeping Bear, and left town when she got pregnant with Dearl."

Al frowned at him. "That's right. Who told you?"

"The Lord." Zechariah sliced off a section of his chevon. "Odd thing is, He gave me the wrong address for some reason. Is the Simmons place where she grew up by chance?"

"Yeah, that's where they lived when Maureen was born."

Luther cast him a cynical grin. "How did the Lord tell you the Simmons address, by a phone call?"

Cooper laughed and fired two imaginary pistols at the Indian, using his index fingers as barrels. "Good one, Luther."

"Can it, Cooper," said Al.

Unfazed by Luther's verbal jab, Zechariah put a finger to the side of his head. "The Almighty speaks to me in here."

That put Luther and Cooper in stitches, but Al didn't seem to find it funny. He focused on the rancher. "Maureen Tipps returned to Sleeping Bear less than a month after your wife died if I recall the Lord's words on the matter correctly."

Al rose from the table. "All right, where'd you really hear that?"

"True enough ain't it?"

"Yeah, but it wasn't the Lord that told you."

"You willing to make book on that? Like I said before, we need to discuss all this alone, just the two of us. And as for your unbelief, Luther, how is it I know you were an only child raised on a reservation by a Cherokee widow who was no relation to you? She pretended to be your mother when she signed the release form that allowed you to join the army at seventeen. Your real mom died of a heroin overdose when you were six and never married your alcoholic dad who eventually succumbed to cirrhosis of the liver. I didn't hear a phone ring, did you?"

Zechariah let that sink in, watching Luther's jaw loosen, even though the big man was trying his best to appear unimpressed.

"You might be interested to know He just now this minute told me to tell you that, so you'd come around to His way of thinking. I didn't know a lick of it until now."

No longer trying to disguise his shock, Luther scooted his chair back and stood up. "Who are you?!"

He shrugged. "I'm nothing and nobody, just a feller with a call on my life I have no choice but to follow."

For several long moments Luther gaped at him in silence, then turned to Al and said, "The only person that knew that outside the reservation was your dad, and I swore him to secrecy after I told him. Our friend here is telling the truth. I'm going to leave now so the two of you can be alone. Come on, Cooper."

After Luther and the boy left, Zechariah took one last bite of chevon and called it quits. "Sit back down, Al."

The rancher nervously returned to his chair.

"First off, understand that I'm just a messenger, nothing more. After I completed the other chores God gave me to do around the area where I'm from, which took quite some time, He told me to walk to Sleeping Bear and not to travel in any form of vehicle until that mission was complete. That's why I couldn't accept your offer of a ride to town that day. God sent me here to tell Maureen Tipps that He wants her son to know who sired him, and gave me a very clear mental image of her, the boy, and his dad. She died before I could tell her, so are you going to tell the boy or am I?"

"Tell him what?"

"Who his father is."

"How can I tell Dearl something I don't know?"

He studied Al for several moments and reckoned he'd spoken the truth. That made him wonder why he'd gotten nervous before. "She left town because of you. Did you know that?"

Al's eyes widened.

"Maureen didn't want to cause trouble, Al. She never told a soul because she didn't want to hurt you."

"Dammit—" he slapped the table and stood back up. "Who told you all this?!"

"God, like I said. While I was in jail The Almighty gave me a lot more details which I'll share with you now. You were a college sophomore on spring break and had a fight with your wife. Neither of you knew she was pregnant at the time. You left her in Austin and came back to Sleeping Bear to spend a few days thinking things over. Maureen, then in her last year of high school, was selling kisses at the Easter Bunny Fair and you bought one, only it wasn't at that booth.

"You told Maureen it looked like the end for your marriage and you two wound up in your old bedroom, knowing you'd have the house to yourselves for a couple of hours because everybody who lived on the ranch was at the fair. That's the only time you ever cheated on your wife. Maureen didn't know she was carrying your child until a week after she graduated. That boy has a right to know you're his father, Al, and Cooper needs to be told he has a half brother."

Tears pooled in the rancher's eyes. "Are you sure I'm Dearl's father?"

"Dead certain."

Al started bawling. "You're right . . . I did sleep with Maureen but she never told me I'd knocked her up. The guilt was so overbearing I haven't touched a woman since Cooper's mother died of encephalitis. And now . . . to know that I'm the reason she left Sleeping Bear and got disowned by her father . . . I don't know if I can handle it."

Zechariah's heart smote him for Al's sake, making him wish he'd relayed everything more sensitively, though he didn't know how that could have been accomplished. "The truth is the balm that'll heal everything, Al. Just tell the boy. He has a right to know. More importantly, God wants him to know."

"Do you know if she really got married . . .?" Al grabbed his napkin and blew his nose.

"Yeah, the Lord told me Maureen moved to Lubbock and got a job at a grocery store where she soon met a soldier named Earl Tipps, who said he'd be going overseas in three months and asked her for a date. She hadn't started showing yet, and seeing an opportunity to give her child a legitimate last name, Maureen accepted, knowing Earl wanted to sleep with her. Six weeks later Maureen lied to him, saying he'd gotten her pregnant, and he married her before shipping out. He and Dearl never laid eyes on each other because he got killed. Earl's parents died in a house fire in Lubbock before Dearl was born, so he never saw them either."

Tossing the napkin on the table, Al inhaled a deep breath and slumped onto his chair. "I wonder why she never told me."

"I wasn't informed. Just like I wasn't told you knew Dearl was your son, that was just presumption on my part—I was surprised to hear you didn't. All I know is the Lord wanted Dearl conditioned to be non-materialistic, and now that he's achieved the character God wanted instilled in him, knowing he has a rich father won't dilute it a bit. Maybe it hurt Maureen so bad when her dad turned his back on her she refused to be dependant on a man ever again. Could be she was afraid you might leave her for another woman that kept her from telling you Dearl was your son when she moved back to Sleeping Bear. Knowing you'd want to do the right thing by marrying her."

Al looked off into space and said, "Maureen must've thought I'd only want to marry her out of obligation and that's a travesty because that wouldn't have been the case at all. When she moved back to Sleeping Bear I tried to woo her but couldn't get anywhere." The rancher slowly turned his eyes back to him. "Zechariah, you're obviously a prophet. You should be tending to people not cattle. You're a man of the cloth."

He shook his head. "I'm just a messenger, pure and simple. If you want to call that being a prophet, fine by me, but I need a job and sure hope to work here a spell. I'm looking forward to being a cowboy. Besides, once Dearl knows who his daddy is my vow will be fulfilled and I can finally cut my hair and get rid of this damn beard."

◆◆◆

They were watching television. Emma had just put out a cigarette and her last puff hung in the air like a dissipating ghost. Rex gulped coffee to ward off nicotine cravings, but as always, it wasn't as satisfying. When the Monday night news from Amarillo went off, he hit the power button on the remote.

"What, no talk shows tonight then?"

"Not tonight, Emma, I've got some writing to do. You can

watch one if you want, I'll work in my bedroom."

Emma rose from the couch and stretched. "Think I'll have a spot of tea, then turn in me-self. So what are you writing about?"

"I want to do an article on the derelict that got accused of killing Simmons."

"That Zechariah feller?"

"Mm hmm. A few minutes ago it dawned on me getting his side of everything might make for an interesting story."

"Wonder how long he'll hold down that job Al Pond offered? Not long I'll wager. Bet the bloke hits the road after he gets his first paycheck."

"Maybe." He took a big sip of coffee. "I'll call Al tomorrow and try to set up an interview Wednesday night. Right now I want to do a first draft on the preamble."

◆◆◆

Jetti stood in the pervert's study staring at the door of the walk-in closet. All his molestations had taken place behind it. Now he was in hell and she'd never have to suffer another bout of such repulsive agony for the rest of her life. How fitting he'd died in this room, the very place where it all started two days after her fourteenth birthday. Grandma went to Amarillo for her weekly pedicure, which meant she'd be gone no less than four hours. Within minutes of her departure he'd laid out his demands and the threats of what would happen to her if she dared refuse. A part of her had died that day, but God had providentially resurrected it.

Now she knew the real destination of Grandma's weekly trips had been an alcove behind Tornado Hill where Maureen clipped and painted her toes in the car so Grandpa would never doubt her story. Two years ago, when Maureen couldn't drive anymore, Grandma quit getting pedicures. Since everybody in town knew her car she couldn't sneak over to Maureen's in it without Grandpa eventually finding out, so she took up bike riding, pretending her twice-weekly ninety minute rides were for exercise. In actuality she only rode for twenty minutes: the ten minute ride to and from Maureen's house while Dearl was at school. The bicycle stayed hidden in Maureen's backyard while they visited.

That had cut into the pervert's molestation time considerably because she was also at school, but whenever Grandma went somewhere while she was home he ordered her into his study and the nightmare continued.

He couldn't attain a full erection and the doctor warned him his heart was too weak to handle Viagra or any other such remedy so intercourse hadn't been an option, thank God. The other thing that had been in her favor was his inability to last, due to how much she excited him. She'd never had to withstand the horror of having his limp weenie in her mouth for longer than half a minute, and usually not even that long.

But whenever the bastard didn't have to hurry he'd French kiss her for long periods, sometimes well over an hour while groping her body, and his tongue had grossed her out even more than his penis.

She opened the closet door, spit on his smoking jacket— whose inside coattails always had dried semen on them between cleanings, unbeknownst to the pervert who'd assumed she always swallowed it—closed it for the very last time, and went to her room, ready for a good night's sleep.

◆◆◆

Not only did Dearl not dread Tuesday's algebra two class because of Jetti, he actually looked forward to it for the same reason. This time he smiled back each time she grinned at him. Cooper looked thrilled about it. Tornado Hill seemed pleased too. In fact everything seemed to be dripping with joy.

"Dearl," his mother's voice invaded his ruminating, "I have a bone to pick with you."

"What, Mom?"

"Why didn't you tell me about Jetti?"

The daydream vanished, leaving him bitter that he'd lost her before he could finally open up about Jetti. Did God allow her to look down from heaven and see how happy he was? He examined the other side of the coin. How had his mother felt about Jetti being raised by the father who'd cast her out?

Happy for Jetti, that's what, he concluded. His mama had a heart of gold, especially where kids were concerned— Cooper had always thought of her as his second mom. She must have confided her feelings on the matter to Gwendolyn, so he'd find out in time, when he finally got to know his grandmother.

An eight-year-old memory overtook him: the goat cook-off at Al's ranch on a cloudy summer's day, Cooper telling her she was the prettiest woman there. Coo had been a smooth talker to the opposite sex even as a little kid. His mother had tousled Cooper's hair while saying how much she appreciated hearing that. Dearl couldn't be objective on the matter, but a lot of people thought his mother was beautiful. Al certainly did, any observer could tell it by the way he looked at her, though Dearl had never heard him actually say it.

His mom had liked Al more than she had anyone else in Sleeping Bear. She'd never put it into words but Dearl had always known it just the same—yet she'd never once accepted an invitation from the wealthy rancher to go out on a date. And there'd been plenty of them.

She'd never dated anybody, her life had been centered on him. Why? What had prompted her to shun every suitor? Having a husband to provide for the two of them would have made everything so much easier, yet she'd sacrificed her love life and had chosen to bear that burden alone. Why? What had turned his mother into such a complicated woman?

Nobody but Maureen Tipps could answer that, and he suspected she might not have been able to fully explain it herself . . . .

He walked Jetti out the door when the bell rang. Cindy Shane was waiting for Cooper in the hall and the four of them strolled to the gym, where Cooper and he kissed their girlfriends goodbye . . . .

After calisthenics the coaches put them through specialty drills before Rainey whistled for everybody's attention.

"Okay, girls, it's time to learn another new play. This one's designed to take advantage of Kenny Higgins' over aggressiveness. Higgins will be keying on Dearl in this formation because it'll appear to be an obvious running play, which it is at first. Cocker, you're the wildcard in this one."

Jimmy Cocker, who played right tackle on both sides of the ball, had a shocked look on his chubby face. "Wildcard, Coach?"

"Yeah. We'll line up strong side right. At the snap you're going to pull and head left to make Higgins and the defensive end think it's a weak side sweep with Tipps totin' the rock—but he'll only stutter step left, then head right. Smith, your blocking assignment is the middle linebacker. Tipps, if Higgins shoots laterally commit to the run and gun it through the three-hole if the defensive end also bites on the sweep. If Higgins charges forward, lateral back to Holt and run a wheel route. Holt, you'll be back-stepping. Hold the ball as long as you can then sling it downfield towards the sideline and let Tipps worry about getting to it. Pond will block the defensive end when he realizes he's been fooled. Vaughn will run an out pattern weak side to occupy at least two defensive backs. Hutch, you'll run a short curl through the four-hole to force the weak side linebacker your way. Whitney, your route is a right slant to lure the cornerback covering you out of the play. We'll call it 'twenty three-vac black fake sweep'. Is that easy enough for you girls to understand?"

"Yes, sir!" shouted every player on the team.

"Good, let's walk through it."

Dearl had been amazed yesterday when Coach taught them a new play on the field without handing out diagrams and carefully going over it in a chalk talk beforehand. Now Rainey had done it again. He wondered if they'd be similarly surprised at tomorrow's practice. Then he recalled it'd only be a walkthrough since the game was on Thursday.

After a few mishaps, everyone got the hang of it and Coach called for repetitions of the play until *twenty three-vac black fake sweep* was ingrained in everyone's brain. Mike Vaughn, a junior who played left wide receiver, was gassed, running all those out routes full speed. He filled the left cornerback slot on defense.

Jetti met him outside the locker room and he rode with her to the lone café still operating in Sleeping Bear. They went Dutch treat on burgers and fries. After supper she drove them to Tornado Hill.

He wanted to make out with her but feared starting something she'd insist he finish, so he got out of the car and ambled to the base of the stationary cyclone.

"Tornado Hill really is amazing, isn't it?" he said when she joined him.

"Mm hmm."

Gazing up the spiraling tower, he eyed the underside of the plateau jutting out above. "Really seems to defy gravity."

"Yeah, it's a real marvel, but I've had enough of Tornado Hill, Dearl. Let's go back to your house and make love."

He lowered his gaze and faced her. "Remember what I told you?"

"Yeah, when it's the right time we'll both know. But you know what? I think you're just afraid."

"I am afraid. I don't want to get my heart broke, Jetti." He couldn't bring himself to tell her the real reason, bad as he wanted to. If she blabbed to anyone about him being a virgin he'd be humiliated. But what he'd said had hardly been a lie.

A warm smile crossed her face. "I would never hurt you, Dearl. I love you."

The look in her sexy eyes demanded an *I love you* from him, but he couldn't muster the courage to do that either.

Her smile waned. "You won't make love to me, and won't even say you love me. I don't understand."

"Look, Jetti . . . I'm not much of a romancer. I think you know how I feel about you. Don't think I don't, you know, because I do."

"Love me?"

He nodded.

She giggled. "Dearl Virgil, I've never known until just this instant that you're shy. How sweet!"

Though he took it as an insult, the notion cheered her up, so he didn't respond. Besides, she was right. "Guess we should be getting on home."

Jetti dropped him off and left for her house. Before he got to the door Al Pond drove up with the tramp he'd hired. Dearl invited them inside.

# 13

AL SEEMED NERVOUS. "HOW ARE you fixed for supplies, Dearl? Do you need anything?"

"I'm pretty well stocked up on everything, but thanks for asking." He looked Zechariah over. The dude was clean as a whistle and had on new clothes.

"Son, I can tell I make you uneasy," the man said. "Please relax and have a seat. We've come to tell you something."

Confused and troubled by this surprise visit, he remained standing.

Al took off his cowboy hat and held it stiffly against his chest. "Dearl, I've always thought the world of your mother, and would never have intentionally done her any harm but . . . last night I found out I did. Are you sure you don't want to sit down?"

He felt queasy, he'd never seen Al this edgy before. "Mom never mentioned you doing anything against her. How do you figure you harmed her?"

Instead of answering him, Al turned to the bearded man. "Maybe this isn't the right time, Zechariah."

Dearl's gut twisted as an intuition nudged him. He didn't know what this Zechariah dude had to do with it, but he somehow knew Al had come to inform him of what he'd suspected for a long time. "If you're here to tell me Earl Tipps wasn't really my father, believe me it *is* the right time. My mother made him up, didn't she."

Al nervously moistened his lips. "No, Dearl, she didn't make him up. Earl Tipps married your mom."

The intuition had been so strong, Al's correction stunned him. "So my father really did die like Mom said?"

Zechariah heaved a sigh and gazed at him with eyes reeking of deep sympathy. "Earl Tipps married your mom all right, but he wasn't your biological father."

The statement hurled him into another world—a place where nothing had ever really made sense, a discombobulated cosmos he'd been condemned to revisit over, and over, and over: the realm of his mother's past. Gathering his strength, Dearl fixed his gaze on the man he'd known since kindergarten and had always greatly admired. "Why are you so nervous, Al? What is it you're having such a hard time telling me?"

Tears rolled down Al's face, his hat shook in his hand.

"Talk to me, Al!"

Al propped his Stetson back on his head with one hand while wiping his eyes with the other. "My third semester at Texas Cooper's mother and I got into a vicious argument, Dearl—the worst fight we ever had. I took off and drove to Sleeping Bear, thinking my marriage might be over. My parents talked me into going to the Easter Bunny Fair with them and Luther. Maureen was there and I . . . I asked her to come out to the ranch with me, and we . . . aw hell!"

His mind reeled with the many recollections of people saying he and Cooper could pass for brothers. The stark realization that his intuition had only been half wrong rattled him. "Are you trying to tell me you're my father?"

"Dearl, I swear I didn't know I was until last night when Zechariah told me."

He cut his eyes to the transient and back to Al. "When *he* told you?! How would he know?"

"Son, Al's telling you the truth. I know this is a shock and all, and what I'm about to say will sound strange to you, but God sent me to Sleeping Bear to inform your mother that

He wanted her to tell you who your real father is."

Dearl didn't bother looking at the weirdo, just glared at the man he thought he knew so well until now. "Give me a break! You don't believe that bullshit do you, Al?"

"Yes, Dearl, I sure do. I didn't believe it either at first, but he proved it to me, and Luther as well. Zechariah is a bona fide prophet of God."

A gleam appeared in the strange dude's eyes. "Need convincing, huh? Well God just told me something that should clue you in, Dearl. There's a little secret you're carrying that you'd flat out die of embarrassment if anyone found out. You've toyed with the idea of sharing it with your new girlfriend, but haven't as of yet. That enough convincing or do I have to spell it out?"

Dearl numbly scratched at his head. It could be a bluff, but what if it wasn't? He thought it over carefully before responding. "Okay, maybe I do have a secret, but you'll have to tell me what it is before I'll believe you. And in case you *are* telling the truth, I want to hear it alone, just me."

"No problem," said Al, "I'll step outside. Holler when you're done, Zechariah."

When Al closed the front door behind him, Zechariah grinned and said, "Being a virgin at eighteen ain't nothing to be ashamed of, son. And believe me, the sooner you tell that pretty young lady the facts, the sooner she'll quit pressuring you to make love. Another thing just came into my head from the Lord—the girl's grandfather was molesting her, and other than that pervert, no one else has ever gotten further than kissing her because she wouldn't let them, even though she told you otherwise. Need more convincing?"

Dearl's knees buckled and he had to lean against the wall to keep from falling. Cooper had teasingly referred to the tramp as Moses, but he hadn't been far off—Zechariah *was* a prophet. The man's hair had been dirty and oily then, matted to his scalp, and his beard appeared to be a haven for fleas. Now they were both clean and flowing, enhancing an otherworldly air that seemed to surround him the instant he spoke the secret. "You won't tell anybody will you?"

The prophet put a hand on his shoulder. "Your secret's safe, but you really need to tell your sweet thing about it and get the air cleared up."

Dearl gave a single nod. "I will, sir."

"Don't call me that. The name's Zechariah."

"What's your last name?"

"I just go by the one name, son." He opened the front door. "Al, you can come back in. The boy believes us now."

Al stepped awkwardly into the living room. Dearl also felt nervous, seeing Al as his father for the first time.

Zechariah must have sensed their tension because he said, "Now it's time for *me* to step outside so you guys can talk."

Al opened the door for him and closed it after the prophet left them alone. "Dearl, I . . . I really don't know what to say. After I became a widower I wanted to marry Maureen but couldn't even get her to go out with me. I wish I'd known. If I had, I wouldn't have taken no for an answer. I hope you believe that."

He managed a nod.

"You know, it's ironic. Cooper always hated he was an only child. I can't tell you how many times he's told me you were the brother he never had. Funny, all this time you really were and none of us knew it. You want to tell him, or do you want me to?"

Dearl sniffled and wiped his wet eyes dry. "Zechariah will have to tell him something to convince him, the same way he did me. Coo won't believe we're not pulling his leg otherwise."

Al let out a nervous laugh. "Reckon Cooper's got a secret too?"

He grinned. "No telling."

"I'm so glad you finally gave in and let me pay for Maureen's funeral instead of having the county bury her. I tried to help her so many times but your mama was a proud woman."

"I know—" he started bawling and soon felt two strong arms embracing him.

"I've always loved you like a son, Dearl. I think you know that."

"Yeah . . . reckon I do. I've always loved you too, Al, just like I do Coo."

A light snicker emerged as Al backed away, hands still on his shoulders. "So, are you gonna start calling me Dad?"

Dearl chuckled. "I reckon not, it'd sound too weird."

"Reckon it would at that." Al gave him a big hug, patted him on the back, and stepped away.

"I'd like to get this over with right now, Al, if you don't mind."

"Good idea. Come on, let's go see your brother."

◆◆◆

Cooper was slouching in a recliner watching television when they arrived. Dearl greeted him and plopped down on a sofa. Zechariah and Al remained standing. Luther appeared and asked if anybody wanted something to drink. Everyone declined, Al nervously motioned for Luther to follow him, and they left the room.

Cooper frowned. "What's going on, Dearl—why's Dad acting so weird?"

Dearl appraised his half brother for a few moments before answering. They'd gotten their hair and skin tone from Al without doubt but Cooper's eyes had come from his mom as evidenced by the many photographs he'd seen of her. Dearl had no idea which side of the bloodline his stemmed from. "Coo, you know how people are always saying we could pass for brothers?"

He nodded, still squinting with curiosity.

"Well, rich boy, that's because we are. That's what's up with Al."

Coo snickered and shoved a handful of popcorn in his mouth. "Well I'm glad I got all the looks, poor boy."

The remark had an odd effect. For the first time since learning his paternal genes came from Al it occurred to him he had the same social status as Cooper. As much Pond blood flowed in his veins as his best friend's. He cleared his throat and leaned forward. "I'm serious, Cooper."

He looked at Zechariah. "Is that what you needed to tell Dad at supper?"

The prophet nodded.

Cooper bolted upright, face beaming with elation. "No shit?!"

"No shit," Dearl answered for the prophet.

"God told you that, Zechariah?"

The bearded seer nodded again.

Now Dearl was frowning. "Sure didn't take much to persuade you."

"I know he's a prophet, Dearl—Luther convinced me. So why did Dad sleep with your mom, did he say?"

"Yeah but I think it'd be better if you heard it from him."

Zechariah stepped out of the den and returned a moment later with Luther and Al.

Cooper glared at his father. "You ran around on Mom?"

The nervous rancher rubbed his eyes and heaved a deep sigh. "Cooper, I never stepped out on your mama. Maureen and I were only together once, and that never would have happened if I hadn't thought at the time it was over between me and your mom."

Dearl watched Cooper closely as Al recounted his infidelity. Unlike his brother, who'd been conceived in Austin, he'd actually sprung into being on the ranch. He made a mental note to razz Coo about it in the near future when things got back to normal. Looking around the den at the fine furnishings, he decided to accept Al's offer to move in.

This was home now.

Tears pouring, Cooper rose from the recliner and gave Al a big hug. "I love you, Dad . . . ."

# 14

THE THREE OF THEM AGREED to wait until after the big game to go public with their relationship. Luther and Zechariah promised to keep it to themselves in the meantime. Such incredible news might be distracting to the players as well as the coaches, and everyone on the team had to stay completely focused on defeating the Lions. For the same reason Dearl decided to remain in his house until hanging up his Kodiak uniform for the last time—keep his daily routine exactly the same so he could concentrate on the game plan.

Sitting in the film room watching Langton take apart their semi finals' foe, Dearl grimaced as Kenny Higgins stripped the ball from a running back and raced to the opponent's end zone.

Coach Rainey reversed the projector and froze the frame where the ball got stripped. "I don't have to tell you this is what you have to watch out for. Higgins will be All Pro someday. Tipps, Hutch, and all you receivers, listen up. Pull your elbows to your body and clamp down on that rock with both paws when that bruiser gets anywhere near you. If Higgins manages to get a hand between your arm and body, you're done for."

Coach then reeled it forward to a running play where star tailback Allen Pierce, 42, broke four tackles on a fifty-five yard run for a score. After reviewing it several more times, he again paused the projector.

"You can't tackle Pierce hitting him above the waist, he's

too strong. Hit him low and wrap up. Hard as it is to believe, he's stronger and quicker than he was last year. Note the formation they ran this particular play from. Wildemont's lined up as an extra tight end. Ninety percent of the time they run with this lineup, but they usually score when they go play-action on it and pass to Wildemont."

He set the machine in motion again and stopped at a play-action pass that went for six points when huge and speedy wide receiver Hugo Wildemont caught a pass from the amazing arm of Langton quarterback Jerry Lane.

"As you can see, they faked to Pierce here and threw to Wildemont. Notice eighty-four's stance." Coach reversed to the beginning of the play. "See how Wildemont's fingers are extended to the turf? Can anybody tell me why that's important?"

Dearl raised his hand.

"Tipps?"

"He set with his knuckles on the run."

Coach Rainey grinned. "Good eyeballing, Pearl. Watch number eighty-four's paws any time they line up in this formation. When he leans on his knuckles he's getting ready to knock the shit out of somebody because Pierce is going to run with the ball. When he sets on the tips of his fingers he's going to run a pass route. Okay—Hutch, when they use this formation with Wildemont weak side, if you see his knuckles on the turf holler 'Window!' to let everybody know it's a run. Tipps, you holler 'Door' if Wildemont sets with his knuckles strong side. If the rest of you girls on defense don't hear a peep out of Hutch or Tipps in this formation, it'll mean a pass is coming so don't bite on the fake handoff."

Middle linebacker Abel Norris stood up and said, "I could call it, Coach."

Rainey frowned at the junior. "When I'm ready for you to coach this team, Norris, I'll let you know. Until then you keep your mouth shut and listen. That'll be fifty pushups after the film session. Interrupt me again and I'll make it a hundred."

Snickers rose around the room as poor Norris hung his head. The big dude had great instincts, strength, speed, and agility, but any sort of savvy strategy went over his head. Dearl marveled at Norris's inability to grasp the obvious: Jerry Lane would soon figure out the Kodiaks somehow knew whether the play would be a pass or run if the middle linebacker barked out the signal each time. Once that happened, the quarterback would audible to change the play and the edge would be lost. All Lane would think with Hutch screaming 'Window' and him hollering 'Door' was that they were planning a stunt and alerting the defensive line to which side Wildemont lined up on.

The door opened and the high school principal said, "Coach, could I have a word with you?"

Dearl didn't like the look on Rainey's face when he came back a couple of minutes later.

"Today's practice won't be a walk through after all, and there won't be a bus ride to Arlington at three. You girls got to miss your afternoon classes today for nothing. The Thursday games have been canceled due to a bomb threat. The authorities think it's only a bluff but a bomb squad will be going through AT&T Stadium tonight and tomorrow to make sure that's all it is. We're still slated for one o'clock, but it'll be on Saturday . . . at Pirate Stadium in Woodrow."

Several of the players groaned, including Dearl.

"Norris, you'll be giving me those fifty pushups after practice. Having to do 'em after wind sprints ought to help you remember never to interrupt me."

When the film session ended Dearl put his arm around Abel's shoulders as they walked to the locker room to suit up in their practice whites, and explained why the middle linebacker couldn't signal Wildemont's stance.

"I wish I had your brains, Tipps."

Dearl winked at him. "Never forget, football's a mental game."

"Yeah, so Coach keeps telling me . . . ."

The student body had been notified of the schedule change and Jetti drove him home after practice. Dearl whipped up a chicken casserole for the two of them, teaching her each step of the way.

He slid a fourteen by nine roasting pan containing the concoction into the oven and grinned. "Think you can do it on your own now?"

A proud smile appeared. "Without a doubt, thanks for showing me. How long in the oven?"

"Forty-five minutes," he answered while setting the timer.

They went to the living room, each holding a Dr Pepper. Jetti took a seat on the couch and he sat beside her.

"As much as I hate having to face the Lions on the same field again I'm glad we'll be getting the two extra workouts." He took a sip of Dr Pepper and sighed. "Coach Rainey's come up with a couple of new plays for Langton. I sure hope they work."

"Such as?" she asked with an inquisitive smile.

"I doubt you'd understand, but basically they're trick plays."

"Tell me, I might surprise you. I know my football, Dearl."

He laughed. "Well you dang sure know my stats, I'll give you that. Okay . . ." he explained the two new plays they'd learned. Jetti listened intently.

"I bet that double pass play will go over big. It'll be great to get to see you passing the ball for once."

"Well, technically I'll be tossing a lateral to Hutch, waiting behind the line of scrimmage."

"I know that, Dearl. Still, you'll be throwing the ball to Delbert like a quarterback even if you won't get a pass on your stats."

"Yeah. Only Hutch will be credited with a pass on that play. It's called 'eighty-nine black motion red sweep double lateral'."

She giggled. "That's a mouthful."

"Yeah."

"Sounds pretty sophisticated. Okay, Cooper's number eighty-nine and he's the one who's supposed to catch the ball so I get that part, but what does the rest mean?"

"Black means strong side right, motion red means—"

"Back up. What does strong side mean?"

"Whichever side the tight end lines up on is the strong side. The other is called weak side."

Her eyes flared. "Oh, I get it—there's an extra lineman on that side, hence the term strong."

"Right. And he'll go in motion to his left, the weak side, codenamed red. That's what motion red means."

She gleefully clapped her hands. "I understand, this is so cool! Double lateral is what you and Rick are going to do. Rick will lateral to you and you'll lateral to Delbert."

"That's right, way to go." He gave her a big smile and took a pull of Dr Pepper.

A pout jumped on her face. "I forgot about sweep. What does that mean?"

"We're running wide like an option sweep. When Holt laterals to me the Lions, hopefully, will think I'm going to run around the corner."

Her eyes once again ignited with the excitement of learning something new. "Yeah, only you won't be—you'll be throwing to Delbert Hutch instead. This is so cool!"

Dearl had never known a girl who really understood football. Jetti's grasp of it amazed him, and he told her as much.

"I'm pretty good at getting to the bottom of things that fascinate me, and football always has. I wish I could play."

"Oh yeah?" He hopped up from the couch. "We've got half an hour to kill before supper. Come on, let's play some ball . . . ."

Every pass he threw to her fell incomplete, and it embarrassed Jetti. "Haven't you ever played catch with a football?"

"Not regulation size," she said, "just those toy ones you can wrap your fingers around."

"You're trying too hard. Let the ball come into your hands, stop trying to catch with your fingertips." He handed her the football and backed away a few yards. "Here, toss it to me and I'll show you."

He exaggerated his motions as he caught the ball. "See how I used my palms before wrapping up with my fingers? Now you try it."

She dropped the first one but snagged the second, after which she spiked the football and raised her arms. "Yes! Yes! I did it!"

Laughing, he trotted over and hugged her. "Now let me show you how to throw it right, then I'll teach you how to run with it and how to tackle . . . ."

During supper he thought about telling her Al was his father and coming clean about being a virgin but did neither, opting instead to tell her about Zechariah's amazing ability to hear the voice of God inside his head.

"You don't really believe that do you?"

"He proved it to me, Al, Luther, and Cooper. It's the truth, Jetti. Zechariah's a prophet."

A disbelieving scowl indicated she'd have to have proof, so he offered it. "He told me something about you that he couldn't have known unless somebody told him. Would you like to know what he said?"

Her frown lightened with a touch of curiosity. "What did he say?"

"That you've never gone any further than kissing with anyone but that old pervert."

She pursed her lips and looked down at her plate. "That's right, and I'm still a virgin intercourse wise. I wonder how he knew."

"God told him."

"You really believe that?"

"Yeah, not a doubt in my mind. He told me something nobody but me knows, that's how he convinced me."

"Which is?"

"I'll tell you after the game."

"Why not now?"

"Because I don't need the distraction of worrying about you telling somebody else. I know you wouldn't do it intentionally, but I'd be worried about it slipping out of your mouth accidentally. Jetti, I've got to stay focused on the game plan. We've got to beat those guys this time."

Jetti pouted but didn't press any further.

After they finished eating he kissed her goodnight at the car and watched her drive away.

◆◆◆

Grandma looked up from her knitting when she stepped into the living room.

"You're home early, Jetti. Did you enjoy your dinner?"

"Did I ever. Dearl taught me how to make a chicken casserole and how to catch a pass."

A flash of concern streamed through Grandma's

spectacles. "How to catch a pass? Did he get fresh with you?"

"A football, Grandma. That kind of pass."

"Oh," she chuckled. "Speaking of passing, did you pass my offer on to him?"

She slid onto the recliner. "Mm hmm, told him the other day. He said to tell you thanks and he really appreciates it, but he's doing okay. Sorry I forgot to tell you before. Would you believe I now know how to run with a football and how to tackle someone else running with it? I actually tackled the great Dearl Tipps. Of course he let me do it."

"You really like him, don't you."

"Mm hmm. We're gonna get married."

"He proposed?"

"Not yet."

Grandma laughed. "Well does *he* know?"

"Yeah, pretty sure he does."

"Have you two talked about it?"

"Technically, no."

"I see . . ." she put down her knitting needles and dropped her hands on her lap. "Love is a two way street, dear. He might not feel the same as you."

"Oh Grandma, of course he does."

"Has he told you as much?"

"Mm hmm." She giggled over having to translate his nod into the words for him.

"What's so funny?"

"Oh, just thinking about something cute that happened with Dearl."

She watched TV with Grandma for awhile and went to her room. While undressing for bed Dearl's statement he'd left unfinished when she'd first gone to his house came back to her verbatim: "Jetti, you're not going to believe this, and if you tell anybody I'll deny I ever said it, but . . . ."

Whatever he'd started to tell her had to be what the

vagrant said that convinced Dearl God revealed his secret to him. None of the girls he'd gone with appeared to be the type that put out. His big secret just might be that he's never had sex. If so, how romantic and special it was that they'd been destined to remain virgins until the consummation of their love.

The flowery, giddy feeling induced by that possibility flittered away as thoughts of being abandoned by her mother intruded, followed by the empty ache of not knowing who her father was. Did he know, or had the whore never told him he had a daughter? She wished the bitch knew what fate she'd been left to.

"She did it for your sake, Jetti," Grandma had said countless times. Grandpa wouldn't even discuss it.

Borne by a prostitute, abandoned to a depraved oppressor, surely God would bless her with a wonderful future to balance the scales. She'd never blamed herself like so many other girls had she'd read about—especially daughters molested by their own fathers. At least the sick bastard hadn't been a pedophile, he'd never acted indecently before her figure developed. For the first fourteen years of her life she'd loved Grandpa, though never as much as Grandma because of his self-centeredness. Grandma had always been a giver, Rutherford Simmons was a taker who'd turned his back on his own daughter. *Like my mother turned her back on me*, she thought, angrily.

Anita Fury was the slut's name. Why had she chosen to be a prostitute? Grandma said Anita made the honor roll all three years she'd attended Sleeping Bear High and graduated as salutatorian—eight months pregnant with her—only one notch below valedictorian Rex Winters, so she certainly hadn't chosen to sell her body for lack of options.

Grandma said Anita came to see her when she was seven but left immediately because, according to Grandma, "For some reason you were scared of her, Jetti." She didn't remember anything about it but believed her grandmother. The woman had never lied to her.

After she learned how to read, Grandma gave her the greeting card Anita left in her bassinet. Upon it was written:

My name is Jetti Louise Fury and my mommy, Anita, loves me very, very, very much! I was born 50 days ago on July 10th and a copy of my birth certificate is on its way to you by mail. My mommy hopes that you'll be my new parents so that I'll grow up in a secure, stable environment where I won't have to spend more time with a babysitter than her, and won't have to worry about mommy not coming home because some bad man hurt her at work. If you don't want to raise me please notify Burly Swain and he'll see to it my mommy comes back for me.

# 15

IT WAS WEDNESDAY NIGHT AND he still hadn't done a lick of work for Al yet. His new boss insisted he have two days of rest after his tiring Monday in Amarillo. Sitting on a stool surrounded by a furry pile on the kitchen floor, he kept feeling the smoothness of his face and running his fingers through his short hair. "I can't tell you how great it feels to finally get shorn, Luther. You did a wonderful job."

"You look good, Zechariah. By golly I dare say you flat out look handsome."

He grinned at his reflection in the big Cherokee's hand mirror. "Sorta do, don't I."

"I enjoyed the challenge." Luther took the mirror and handed him a dust pan with a brush snapped to it. "Now you get to clean up this mess."

"Guess I won't have to worry about taking a ribbing from the cowboys now."

Luther looked at him funny.

"What's the matter?"

"There's been a change of plans. Al doesn't want you living in the bunkhouse, you're going to stay here and help me take care of things. I agree with his decision, Zechariah— a man of God shouldn't be digging horse manure, and Lord knows I could use the help."

He sighed with disappointment.

"You don't want to work for me?"

"It's not that. I was really looking forward to becoming a

cowboy. I've never got to ride a horse before."

Luther grinned. "You don't have to worry about that, I'll turn you into a cowpoke. First thing tomorrow I'll teach you how to ride, after you help me cook breakfast of course. By the way, can you cook?"

"Not like you, but I look forward to your schooling on the matter. When did that newspaper guy say he was coming?"

"Rex said he'd be here by nine, so I got you presentable with ten minutes to spare."

◆◆◆

Rex had seen the man accused of killing Rutherford Simmons when he was in lockup, but Myles wouldn't let him interview him then. Emma, who'd been with him at the time, stood slack-jawed seeing the tramp with a haircut and smooth cheeks. Zechariah with no last name looked like a totally different person. Emma's reaction sent a bolt of jealousy through him for some reason.

Luther excused himself, leaving the three of them alone in Al Pond's den.

"I'm Rex Winters and this is my associate Emma Riley."

The cleaned up transient shook their hands. "Pleased to meet you."

"I'll get right to the point, Zechariah. I'd like to do an article on you—what brought you to Sleeping Bear, how you felt about being falsely accused of murder, why you've chosen to work for Al Pond, that sort of thing."

Zechariah, who now looked forty instead of sixty like he had in jail, shrugged his shoulders. "I doubt you'll want to print it, but I'll tell you everything you want to know."

Emma was still enthralled, and Rex wished he hadn't

brought her along. He didn't know why he felt so resentful but the emotion refused to subside. Activating a hand-held digital recorder, he began the interview. "Where are you from?"

"A little town in Arkansas."

"What's the name of the town?"

"Doesn't have a name. It's a little township south of Little Rock. I grew up on a farm near there."

"And you claim not to have a last name as well, right?"

The man nodded.

"Why did you come to Sleeping Bear?"

"God told me to walk here."

Emma giggled. "You walked all the way from Arkansas to Sleeping Bear?"

"Yes, ma'am."

"Oh please, call me Emma."

Rex's irritation mounted. He'd never been this angry with Emma before, but the way she so blatantly admired their interviewee really chapped his hide. He continued the interview. "Why did God want you to do that, Zechariah?"

"He told me to tell Maureen Tipps something."

"Like what?"

"Can't say at the moment."

"Why not?"

"Just can't."

"Well did you tell her?"

He shook his head. "Got there too late. She'd passed away."

"When I saw you at the jailhouse you had long hair and a beard. Did Al ask you to cut it?"

"No, I was aching to get that fur off me. I was under a Nazarite vow that I finally fulfilled after two years."

"Ah," Emma sighed, "the vow of the Nazarite. Have you always been a man of God?"

"Since birth, ma'am."

Emma seemed very impressed. "Were you born with a caul over your face by chance?"

"As a matter of fact I was."

Rex couldn't believe Emma was taking all this bullshit to heart. "Um, Zechariah, how did it feel being accused of killing Rutherford Simmons?"

"Indescribably awful. I wouldn't wish a thing like that on my worst enemy."

"What do you do for a living?"

Zechariah smiled. "I've just been assigned to assist Luther as a matter of fact."

"No, I mean before you came here. What did you do then?"

"What I've always done. Follow the command of the Lord."

He heaved an impatient breath and scratched aimlessly at the side of his neck. "No, Zechariah, I didn't mean that. How did you earn your living, that's what I mean."

"I told you. The Lord always provides. He took care of me then, just like He's doing now by seeing to it I got this job."

"How exactly did He provide before Al hired you?"

Emma scowled at him. "What's with you, Rex? The man told you, move on to another question."

Rex ignored Emma—he'd bite her head off if he didn't. "You know something, Zechariah, I don't believe you don't have a last name, and I don't believe you came from a town with no name, just like I don't believe you're a man of God."

Zechariah merely shrugged again. "What you believe or don't, doesn't concern me. You're not the first person to think I was crazy, and you certainly won't be the last."

"Oh, I don't think you're crazy, my friend. I think you're some sort of hustler, that's what I think."

"Speak to him like that again, Rex, and I'll throw you out

of my house."

He spun around to see Al enter the room. Had the whole world gone mad? Emma had the hots for the tramp and Al seemed hell-bent on defending him. "We're done anyway. Come on, Emma."

"I most certainly will not! Not until you apologize to the gentleman."

The vagrant smiled at Emma. "Oh that's all right. I've been called a lot worse, believe me. The Lord just gave me a message for you, Mister Winters. Lay your jealousy at His feet and let Him deal with it. You'll feel a lot better, and as a reward the Lord will take away your craving for nicotine."

Stunned by the incredulous disclosure, he gawked at Al. "Did you tell him I used to be a chain smoker?"

"Nope. Believe me, Rex, when Zechariah says he has a message from the Lord, *he has a message from the Lord.*"

Emma squinted at Zechariah. "What's he jealous about?"

"Don't know, the Lord didn't tell me."

She turned to him. "So what are you jealous about, Rex?"

His insides squirmed with anxiety. She'd never believe he didn't have a thing for her if he told the truth, and she might leave him. He loved Emma, she was his dearest female friend. For the life of him he didn't know why the green demon had latched on to him so severely. Sniffing a lungful of air through his nose, he switched off the recorder, slipped it into his shirt pocket, and defiantly folded his arms across his chest. "I don't recall agreeing that I was."

"You must be, Rex. He damn well knew about your struggle to stay off cigarettes, old boy."

"Please let it go, Emma," Zechariah urged. "That's strictly between him and the Lord."

"All right, if you say so. I've got an aunt in Ireland who has a remarkable gift of healing certain people of dyslexia. She was born with a caul as well."

Making Emma back off caused him to like the tramp for a moment. But that feeling vanished when she donned a flirtatious smile and said, "So you're single, I take it."

Zechariah nodded.

"Ever been married then?"

"Nope."

"I'm a widow me-self."

Rex couldn't take any more. "Emma, why don't you just ask him out and be done with it?!"

Emma's eyes ripped wide as her hands flew over her heart. "Plow me shamrocks, you're jealous over me!"

"No, that's not true. Irritated, yes—jealous, no. You've been blushing like a star-struck groupie ever since we got here. Now go ahead and make a date with him so we can go home."

She smoothed her hair and smiled at him. "So how long have you fancied me, Rex?"

"Emma, I love you as a friend, that's all—I promise that's all. I don't know why I got so wound up over this."

Zechariah chuckled, deep and raspy. His yokel bearing suddenly turned erudite with a strange smile. "He's telling the truth. The Lord just told me the jealousy you feel, Mister Winters, is more akin to a concerned brother rather than a lover."

A tingling sensation trickled over his skin—the man had astonishingly solved the mystery for him. "Exactly! Thank you, Zechariah, that's precisely what I feel like, a concerned brother. My apologies to you for what I said earlier, sir, and please call me Rex."

Emma donned a peculiar expression he couldn't interpret. "So you don't fancy me then?"

"No, I promise."

"Humph, feel a bit put off about it for some reason."

"You'll get over it, I'm sure." He cut his eyes to Al. "How

did Zechariah convince you God speaks to him?"

"It's on ice at the moment, but after we win State I'll tell you. I'm sure you'll want to publish it in The Hibernator as a matter of fact."

The prospect excited him. "You'll let me write about it?"

Al nodded.

Rex again stuck a hand out for Zechariah to shake. "Sorry we got off on the wrong foot."

After the handshake, the prophet tossed Emma a grin and said, "So are you going to ask me out or not?"

Emma was speechless, a phenomenon Rex hadn't witnessed for as long as he'd known her.

"Okay, Emma, I'll ask you out then. When I draw my first pay I'd like to take you to supper. Suit you?"

She gave him a big smile and nodded.

"Great." Zechariah ran his hands up and down his chest, grinning proudly.

Al pulled out his wallet. "I'll advance you whatever you need, Zechariah. Reckon a hundred will cover it?"

"Don't know, better ask her. She's the one's gonna pick the place."

Finally pulling herself together, Emma said, "I want to drive you to a big steak house in Amarillo. And I'll be paying for it, not you."

Her new paramour frowned. "I couldn't let you do that, it ain't proper."

"You can pay the next time, and we'll eat at the café here in Sleeping Bear then."

"Well since you're guaranteeing me a second date, I accept. So when are we going to Amarillo?"

"Tomorrow night sound okay?"

"Sounds fine to me." Zechariah glanced at Al. "Unless Luther needs me to hang here, that is."

"Won't be a problem."

"I'll pick you up at six," said Emma, eyes gleaming with anticipation.

◆◆◆

The jealousy he'd experienced made Rex think of *her* during the drive home, and he continued stewing on the bitch after telling Emma goodnight. He refused to even think her name much less say it out loud. Kelly Newly knew about her but no one else. Seven years had passed since he found out she was living two lives: one with him, the other with her husband in Muleshoe.

He met her at an Amarillo car lot on a Saturday afternoon. They'd both been car shopping and wound up looking at the same price-slashed-to-the-bone Acadia, which she'd purchased at his insistence. To show her gratitude she bought him a drink at Hooters. When she found out his life was wrapped around The Hibernator as they got further acquainted, she asked to see it.

She followed him to Sleeping Bear in her new vehicle and after he showed her around the newspaper she wanted to see where he lived. The following Monday the doorbell woke him at midnight and he answered the door to find her standing there.

"May I come in?"

"Sure," he said, aroused by the surprise. "What are you doing in Sleeping Bear this time of night?"

It was only a tease. She claimed to live in Amarillo and he had no reason to doubt her at the time. She'd obviously made a late-night trip just to see him.

"Rex, let me be frank," she said after a few minutes of small talk over a drink. "I'd like to come see you each night I can. Would you mind?"

Excited over the request, he said, "I'd love the company if you promise to come at a decent hour."

"That's just it," she replied, "this time of night is the only time I can make it. And I'll have to leave by two a.m."

"Why?"

"I'm a live-in nurse, and the woman I tend to can't be left alone except when she's asleep. Her medication schedule only allows me to be gone during that time and I can't get away on weekends."

"How were you able to go car shopping then?"

"A friend sat with her for me."

"Why can't you get away on weekends?"

"Because we go to her son's house in Oklahoma City every Saturday and return Sundays except when he's away on vacation, which he was this weekend."

Certain they'd soon be lovers, he agreed to the arrangement.

"One more thing," she insisted. "You can't tell anyone about me. Promise me you won't."

"Why?"

"Because I'll get fired if the lady's son ever finds out I leave her alone for a few hours every week night. He pays me more than I could get caring for anyone else, and I don't want to go back to nursing at the hospital or a clinic. I can dress as I please—no uniform—and the lady lives in an extremely nice home. I pretty much have the run of it."

"Okay," he said, "but I want to introduce you to my best friend. He won't tell anyone about you, I guarantee it."

She was unnerved by it but he wouldn't back down, wanting Kelly to see the pretty woman who'd chased *him*. Kelly had all those bragging rights back in school—no girl had ever come on to the scrawny nerd that hung with the stud: him. They'd been sleeping together over a month when he showed her off to Kelly after midnight one Friday.

Almost two years went by with her rarely not showing up at midnight Monday through Friday, then Kelly spotted her sitting with a man at the Muleshoe Livestock Auction one Saturday. She hadn't seen him so he went outside and waited in his pickup. When she left with the man, Kelly followed them to a house and drove on as they walked to the door. Kelly told him the address and he did some snooping around in Muleshoe where he soon learned she lived in that house, with a husband.

She left Sleeping Bear the following Monday at 12:15 a.m. bawling her eyes out after he confronted her, and he hadn't seen her since.

Her husband sold insurance and supplemented his income as a bartender in Hereford on weeknights. It was his job to supervise cleanup after closing time, so he never got out of there before two-thirty.

Rex would always hate her for deceiving him, but missed the sex. He hadn't been with a woman since.

♦♦♦

Zechariah couldn't sleep. His thoughts were held captive by the Irish redhead. Little did she know how perfectly the Lord timed their first meeting. Because of his commitment to the call of God, he'd never been able to seriously entertain the thought of any sort of love life. He'd never expect a woman to eat crickets or grasshoppers when a rabbit or rattler couldn't be found. But all that had changed.

The Lord evidently sent him to Sleeping Bear not only for the mission's sake but so that he could also put his John the Baptist days behind him. God had seen to it he got arrested, that's why he'd been told to talk to Maureen on the third day of the week, and God had blocked him until the right Tuesday came along—the day of her funeral. The Almighty hadn't told him so, but that had to be the reason.

His arrest led to a steady job through Al, and he had a hunch he'd be working for the rancher the rest of his life. Al hadn't mentioned salary but surely it would be enough to start a new life with Emma. The Lord had really blessed him tonight. He'd met the woman he planned to marry.

# 16

THEIR HORSES WERE MOVING AT a walking pace. The gentle mare Luther taught him to saddle up was a palomino named Buttercup. Zechariah held the reigns with one hand and stroked her mane as he rode beside the Cherokee, mounted atop an Appaloosa. He didn't feel right about wearing his new Stetson in front of real cowboys, so he traveled along bareheaded like Luther. It was a chilly morning but Luther hadn't bothered zipping his coat. A gust of wind blew the bottom half back like a cape and Zechariah noticed a long knife dangling from his belt.

They came to a group of cowboys taking a break beside a huge pond, fed by a windmill. There were over a dozen of them and several were Mexicans. One of the white men—a muscular, mean-looking fellow with close-cropped gray hair—got up, put a battered black hat on, and started towards them. The dusty chaps he wore made a swishing sound when he walked.

Luther reigned to a stop and dismounted. "Kelly, meet Zechariah, my new helper. Zechariah, this is Kelly Newly, Al's foreman."

The guy didn't look very glad to see them but Zechariah gave him a smile just the same and said, "Pleased to meet you."

"Don't be too sure about that," Kelly responded before cutting his eyes to Luther. "Is this the new hand I was supposed to get?"

Luther grinned. "Yeah, but I stole him away. What are

you gonna do about it?"

The foreman spit a stream of tobacco at Luther's feet.

In a flash Luther pulled out his knife and threw it—pinning it to the ground between the man's boots.

Kelly Newly calmly reached down and pulled it from the sod. "Not bad, Luther."

"I missed. Meant to stab you in the nuts."

"Maybe next time." Kelly whisked the knife around and handed it to Luther handle first. "So, Zechariah, how you like working for this redskin?"

"Um, fine, though I just got started. You guys always fool around like this?"

"Who's fooling?" said Luther.

"I got no use for this renegade and he ain't got no use for me."

Zechariah couldn't tell if Kelly said it in jest, but was relieved he wouldn't be working under him.

Kelly turned to the other hands. "Come on, boys, time to get back to work. We can't all be pussies like Luther."

"You need a stepladder to kiss my ass, Newly, and you know it." Luther got on his horse.

Right hand raised in the air with middle finger extended, Kelly walked away.

Luther chuckled. "Okay, Zechariah, it's time to show you what that horse can do. Give her a gentle kick in the haunches and she'll hit top end for you. Like this—" he gigged the Appaloosa and galloped off.

Zechariah did likewise and found himself on the ground after the horse reared up on her hind feet.

The other cowboys were laughing but Kelly ambled back and helped him up. "Buttercup used to be a stunt horse. Luther knew that's what she'd do, got to watch that boy. To make her lope, just pop the reins like you're spreadin' out a sheet on a bed and she'll go."

Zechariah climbed back in the saddle and tried it. Kelly had told the truth, and before long he caught up with Luther, waiting for him by a cluster of elm trees. He found the fast ride invigorating and once again began to miss the idea of working as a cowboy.

After showing him around the key points on the ranch, Luther led him to an area of pasture where a herd of Buffalo were grazing.

"Al's got close to two hundred of these beauties. His dad once had a thousand, but destroyed them all after they killed his other two boys in a stampede."

He grimaced, picturing the awful scene. "Holy Moses, that poor man. How old were his sons when they died?"

"Seventeen and fifteen."

"Man … Why didn't he just sell those buffaloes?"

"They spooked too easy, somebody else could have got stomped to death, and he didn't want anyone eating meat from an animal that killed his boys. He bought them from a man who rented them out to movie makers. When very few westerns coming out of Hollywood required buffaloes anymore, the guy was forced to sell them, and didn't bother mentioning he'd trained them to fly off the handle at the drop of a hat."

Watching a little bull help himself to his mother's milk, Zechariah said, "Where did these buffalos come from?"

"Al bought a handful of calves and you're looking at their descendants. By the way buffalo is a misnomer. What we have here are American bison. Real buffalos are indigenous to Africa. Al keeps these as pets. He's got twenty-five hundred beefalo that are part of the moneymaking livestock on this ranch, along with three thousand goats and seven thousand head of Beefmaster cattle."

"Beefmaster? Never heard of that breed."

Luther hacked a gruff snicker and cut his eyes to him. "I

thought you were raised on a farm?"

"I was but we didn't have any cows or horses, just sheep and pigs."

"Oh. Well Beefmaster is a cross between Hereford, Shorthorn, and Brahman. Al owns two sections in southwest Texas that an extended Mexican family lives on free in exchange for looking after another herd of 'em. That's where the oil wells are that made Al's great grandfather rich. The Ponds were already pretty well off before then though. This land was purchased by Cooper Forrest Pond in eighteen thirty-eight. Cooper's named after the patriarch."

"Where do Al's parents live now?"

Luther looked up at the sky as if watching a bird fly, but there wasn't even a cloud to view. The big Cherokee's profile made him think of an Indian brave silently praying to the Great Spirit.

"They died in a plane crash," he said with a slight tremor in his voice, "a jet chartered to take them to Austin to see Al graduate college. Wind shear took it down while they were landing. I'd have been with them if I hadn't caught the flu."

He could plainly see Luther felt guilty about being spared.

They rode back to the ranch house and Luther showed him how to make menudo, using tripe from a freshly slaughtered Beefmaster steer.

"Do you and Kelly Newly really dislike each other?"

Luther frowned at him. "Why would ask such a thing?"

"The way you two went at it. I thought you were razzing each other at first but then it seemed like it was real."

Luther's expression showed no signs of humor, or loathing. "You want to stay on Kelly's good side, he's a throwback to the old west and acts before he thinks."

Zechariah didn't ask again, seeing he wasn't going to get a

straight answer.

"Congratulations on winning over Emma, she's a pretty thing. One must be careful when acquiring pretty things."

"You said that like there's something I should know. Is there?"

Luther folded his arms and replied, "You're the prophet, you tell me."

"As I said before, I'm nothing and nobody. I only know things when the Lord informs me."

♦♦♦

Rex stood outside the chain link fence surrounding the practice field watching Thursday's workout. A few trick plays had been added to the repertoire and one in particular really impressed him. After catching a lateral from Rick Holt on what appeared to be a sweep to the right, Dearl Tipps threw a backward pass to Delbert Hutch, who then passed the ball to Cooper Pond downfield.

When they ran the play again he muttered, "That might just be the game breaker."

"Damn sure might at that."

He turned to see Kelly Newly walking up. "Well hey there, cowboy. Haven't seen you at a Kodiak practice in a long time."

"Yeah," said Kelly, "been a while."

Emma wasn't with him, thank God, and he hoped Kelly wouldn't bring her up. He never did at any of their weekly poker games because of Luther, but seldom failed to when they were alone, like now.

Delbert Hutch busted one up the middle and ran full speed until Coach Rainey blew his whistle. It would've been a touchdown in a real game.

"I remember seeing you make a lot of runs like that back when we were in school, Kelly."

"Seems like a century ago, don't it?"

"Yeah . . . sometimes it sure does."

They'd grown up together as the odd couple of Sleeping Bear: Kelly tough, quick tempered, and built to back it up—him, the skinny diplomat. He envied Kelly's hair even though it'd turned prematurely gray in their early twenties. Now thirty-six, his may have still been brown but it was gradually bidding farewell to his scalp. Kelly still had all of his. He used to be a Kodiak star back in their high school days, playing fullback. Rex had thought for sure he'd play college ball but the natural born cowboy decided to stay in Sleeping Bear and work on the Pond Ranch.

"So how's Emma?"

*Aw crap, here it comes.* "She's doing fine, Kelly. Please don't do this to yourself."

"Can't help it. The girl did me in."

"Like I've told you a thousand times, you've got to let it go."

Kelly pulled out a bag of Beechnut and stuffed a big wad of chew in his mouth. "It never happened to me before. Beats the hell out of me why I couldn't get it up."

Like he'd done before at least a dozen times Rex told him, "You've got to quit letting this haunt you."

Squinting at the practice field Kelly said, "Funny how she wouldn't give me a second chance but never went out with nobody else after that. Wonder what makes that gal tick?"

Rex hated being the one to break the bad news, but Kelly was going to hear about it soon anyway. He put a hand on his best friend's back and said, "Don't lose your head now, but Emma's going on a date tonight."

Kelly hiked his brows. "Anyone I know?"

"Maybe, since he just started working for Al."

"You talking about that new feller Zechariah?"

"That's the one."

"Well I be damned." Kelly spit and worked his jaw a minute. "Does Luther know?"

"Yeah. Emma and I went out to the ranch last night to interview Zechariah. They arranged their date before we left." He shoved his hands in his pockets, surprised how well Kelly seemed to be taking it.

Kelly spit again and sighed. "Might as well wish 'em the best I guess."

"Now that's the right attitude."

"What does she see in him I wonder?"

"Darned if I know."

◆◆◆

Lungs on fire, Dearl forced his empty legs to motivate, longing to hear the whistle. When it finally blew he leaned over, hands on knees, heaving. Wind sprints were over, hallelujah.

Rainey had installed a third trick play yesterday, taking advantage of having a full workout rather than the anticipated walk-through. On it, Hutch lined up to the left of Holt instead of behind the quarterback, and Gilbert Smith hiked him the ball. Hutch had the option of running with it or passing, and he'd fired a beauty to Mike Vaughn before Coach hollered it was time for wind sprints.

In the shower Hutch kept ragging Holt about being a better passer than him, then Cooper got in on the act and he joined in. Holt shot them all the bird, but for a moment at least, the super-stud quarterback had actually seemed to doubt himself.

Coach Rainey came over while everyone was drying off.

"Listen up, girls. Just got word we've been designated the home team. Now I know some of you are going to see that as a jinx since we've drawn the same lot every time we've played the Lions, but you can't let it get you down. Nothing about the last three games against them matters now. Keep your focus on this coming Saturday and forget what happened before. I want all your butts in bed by ten. No booze, no sex, no fun of any kind. You can all cut loose to your heart's content out on the Pond Ranch after we bring home the state championship, but until then I want you as disciplined as marines on the last day of boot camp."

♦♦♦

Delores Kaye lived next door to Lyle Whitney. His dad was the school superintendent and his mom taught fifth grade. Her daddy owned KAYE'S SADDLE & FEED on the western edge of town. Her mother worked at the only bank in Sleeping Bear. Delores wished they'd had more children after she came along, but her identical twin dying of pneumonia as an infant had so devastated her dad that he'd gotten a vasectomy.

He spoiled her, gave her anything she wanted that was affordable, so she'd had no concept of having to work for something until trying out for cheerleader in ninth grade. She didn't make the cut, got only enough votes to be named alternate as a sophomore, but this year she'd finally succeeded. Now her goal was to make head cheerleader. Darlene, Bibi, and Marybeth were seniors, so the stiffest competition would be gone, but she'd have to outwork incumbents Joie and Pat next year. Surely no rookie could beat her.

However, that goal was secondary to a desire she'd had since sixth grade: marry Rick Holt. Darlene had him now, and he'd gone steady with nothing but seniors since he started high school. This time next year Rick would be in his first semester at Texas Tech, thus leaving her no option but to go there after she graduated.

She had thought no one could alter her desire to be Rick's wife, but if Cooper Pond was to propose she'd marry him in a heartbeat, even drop Rick if she happened to be his at the time. Cindy Shane wouldn't hold him long, no girl could, herself included. The appeal didn't have a thing to do with him being Al Pond's only heir. Cooper's greatest talent couldn't be displayed while playing football—outstanding as he was at it—but in bed. Many heartbroken ex-wives lay in his future, she figured. A guy that good at sex couldn't possibly stay satisfied with only one woman.

Ten times she'd gone out with him in the last twelve months, at least thirty times he'd made her come so hard she'd lost her breath, and that without letting him go all the way on their first date.

Sitting on the front porch reading yesterday's edition of The Hibernator, Delores looked up when a horn honked.

Lyle waved at her while pulling into his parents' drive. They'd both lived on this street all their lives and were each other's first sweethearts. That relationship faded before their ages reached double digits. Now they were too close as friends to even think about dating each other. He often called her Kaye, and she always retaliated by using his last name as well.

He got out of his car and a Manx tomcat, who'd been prowling the neighborhood lately, jumped on the hood. Lyle gave him a good back scratching and crossed her lawn.

"Whatchadoin?"

"Reading . . ." she folded the paper and laid it on her lap. "How was practice?"

"Tiring as hell," he answered, grinning. Lyle's chipped left front tooth helped offset his freckled-little-boy cuteness, giving him a slightly tough look.

"Mind if I ask you something, Lyle?"

"Of course not."

"Why is Cooper going with Cindy Shane?"

He shrugged.

"You've never heard him mention it?"

"No."

"Why do you think he is?"

"Are you jealous about it, Kaye?"

"No, Whitney, just curious."

"Well, I figure she must be pretty good in the sack with Cooper being such a ladies man and all."

*That's what I was afraid of,* she thought. Lyle was bound to be right. The bitch would probably monopolize him until he left for college, taking away any chance of him asking her out again.

"That do it for you?"

"Yeah, thanks. How come you never asked her out, Lyle?"

"Because of Cooper, stupid."

"No, *stupid,* I mean before he started going with her."

"Oh. I thought about it a time or two but just had the feeling I didn't do it for her."

Pat Queen honked while driving by.

They both waved at her.

"Are you ever going to ask that girl out?"

"Pat?" said Lyle.

"Yeah."

"Nah, Abel's got his eye on her. I don't want that big boy mad at me. He'd break me in half."

# 17

ZECHARIAH ADMIRED EMMA FROM THE corner of his eye as she drove them down I-27, heading north to Amarillo. Conversation had fluctuated between her life history, rich with events, and his simple life as an itinerate messenger of God.

"Okay, Zechariah, I want the truth. Nobody goes round without a surname, now what's yours?"

"I really don't have one."

"What, were you abandoned as a baby, is that it?"

"Nobody knows."

She glared at him. "Now you're having me on."

"What do you mean by that?"

"You know. You're teasing me."

He grinned. "Learn something new every day. I was raised by a religious hermit who found me crying in his cornfield. He said I couldn't have been more than a few hours old and it was like I'd been miraculously placed there. A few months later I was lying on his chest while he read to me from the book of Zechariah in his Bible. I tore a page from it and he saw it as a sign from God he should name me that. Of course I don't remember any of it."

"That's amazing," she said in an awestruck tone. "So he's the one who told you about the caul I suppose."

"Mm hmm. Said he knew God had sent me to him to raise."

Emma passed a young couple riding a motorcycle and frowned at him when she got back in the right lane. "How'd you get through school without a last name? Surely the authorities must have looked into it, tried to locate your real parents and all."

"Never went to school. I was educated on the hermit's farm. His name was Noah Adams and he knew the government would take me away from him if they found out I existed. Noah wouldn't let me take his surname because he believed God had called me for a special purpose and feared he'd be infringing on The Almighty's will that I be totally separated from society."

"Why that's horrible, he'd no right to do that!"

Her reaction struck his funny bone but he managed not to laugh. "Emma, my upbringing went exactly the way the Lord intended. Noah had a doctorate in theology and was the president of a seminary. He grew disillusioned with so much of modern Christianity spiraling into mere formality, rigid legalism, or worldliness, so he resigned."

Emma made a sour face. "Aye, it's a bloody clutter all right. That's why I'm not affiliated with any religious organization, though I was baptized in the Church of Ireland. I fear it's a sign judgment day's approaching. Go on then. What happened after Noah resigned?"

"He bought a farm in Arkansas and went into seclusion. Once I came along Noah felt his mission in life was to train me in the knowledge of the Lord. After I grew up he purchased a small house in that township I told you about and made me move into it. I hated to leave the farm."

"So he's still there then, I take it."

"Well his remains are. He died ten years ago."

"Oh," she said with an apologetic smile. "Sorry for being so critical of him."

"Apology accepted. Noah was a great guy, the world could use a lot more like him. He had the highest degree of integrity of any man I've ever met, or expect to."

She shot him a grin. "Except you, of course."

"Yes, I'm a man of integrity, I'd be lying if I said otherwise—but I learned it from him. You strike me as a woman of integrity."

A light blush colored her cheeks. "Thank you. I like to think I am, though I'm as bloody human as anyone else."

"We all are."

"So tell me about the women in your life."

"There haven't been any."

"Oh you must be joking—such a special bloke like you?"

◆◆◆

Rex pulled into The Kodiak Cave and spotted Coach Rainey's Jeep in the parking lot. The restaurant was built seventy years ago and had gone through several owners and renovations since. The name had changed many times as well. Burl Swain gave it its present title upon acquiring it as a pet project after moving to Sleeping Bear from Dallas, where he'd made a killing in real estate and stock ventures. Burly, Burl's son, owned it now. Burl had wanted to raise his kids in a small town and chose Sleeping Bear because his brother lived here at the time. Rex had been in second grade along with Burly when Burl changed the name of what then was known as SLEEPING BEAR CAFÉ.

Burl's wife died of anorexia nervosa, then he got killed in a hunting accident, leaving a very handsome inheritance for Burly and his older sister Ruthie to split seventeen years ago. Ruthie let Burly have the restaurant in exchange for Burl's house, which she sold before moving to Austin.

There were three names synonymous with wealth in Kodiak County: Pond, Simmons, and Swain, in that descending order. Rutherford Simmons had been the richest Sleeping Bear resident, but Al Pond's assets were passed on to him by the wealthiest man in the county. Rutherford  got rich through an inheritance as well. His daddy made a fortune with numerous Dairy Queen franchises in south Texas. Gwendolyn—born and raised in Sleeping Bear—met spoiled only-child Rutherford at Texas their first year of college and married him before they graduated. When Rutherford no longer had to work, they moved here while Gwendolyn was pregnant with Maureen, who'd been a grade ahead of him in school.

An empty plate with a wadded up napkin on it sat before the coach, while his wife Annabel had pushed a half-eaten chicken fried steak to the side of a table for four.

The tough-faced marine vet looked up with a smile. "Hello, Rex, won't you join us?"

"Thanks, believe I will." He took the chair to Rainey's right, across from  Annabel.

"Where's Emma this evening?" she asked, fluffing the sides of her frosted hair.

"On a date. She's treating the man Gwendolyn thought killed Rutherford to a steak dinner in Amarillo. We got to know him last night, and he's quite an interesting character. Seems he's a prophet."

Rainey gave him a 'Come again?' frown.

"I know it sounds crazy, but the guy really is one." He explained how he'd been convinced. "I'm going to do an article on him as a matter of fact."

"Wonder if he can tell me Langton's game plan."

Rex laughed. "Now that would certainly give us an edge wouldn't it, Coach?"

"Actually, it doesn't take a prophet to know their game plan will center on stopping Dearl Tipps."

"I know mine would. Been watching the practices and

noticed you've thrown in some new wrinkles on offense. I'm very impressed. I suppose we're going to lose you to a larger school soon. A coach with your expertise should be handling a Five or Six-A school or coaching in college. I bet you've been getting offers haven't you?"

"I've turned down quite a few since my first season here as a matter of fact," said the couch. "Every one of them willing to top my current salary."

"So what's keeping you here?"

"Tipps, Rick Holt, Delbert Hutch, and Cooper Pond. Those four boys deserve to win it all, and I feel like I'm the right guy for the job. Being that I'm o-and-three in getting them there, if we don't take down Langton this time, I might just hang it up."

Annabel shook her head. "Don't listen to him, Rex. He'd go crazy if he couldn't coach."

"No, sugar, I'm serious. Truman Jette has always had my number. I've never beaten him."

He was referring to Langton's head coach. "You mean you've coached against him at other schools?"

"Sure have, and I'm o-and-six against him. But don't let any of my players know that. We've already been jinxed by that damn swap from AT&T Stadium to Pirate Stadium, and being designated home team again on top of that. Some of them would really panic if they knew I've lost to him twice as many times as they know about. Talk about getting offers, Truman will definitely wind up coaching in the college ranks."

Scowling at her husband, Annabel took a sip of iced tea as if to cool herself off. "You're every bit as good as he is, dear, and even better. What he's not telling you, Rex, is that those other three games were hopeless mismatches. Truman Jette had far superior players and it was only my hubby's ability to make young boys play beyond their capabilities that got them to the playoffs in the first place. Now he's got some real talent to go against him with, and should have beaten him last year."

Rex raised his brows. "Those other three were playoff games too?"

Rainey nodded.

"Well maybe seven times is a charm."

"Let's hope so."

♦♦♦

Dearl ran *eighty-nine black motion red sweep double lateral* over and over in his head—sometimes at full speed, other times in ultra slow motion. He felt in his gut that play would put them over the top if he could only control his adrenaline enough to not overthrow Hutch on the lateral. He'd mastered it in practice but that was without the pressure of a playoff atmosphere. Coo would catch it if the fullback could heave it anywhere near him—that was a given—but would Hutch be up to the challenge when the marbles were really on the line? It occurred to him the whole game might rest on his and Hutch's shoulders.

In his mind's eye he watched himself run to the right side one more time. Holt tossed him the ball, he took a few steps, then planted his right foot. Slowly, he turned and threw a backward pass to Hutch, who snatched it from the air and rifled it downfield towards Cooper. Dearl watched the ball—spiraling, spiraling, spiraling, until two hands reached up and grabbed it.

He jerked upright in bed when he saw they were Kenny Higgins' paws . . . .

♦♦♦

Emma turned onto the ranch road, drove about a quarter of the way up it, and pulled off into pasture. Then she turned again so the car faced the direction of Al's house and stilled the engine. Zechariah's nerves were tingling. Knowing she expected him to kiss her, he wished he had some mouthwash to gargle. The aftertaste of a marvelous beef steak still lingered in his mouth and he feared his breath would be foul because of it.

"*Ahem* . . . Zechariah, isn't it lovely sitting out here in the country under the shimmering stars on such a clear night?"

"Uh, yes it is." He nervously pursed his lips.

"So you've really never been with a woman before?"

He shook his head.

"Well, I can show you what it's like if you won't think me too forward."

"Here?"

"Yes, we can use the back seat. My first time happened on one as a matter of fact."

Zechariah took an apprehensive look at the proposed site and turned to her. "We shouldn't do it there, it seems inappropriate. Besides, don't you think we should wait until after we're married?"

A shrill giggle rose from her throat. "Married?! Who said anything about getting married?"

His heart sank. Had he totally misread her intentions? He begged God for the answer.

"Um, Zechariah there's something you should know about me that I haven't told you. Haven't done it until now out of respect for you being a man of God, but I smoke. And to tell you the truth, I'm dying for a cigarette. Would you mind terribly? I'll smoke it outside so as not to offend you with the smell."

"No, not at all."

She pulled a pack of cigarettes and a lighter from her purse and got out of the car. Waiting for The Almighty to answer him, he watched her repeatedly blow smoke into the night. As often happened, the still small voice refused to speak. When she turned her back to him, continuing to enjoy her cigarette, he gazed across the country side in the direction of the towering oddity he'd learned was called Tornado Hill. He couldn't see it through the darkness but knew its location well, having glanced at it off and on while trekking to his camping spot on the Pond Ranch after first spotting it.

Emma got back in the car and sat sideways with her blouse opened. Her breasts were pointing at him like two lethal cannons.

"Thought having a look at the girls might move things along. Have you ever seen a woman's breasts before?"

Throat restricted, pulse racing, unable to take his eyes off the incredible globes of flesh with their stiff, red nipples—he shook his head.

"You can feel them if you like, Zechariah."

He almost gave in to the temptation but God finally spoke to him and he immediately covered his eyes. "Emma, I have a word for you from the Lord. Please button up your blouse and I'll pass it on."

"You don't like them then?" she asked in a tone of utter shock.

"Oh no, they're beautiful, but please . . . they're distracting me."

"Drop your hands and have one last look, then I'll do as you ask."

After he complied Emma pulled up her bra which she'd folded beneath her spectacular mounds, and buttoned her shirt—staring at him the whole time, eyes dripping with disbelief. "Okay, what's the word?"

"Kelly Newly isn't homosexual."

Emma's face reddened as if she'd been slapped hard on both cheeks. "Please tell me Kelly put you up to this and you didn't really hear it from God, Zechariah."

"The Lord said those exact words to me just a moment ago."

She vented a huge sigh and turned towards the windshield, hands clutching the steering wheel. "That's devastating to hear . . . I was certain Kelly must have been a gay man trying to force himself to turn hetero, because he's the only bugger that didn't immediately sprout a tree at the sight of my body. Now here you go telling me to cover me tits. I guess I have to face the fact I'm no longer the woman I used to be."

Watching a tear meander down the side of her face, he thought about two things Luther said: "You want to stay on Kelly's good side" and "One must be careful about acquiring pretty things." He'd been subtly warned that Kelly wouldn't take kindly to him dating Emma.

"Gawd I feel awful. I haven't noticed any changes in me body at all. Guess my mind plays tricks with my vision when I look in the mirror to keep me from noticing them. Perhaps no woman realizes she's losing her physical charms at first."

"You're not losing anything, Emma. Don't take my reluctance to make love to you as a sign I don't want to."

She cut her eyes to him. They were questioning, yet hopeful. "So you do want me then?"

Zechariah nodded.

"But only if we're married, is that right?"

He nodded again.

"Right . . ." Emma silently gazed through the windshield for several minutes.

If she didn't want to marry him there was no point in pursuing her. As aroused as he'd been when seeing her breasts, he knew if he gave in, that moment of carnal pleasure would bite at his conscience with the bitterness of a serpent's venom for the rest of his life. At length he told her so.

Emma sniffled and again turned sideways in her seat. "Here's how it is, Zechariah. I'm very attracted to you— enough that I want you to make love to me—but I'm not in love with you. And that's what I'd have to be in order to marry you. Could it happen? Of course. Will it happen? I've no way of knowing. If you want, we can continue seeing each other and I'll respect your feelings on abstinence and won't try to seduce you. Got me word on that. And if in the process I find myself falling in love, I'll marry you."

He felt warm inside. Surely it would only be a matter of time before she saw what he did: that they were meant to be man and wife. "Sounds like a perfect solution to me."

She turned firm and said, "Got one condition though."

"Okay."

"You'll have to put up with me smoking in front of you, and you can't ever ask me to quit. If and when I ever give up the habit, it'll be because I want to, not because someone else wants me to. If that sounds reasonable to you, we're on. If not, we're off, simple as that."

"Sounds reasonable enough to me."

"Can we at least kiss?"

"I'd like that."

She leaned over and put her lips on his. Instinct took over and Zechariah thought he had it all figured out until Emma stuck her tongue in his mouth. Flabbergasted at the emotion it pulled from him, he realized she expected him to respond in kind . . . and so he did.

# 18

LUTHER DEALT THE CARDS: TWO face down, the third exposed for all to see in another round of seven card stud. Rex peeked at his hole cards, pleased to see a pair of fours to accommodate his ace. This Thursday night poker game consisted of Luther, Al Pond, Myles Grange, Kelly Newly, and himself. It was his week to host the game and on the one hand he hated Emma wasn't there to keep them supplied with refreshments—on the other, if she had been, they'd be a player short because Kelly wouldn't have shown. They were in the living room, where he'd set up his professional poker table, a Christmas present Emma had bought for him in Amarillo two years ago.

"Ace bets," said Luther.

Rex tossed two quarters in the pot. "Four bits."

"I'll see your four and raise you four—" Al threw a dollar bill on the pile.

Luther looked across the table. "Waiting on the high sheriff."

Myles thumbed up the edge of his unseen cards and placed a five on the center of the table, making change from the quarter antes and bets. "Call."

"Same here," said Kelly while making the pot right.

"Dealer also calls."

After Luther contributed the correct change, he dealt another card to each player face up.

Trying to come off like he was merely bluffing when Luther tossed him another ace, Rex said, "The price of poker just went up, gentleman. Wish this wasn't dollar limit. I'll bet the max, half a buck on each bullet."

Al and Myles both called.

Luther grinned at Kelly. "What's it gonna be, limp dick, bet or fold?"

"Up your butt!" Kelly belted, glaring at the big Cherokee.

"Well by all means, if you can get it up."

Kelly picked up his cards and threw them down. "Fold."

"A thing he does well. Dealer calls."

The next round Rex drew a queen of hearts. Fearing his full house might not materialize, he checked. Al bet a dollar and everyone called.

After such a sweet deal of the first four cards it looked like lady luck had abandoned him because Luther tossed him a nine next, but on the final round Rex had a hard time concealing his excitement when he checked the last card, dealt face down, and saw another four.

"Aces still bet."

He cut his eyes to Luther, who'd spoken. The Cherokee had a pair of deuces, a jack, and a king showing. Al seemed to be trying to fill up a high straight and Myles was obviously hoping for a spade flush. With no other deuces showing, Rex knew there was an outside possibility Luther had two more in the hole, but decided to risk it and bet the maximum.

Al raised a dollar, as did Myles.

Luther frowned. "Hmm, that's three bucks to me. Tell you what I'm gonna do—I'll see your three and raise. Make the pot right if you wanna stay in this game, newspaper man."

Rex dropped a five dollar bill on the pile and took out a one. "Raise the max."

Al also raised a dollar and Myles bumped it to six.

"Dealer raises."

Rex matched the raises and bumped another dollar. Al

also raised the maximum, then Myles did likewise and so did Luther.

"Leave it to the redskin to deal me such a shitty hand I had to bail," Kelly bitched with a mournful scowl. "Oh what a sweet pot."

Luther grinned. "Almost enough to give an ol' boy a stiff, ain't it."

Kelly gave him the finger.

Feeling confident, Rex raised another dollar. "I'm going to keep raising all night, gentleman, so you'll all have to call me if you want to see this gorgeous hand I've been dealt."

Al turned to him with a snicker. "Why don't I do just that. Call."

"Call," said Myles, fattening the pot.

Luther gave him a wry smile. "You can't beat my four deuces, Rex. Al has an ace and queen showing, and Myles has your nine so there's no way you've got four of a kind. Best cut your losses and fold. Dealer raises eight bits."

Rex immediately matched Luther's bet and raised again.

Al and the sheriff called but Luther bumped the bet another dollar.

The cocky dealer wouldn't back down and kept raising the maximum while Al and Myles continued calling his dollar raises as well. So when Luther raised again, making the bet twenty-five dollars, Rex finally called. "Let's see that pitiful hand you're bluffing with, Luther."

Emma walked in and brought a hand to her throat. "Gawd, would you look at that pile of money?"

Kelly's face paled, as did Emma's when she saw him sitting there. They stared at each other and no one uttered a word, not even Luther, who rarely passed up an opportunity to pop off in tense situations.

After what seemed an eternity of awkwardness, Emma heaved a nervous sigh and said, "Well, I'm knackered, so I'll be off to bed. You gents enjoy your game."

Kelly watched her walk away and got up. "I'm going to settle this damn mess once and for all."

Myles shot him a cautionary frown. "You don't do a damn thing without her permission, hear?"

Kelly nodded.

Luther donned a look that almost appeared sympathetic. "Don't do this to yourself, Kelly—sorry for poking fun at you about it. Emma likes someone else now, leave her be."

"Don't much think I could live with myself if I did."

Rex knew he couldn't change Kelly's mind, so when the tortured cowboy left the table he turned to Luther. "Let's see what you've got, big shot."

Gaze focused on Kelly ascending the stairs, Luther turned up his hole cards. Rex groaned. So did Al and Myles. The lucky bastard had four twos after all.

◆◆◆

After Friday morning's breakfast dishes were taken care of, Zechariah asked Luther if he could go talk to Kelly Newly.

He seemed taken aback by the request. "Why would you want to do that?"

"The Lord gave me a word for Emma last night that involved him, and I feel like he might could use some ministering to."

"Oh? What did the Lord say?"

"I'll be glad to tell you if Kelly says it's okay. I'm not sure at the moment he'd want you to know."

Luther crossed his arms. "He won't want you to tell me, you can bet on that."

"So you don't want me to ask if he minds then?"

A trace of a grin appeared. "I didn't say that now, did I."

Zechariah chuckled.

"Remember how to saddle up Buttercup?"

"Yeah, I think I can manage it okay."

"Ride to the watering hole and head due north until you come to a corral sheathed with chicken wire. If nobody's there just wait, Kelly will show up before long. They're culling goats for auction."

He didn't have to worry about finding the corral. Kelly was at the pond by himself, watering his horse. Zechariah dismounted and walked towards him, holding Buttercup's reigns. "Hey there, remember me?"

Kelly squinted at him. "Yeah, you're the man trying to steal my woman."

Freezing in his tracks, Zechariah uttered a silent prayer for deliverance in case he was about to be assaulted. "Emma doesn't want to marry me, and that's the only way I could ever be intimate with her. We're just socializing, that's all. You don't have anything to worry about with me unless she changes her mind, which I hope she will."

Several moments of awkward silence rolled by, then Kelly said, "I talked to her last night after she dropped you off. She tells me you're a man of God—a prophet."

"I'm just a messenger, nothing more. Did she tell you about the word the Lord gave me?"

"Yeah, that I ain't queer."

"That's right. I came to see you because I thought you might want to talk about it."

Kelly spit out a plug of tobacco, dropped to one knee, and rinsed his mouth out, scooping water from the pond with a cupped hand. "She tell you what happened between us?"

"Not exactly, only that she failed to get you excited enough to . . . you know."

A dry laugh escaped Kelly as he stood up. "Like hell. She didn't fail, I did."

"Care to talk about it?"

"It was the damndest thing, Zechariah. I couldn't wait to get in her pants but when the time came I couldn't get a hard on to save my life. It's never happened with anyone else before, and she refused to see me again—wouldn't give me a chance to redeem myself. I made the mistake of telling Luther and the boys about it, and that damned ol' redskin won't let me live it down. Anyway, the tale got to floating around Sleeping Bear and sparked a rumor that I was homosexual. Now that's a mighty hard thing for a man like me to live with. I was at Rex's last night when she came home, and begged her to let me give it another try but Emma wouldn't do it because she figures she's just not my type and besides that she was dating you now."

Kelly's eye color caught his attention. He'd never seen anyone with irises that particular hue. "When did it happen?"

"Four years ago, not too long after she moved in with Rex Winters. Me and Rex have been tight all our lives. For whatever reason the two of them knew right off they'd never be more than friends, and Rex introduced me to her, thinking we might hit it off and we did. Big time. I asked her out, and at the end of our first and only date she said she wanted me and started yanking her clothes off like a maniac.

"No woman's ever done a thing like that with me that soon after getting acquainted and I guess it got to me somehow. That's the only thing I can figure that caused it to happen, or not happen rather. It screwed me up so bad I've been scared to try it with another woman outa fear I'd fail again, which really stoked the fires of that nasty rumor. Say, why am I telling you all this shit anyway?"

He shrugged. "Maybe because sometimes it helps to tell a stranger what's too embarrassing to share with friends."

Another dry laugh. "Hell, I did share it with them, and that was the worst mistake of my life. Anyway, damned if I know what can be done about it since Emma won't give me another chance."

*Holy Father, please quicken to my spirit the advice this man needs.*

"Why are you standing there with your eyes closed?"

"Shush, I'm listening."

"Listening? To what?"

"To the Lord, now shut up—I can't help you if I don't hear Him right."

◆◆◆

Everyone's last class of the day had been canceled because of a pep rally, the second one this week. There'd been one at noon Wednesday for the Thursday game that got canceled. Dearl stood with his teammates on the auditorium stage as the band played and the cheerleaders led the school body in the Kodiak fight song.

Cooper elbowed him as they exited and said, "Dearl, I don't think I've ever been so damn nervous in my life as I am right now."

"Yeah, me too, but we can't allow ourselves to get too hyped up or we'll be exhausted before the game even starts tomorrow."

Jetti and Cindy appeared in the crowded hallway and walked with them to the gym. They were standing outside the locker room door when Cooper and he came out in their blue game uniforms.

"Can I walk with you to the field?" Jetti asked.

"Coach wouldn't like it. Listen, I don't want to hurt your

feelings but this is the last I want to see of you until I board that bus tomorrow. I can't afford any distractions."

She pouted. "I understand. I'm so proud of you."

He put his helmet on. "Hope you still feel that way this time tomorrow . . . ."

The pre-game workout took place at the stadium as always. They walked through the new plays several times, then rehearsed some of their old ones. After a walk-through of the defensive scheme, practice was over—they didn't have to do wind sprints the day before games. Dearl halfway wished they did because he grew more tense and anxious by the minute, and figured an exhausting running marathon might take some of the edge off. He could tell by the expressions of his teammates they were just as wired.

This didn't bode well and he wished Coach would say something to loosen everybody up, but Rainey seemed equally uptight. So did the three assistant coaches.

A dead weight lodged in his stomach and he pictured Higgins once again stealing victory from them. Now pissed off as much as he was frustrated, Dearl took off his helmet and threw it to the ground, despite knowing it would draw severe punishment. No one was allowed to remove their head gear without permission until they got to the locker room, and they were only half way there.

Coach Rainey stopped, turned around, and glared at him, hands on his waist. "Something on your mind, Pearl?"

"Yes, sir!" he barked out like a new recruit answering his drill sergeant.

"Hold up, girls, I believe one of the captains wants a word with you! Take off your helmets, drop to a knee, and listen."

Dearl couldn't believe how slick Rainey was. The way the corners of the sly dog's mouth turned up before he spoke could only mean he'd engineered this. He no longer seemed edgy—neither did the other coaches—it had all been an act to get one of the team leaders frustrated enough to react and address the problem.

"You have the floor, Tipps."

He licked his lips but the action failed to moisten them. Nervously crossing his arms across the white twenty on his blue jersey, Dearl sucked in a deep breath and blew it out. Coo, Holt, Hutch, all the guys looked up at him expectantly, and he dared not let them down.

"Most of you have known me since first grade and you know I'm not much of a speaker, but we're all way too keyed up and that just ain't gonna get it or we'll get our butts kicked tomorrow. In the end all that's gonna happen is a football game, and that's how we've got to look at it now. We all know what's at stake but if we don't take that field tomorrow loose and confident, expecting to win like we have every other game this year, we're going to lose, I guarantee it."

Dearl dropped his hands to his sides and sniffed another long breath through his nose. "It's my fault, and my fault alone that we lost to Langton last year. Well, guys, I promise you it won't happen again. Kenny Higgins is a damn good linebacker, probably the best in the whole state, but I'm gonna make him pay the price every time he tries to tackle me tomorrow, you've got my word on that. Jerry Lane is a gifted quarterback, no doubt, and Allen Pierce *is* fierce like the Langton cheerleaders love to scream, but they haven't faced us this year have they. We're better, we're stronger, and we're a hell of a lot smarter now, thanks to our coaches. More importantly, we're hungrier than Lane and that running back. Hugo Wildemont may be an All-State receiver but we're an All-State defense, and don't forget that.

"I want to remind my fellow seniors what we swore we'd do after that shitty seventh grade season. Well, we finally made it to the big ride and this is our last chance to do it, guys. Confident and loose—eager to take that field—that's what we have to be. All we have to worry about is executing the game plan, that's all. We do that, we win, I guarantee it." He looked at Rainey. "Guess that's all I wanted to say, Coach."

Rainey grinned and told him to take a knee with the team. "What Tipps said is dead on the money, girls, but I want to add one thing. Every one of you has the heart of a champion, and you keep telling yourselves that tomorrow, especially if things don't appear to be going our way at times. Stay with the game plan but don't over-think it, and don't be afraid to go with your gut instinct on any surprises the Lions might come up with.

"Now there won't be any fancy locker room speeches in Woodrow tomorrow. Each of you will have to motivate yourself, and I know you will. Why? Because you know, deep down inside your gullets, that you deserve this. We coaches wouldn't have pushed you so hard if we didn't believe you could do it. Tomorrow will be the last time this squad will play together as a football team. Next year almost half of you will be attending different colleges, and a few of you will be representing those universities on the football field.

"When I came to Sleeping Bear I remember some arrogant freshmen telling me they weren't going to settle for anything less than a state championship. I won't mention names but their initials are Dearl Tipps, Rick Holt, Cooper Pond, and Delbert Hutch. Well, they made a believer out of me and now, girls, I won't settle for anything less either. What are we going to do tomorrow?"

"Win State!" hollered every member of the team.

Coach put a hand to his ear. "What's that, I barely heard you. What are we gonna do tomorrow?"

"Win State!" everyone shouted at the top of their lungs.

"What are we gonna do tomorrow?"

"Win State!"

"I said, *what are we going to do tomorrow?!*"

"Win State!!!"

"Damn right. Now hit the showers . . . ."

# 19

STANDING AT ITS BASE, ZECHARIAH looked up at the plateau atop Tornado Hill. Luther hadn't pried when he'd told him he needed the rest of the afternoon off in order to speak with Emma, and had informed him where she lived. He'd ridden here first, in the hope that seeing the structure up close might arouse enough childlike wonderment over the odd-shaped edifice to override his other emotion.

It didn't.

His eyes were misty and his heart ached. Nonetheless he felt grateful his affection for Emma hadn't grown any stronger before learning the truth. He gave Buttercup a love stroke on her powerful neck and mounted her. Never one to see the glass as half empty, always half full, he resisted the temptation to wallow in self pity and give in to anger. Solitude was nothing new to him, but meeting that Irish redhead had made him think those days of isolation were finally behind him. Though in a way they were since he now shared the company of Al, Luther, and Cooper, in a deeper sense they never would be.

As Buttercup moseyed along in the late afternoon his mind stayed locked on this morning when he'd spoke with Kelly Newly at the watering hole. He'd asked the Lord for advice so he could minister to the foreman, and God granted his request. But only after delivering a jarring message not meant for Kelly, only him.

Kelly had been frowning with anticipation when he'd finally opened his eyes after receiving the word.

"Well?" the foreman had asked.

"You figured right," he'd said. "Emma's aggressive, uninhibited nature overwhelmed you, causing your impotence. I'll speak to her and share what I just told you, and I've got something else to say to her alone beyond that. After I do, I'm sure everything will be okay between you two."

"You saying you're backing off from her?"

"Yeah . . . I'm out of the picture."

After a grateful handshake and pats on the back from the ecstatic foreman, he'd gone back to the ranch house: happy that Kelly had been liberated from the emotional cancer that'd eaten at the cowboy for so long, yet deflated over what God said to him.

*You are not to take a wife or ever defile yourself with a woman,* the Lord had commanded.

Emma's breasts would be the only female's he'd ever see uncovered, at least in real life. He wished he had accepted her offer to feel them so he could relish that memory as he always would her wonderful kisses.

♦♦♦

They were sitting at the dining table after a savory Irish stew and soda bread supper. Emma stubbed out her cigarette on a saucer and reached for the tea. Rex eyed the lipstick-stained butt with awe. It hadn't occurred to him until that moment that he'd felt no compulsion to light up while she'd smoked the beastly thing. Smiling, he raised his coffee cup and savored the rich nectar of his only addiction, caffeine. Zechariah had been right, the Lord took away his craving for nicotine.

The doorbell rang and Emma went to answer it. A moment later she walked in with the prophet.

Rex grinned at him. "Well hello there, I was just thinking about you."

"You were?"

"Yeah, just a second ago I realized God healed my craving for cigarettes just like you said He would. I didn't know you guys had a date tonight."

"We don't. I came to speak with Emma about a word from the Lord."

He pushed away from the table and stood up. "Guess I'd better leave you two alone then."

"No, Rex, please stay," said Emma.

The seer cleared his throat. "You might not want that, this is on the personal side. You know, about as personal as you can get."

That put a smile on her face. "Oh, you're here to romance me, is that it?"

"Uh, no," Zechariah answered with a touch of sadness in his voice.

"Then I want Rex to hear too."

"It concerns you and Kelly Newly, Emma."

Emma's perpetually flaming gaze turned ice cold. She pulled absently at the unbuttoned collar of her pink-and-white checkered shirt with one hand as the other found its way to her waist. Her right knee began rocking back and forth like a singer's keeping time to a beat. At length she said, "Well I still want Rex to stay. Go on then, tell me."

"I'm afraid I can't date you anymore, the Lord has other plans for me, but please give Kelly another chance. He wasn't unable to perform because he didn't desire you—your aggressive, uninhibited nature was the culprit."

Exhilaration turned Emma's naturally pink-tinted face a light crimson. "Are you certain of this, Zechariah?"

"Yeah, it came straight from heaven. Now I've got something else to say. If you'll let him do all the initiating, everything will be fine."

"Did God tell you that too?"

"No, it's just a hunch I have."

Rex patted her on the shoulder. "I think you should do it, Emma, and follow Zechariah's advice, hard as it will be to go against your natural instincts."

"Most assuredly I will!" Emma planted one on the prophet's cheek. "Oh thank you, Zechariah, thank you so very much."

♦♦♦

Bluish white lights twinkled on the dark horizon: Sleeping Bear, the place where her heart lay. Anita hadn't been there in ten years, the last time she'd seen Jetti. When the precious little seven-year-old was frightened to speak with her—despite being prompted to do so by Gwendolyn Simmons—she'd driven away in tears, swearing never to return. But Jetti would turn eighteen in July and she wanted to see what her daughter looked like as a grown woman.

Not wanting Jetti to bear the stigma of having a prostitute for a mother, she'd left her on the Simmons' doorstep in a basinet with a note pleading for them to raise her. She'd counted on Gwendolyn taking Jetti in because it was no secret she'd been dead set against Rutherford disowning their daughter Maureen. Her plan worked, but it hurt so bad not having her baby she couldn't take it any longer after four miserable years, and tried to get Jetti back—promising the judge when the Simmons brought the matter to court that she'd turn over a new leaf. But the judge hadn't believed her.

Born and raised in El Paso, if she hadn't lost *her* mother to an accidental overdose of a prescription medication, the events that lead to her becoming a hooker wouldn't have happened. The instructions called for two tablets every eight hours but her mom had mistaken the eight for a three. Her dad hadn't checked the label until calling for an ambulance when he came home for lunch to find his real estate agent wife lying unconscious on the kitchen floor. What looked like a 3 was in fact an 8 with the left side barely visible. She'd never read the accompanying leaflet which clearly stated: TWO TABLETS EVERY EIGHT HOURS. The life insurance company won a battle to withhold payment due to the manner in which she died.

Her father worked at a lumber yard at the time and didn't earn enough for them to remain in the nice house she'd lived in since preschool, so he'd been forced to move them into a modest apartment. To supplement her reduced allowance, she babysat for a young widower whenever he wanted to spend an evening out. His toddler daughter stayed in a daycare while he was at work.

He made good money and lived in the ritzy part of the same complex. On a Friday night in May of her eighth grade year he offered her twenty dollars for a hand job. Curious to see what the handsome guy's penis looked like, she'd let him show her what to do and marveled at how quickly she'd earned the money. Before long he was handing her fifties for letting him finger her while she jacked him off, and that led to hundred dollar bills for using her mouth.

A distant aunt of her dad's passed away and he'd been greatly surprised to learn she'd left her lovely house in Sleeping Bear to him. By the time they moved into that home and he went to work for the county, driving a road grader, she'd branched out to other men and knew how to spot a potential client a mile away.

Her dad thought she'd afforded all her nice clothes because of babysitting, and never knew the only real gig she'd ever had as a sitter was for the man who'd enticed her to sell him sexual favors. When a john wanted an all-nighter she'd tell her father the parents had an emergency and needed her to spend the night with their children, always using made up names he never checked up on. She'd been a sophomore when they moved to Sleeping Bear, and he'd suffered a fatal asthma attack near the end of her junior year, never knowing what kind of daughter he really had. Now thirty-six, Anita regretted the path she'd chosen and planned to find a legitimate vocation, even though she sometimes garnered more cash in an hour than a high-priced lawyer. It wasn't because of Father Time, she looked ten years younger than her age and could easily demand top dollar for at least another ten, if not twenty.

At first she'd been a popular kid at Sleeping Bear High, but being such a small town, her extra curricular activities eventually became known by everybody and most of the students shunned her.

Driving by the old Piggly Wiggly, she sadly noted all the windows had been boarded up with plywood. The store looked like it had been closed down a long time. A smile came to her when she saw The Kodiak Cave still open for business. Passing The Hibernator, she wondered what Rex Winters was up to these days.

Thinking about the editor took her back to late September of her senior year. While working a rodeo in Amarillo the weekend before, she'd reeled in two local boys who'd paid a hundred dollars apiece to gangbang her. The next Saturday they came to Sleeping Bear wanting a repeat performance. They'd driven up while she was watering her flower bed and made the proposition in her front yard, refusing to say how they'd found out she lived in Sleeping Bear.

They'd roughed her up in Amarillo so she refused, even though they were willing to throw in another hundred. Rex drove by and saw them trying to force her into their car. He pulled over and tried to defend her, only to get stomped. However, his brave action caused the boys to flee afterwards out of fear of being arrested for assault. Later that afternoon she ran into Kelly Newly at the drug store and told him about it.

"Can you get hold of 'em?" Kelly asked through gritted teeth.

"Yeah, one of them has that new thingy called a cell phone and gave me the number in Amarillo, begging me to call him when I wouldn't tell him my phone number. I wrote it down in my address book before I found out they were a couple of thugs."

"Give him a call," said Kelly, "and say you decided their money's as green as anybody's but you can only fit them in at five o'clock. I've got a plan."

After they picked her up at a roadside park where she'd arranged the meeting, she guided them to the spot Kelly had told her to go: a grassy clearing in the country surrounded by high brush. Per his instructions, she insisted they take off their clothes before she'd remove hers. When they did, Kelly came running out of the bushes and took them down single handedly, swearing he'd kill them on sight if he ever caught them anywhere near Sleeping Bear.

Bruised and bleeding, they'd driven away and Kelly made her promise never to tell Rex what he'd done. "Rex can't help that he's built on the fragile side, but he's got plenty of guts. Why he'd want to take on those two punks over a whore like you, I'll never know, but his pride will be sorely wounded if he ever finds out I heard about him getting his ass kicked."

Recalling the blowjob she'd given Kelly afterwards, Anita smiled while continuing down Main Street.

"I did this for Rex, not you, bitch," he asserted with a hateful scowl after she made the offer.

"I know that but I want to thank you anyway," she insisted. "You're getting it for free if that's what you're worried about."

"Rex is the one that tried to help you. Suck *him* off."

Unbeknownst to Kelly, she'd gotten so hot watching him beat the shit out of the two jerks, her offer had been for purely selfish reasons. Ignoring his scornful frown, she started stripping. He held on to his disapproving glare but his jeans ballooned at the crotch. Lust burned in his eyes and by the time she got naked Kelly hastily lowered his pants.

Kneeling before him, she bobbed her head up and down his thick shaft a few strokes then laid down on the soft grass with legs spread, demanding he stick it in her. He tried to pull out at the moment of climax but she grabbed his butt and cried, "Pump it in me, Kelly!"

Even now she didn't know what had possessed her to do that. Only one other time had a man ejaculated inside her without wearing a condom and that was because he'd raped her.

The treasured memory of screwing Kelly vanished, along with her smile, as she pulled into the Simmons' drive . . . nervous as hell.

◆◆◆

Jetti hated having to sit at home watching TV with Grandma but understood why she couldn't be with Dearl tonight. He mustn't have any distractions. But that wouldn't be the case tomorrow night, and she smiled at the thought.

"I tell you, Jetti, I'm so nervous about tomorrow's game you'd think I was playing in it."

"You're not the only one, Grandma, but I'm more excited than I am nervous. Let's not mention it again tonight, that way maybe we can both calm down enough to get some sleep."

The doorbell rang.

"Well I wonder who that could be." Grandma put her knitting down and started to get up.

"Keep your seat, I'll answer the door . . . ."

Standing on the front porch was a beautiful woman that made Jetti's heart lunge to the back of her throat. That *had* to be Anita Fury, they looked too much alike for her not to be.

The lady gawked at her for an awkward moment and started bawling.

"Anita, is that you?" Grandma asked from behind her.

Jetti's pulse raced faster as years of hurt and anger pushed aside the awe of finally seeing the bitch in person. "So you're my mother."

◆◆◆

Emma was on cloud nine and Kelly hadn't wasted any time getting here after she'd called to invite him over. Rex grinned at him and said, "Come on in, Romeo."

Closing the door as Kelly walked past, he noted the laidback air that use to cling to him before he'd gotten emotionally castrated had returned. "Your gal's upstairs doing some last minute primping."

"Rex, you're looking at the happiest son of a bitch on the planet."

He laughed. "Well you sure look like it, I'll say that. Want a beer?"

"Sounds good." Kelly glanced around the living room. "Where's Zechariah? Emma said he was over here."

"He was when she called you, but left right after. Have a seat and I'll grab us a couple."

When he returned with their beers, Kelly had made himself comfortable on the couch. He handed the exuberant cowpuncher a bottle and raised his own. "Congratulations, old friend."

"Thanks . . ." Kelly downed a swallow. "Our Kodiaks have some serious shit to take care of mañana, huh."

"They sure do."

"I wouldn't miss tomorrow's game for all the pussy in Acuña, would you?"

"Damn sure wouldn't. It's good to hear you cut up like that again."

Kelly snickered. "Luther would have a field day if he heard me say that, wouldn't he?"

"Not any more."

"Well, technically he still could, but he won't be able to after tonight."

Rex hoped Emma could keep her part of the bargain. She was so hyper over Kelly being able to seal the deal, he knew she'd have a hard time subduing her aggressive tendencies long enough to let him make the first move and lead the way from there. If she couldn't, and it made Kelly impotent again, a serious nightmare lay ahead for the cowboy. *Emma want, Emma get* could be engraved on her tombstone with brutal accuracy.

Rex had always known the gay rumors were completely unfounded. They didn't come any more macho than Kelly Newly, and a woman Kelly slept with several times before Emma entered the picture had confided to him what a great lover he was. Rex had promised her he'd never tell Kelly he knew they'd dated on the sly. Why Kelly felt compelled to keep it from him would forever be a mystery, for he couldn't learn the reason without breaking his word. His conscience wouldn't let him do that because she'd told him all about her relationship with Kelly on her death bed, and bound him to that promise the day she lost her battle with liver cancer.

That woman was his little sister, and she'd wanted him to know because there'd never been any secrets between them save that one, and also made him swear not to tell anyone else because it would eventually reach Kelly's ears.

Losing his only sibling had been the saddest chapter of Rex's life so far. They'd grown up together in this house his dad had sold him dirt cheap when he retired from the railroad commission. His parents now lived in Florida and couldn't make it to the game tomorrow because his dad was recuperating from hip surgery and had to be waited on hand and foot.

# 20

ZECHARIAH QUESTIONED THE LORD'S TIMING many times but never disobeyed. It was getting close to nine o'clock, nonetheless he'd just been commissioned to go back to the address that caused him to be arrested when he'd gone there before. He was watching a movie with Al and Luther and hated to miss the ending. Luther would have to miss it too unless he refused to help him. He'd ridden Buttercup to Rex Winters' house, but while heading back to the ranch Sheriff Grange had spotted him and warned that horseback riding inside the city limits was frowned upon.

"I've just got a word from the Lord and have to go to the Simmons' place right away. Can I impose on you to drive me, Luther?"

The big Cherokee frowned. "It can't wait?"

"I'm afraid not. I'll go on foot if you don't want to chauffeur me, but I have to head that way now."

"Take my pickup," said Al without looking away from the television.

"I'd rather not. Besides not having a license, I'm not a very experienced driver."

Now the rancher was frowning. "Well how much experience do you have?"

"Outside of driving around the farm I grew up on, none."

"I'll drive you then. Record the rest of the show, Luther. Zechariah and I will finish watching it when we get back."

◆◆◆

She sat across from her daughter at the Simmons' lavish dining table. Jetti had grown up to become an extraordinarily beautiful woman and Anita was glad the judge had denied her request to regain custody—she deserved to live in these nice surroundings, purchased with honest money rather than a whore's income. Gwendolyn had made a pitcher of tea before graciously excusing herself a moment ago, leaving the two of them alone when Jetti asked why she'd been abandoned.

"I figured you'd been told as soon as you were old enough to understand. I left a card in your basinet explaining why."

"Yeah," she said disdainfully, "I know it by heart. But what I want to know is why you didn't go straight once you had me instead of leaving me here. You could have, you know."

Anita wanted to crawl under a rock and die.

"I'm waiting, lady. Tell me why you didn't love me enough to do that."

*Lady,* killed her inside. "Jetti, I love you more than my own life. I didn't know how to do anything else, and I couldn't stand the thought of you being poor, which you'd have definitely been had I got an honest job. I started hooking at fourteen and was only eighteen when you were born. I hadn't finished growing up emotionally, and it took a long, long time before I finally did. Now I *am* planning to go straight. I've got plenty of money to live on while I learn a new career and I want to be a part of your life."

Her daughter sat still and silent, glaring at her—the look on her face not indicating one way or the other what she thought about the matter. But her anger was painfully evident.

"Jetti, please. Give me the chance to start over with you."

"Forget it," she retorted. "There's only one more thing I want from you, lady. Who's my father?"

She fought hard to keep from crying again but felt a hot tear roll down her cheek. "I don't blame you for not wanting anything to do with me, but you are *so* wrong if you think I don't love you. What I did, I did for your sake, not mine. It hurt so badly not having you with me I tried to get you back but the judge ruled against me. I came to see you when you were seven but you were frightened of me. That so tore me up inside that I didn't have the nerve to try again."

"Until now." Her voice reeked of skepticism.

"Yes. Because I want to turn my life around, and had to see what my baby looks like all grown up. And I must say, I figured you'd be a pretty woman but you far exceeded all my expectations."

Jetti finally quit staring at her and sipped some iced tea. "Who's my father?"

When she didn't answer, the pretty seventeen-year-old donned a sneer that went through her heart like a dagger.

"You don't even know, do you."

The doorbell rang. A few moments later Gwendolyn came into the dining room with Al Pond and a man Anita had never seen before.

Al gave her a friendly grin. "Hello, Anita. I'd like to introduce you to Zechariah."

"Wow," Jetti exclaimed, "I didn't recognize you at all, Zechariah! You look totally different without the beard and long hair. How do you like working on the ranch?"

The gentleman smiled and winked. "Well, I wound up working in the house instead, helping Luther."

"I like Luther, he's cool. Why are you guys here?"

"Um, I need to talk to you and your mother if you don't mind."

"About what?"

Al turned to Gwendolyn. "Gwen, why don't we go to the living room."

Gwendolyn appeared as confused as she felt, but followed the wealthy rancher.

"Dearl told me you're a prophet," said Jetti.

"That's not what I call myself, but I do have a word from the Lord for you two ladies."

Anita couldn't believe what she was hearing. "Listen, mister whatever your name is, I don't believe in God."

"Zechariah's the name, ma'am."

Jetti shot her a harsh look. "Well I do, and I happen to know this man hears God speak. Dearl convinced me."

"Dearl Tipps? Maureen's boy?"

"Yeah."

She'd always liked Maureen. "How's she doing? I know she doesn't work for Piggly Wiggly anymore because I saw it's been closed down."

Jetti scowled at her. "She's dead."

"Dead?! When did she pass away?"

"Three days before Grandpa."

"Rutherford died?"

"Yeah. Didn't you wonder why he wasn't here?"

The look of contempt on Jetti's face was more than she could bear. Anita covered her own and began to wail.

◆◆◆

Zechariah nervously shifted his weight from one foot to the other. Anita Fury continued sobbing and Jetti sat with arms folded beneath her breasts, looking irritated over her mother's actions and impatient to hear what he had to say.

The surprise he'd felt over the Lord sending him to this

house again had given way to concern that his initial impression about spending the rest of his life on the Pond Ranch might have been a vain vision. Who would God send him to next? Would he have to make another exhausting trek, bound by another command not to cut his hair or beard or accept any offer of vehicular transport? A silent groan welled up inside at the prospect.

He forced his thoughts away from himself and got back to the task at hand. "Jetti, God wants you to know that your mother can't answer your question."

"What question?"

"Who your father is."

Jetti dropped her jaw but Anita merely frowned at him. "How did you know she asked me that?"

"The Lord told me. He also sent me here to tell you the time has come for you to change your ways. You've been with child eight days."

She responded with a cynical laugh while wiping tears from her eyes. "That's impossible. I supply the best condoms on the market and have an IUD."

"Nonetheless, you're pregnant with a son and God has plans for the boy."

"You're crazy."

"No he's not," Jetti reprimanded. "Can you tell me who my father is, Zechariah?"

"I'll ask the Lord, and He may or may not inform me. I don't know anything other than what I was sent here to tell you and Anita tonight. Now that I've done that I'll be on my way. If God tells me who your daddy is, I'll let you know."

The pretty girl turned to her mother. "Don't you have any idea who he is? Surely you must have someone in mind."

Anita began to tear up again. "I'm pretty sure I know, but since I'm not certain, it wouldn't be fair to you—or him—to tell you, Jetti."

"Would I know him?"

"I can't imagine he'd ever move away so I'm sure you've heard of him even if the two of you haven't met."

Zechariah examined Jetti closely, taking note of the tint of her eyes. They appeared gray at first glance, but close inspection revealed them to be a unique silvery-blue like Kelly Newly's. However, Jetti's lovely orbs where shaped far different than Kelly's. His were much smaller, squinty, and threatening.

He said goodnight and went to the living room to tell Al they could leave.

♦♦♦

Dearl studied the three figures on the blackboard, feeling they must have great significance, yet clueless to their meaning. He didn't know who'd drawn them. Sitting alone in algebra two class, he looked out the window towards Tornado Hill, somehow visible in the dark night. It seemed to be conveying a secret, whispering it indecipherably.

"Come up here, I want to talk to you." The voice came from the direction of the blackboard.

His mouth hung open as he gawked at Jesus, sitting on Coach Rainey's desk, wearing a flowing robe that almost obscured it.

Adrenaline pumping, he nervously obeyed the command.

Jesus put an arm around him, whispered something, and Dearl found himself standing on top of Tornado Hill, alone.

Whatever Jesus said was extremely important, but he couldn't remember it. His feet carried him to the edge of the plateau against his will. Terrified he'd fall if he dared look down, his head bowed anyway.

Throngs of people stood below, looking up at him. They were in trouble and needed his help.

"Here!" he heard a voice say from behind him.

Dearl whirled around to see Zechariah toss a blanket. He caught it and turned back to the people. A tidal wave at least a mile high was heading towards Sleeping Bear from the far south, and he shouted with all his might that it was coming, but nobody seemed to hear him.

# 21

SHE COUNTED THE MONEY AGAIN. Five thousand dollars for only a few minutes work. This stupid, hick, football-worshiping town deserved to be burned and her only regret was that she wouldn't be able to take the credit for seeing to it their precious team lost the state championship tomorrow. Cooper would break up with her if he knew, and that would kill her.

It all started when he'd taken that nap after making love to her in his room the night of the first victory celebration over the Kodiaks winning Bi-District. Cindy hadn't planned on stealing anything, merely wanted to see what Cooper considered worthy of keeping in his sanctuary, and couldn't resist the opportunity to find out. Using a penlight she kept in her purse, she'd gone through his desk, coming across typical male paraphernalia in all the drawers, but one contained his playbook.

Not expecting them to go any further in the playoffs because her dad said they'd only won Bi-District due to the opponent missing their best player, the idea hadn't occurred to her until Sleeping Bear won Semi Finals. During that victory celebration she'd faked a trip to the bathroom and snuck to Cooper's room while he whooped it up with the other players by the beer kegs. Using his printer which had a copier, she'd duplicated all the Kodiak's plays and stashed them in an over-sized purse she'd purchased for the occasion.

The only shady member of her entire family was a cousin who sold used cars in Langton. She'd called him the next day, explained what she was up to, and asked who to contact to negotiate a deal. He'd promised to nose around and get back to her.

Less than an hour later he'd called and said, "Someone on the coaching staff who must remain nameless is very interested. Since this is a state championship you could probably name your price, within reason, and I get half or it's a no go. So how much do you want for it?"

"Five thousand," she'd replied, "not a cent less."

"Okay, I'll call you back in a few minutes and let you know if he's willing to go as high as ten grand."

The unnamed coach had been willing and said it would take a few days to raise the cash but he had to have the playbook immediately. She'd faxed it to her cousin, warning she'd blab if the money wasn't in her hands by Friday.

He was downstairs chatting with her parents, who'd been told he'd decided on the spur of the moment to pay them a surprise visit like he used to do when they lived in Lubbock. An hour ago he'd pretended he wanted to show her his CD collection in his car, and slipped the money to her.

♦♦♦

Anita pulled at a Singapore Sling, set it on the bar, and glanced at her watch. Ten fifty-five. She planned to stay until the joint closed at two. Gwendolyn had offered her guest room, but not wanting to upset Jetti any further than she already had, she'd checked into the only motel in town before coming here: Sleeping Bear's lone night club.

Burly Swain ambled over, running a hand over his wiry brown hair. "Damn it's good to see you again after all these years! I've been one lonely tomcat since you left."

"I'm not open for business tonight," she warned.

He brought a mug of beer to his mouth, dumped a goodly portion of its contents down his flabby throat, and wiped his thin lips with the back of a hairy forearm. "I've really missed you, Anita. We had some great times together."

Ignoring his remarks, she spun around on the barstool and looked the place over. "Who's the redhead sitting with Kelly Newly?"

"Emma Riley. Saucy little number, ain't she?"

Anita returned to her drink. "Are you still running The Kodiak Cave?"

"Mm hmm . . ." he took the stool beside her.

"I'm not in the mood for company, Burly."

He tossed her a cheesy grin. "Now that's no way to talk to an old friend. What did I ever do to deserve such a snide remark? I must have shelled out over twenty grand to you before you moved away."

Looking straight ahead, she downed the rest of the sling. It did little to appease the emptiness she felt. "I'll have another, Bart."

Bart Newly, Kelly's uncle, soon had her fixed up. She raised the glass and smiled at him. "Still spelling Myles on weekends?"

"Why, are you planning to spend the night in the pokey?" Bart teased.

"Myles only had the goods on me that one time."

"You were always a crafty gal."

"You know it, Bart. If that damned carpet bagger hadn't been such a chicken shit, I wouldn't have a record. At least Myles wrote it down as public intoxication."

"He always thought you'd clean up one day, and didn't want your past to haunt you more than it had to."

That compounded the misery she already felt. Except for her father, who'd never known about her scarlet side, she'd let down everyone that ever cared for her after he became a widower. "How's the sheriff getting on?"

"Fine. Your daughter kept him from unknowingly committing a grave injustice. You ought to see what a pretty gal Jetti turned out to be."

Tears instantly blurred her vision. "I've just come from seeing her. Oh, Bart . . . I fucked up so bad."

"Sorry, Anita, didn't mean to upset you."

Burly put a hand on her shoulder. "Drink up, you'll feel better after another round."

"If you value your life, you'll remove your hand and refrain from touching me again. I mean it, Burly, *leave me alone.*"

He obeyed and emptied his mug. "Need to call it a night anyway. In case you haven't heard, we're playing for State tomorrow and I want to get an early start for Lubbock. What's the damage, Bart?"

Her Kodiak spirit rose from dormancy and stirred her up so mightily Anita felt like she was back in high school. She took another quick look at Kelly, recalling how disappointed the whole town had been when he and his fellow Kodiaks had been edged out of an opportunity to make it to the quarter finals, losing to Seagraves by one point. It was the farthest any Sleeping Bear team had advanced at the time. Hearing her alma mater had finally broken the barrier and would be playing for the state championship changed her mind about getting drunk. "What time are you leaving in the morning, Burly?"

"Around eight."

"When does the game start?"

"One, but I'm going early so I can get a good seat. These playoff games have been packed to the hilt. You wouldn't believe how many people have been attending."

"Mind if I join you? Or did you finally get married while I

was away."

His jowls flapped with laughter. "Nope. Like I told you the first time we were together, I've got no use for a woman other than sex. Haven't been able to find that special one who can understand that."

"Gee I can't imagine why," she said dryly.

Bart cleared his throat. "Don't let me hear you solicit him, Anita, or I'll have no choice but to run you in. That goes for you too, Burly, if you take her up on it. You two should probably continue this discussion out of my earshot."

Anita rose from the stool and hooked her arm around Burly's. "I wanna say hello to Kelly anyway. Come on, Casanova . . . ."

Kelly still had his looks, and the frown he donned when she approached showed the cowboy still couldn't stand her.

"Well if it ain't Anita Fury. Figured you'd come back some day if you didn't die from AIDS."

His date scowled at him while exhaling cigarette smoke. "Don't speak to the lady like that, Kelly! Sorry, miss, allow me to apologize for him."

"Thank you. I'm Anita."

"Emma Riley. Won't you and Burly have a seat?"

She glanced at the two empty chairs, then at Kelly. He obviously didn't want her occupying one. "Um, just wanted to say hello. We'll be on our way."

"Nonsense. Tell them to sit down, Kelly."

He responded by turning up his beer.

Meanwhile Burly plopped his chunky butt on a chair, leaving her no choice.

Anita placed her drink in front of the other and eased onto it. Noticing a package of Winston 100s sitting by the lady's purse, she pointed at them and said, "Could I bum one of those?"

"Oh please." Emma moved the ashtray between them and

laid her cigarette on it. Then she popped one from the pack, handed it to her, slid her lighter across the table, and resumed smoking.

Burly chuckled. "Anita has the remarkable ability of being able to smoke like a freight train on occasion without getting hooked. Or did you finally?"

"Nope, I can still take 'em or leave 'em. I sometimes go weeks on end without indulging. "

Emma giggled. "Don't let my employer hear that, he'd burn with envy."

"Who's your employer?" She lit up.

"Rex Winters."

"Not a problem for him anymore," Kelly informed Emma. "While you were getting ready for our date he told me God took away his addiction."

"Aye, but he'd burn with envy if he knew there were people that can have their cake and eat it too."

Anita exhaled and smiled at her. "Oh he knows. Rex has told me several times how much he hates me for it. What did you mean about God taking away his addiction, Kelly? Rex doesn't smoke anymore?"

"He quit five years ago," said Emma when Kelly didn't answer. "But his craving for nicotine stayed strong as ever. Now don't laugh, but what I'm about to say is true. A man of God told him he'd be rewarded by having that craving removed, and by Jove it happened this very day as a matter of fact."

It amazed her how believers spoke so pragmatically about a being that didn't exist. She could believe in Santa or the Easter Bunny before buying into the idea that God sat up in heaven doing nothing about all the evil and injustices in this world. "Do you live in Sleeping Bear?"

"Yes. Moved here four years ago."

"I've been away for ten. So how's life been treating you,

Kelly?"

He took another swig of beer.

"Sorry. Guess you've got nothing to say to me."

"As a matter of fact I'm on top of the world at the moment because of this pretty lady here."

She almost fell off the chair—he actually spoke to her. "Good for you. Emma, that's quite a guy you've got there."

"Thanks, I certainly think so. So you two have known each other since when?"

"Since high school," said Kelly. "Miss Fury here was a prone Joan even back then, but at least she was smart enough not to give it away."

Emma glared at him for a moment, then turned to her. "You're Jetti Fury's mum, aren't you?"

Hearing the name after Kelly's cruel jab instantly threatened to bring back tears, but she refused to cry. Wondering what Kelly would say if she mentioned her suspicion that he'd impregnated her that one time they'd had sex, she forced a smile. "Yes, I'm Jetti's mother."

"She's quite an exceptional young lady." Emma stabbed out her cigarette. "You should be proud."

Kelly grimaced. "Proud?! She dumped Jetti off on the Simmons."

The redhead's stunning eyes turned menacing. "Kelly, I'm going to slap you if you make one more rude remark, and I mean it. Now stop being so bloody high and mighty. Let me apologize for him yet one more time, Anita."

"I do my own apologizing, Emma," Kelly blasted, "and don't ever try to speak for me again. You don't know Anita, I do. She's a whore, pure and simple. That's just the way it is."

"He's right," she hastily agreed, fearing Emma would retaliate and a serious fight would erupt between the two lovebirds. "I chose the profession and am fully aware of what I am."

Burly scooted his chair back and got up. "I need to get to bed."

She snuffed the cigarette and rose from the table. "Thanks for the smoke, Emma, it was a pleasure to meet you."

◆◆◆

Bibi was too nervous to sleep. She got out of bed, put her bathrobe on, and crept into the hall. Light bled into it from the bottom of Gilbert's bedroom door. Tapping the signal used since they were six to let one know the other was also awake late at night, she waited.

Gilbert soon opened it and she stepped inside.

"Couldn't sleep either, huh?" said her big brother. Big didn't refer to him being older, they were twins, but to his size. He was six-six, a foot taller than her, and weighed three hundred pounds.

She shook her head.

"Let's go to the kitchen," he said, "so we won't wake up Mom and Dad. Maybe a snack will help us doze off."

Mom had made spaghetti for supper. Gilbert filled a big bowl with the leftovers and stuck it in the microwave. She grabbed an ice cream sandwich from the freezer.

"Gilbert, I'm gonna die if you guys don't win tomorrow."

He grinned. "Don't tempt me to blow the game, sis. I'm the center, I could really screw things up."

"You're also the left tackle, so you could screw things up on the other side of the ball as well. Now stop teasing me, and swear you won't let the Lions beat you this time."

"I swear this, Bibi, the only way we'll lose tomorrow is if Dearl gets hurt, and *only* if he gets knocked out of the game early."

♦♦♦

Burly had shelled out a grand, the price for a whole night. Knowing he wouldn't be able to go more than one round, Anita considered it little more than a hand out. As always, he'd ejaculated mere seconds after his condom-sheathed cock penetrated her, and a few moments later drifted off to sleep. When he began to snore she'd slipped out of bed to take a bath in his exquisitely deep antique tub. Burly slept soundly and never woke up during the night. After discovering that way back when, many was the time she'd snuck off to pleasure more johns on his dime, crawling back in bed with him before dawn. Anita had no such plans tonight, but she'd steal away to her motel room after the bath in order to get some sleep—which she'd never be able to do with his snoring—and be back in his bed by six a.m.

Relaxing in the hot water she thought about the oddball who claimed to be a prophet. What had prompted him to think she was pregnant? Eight days, he'd said. She'd worked a convention in Houston the night in question, and like Burly, the guy had purchased her for the whole night.

A lot of johns said "I usually don't do this sort of thing" but Eli Adams maintained that he'd never been with a prostitute before. Careful to memorize their names to prompt them into paying more by making them feel like they stood out from the rest when they sought a repeat, she'd have remembered Eli's regardless because of the gentle, romantic way he'd treated her.

He'd walked up to her at a computer exhibit where she'd been loitering, and introduced himself. A distinguished looking man who appeared to be in his forties, he'd said, "Do you mind if I ask your name? I can't help but wonder if you might be related to my wife, you look so much like her."

"Oh really, is she here?"

"No, she passed away."

She'd already known he was alone, having slyly kept an eye on him because he'd been ogling her and looked to be a good prospect. After offering her condolences, she'd told him her name and asked if there were any Fury's in his wife's family.

"Not that I know of, but let me show you her picture, you'll see what I mean."

He'd produced a photograph and she'd been impressed to find he hadn't merely made up a line. The lady *had* looked a lot like her.

Long ago she'd learned when a man's attraction for her stemmed from his heart and not just his genitals—a certain look on his face gave it away. Eli's had dripped with it. So when he'd asked if she'd like to have a drink, her conscience hadn't allowed her to let the misunderstanding to go any further. "I'm not available in the manner you're looking for, Eli. I'm a pro if you know what I mean, and don't want to mislead you into thinking there could be any future for us."

The revelation had startled him and he'd been speechless for several minutes, jaw sagging with disappointment. Then he'd finally spoke again.

"What are your rates?"

"Depends on what you want."

"I want to spend time with you—lots of time."

"If you want me to stay the night, I'll need a thousand."

"Even if we only talk?"

"Even if we only talk."

She'd accompanied him to his hotel suite and for two hours talk was all they'd done. During that time he'd doled out his life story. He'd made a fortune from computer programs he'd created, some of which were used by the military, and continually added to his wealth by designing more. She'd sat patiently as he spoke of his entire family and rattled on at length about a dead uncle who'd been a renowned theologian that turned eccentric and went into seclusion.

Providing johns with a makeshift psychiatrist was the one part of her profession she actually felt proud of. Eli had badly needed someone to talk to after losing his wife, and when the conversation finally got around to her death, he wound up crying.

He'd sat on a sofa and she'd listened from a chair. Face in hands, shoulders heaving, the poor man had desperately needed comforting. She'd instinctively moved next to him and brought his head to her bosom, cradling it in a motherly hug. Soon he'd looked up with grateful eyes and tried to kiss her.

Turning so his lips collided with her cheek she'd stated, firmly, "That's the one thing I don't do, Eli."

"Can't you make an exception?"

"I'm afraid not."

The pitiful look on his face had tugged at her heartstrings but she couldn't afford to give in. Instead she'd unzipped his pants and tried to go down on him.

"No—" he'd hissed through a heavy breath "—not this way. Take off your clothes so I can make love to you."

Tenderly and lovingly, he'd done precisely that, even bringing her to orgasm, an extremely rare occurrence with a john. At the time she'd put it off to having gone so long without a boyfriend, but as she soaked in Burly's tub, she wondered if she might actually have feelings for Eli Adams. Soon reality set in and blew that notion away. Eli's wealth and genteel ways made her wish the emotion he stirred in her was more than friendship, but she'd merely been romanticizing the situation in a phase of wishful thinking. In reality, that's all she felt for the man, and all she ever would.

She'd lied about having an IUD, wanting to make the so called prophet look foolish, but she'd made Eli wear a condom—one of her high-quality prophylactics, as she never took the risk of a john using an inferior rubber. Only one thing troubled her over that weirdo saying she'd gotten knocked up eight days ago: until tonight, she hadn't serviced another john since.

# 22

THE LION KEPT CIRCLING DEARL, standing with his back against a tree, bound to its trunk by heavy ropes. Slowly decreasing the radius of the loop, the beast repeatedly bared its teeth in angry growls. Viewing the scene from an elevated position, suspended in mid air about twenty feet above ground and unable to descend, Zechariah tried to cry out but had no voice. Mysteriously, Dearl seemed unperturbed.

Though aware he was only dreaming, Zechariah recognized it as a symbolic warning from God.

But about what?

When it got within five feet of Dearl, the lion let out a savage roar and leapt at the youth, tearing at him with its fangs and claws, moving so fast Zechariah could only see a furry blur, yet Dearl didn't so much as whimper.

Zechariah tried to look away but couldn't move his head or close his eyes. Certain the poor boy had been torn to shreds by now, he began to weep. Then the ropes snapped as Dearl transformed into a huge angry bear. Frightened by the transformation, the lion turned to run, but talons elongated on an enormous right paw like a row of switchblades, and with one mighty swoop the big cat was decapitated.

Its body keeled over and Zechariah gasped as it turned into a headless woman with blood gushing from the jagged stump of her neck. That scared the bear and it ran away on all four limbs. A moment later, the nude feminine form jumped to its feet and took off after the bear.

They disappeared into the horizon and Zechariah winced

when he heard distant howls of agony, because it appeared the lady with no head had somehow felled the bear.

He heard a cheering crowd but couldn't see the people as the headless female marched back to the tree, carrying a drum major's baton. A huge spray of blood shot upwards from her torso and when it finally dissipated, a face appeared: the female's head had somehow been reattached to the body. She now looked like a pretty teenage girl.

Seemingly unaware of his presence she marched in place, rhythmically raising and lowering the baton. Her bare breasts undulated with the motion and knowing he mustn't look directly at them he focused on the tree, still seeing her bouncing bosom in his peripheral vision while weeping over the bear's apparent demise.

Her face suddenly covered his entire field of vision, framed by light-brown hair. Something white was wrapped around her neck, where the image faded into obscurity. She closed her eyes and he woke up with tears in his. He wiped them away with the open end of the pillow case and went back to sleep.

# 23

DICK PARSONS HAD BEEN STUDYING the Kodiak's plays all week, adjusting the defensive scheme accordingly, but was going back over them to make sure he hadn't missed anything. He'd been Truman Jette's defensive coordinator for the last five years and they'd had an incredible run of success. But the more he'd viewed Sleeping Bear's game films the more convinced he'd become they couldn't manage a fourth victory over them without some sort of edge. He'd hoped and prayed the Kodiaks wouldn't make it to the state championship game, all the while knowing they would.

When Will Amarod called and told him he could provide the playbook, Dick had seen it as an act of God. Since he couldn't let anyone else know, he'd had to raise the money himself—selling his boat and camping trailer to pad the six thousand he had in savings. It was a small price to pay because a fourth state championship virtually assured Truman would be moving up to the college ranks and he was the logical choice to succeed him at Langton.

The playbook revealed everything the Kodiaks would do from each formation, and the alternative plays they'd run if the quarterback audibled.

Truman would have a stroke and get him fired if he found out why his defensive coordinator would be able to call the perfect defense at least ninety percent of the time tomorrow. Of course that didn't guarantee stopping Dearl Tipps. What he really needed was another providential act—

some sort of accident that would prevent Tipps from playing altogether.

When the idea of hiring some goons to break the boy's legs sprang to mind, he jerked his head back and forth to make the stupid thought go away. *Get a grip, idiot, you're no mafia don . . . .*

◆◆◆

Jetti lay wide awake in bed, wondering why Anita had chosen the life of a prostitute. She'd refrained from asking, not wanting the whore to think she had any interest in her. Easy money was obviously the strongest motivation, but to her way of thinking, allowing a man she didn't love to use her body would be the hardest way to make a living imaginable. If she'd had any choice in the matter she wouldn't have allowed her fucked up grandfather to touch her for a million dollars.

Thinking about him made her feel greasy inside, intensifying the anger she felt towards her mother. If the bitch hadn't abandoned her to the sleazy bastard, he wouldn't have had the opportunity to molest her. She hoped Grandma had told Anita about it after she'd left the two of them alone, so the bitch could see how her selfish act had set the stage for a fourteen-year-old girl to be defiled by a perverted old man, who'd done it countless times since.

She fluffed her pillow and turned over on her side, thinking about the irony of Dearl not knowing who his father was either. A smile came to her at the realization their children wouldn't have to deal with that issue. *Maybe one of them will be conceived tomorrow night,* she thought with a giggle. Dearl didn't know it but she planned to see to it that neither of them woke up a virgin on Sunday. It had crossed her mind she could be wrong about him being one, but what else could his big secret be?

Cindy Shane confided to her that she'd fallen in love with Cooper and they had sex regularly. Jetti so longed for Dearl to make love to her she'd resented hearing it.

Despite his faults she'd always be grateful to Grandpa for teaching her about football, which she'd been passionate about since seeing her first game as a little child. She'd impartially rooted for all the players in her grade through junior high, but their freshman year she'd been mesmerized by number twenty, whose superior talent had begun to manifest. Before the football season ended she'd fallen in love with him. Besides collecting newspaper clippings, she'd started a journal, jotting down all Dearl's accomplishments during every game, and committing them to memory.

He'd been going with a senior at the time, making her afraid to make a move, being a mere ninth-grader. That girl broke up with him when she left for college, and another senior got her hooks into Dearl before she could their sophomore year. That girl also called it quits after graduation and he'd gone steady with yet another senior when they were juniors, and she too had cut him loose when summer came. All three had been straight-laced socialites and she'd always suspected they'd used Dearl as a means to bask in the limelight. That was probably the reason for him being paranoid about whether she'd still like him if he wasn't a football star. Perhaps he'd figured out his status had been what appealed to those girls, who were the only ones he'd ever dated that she knew of. Thank God that was all in the past now and she had him all to herself as fate intended.

A hollow ache welled up inside as her mother crept back into her mind. Being a salutatorian, Anita had to be as intelligent as she was beautiful, and the distinct aura of a winner shrouded her. Why had she chosen to be such a loser?

♦♦♦

Rex awoke to the sound of arguing downstairs. Emma sounded like she was reading Kelly the riot act and he was obviously just as pissed. He got out of bed and opened the door so he could make out what they were screaming about.

"I don't give a bloody damn about that, she's still a human being and you had no right to speak to her that way!"

Kelly shouted that he'd speak to anybody any way he damned well pleased and she could just kiss his ass if she thought she could change him.

"So that's how it is then?!"

"That's how it is!"

"All right, fine! We're through, Kelly, it's over!"

"If that's the way you want it, that's the way it'll be!"

He heard the front door slam and a moment later the sound of Emma wailing as she ascended the stairs. Rex stepped outside and grabbed her arm when she passed. "What happened between you two?"

Mascara streaming down her cheeks, she shrieked, "I found out he's a bloody caveman, that's what! . . . I've never seen you in your underwear before, Rex."

"Oh *man,* sorry! Let me get dressed and we'll talk about it."

"Humph! Nothing to talk about, Kelly and I are done for good. Sorry we woke you, go back to bed."

"Emma, please don't be like that. At least tell me why you think he's a caveman."

"Let me blow my nose first."

She went to her room and he hurried into his own to put his pants on. A moment after he stepped back in the hall she returned, daubing her eyes with a Kleenex.

"We were having a pleasant drink at Bart's place when Burly Swain and this woman came over to say hello. The woman turned out to be Anita Fury, and Kelly called her a whore to her face. Can you imagine, Rex, right to her face! I said 'Let me apologize for him' and it went all over Kelly. The poor woman wound up basically apologizing for him, the cretin, and left.

"I sat there stunned for several minutes because he continued sipping beer as if nothing had happened. So I finally told him I never wanted to hear him talk to anyone that way again, and he just exploded. Well, I gave as good as I got. Bart finally had to ask us to leave, we'd gotten so rowdy. I never want to see that bloody bastard again for as long as I live."

Rex heaved a weary sigh. "I can't believe this. After all the two of you have been through, you're going to call it quits over Kelly calling Anita a whore? Emma, Kelly and I have known Anita since high school and she was a prostitute even then. Kelly has never made any bones about not liking her, and he always calls a spade a spade, and you're never going to get him to do otherwise. Myself, I've always been fond of Anita, but the plain truth is she *is* a whore. No one forced her to become one, it was her choice and she has to live with the consequences."

Emma glared at him. "I understand what she is, but have you ever called her that to her face?"

He shook his head. "I never have and never will, but Kelly always has, and you can't let that drive a wedge between you. Kelly's as straight a shooter as they come, and speaks his mind without a thought of worrying about being politically correct, something I've always admired."

Her jaw dropped. "Oh have you now? Well all I can say is you must be as thick as he is then."

It dawned on him Emma and Kelly were as incompatible as oil and water. Zechariah had gone out of his way to mend a lost cause. "It's probably for the best that you two go your separate ways."

"What makes you say that?"

"Are you kidding me? You're both stubborn as mules and your ways are set in stone. You're yen and he's yang, as different as night and day. You'd wind up killing each other. I'm going back to bed . . . ."

♦♦♦

When Anita pulled into the motel parking lot the pickup that had been tailing her for the last few blocks screeched to a halt beside her. She glanced over to see Kelly Newly turning up a bottle of whiskey. He was alone and looked mad as hell. A cold wave of fear rolled over her when he got out and slammed the door so hard it rocked his vehicle.

She opened her own and stepped onto the pavement, hiding her anxiety—an act she'd mastered in her late teens. "Something I can do for you, Kelly?"

"Yeah, get the fuck out of Sleeping Bear, bitch. You ruined my life tonight."

Stunned and confused, she asked how.

He stepped towards her. "Emma broke up with me for calling you a whore."

Anita backed up against her car. Kelly had always been a bad ass but she'd never known him to be an unfair one, and didn't think he'd hit a woman—but he was so angry and possibly drunk, she feared he might be planning to use her as a punching bag to take out his frustrations on. "I'm really sorry to hear that, but I don't see how you can blame me for it."

Kelly stopped to take a long pull from the bottle, then lowered it to his side. His lips glistened wetly under the lights of the parking lot before he raked the sleeve of his free arm across them. "Why *did* you come back anyway?"

His voice sounded much calmer and she could tell his intentions weren't to harm her, at least not physically. "To see Jetti."

A derisive grin formed. "That's what I figured."

Drawing a deep breath, she placed her hands on her hips and fought through the pain his sarcasm evoked—refusing to let him get to her this time like he'd always done in the past. "Why do you hate me so much, Kelly?"

He leered at her, contemptuously, as if she owed him a debt that could never be paid in full. "You had way too much going for you to be a whore, that's why. What a waste."

Her stomach cramped as moisture loomed in her eyes. Not about to give him the satisfaction of making her cry, she waited until the emotional hit waned enough she could speak without doing so. "You're right, I made a bad choice, but I've never done anything to you. Not once have I ever bad-mouthed you, to your face or behind your back, so I don't understand why you feel the need to constantly put me down."

A light came on in a nearby window and she realized they were talking too loud. "Let's go to my room. We're disturbing the guests."

Kelly took another gulp of whiskey and burped. "All right, let's talk in there."

He followed her inside and seated himself in an armchair nestled in a corner. She went to the bathroom and ripped the plastic off a disposable cup, filled it with water, and carried it to the bed. Sitting down on the side nearest him, she noticed he wasn't fuming anymore, but looked sad.

"I really am sorry, Kelly. I was afraid a fight might start over her wanting you to apologize so I tried to avert it."

"Yeah well, it didn't work."

She took a sip of water and set the cup on the nightstand. "Well what more could I have done?"

"Stayed away from our table, dammit, that's what you could have done." Kelly looked pissed again, but only for a moment before his eyes turned sad and he lowered them to the floor. "You know me, Anita. I can't go against my grain, and that's what she wants me to do."

The way he said 'Anita' surprised her because it almost sounded deferential. In all the years she'd known him he'd called her a whore, bitch, or slut far more often than by name—and on the rare occasions he'd used it, his tone had never contained the tiniest modicum of respect. Seeing he was really hurting, she wished she'd stayed away from his table all right. The motherly psychoanalyst in her kicked in. "Why don't you tell me about it?"

Still somberly gazing at the floor he said, "Emma wants me to change . . . and you and I both know that's never gonna happen."

She stifled a giggle. Truer words had never been spoken. "How so? What is it she wants you to change?"

He looked up. "Right now it's one thing, but I know there'll be another after that, and another after that, and it won't stop until she has me pussy whipped."

The thought of Kelly Newly being pussy whipped was more than she could bear and this time the laugh escaped, which brought a scowl to his face.

"I'm sorry, Kelly, it just hit me funny. You're not a man that any woman could hope to control. She must not know you very well or she'd be keenly aware of that."

A trace of a smile surfaced. "She's a stubborn Irish woman, used to getting her way. And I wouldn't mind her getting her way most of the time if she just didn't want to change me."

"I must say you two really make a lovely couple. I doubt she's wanting to change you so much as trying to get you to meet her halfway."

His sun-darkened face turned grim. "The hell she's not— telling me what I can and can't say. That's not meeting in the middle, that's ordering me around."

"Well what exactly did she ask you to do?"

"She didn't ask me to do anything, she *told* me I wasn't going to speak to people the way I did you."

Kelly still had all his prematurely gray hair, which she'd always thought enhanced his ruggedly handsome features, and his sexy body looked as muscularly lean and mean as it had ten years ago. If Emma Riley was smart she'd find a way to hold on to this cowboy. "How long have y'all been dating?"

He set the bottle on the floor and leaned forward, elbows on knees. "We've known each other for four years and tonight was our second date."

She gaped at him with utter shock. "Two dates in four years, and you were on top of the world because of her?"

"Yeah . . . sounds funny, don't it. Long story."

"I'm all ears."

A pained expression draped his face, she'd inadvertently hit a nerve.

"I'm sorry, Kelly, I must have just poked my nose where it doesn't belong. I'm sure it's none of my business."

For several seconds he stared at her with pain-filled eyes, then something seemed to occur to him that caused them to widen. "Hell it just dawned on me this is *exactly* your business. You haven't contracted any social diseases have you?"

Her jaw fell. "Are you propositioning me, Kelly?"

"I am if you're not going to give me the clap."

She'd love nothing more than to have that stud screw her again, but not like this. "Listen, I don't know what brought this on but sleeping with me will only make matters worse. You don't want to do it, believe me."

Kelly reached for the bottle, turned it up, and set it back on the floor. "Wouldn't have propositioned you if I didn't. How much will it cost me?"

"You couldn't afford me, but I'd never charge you anyway so that point is moot. Why do you suddenly want to have sex with me?"

All energy seemed to drain from him as he slumped back in the chair, looking morose and defeated.

"What's wrong, Kelly?"

"Would you believe me if I told you I haven't been with a woman in four years?"

"Four years?!"

"Yeah, and that prophet Emma told you about? Well, I thought all my troubles were over because I really thought the dude heard God on the matter, but something got fouled up somewhere, because he sure missed the mark when he told me that Emma and I would mend fences. Since he was wrong about that I'm afraid he might be mistaken about my problem getting fixed."

She squinted with curiosity. "What problem is that?"

He grabbed the bottle and took another big swallow. "I need help, Anita, and you're just the one that can do it. I need to be with a woman tonight—need to know I *can* be with a woman tonight."

Dumbfounded at the statement, she leaned forward and cocked her head. "Are you trying to tell me you're afraid you're impotent?"

"I ain't *trying* to tell you that, I'm telling you I'm slap dab scared to death I am. Emma wanted me to fuck her four years ago and I couldn't do it. Been too scared to try it with anyone since, after she wouldn't give me another crack at it. Zechariah got things straightened out between us, but we got into that damn fight and she wrote me off again."

Patience, a necessary trait for any woman that fancied Kelly Newly to possess in abundance, obviously wasn't Emma's strong point. "Did it ever occur to you that maybe deep inside you knew the two of you were incompatible and it messed with your libido? I mean, if she really is trying to change you, you know she's not the one for you. Maybe you knew that then, subconsciously, and it caused the communication line between your brain and gonads to short circuit."

"Nah, it was her over-aggressiveness that caused it, I think Zechariah nailed that—but I'm afraid it might have fucked with my head so bad it crippled me sexually. I used to wake up every morning with a hard on, but haven't done it one time since that night I couldn't get it up with Emma."

Seeing there was only one way to put this broken cowboy back together again, she rose to her feet and pulled off her shirt. Reaching for her bra snap, she said, "You're not impotent, Kelly, and your drought is about to come to an end."

By the time she slid her panties down her legs and left them on the floor, Kelly's face was a portrait of feverish lust. But he just sat there, apparently too scared to make a move.

Standing before him completely naked, she put her hands on her hips and smiled. "Remember our little episode on the grass after you put the hurt on those two Amarillo boys?"

He nodded.

"I want you as badly now as I did then, Kelly Newly. God you were so hard, and you'll get just as stiff now, I promise.

Take off your clothes, cowboy, and let's put this bed to good use."

For several seconds all he did was continued to ogle her body, so she fondled her breasts in an effort to urge him on, and it worked. Kelly pulled his boots off and started unsnapping his blue jean shirt, then suddenly leapt from the chair.

Before she could stop him he covered her mouth with his.

The one time they'd been together he hadn't tried to kiss her so it hadn't been an issue. She couldn't allow this, especially not with Kelly whom she'd always been so strongly attracted to despite knowing he didn't give a damn about her. It would plant emotional seeds in her heart that would grow like cancers. She tried to push him away but he grabbed the sides of her head and forced her face back to his. The hot thrill that shot through her when his tongue entered her mouth made it impossible not to kiss him back. Whimpering from the emotions flooding her, she popped the rest of his shirt snaps while he unfastened his jeans.

Kelly stopped kissing her just long enough to strip, then glued his lips to hers again. Left hand on the back of his neck, she lowered the other and stroked his penis as he squeezed her breasts, driving her wild with passion.

"Is it gonna do it?" he hissed in her ear after finally ending the long, wet kiss.

"Oh yeah."

He shoved her onto the bed and gaped at his erection with macho pride. "I love you, Anita, you saved me! I haven't seen ol' Shorty in this condition in four fucking years. Spread your legs, woman, you're in for the ride of your life."

She eagerly complied and in seconds he was throttling her, the intense pleasure forcing her to writhe and pump and moan like a wild animal. He made her come and she ecstatically cried out his name, begging him to climax with her. Kelly moaned and ejaculated, gorging her canal with hot semen, and only then did she realize her frenzied ardor had made her forget to give him a condom.

Kelly collapsed on top of her.

Running her hands over his back, she exulted in the erotic sensation of his chest merged with her breasts, his cheek pressed against hers—the stubble of freshly sprouting whiskers tickling her smooth skin, the masculine scent of aftershave mingling with his natural musk. She knew he hadn't meant it when he'd said he loved her, so she should have kneed him in the balls, or ran to the bathroom and locked herself inside—done *something* to force him to stop kissing her so she wouldn't wind up kissing him back— because she'd really fucked up by doing so. It had given birth to something inside that shouldn't have been born until the right man came along.

She'd fallen in love with the very one she could never have.

# PART 3

## Revenge is best served from the Wishbone

# 24

REX CHEWED A BITE OF scrambled eggs while examining Emma, who hadn't touched her cheese omelet. She took a sip of coffee and noticed him looking.

"Stop staring at me, Rex, you're making me feel more miserable than I already do. You know I can't stand people feeling sorry for me."

Yeah, he knew—but pity hardly described what he felt. Last night she'd gotten even more upset when he'd refused to discuss the matter any further and started for his bedroom. She'd rushed into hers and it made him feel guilty. He'd stood in the hall mulling things over and finally decided to apologize. By the time he opened her door to do so, she'd taken off her clothes and was about to get under the covers naked. Instead of covering herself in a panic, she'd calmly turned towards him and said, "Yes?"

He'd tried to turn away while saying "Sorry, I should have knocked" but hadn't been able to take his eyes off her astounding body.

"So what did you want to tell me?"

"Huh?" he'd mumbled, blown away she'd been so unperturbed by the intrusion.

"Well you must have something else you wanted to say, Rex, or you wouldn't have come into me room."

"Uh, I just wanted to apologize for being so sharp with you."

"Oh don't worry yourself over that, go on back to bed.

We'll talk more about it in the morning."

Overwhelmed with lust, he'd returned to his bedroom and whacked off, fantasizing about Emma from start to sticky finish.

He'd always known she thought of him as a brother. They'd become close friends soon after they met, and the platonic bond that forged their relationship had naturally kept him from entertaining any ideas of romance, even though he found her very attractive.

Seeing her absurdly beautiful breasts and scarlet pubic hair last night had changed that.

When Emma agreed to work for him she'd planned to buy a house, but there hadn't been any available that met her standards. His being very roomy, he'd told her she could stay with him as long as she liked. When Emma discovered he ate out most of the time because of his culinary ineptitude, she insisted on remaining with him to make sure he stayed "properly nourished". Their arrangement had been ideal. She didn't have to make house payments and he didn't have to dine at The Kodiak Cave unless he wanted to. Being emotionally untethered made them free to come and go as they pleased.

Now he wanted her badly and couldn't stand the thought of her being with another man. Since Emma didn't feel the same about him, he had no choice but to insist she move out. He'd have to fire her as well—cut all ties with the striking redhead—otherwise he'd go insane, unless she agreed to give up men altogether, and that would never happen. But it would have to wait until after she helped him get the next edition out, headlined by today's game, the most important in Kodiak history.

"Got the camera's loaded and ready," she said, eyeing her still intact omelet. "What time are we leaving for Lubbock?"

"As soon as I finish breakfast." He picked up a strip of

bacon and bit into it, imagining as he chewed what it would be like to gently gnaw on her cherry-red nipples.

"You're staring at me again."

"Sorry." He forced his eyes to his plate.

"Reckon I should give Kelly a ring?"

Almost choking over hearing that, he managed to force the bite down his throat and cleared it. "Ring?"

"You know, a call."

"Oh . . . I wouldn't, make him call you. You'll be giving him the upper hand otherwise, and it'll be twice as hard to straighten things out between you two. It would make him lose some respect."

Her pretty lips formed a pout as she considered it. "Guess I do have a few things to learn about the bugger, eh?"

A dollop of guilt gnawed at his gut over betraying Kelly with the unsound advice he'd just given Emma. But his lust soon quelled it, completely.

♦♦♦

Cooper picked him up and they drove to the gym.

Dearl couldn't quit yawning.

Rex Winters and Emma Riley gave them a thumbs up from Rex's car as Coo passed them in the parking lot.

"What's up with all the yawns, man?" Cooper asked.

"A weird dream woke me up during the night and I had a hard time going back to sleep."

"Don't tell me you didn't get enough rest last night. We need you fresh as a daisy, poor boy."

"I'm fine, don't worry."

"So what did you dream?"

"I was in algebra class and Jesus was sitting on Rainey's

desk. Then suddenly I was on top of Tornado Hill and Zechariah threw me a blanket. There were all these people below and I saw a huge tidal wave coming towards us. I was so panicked over the tidal wave it startled me awake."

Cooper parked beside Coach's Jeep and they got out of the pickup.

"Zechariah gave you a blanket?"

"Yeah."

"What did this blanket look like?"

"Can't remember, it was just a blanket."

"First you dreamed of Jesus then Zechariah threw you a blanket, right?"

"That's right."

"Boy are you in trouble."

"What makes you say that?"

"That blanket was a mantle like Elijah gave Elisha before God took him up to heaven. He did that because God wanted Elisha to take his place, so it looks like you're going to be Zechariah's replacement. That means you're a prophet, at least you will be someday."

He laughed and slapped Coo on the back. "Get real, rich boy."

Cooper frowned at him. "I'm not kidding."

"Since when did you start reading the Bible?"

"I don't. Zechariah told me all about Elijah and Elisha a couple of nights ago during supper."

Dearl opened the locker room door and the familiar stench of salty sweat and liniment assaulted his nostrils.

Steve Holt had everyone's uniforms and equipment packed. Each player was responsible for loading his own. Dearl picked up a bulky duffel bag with 20 stenciled on it, heaved it over his shoulder, and followed Hutch out the door.

"Great day to win State, huh, Tipps?"

"Sure is," he answered with a grin.

"If you don't fetch us some touchdowns I'm going to know the reason why, hear?"

"Hutch, if you don't catch my lateral and get that ball into Coo's hands, *I'm* going to know the reason why."

Hutch shot him a horse smile as they tossed their bags in the storage compartment of a chartered bus. "Money in the bank, Tipps, money in the bank."

Practically the whole town had shown up to see them off. He spotted Jetti blowing kisses at him, and waved at her while boarding. Cindy Shane stood beside her, casting air-smooches Cooper's way.

◆◆◆

"So they can have their pre-game meal at Lubbock and rest up for the one o'clock kickoff," Al answered a charming lady who'd asked why the players were leaving so early.

Zechariah spotted Jetti standing near the Greyhound. A girl next to her disturbed him. *Why am I seeing her here, Lord?*

No answer.

"Excuse me, Al, I need to talk to someone."

The rancher grinned. "You got another word from the Lord already?"

"Not exactly." Zechariah made his way to Jetti and asked if he could speak to her alone. The girl he'd dreamed about looked puzzled, but thankfully didn't try to follow as they walked away from the crowd.

"What's the name of that pretty gal you're with?"

"Cindy Shane. Why?"

"I dreamed about her last night, and it was a vision from

the Lord—a warning."

Jetti cocked her head and squinted at him. "Is something bad going to happen to her?"

"No, but I'm afraid she's planning on something bad happening to someone else. How well do you know her?"

"Is she going to hurt Cooper?"

"Please, just answer my question."

She glanced Cindy Shane's direction while shoving her hands in the hip pockets of her jeans. "All I really know about her is she's crazy about Cooper. Just about all our conversations are centered on our boyfriends."

"Would you happen to know if a lion and bear would mean anything to her?"

"Duh!" she chided, now looking at him. "The Sleeping Bear Kodiaks are about to play the Langton Lions for State, Zechariah."

Stupefied, he cast his eyes on Cindy Shane. She looked so sweet, so innocent, so incapable of any form of chicanery. "The team they're about to play is called the Lions?"

"Yeah, you didn't know that?"

"I've only heard them referred to as Langton until now. Dearl was also in the dream and turned into a bear. How important is he to his team?"

Jetti donned a proud grin. "Only the most important player, that's all."

The bus started moving and Jetti ran towards it, joining the crowd in cheering the football team on. Zechariah stood with hands on waist, wondering how a teenage girl who wouldn't even be in the game could cause Dearl and his team to lose.

He knew little about sports because his mentor hadn't cared for them. Noah considered football to be especially undesirable because of its violent nature. This would be the first time he'd get to watch a game. Perhaps he'd finally understand why Al, Luther, and Kelly had so eagerly looked forward to this day as much if not more so than Cooper, who'd be playing in it. High school bands were led by a drum major and marched on the field while the football players rested—he knew that much—so he figured Cindy Shane high-stepping in place with a drum major's baton had to pertain to today's game.

Silently beseeching the Lord for an answer to the mystery, he walked back to Al and Luther. Cindy Shane cheered as boisterously as Jetti and the rest of the crowd.

"What time are we heading for Lubbock?" Luther queried Al.

"Our tickets have been set aside for us, three front row seats on the fifty yard line, so we won't have to get there early like everyone else to get a good spot."

"Being on the school board has its privileges doesn't it."

"No, Luther. Having a son who Texas Tech wants to become a Red Raider does. One of their scouts arranged it in return for one more crack at trying to convince Cooper to go there instead of Texas."

Luther winced. "That's not like you, Al—I've never known you to be underhanded."

"Nothing underhanded about it. I told him I'd ask Cooper to check out their facilities and meet with the coaches like he requested, but warned him they wouldn't be able to convince Cooper to change his mind."

Zechariah didn't want to inadvertently bear false witness, which he feared he'd be doing by voicing his suspicion about Cindy Shane, but she was definitely up to something amiss and he needed help figuring out what, since the Lord hadn't spoken to him about it. "Al, I'm pretty ignorant about football so would you explain to me how someone could go about fixing things to make sure the team they wanted to win did?"

Al chuckled. "Why, got a big bet with somebody?"

"No, I'm just concerned, that's all."

"That the game's been fixed?"

"I'm afraid so."

"God told you that?"

"Not in words, but I had a prophetic dream last night about Dearl, a lion, a bear, and a girl I'd never seen before until a few minutes ago. She's standing by Jetti."

Al hooked his thumbs on a large belt-buckle with a gold image of Texas slightly elevated from its silver background. "Is that what you were talking to Jetti about?"

"Yeah, and she told me the girl is Cindy Shane. I don't want to falsely accuse her, but let me tell you what I dreamed and see if you can put the pieces together."

♦♦♦

The cheerleaders normally road to away games on a school bus with the band but Mrs. Rainey was driving them to Woodrow in an eight-passenger minivan, courtesy of the First Baptist Church. They'd change into their uniforms in the ladies room of a truck stop where they'd also be eating lunch. Bibi had learned none of the others had gotten much sleep last night either.

"I'm gonna nap all the way home," said Darlene, yawning. "At least the jitters are gone . . . for now."

"They'll come back when we get to Pirate Stadium," Marybeth predicted.

"Oh once you girls start cheering none of you will be nervous at all anymore," assured Mrs. Rainey. "I cheered for my hubby in a Permian Panther outfit when we were in high school. We won State our senior year."

"Odessa Permian's won State tons of times," Delores said.

"True, but only that once while we were there."

"What position did Coach Rainey play?"

"Middle linebacker."

"Was he as good as Abel Norris?"

"Abel reminds me of him."

Delores giggled. "Well that doesn't answer my question."

"I'd call it a draw. My husband sees a lot of himself in Abel. His football smarts weren't as sharp as his talent until after his first year playing college ball after he got out of the marines. Unfortunately a hip injury ended his time as a player for good midway through his senior season."

"Where did he go to college?" Darlene asked.

"Oklahoma State."

"How about you?"

"Texas. We married right out of high school. I earned my degree the same year his hitch was up?"

"Have you always taught English?" Darlene further probed.

"Mm hmm, and he's always taught math."

Bibi wondered if Mrs. Rainey was really as relaxed as she appeared to be. "Do you ever get nervous for your husband's sake?"

"Every game, dear. More so than when he played."

"But especially so today, huh?"

"Mm hmm. Which college do you plan to attend, Bibi?"

"Whichever one Gilbert gets a scholarship for."

"Y'all are that tight huh?"

"Yeah, we've always been super close."

"Well he'll be offered more than one scholarship, you can be sure of that. This season his play has almost reached the level of the four stars."

No one asked Mrs. Rainey who she meant by that. Everyone knew the Kodiaks wouldn't be playing for State without Rick, Delbert, Cooper, and especially Dearl. Pat referred to him as Dreamboat Dearl, but never to his face.

Bibi would always remember the first time she'd seen the cute blonde boy in kindergarten who'd moved to Sleeping Bear from Lubbock. Shy and timid around girls, Dearl was just the opposite with the boys in her class. He and Cooper paired off as best friends for life straight off. They'd looked so much alike in those days anyone who didn't know better would've sworn they were brothers. Cooper had grown taller and heavier than him, Dearl's muscle definition was more pronounced than Cooper's, but they still looked quite similar. Their hair was practically identical, the same dark shade of blonde Al Pond's used to be before so much gray crept in.

Al never married again after Cooper's mother died, nor did he date anybody now. She suspected he must have a secret mistress living somewhere besides Sleeping Bear. She couldn't imagine such an attractive guy without a girlfriend or wife. Her daddy had been a freshman Al's last year of high school and the pictures of Albert Joe Pond in his yearbook depicted a senior even more handsome than Cooper, especially Al's individual football pose as quarterback. He looked much different now but still had tons of sex appeal.

♦♦♦

Anita would have to give Burly a refund since he'd woken up to find she'd bailed on him during the night. But she'd gladly give up any amount of money to be where she was at the moment: sitting on the passenger side of Kelly's pickup as he drove to Lubbock, en route to Woodrow where the game would be played. After making love a second time they'd fallen asleep in each other's arms, and when she'd awakened this morning to see him looking at her, wearing his lazy cowboy smile, she'd scarcely been able to believe it hadn't all been just a wonderful dream.

"I want to thank you for making me feel like a man again," he'd said after nipping the tip of her nose with a kiss.

She'd pulled his face to hers and the moment their lips merged, his hands began exploring her body. It hadn't taken long for them to reach the summit of Mount Ecstasy for a third time.

Gazing at the rugged flat countryside whizzing past her window, she thought about how ugly she once found this part of Texas. Now it seemed beautiful. They could be trapped in the harshest regions of hell and she'd still find the scenery astounding as long as she was with Kelly. She'd been blown away last night when he'd pulled her from the depths of depression into the uttermost heights of jubilation. There hadn't been a doubt in her mind she'd fallen for him in vain, then he'd shared something that changed her whole world.

"Remember when I said you had way too much going for you to be a whore?" Kelly had asked while gently stroking her face. "Well it runs a little deeper than that. I'd heard a man with a teenage daughter had moved to Sleeping Bear, but didn't know she was my age. I was sitting at my desk in English class when this *good looking* gal walked in and old lady Mathews announced we had a new classmate named Anita Fury. You got to me right then, and I mean *got to me.* I bided my time, planning to ask you out, but then I found out what you were. It really knocked my dick in the dirt—went all over me because I'd even saw us getting married some day, and I've resented you ever since. Now tonight, you restoring my manhood and all, its killing me all over again that you're a whore, and I wish like hell you weren't so I could make an honest woman out of you."

An emotional bomb had exploded in her heart and soul, making her feel as if she'd never been truly alive before that moment. Bawling with elation she'd cried, "Don't say that unless you mean it, Kelly."

"Hell I reckon I mean it or I wouldn't have said it," he'd replied. "You know I don't pussyfoot around. But it don't make no difference anyway . . . you are what you are, and there ain't a fucking thing I can do about it."

"Isn't there," she'd weepingly insisted.

"Are you saying you'd give it up if I asked you to?"

"That's exactly what I'm saying. I love you, Kelly, and I'd do anything for you."

He'd shot her a suspicious frown and rolled over on his back. "You've been a pro since your teens, how could you just give it up? You obviously like it or you wouldn't have gone down that road to begin with."

"You're dead wrong there, Kelly. I took that route because of the fast money, no other reason. I'm giving it up anyway, even if you won't have me. By the way your prophet, that Zechariah guy, said the Lord wants me to."

"Thought you didn't believe in God."

"I don't."

"And yet you're going straight because Zechariah told you to? That don't make no sense."

"It's not because of him, Kelly. I want to earn my daughter's respect and hopefully make her love me, and that'll never happen as long as I'm a hooker. Plus I don't ever want any man but you to touch me again because I'm in love with you."

"You sound like you really mean it."

"That's because I really do, I swear—and no amount of money could tempt me to change my mind."

Kelly had pulled her on top of him and said, "Then you're

mine from this moment on. Say it."

Heart thumping wildly, tears still streaming down her face, she'd obeyed her man: "I'm yours from this moment on. And you're mine—say it."

"I'm yours."

They'd sealed their declarations with a deep kiss and fallen asleep still embracing each other.

She admired Kelly's profile as he drove. "I can't believe we're actually playing for State."

"Yeah, how sweet it is," he exuberated, wearing his lazy grin that had always turned her on.

"I remember how much I cried when we lost to Seagraves back when you were playing."

The grin disappeared. "You weren't the only one . . . man that broke my heart."

"It broke everybody's heart. So how many of our mighty Kodiaks would I know?"

"Hmm, you left town ten years ago, right?"

"Uh huh."

"You're bound to remember most of the first string."

"Did the Smith's move away? Gilbert was so big for his size as a youngster I always thought he'd make a good lineman when he got to high school."

Kelly nodded. "Good eye, he's our center and left defensive tackle. His sister's one of the cheerleaders."

"Who's he hiking the ball to?"

"Rick Holt. The star of the team is Dearl Tipps. He's the tailback, plays linebacker on defense, and returns punts and kickoffs to boot. That boy's a gem—he'll make a big splash in the pros when he gets out of college."

It seemed impossible that Dearl's vibrant mother was no longer alive. "Gwendolyn told me about poor Maureen succumbing to MS. You could have knocked me over with a feather when Jetti said she'd died."

"Yeah . . ." Kelly heaved a mournful sigh. "That was a real sad deal. Remember how pretty she was?"

"Oh yeah."

"Well you'd have never known it if you'd met her the last two years of her life. That poor gal looked awful."

She'd last seen Maureen at Piggly Wiggly teasing Joie McClain about her missing teeth. The cute little first-grader was buying gumballs with her tooth fairy money. "Did she ever tell anyone who Dearl's father was?"

"Not that I know of."

"I always suspected it was Al Pond."

Kelly slapped the dash and gave her a big smile. "Hot dang, I'm glad to hear I'm not the only one who's thought that all these years. I've never mentioned it to nobody since I work for Al."

She giggled over his enthusiasm. "Well how could you not, Dearl and Cooper looked so much alike when they were little. I bet they grew up to be lady killers. Jetti's sweet on Dearl, and Gwendolyn told me she thinks they'll wind up getting married."

He sobered and cut his eyes to her. "Darlin', there's something that's bugged me for years. I never asked because I wasn't sure how to take what you might tell me."

"Guess I know what you're talking about. The answer is I think so, but I could be wrong."

Kelly leaned forward and pulled a bag of Beechnut from his hip pocket.

"So you still chew, I see."

"Yep."

Few things grossed her out more than a man spitting out a slimy stream of tobacco juice. Watching him stuff his jaw she wondered if he planned on spewing out the window. A second later he lowered his hand into an elastic holder on the door and pulled out a beer can with the top cut off.

He spit in it and glanced at her. "How many candidates besides myself?"

"Only one." She looked away from him, trying to suppress the ghastly emotion enflaming her because it usually made her cry. Like all members of the world's oldest profession she'd occasionally suffered physical abuse from johns, but never had she been foolish enough to allow any of them a second chance. But one son of a bitch, who'd slapped her face back and forth while coming, hadn't taken no for an answer when she'd told him never to call on her again.

After he left the motel room she'd taken a shower. While drying off, a hand had clamped her mouth closed as the cold steel of a knife pressed against her throat. Not bothering with a rubber, he'd raped her, and again smacked her face repeatedly while ejaculating. Knowing she'd never stand a chance of getting a conviction and would only wind up in trouble, she hadn't bothered calling the police. Relieved the maniac had spared her life, didn't know her real name, and had no idea where she lived, she'd vowed never to work Amarillo again.

It happened the weekend after she'd coaxed Kelly into screwing her. Life was full of ironies but the color of the rapist's eyes being so similar to Kelly's making it impossible to know which of them passed that trait to Jetti still blew her mind, for she'd never seen anyone else with orbs so uniquely colored.

Twice last night and once this morning made it four times she'd had Kelly's semen inside her. If only that bastard rapist hadn't defiled her with his, her body would only have known the seed of her soon-to-be husband. She hadn't seen any logic in asking Kelly to use a condom after forgetting to do so the first time they'd made love last night, since sperm can survive for six or seven days after entering the fallopian tubes. It would be up to him whether or not to risk pregnancy if they'd dodged it this time.

He probably figured she was on the pill, but she'd never do that. The way her mother had died made her afraid to take any type of medication except when absolutely necessary.

"Any particular reason you lean towards me being Jetti's daddy?"

Still looking out the passenger window, she nodded.

"Well, what is it?"

"Because I want you to be . . . ."

# 25

REX OGLED HER FROM HIS peripheral vision as he drove, longing to reach over and squeeze Emma's breasts, straining against a pink blouse pressed tight by the shoulder strap of her seatbelt. She blew smoke through a gap at the top of the passenger window, powered it closed, and stubbed out her cigarette in the ashtray. The action made her bosom jiggle, and the back of his throat turned dry.

"Last night was funny, eh? You catching me in the buff and all."

Neither of them had mentioned it, and he wondered what prompted her to do so now. "I shouldn't have barged in without knocking."

"Nonsense, you had no way of knowing I was naked, Rex."

Hearing her say the word aroused him further. "Nevertheless I should have knocked. I promise it'll never happen again."

She pouted. "Oh boo, hate to hear that. Kind of gave me a thrill actually. Closest thing I've had to sex with a man in years."

Hoping she wouldn't see him growing erect, he cut his eyes to her and grinned. "I could tell you a real heartbreaking story on that subject."

Giggling, she turned partially sideways, the shoulder strap forcing her breasts to undulate during the movement. "So how long has it been for you anyway?"

His pulse elevated at the thought she might be hinting around about the two of them having sex. He was glad his pants were rather baggy or she'd surely notice his emerging hard on. "Longer than it has for you I'm sure."

"Remember the night we went out to Al Pond's to interview Zechariah and I thought you were jealous over me?"

"How could I forget? I was in the doghouse for awhile there."

A light blush sprang to her cheeks. "Well I've a confession to make. I was very disappointed to learn you didn't fancy me."

If she were to glance at his crotch he knew she'd see her statement had hurled his penis to its zenith. "As I recall you said as much that night."

"No, Rex, I said I felt a bit put off—never said I was very disappointed."

He inhaled a deep breath. "I have to confess something too, Emma. I wasn't able to take my eyes off you last night when . . . ."

"You saw me naked." She completed his unfinished sentence grinning.

"Yeah."

Emma looked thoughtful for a moment. "I did a lot of thinking last night after I went to bed, pondering what you said about Kelly and me being like yen and yang. Been thinking about it since I got up this morning as well. You're right, we really are completely incompatible, the two of us. You and I get along as smoothly as hands in gloves. Think there might be a chance for us?"

He groaned with excitement. "Emma, I haven't been able to think about anything since I went into your room last night except making love to you."

"So glad to hear that," she relayed with a seductive smile, "because I've another confession to make. I knew you'd be coming into me room to apologize, and stripped as fast as I could. Of course I thought you'd knock first which would make it obvious what I was up to."

A big lump formed in his lust-dried throat. "Wow, I had no idea."

"Didn't you wonder why I didn't scream for you to get out, or jerk the bedspread off the bed to cover me-self?"

"No, I just thought you were real uninhibited."

"Oh I'm uninhibited all right," she laughed, "but not to that bloody degree. Caught you staring at my tits during breakfast by the way. When we get home after the game I'll let you have a look at them au naturale again."

Unable to believe this was really happening, he didn't want to say it, but knew he had to. "Um, what about Kelly?"

"We're through, it's over. I only asked if you thought I should give him a ring this morning to test your reaction, and that intentionally stupid advice you gave me was exactly what I'd hoped you'd say. And before you ask, no I'm not going to chase after Zechariah. It would only be a rebound and that would be unfair to him. Besides, he said the Lord has other plans for him. I may not be in love with you, Rex, but I do love you, and I think my feelings could easily turn that way. I suspect yours for me could do the same. We owe it to each other to find out, don't you think?"

Rex felt so lightheaded with erotic giddiness he could only nod.

"Good. Now then, I've a grand idea. How 'bout I pull out that hard cock of yours before it pokes a hole in your pants and suck on it while you drive . . .?"

◆◆◆

Leaning back in his seat, Dearl tuned out the droning bus

engine, running all the plays through his head before focusing on *eighty-nine black motion red sweep double lateral.* Catching Holt's pitchout, Dearl threw a perfect spiral to Hutch, and the ball flew from the fullback's hands smoothly into Cooper's, who had nothing but open field before him.

His imagination took on a life of its own and he grimaced as Kenny Higgins stripped the ball from Coo on the one yard line. He elbowed his half-brother and reminded, "Remember what Coach said. If Higgins gets anywhere near you lock up on that ball with both hands."

Eyes hidden behind a pair of shades, Cooper grinned. "That son of a bitch will be too preoccupied trying to stop you to worry about me."

"Not on the trick play he won't."

"It'll never occur to him in a million years that you're not coming around the corner. By the time you get the ball to Hutch I'll be all alone, way down the other side of the field. No matter how fast he catches on to what we're up to, there's no way he can catch me, I'll have way too much distance on him."

◆◆◆

Jetti hadn't wanted Cindy to ride to the game with them because of what Zechariah said, but Dearl would be upset to learn she'd been rude to Cooper's sweetheart so she'd kept her word. Sitting in back behind Grandma, who was driving, the girl seemed preoccupied with something.

*Probably daydreaming about making love with Cooper,* she thought.

Rex Winters passed them and she wondered why Emma

Riley wasn't with him. Shortly after he pulled into their lane his car began to weave erratically.

"For heaven's sakes!" Grandma yelped. "I hope Rex isn't driving drunk."

The statement seemed to pull Cindy from her musing. She yawned and stretched her arms. "Who was that man that wanted to talk to you in the parking lot, Jetti?"

"His name's Zechariah. He's a prophet."

Cindy laughed, taking it as a joke.

"I'm serious." She kept eyeing the car ahead. "Grandma, you ought to slow down—it looks like Rex might flip over any second."

A moment later the weaving stopped and Jetti laughed hysterically when the back of Emma Riley's head appeared.

"What's so funny?" said Grandma with a confused frown.

"Oh . . . nothing." Grandma hadn't connected the dots and she wasn't about to tell her Rex had just gotten a blowjob.

"Well something sure turned your giggle box over."

"I didn't see Emma when he passed us, Grandma, and now that I do he's driving normal again. She must have been doing something to him. Get the picture?"

After thinking on it a few seconds Grandma's face turned red. "Jetti, that's lewd! She was probably only picking something up from the floorboard."

Cindy giggled. "I guess they're not as platonic as they want everyone to think. Jetti, you said you were serious about that man being a prophet. What makes you think he is?"

"Just do." She didn't want to discuss the matter any further, figuring Zechariah wouldn't want her to. He'd said Cindy wasn't going to hurt Cooper, so she couldn't imagine who the prophet thought might be harmed. The girl certainly didn't frighten her in the least—she could take Cindy Shane with one arm tied behind her back.

"How do you like living in Sleeping Bear, Cindy?" Grandma asked.

"It's okay. I still miss Lubbock though."

Jetti turned to her. "You wouldn't have met Cooper if you hadn't moved."

"That's true," Cindy agreed, smiling about it.

"Oh, are you dating Cooper Pond?"

"Yes, ma'am."

"I told you that, Grandma. Are you going senile?"

"Let's hope not, dear . . . ."

♦♦♦

Zechariah felt a little claustrophobic sitting between Al, who was driving, and Luther.

Sensing his discomfort, Luther winked at him. "You'd think a rich man like Al would own a double cab."

"I don't like them," said Al, "and wasn't about to drive to the game in one of my sports cars—folks would think I was putting on airs. Back to your dream, Zechariah, I can only figure someone from Langton has been spying on the Kodiak's practices all week, hoping to figure out Coach Rainey's game plan. But I can't recall seeing a solitary soul I didn't know at any of them, and I didn't miss any."

"Maybe they were using binoculars from a distance," Luther suggested.

"Had to have been something like that as far as I can tell."

"That doesn't explain the girl's part in this," Zechariah pointed out, "and she was the focal point."

Luther leaned forward and looked at Al. "Last Saturday night while I was giving Cooper a refill, Cindy told him she needed to use the bathroom. He hung around the kegs talking to Lyle Whitney, and she was gone nearly half an hour. What if she copied Cooper's playbook and gave it to somebody on Langton's team? Cindy's not a Sleeping Bear native, so she may not have the ol' Kodiak spirit."

Al frowned. "But she lived in Lubbock all her life before moving to Sleeping Bear. Why would she want to help Langton?"

"Don't know, maybe she got paid to do it—but that might be what Zechariah's dream means."

"Dang it," Al seem to say to himself before looking at Luther. "I noticed Cindy seemed a little nervous when she asked me for a wine cooler around nine-thirty. At the time I figured she was embarrassed for requesting another when she'd already had three. Do you remember if her trip to the bathroom was before that?"

"Yeah, about an hour before. Right after I handed Cooper's cup back Lyle Whitney asked me what time it was."

"Oh boy . . ." Al rubbed his forehead. "Well if that *is* what happened at least Langton won't know about the new plays Rainey installed just for them because they weren't in Cooper's playbook. Problem is, there're only three of them. I'll fill Rainey in as soon as we get there. Of course I won't mention I'm suspicious because of a dream. And since we're not certain Cindy copied the playbook, I'll leave her out of it too."

◆◆◆

"Think you can be happy living only on my pay?"

Anita nodded. "I'd be happy even if you only made minimum wage, Kelly. But just the same I want to learn a legitimate vocation. I've got great people skills and being a naturally gifted salesperson, I think I'd like to try my hand as a real estate agent—that's what my mom did before she died. I'd have to do a lot of driving of course, since I'd never make any money in Sleeping Bear."

Pulling onto Loop 289 encircling Lubbock he said, "What if I don't want you to work?"

"Then I won't."

"Simple as that, huh."

"Simple as that."

"And kids?"

She shot him a grin. "You may have already knocked me up, Kelly, I've never used anything but condoms for birth control. I'm confident you didn't but if you want kids we'd better move fast because I'm thirty-six."

"I know how old you are, we're the same age, remember? I'd like to have a couple of sons since you think we've already spawned a daughter."

"Well I'll see what I can do." Watching him raise the makeshift spittoon to his mouth, she sighed. "Don't suppose there's any way I could talk you into giving up chewing tobacco."

"Nope."

"Didn't think so."

◆◆◆

Burly gazed at the artificial turf of Pirate Stadium from his excellent location in the home stands: row five above the fifty yard line. Soon his beloved Kodiaks would be stomping Langton's ass on it and he couldn't wait. Worry over Anita mingled with his excitement, however. She'd always been a woman of her word and had never burned him before, so some sort of emergency must had forced her to leave during the night. He'd still gotten his money's worth, feeling her big tits pressed against him while drifting off to sleep, but had failed once again to get that one thing she wouldn't sell him no matter how much he offered: a kiss. She'd never allowed him one solitary peck on the lips. Every time he'd paid for a whole night it was in the hope she'd fall asleep first so he could steal a smooch, but she never had.

Kelly Newly stepped down the aisle to his right and headed for a ramp. Someone tapped him on the back of his shoulder and he freaked out to see Anita smiling at him while digging into her purse.

"Sorry I skipped out on you, Burly."

"What happened, are you okay?"

"Never been better. You have the honor of being my last client ever."

He gulped. "Anita, please don't say that."

"It's true. You're looking at a new woman, I'm getting hitched to Kelly Newly."

"Oh no, what am I gonna do?! I damn near went crazy all those years you were gone."

"You'll manage just fine. Anyway, here's your money back, one thousand even. Your last ride is on the house."

◆◆◆

Cindy settled into her seat, holding hot-buttered popcorn and a root beer. Several rows below, Kelly Newly sat beside a gorgeous woman that reminded her of Jetti. Further down the stands she saw Burly Swain slumped over, cradling his forehead. Rex Winters and Emma Riley stood by the Kodiak bench shooting pictures of the players doing warm-ups on the field. Other than Al Pond, Luther, and the man Jetti claimed to be a prophet, she didn't recognize any other Sleeping Bear residents. She knew most of the town had to be interspersed somewhere in the crowd because the pagan hicks lived for nothing else.

Watching number 89 stretching his legs on the twenty yard line, she felt her panties moisten. Cooper looked so amazingly hot in that blue uniform.

On the other end of the field, wearing white jerseys above red pants, the Langton Lions were also getting loosened up for the big game. She wondered how many, if any, of the players knew that one of their coaches had received a gift that would ensure them a fourth consecutive state championship.

It would shatter Cooper if he knew, and that spurred a sense of guilt for not feeling ashamed for what she'd done— but football was just a silly game, and someday he'd realize that the way she always had. She'd never confess her diabolical deed of course, because he'd dump her immediately.

Sheriff Grange and Bart Newly appeared at the bottom of the stands. She checked the time ticking down on the scoreboard. Jetti said the game would start when it reached zero, so the fucked up town of Sleeping Bear had only four minutes and thirteen seconds left before its nightmare began.

# 26

HYPERVENTILATING, DEARL STOOD IN THE center of the field on the five yard line, waiting for the kickoff to start this battle for State. The Lions kicker didn't get much height or distance. He bit into his mouthpiece as gridiron instinct took over, and ran forward, snagging the memorial pigskin at full speed. Gripping the ball vice-like between his cupped hand and left elbow, he charged towards his middle blockers, who were trying to open a lane for him.

Kenny Higgins also played on special teams. When the savage linebacker knocked two Kodiaks to the ground who'd tried to double-team him, and sped his way with an ear-splitting roar, Dearl growled with anger. Having already attained good field position, he locked both arms around the ball, lowered his shoulders, and plowed into Higgins rather than try to dodge him—drawing first blood to let the boy know he was in for a long, long day.

Dearl sprang to his feet and offered a hand to help his archenemy up, but the fearful bruiser was moaning, rolling from side to side while clutching his belly. "Get up, Higgins, you're not getting off that easy!"

"Un-sportsmanlike conduct, taunting!" The ref's yellow flag landed near Higgins' feet. "Fifteen yards."

Dearl whirled around in shock. "You can't call me for that, all I did was tell him to get up."

"That'll be another fifteen. You don't sass me, son."

Fearing he might get ejected if he spoke his mind over the outrageous penalties, Dearl gritted his teeth instead and started back downfield. He'd returned the ball to the Kodiak 40, relishing the last few feet as he'd driven the All State linebacker backwards, screaming, "It's gonna be this way all game, Higgins, I've got your fucking number!" But because of the two insane calls they'd have to start from their own ten yard line.

The ref called timeout as the trainers checked on Higgins, still writhing in pain. Ten long minutes went by and they carried him off the field on a gurney. Watching the hurting linebacker being wheeled away, the gravity of the situation seized him and Dearl started bawling. He'd only meant to intimidate his nemesis, not injure him.

"Huddle up!" yelled Rick Holt when the whistle blew and the intolerant head zebra signaled to start the clock again.

"Quit your boo-hooing, Tipps, you didn't hurt him on purpose." Rick glanced around, making eye contact with each player. "You guys are gonna love this, Coach isn't wasting any time. Eighty-nine black motion red sweep double lateral on two. Break . . .!"

Holt stuck his hands beneath Gilbert Smith's ass. "Blue thirty-one! Blue thirty-one! Hut-Hut!"

Dearl saw the ball coming to him through tears as Holt and he ran to the right, Higgins' backup biting on the sweep all the way. Right foot planted, he turned and passed to Hutch.

The ball sailed on him and Hutch had to leap to make the catch, but managed to come down with it. A Lion dove at the fullback's feet as he hurled it to Cooper, hitting him between the numbers. The crowd went wild as Coo raced untouched down field and crossed the goal line. They'd covered ninety yards on their first offensive play from scrimmage.

Heart pounding, Dearl looked at the scoreboard and watched the six points appear. Adrenaline surged as the Kodiak fight song blared in his ears, yet he couldn't quit crying, petrified he'd damaged Higgins internally. He'd intended to inflict as much pain as possible, but not injury. Now he cussed himself for not backing off before pinning him to the turf.

"We're going for two!" yelled Holt.

Coach called his number and Dearl punched it over as Jimmy Cocker leveled the defensive end.

"Two plays, eight points, I'll take it every time," said Hutch, slapping him on the butt. "You damn near overshot me. Good thing I've got flypaper hands, huh?"

Dearl sniffed back a dribble of snot. "Hutch, I feel sick to my stomach. I think I really hurt Higgins bad."

Baring his teeth, the fullback looked menacing behind the bars of his facemask. "What's the matter with you, man, stuff like that comes with the territory. We've got four quarters of football left to play so get your fucking head out of your ass and back on the game . . .!"

Dearl sped downfield on the kickoff. Allen Pierce caught it at the 3 and got to the 20 in two seconds. A bulky kid leading the Lion wedge tried to take him out but Dearl laid a spin move on him and had Pierce in his sights a second later. Coach had instructed them not to hit the All State running back high but Hutch had gotten a hand on the ball as Pierce stiff-armed him, causing it to bobble, so Dearl reamed it with his helmet, making it squirt out from Pierce like a hardened whitehead shooting from an overly ripe pimple being squeezed.

It flew right into the waiting hands of Abel Norris and he took it to the house.

Coach called for another attempt at a two-point conversion. Listening to Holt bark out a fake audible, Dearl took note of the faces beneath eleven red helmets. Instead of the confident, arrogant expressions he'd witnessed three years in a row, the Lions defensive squad looked petrified.

They'd lost their star, and along with him, their swagger.

"... Hut-hut-hut!"

Dearl ran to his left. Holt faked a handoff to him and tossed the ball to Hutch, who went up the middle behind Gilbert Smith. Despite the fact not a single Lion bit on the fake, Hutch managed to plow his way to pay dirt.

"Sixteen to nothing, sixteen to fucking nothing!" Cooper howled ecstatically, pounding his chest like King Kong as they trotted towards their end zone preparing to kick off again.

Dearl's eyes finally dried up but not the horrible guilt. He wished the announcer would comment on Higgins' condition. The trainers had wheeled him to the locker room, and he prayed they hadn't been forced to take him to the hospital from there.

This time Allen Pierce held on to the ball and it took him, Abel Norris, and Cooper to finally drag him to the ground. The Lions offensive drive would commence on their own forty-eight.

Heaving for breath, Dearl watched Hugo Wildemont closely as the Lions came to the line of scrimmage with the speedy wide-out lining up strong side as an extra tight end. That formation alerted him to check 84's hands. The All State receiver's knuckles merged with the turf.

"Door! Door! Door!" Dearl shouted.

Sure enough Jerry Lane handed off to Pierce instead of faking it, and the tailback went off-tackle weak side. Alerted the play would be a run, left cornerback Mike Vaughn teamed up with Hutch and Abel Norris to stuff Pierce at the hole, giving Coo and him just enough time to pile on before the fearsome Lion could break through. The five of them managed to hold the beast to a minimal gain.

"Second and eight!" declared the official.

When Langton broke huddle they lined up in the same

formation but with Wildemont weak side.

"Window! Window!" screamed Hutch.

84 had flipped sides but they'd called the same play, and Pierce got brought down at the line of scrimmage.

For the third time the triple-champions used the same alignment, sending Wildemont back strong side. Dearl kept quiet when he saw the receiver stretch his fingers out, barely touching the ground. If they'd keyed on Pierce again, Hugo Wildemont would have made an easy touchdown. But knowing not to, the defensive backs played pass all the way, and when 84 turned for the ball, Lyle Whitney had beaten him to it, snagging himself an interception. Wildemont pulled him to the ground, preventing any return yardage.

The ref pointed towards the Langton end zone and spotted the ball at the Kodiaks' 18.

Jerry Lane's perpetually cocky look evaporated, and for the first time since Dearl had faced the amazing quarterback, he saw fear in number 12's eyes. Head lowered, Lane made his way to the Lions' bench.

Despite not having Kenny Higgins, Langton's defense managed to force a three-and-out, and Allen Pierce returned the punt for a touchdown, crossing the goal line wearing only one shoe because the other had slipped off in Dearl's hands while attempting a shoestring tackle. They nailed the extra point, cutting the Kodiak lead to nine. After going three-and-out again, Dearl only netting a total of four yards on two carries, they punted out of bounds to prevent a return and managed to send Jerry Lane and company off the field after three downs.

Awaiting the Lions' punt, Dearl marveled at how well prepared Langston's defense was, and hoped he or one of his teammates wasn't guilty of telegraphing intentions like Hugo Wildemont. The punter had obviously been warned to keep the ball away from him, and the directional kick was fielded by Hutch, who got brought down at the Kodiak 31.

A pass to Whitney running a fade route got broken up. Dearl ran up the gut on second down and every damn Lion seemed to be aware if it beforehand, limiting him to a three yard gain. Knowing Langton expected them to pass on third and long, Coach called his number again. The Lions didn't bite on the play-action fake but he refused to go down, dragging three of them for first down yardage.

"Shit!" Hutch bellowed. "It's like they know what play we're gonna run as soon as we do."

"Stop bellyaching and listen up," commanded Holt. "Twenty three-vac black fake sweep on one."

Coach had designed the play to trick the quick-reacting Higgins into biting on a run only to have Dearl lateral back to Holt and sneak downfield for a pass. Dearl's stomach twisted with anxiety because he still didn't know if he'd seriously injured the linebacker or not. He leaned forward, hands on his thigh pads, as Hutch got set in front of him.

"Forty-thirteen! Forty-thirteen! Forty-thirteen! Hut!"

Not being able to study this play because it wasn't on any game films, it came as no surprise to Dearl the Lions reacted solely to a run, leaving only the free safety as a security back should Hutch or he get past the other ten defenders. Higgins' replacement, number 50, stormed for the three hole vacated by Jimmy Cocker, who'd pulled as if blocking for a weak side sweep. Dearl tossed the ball back to Holt and sped down the sideline.

Holt rifled the ball ahead of him and Dearl caught it in full stride. The free safety tried to tackle him high but he swatted him down like a fly. Heading towards the same end zone where Higgins had stripped the ball from him last year, he swore to himself he'd give up football if he'd seriously wounded his old foe.

He never wanted to feel this way again.

Crossing the goal line, Dearl managed to toss the ball to the official before getting bombarded by his teammates. Coach called on him again and he harvested another two points.

For the rest of the first quarter and deep into the second neither the Kodiaks nor the Lions could manage a first down or any decent punt return yardage.

After two pass plays went nowhere, they ran a draw on third and long. Dearl missed the first down marker by a short yard. Holt called timeout and went to the sidelines to confer with Coach Rainey about possibly going for it. Though certain he could have gotten them a fresh set of downs, Dearl wasn't surprised to see the punter trot onto the field. If they didn't make it, the shift in momentum at this juncture might have proved insurmountable.

Pierce lateraled to a small speedster after fielding a shanked punt. The trick worked and Langton put up another six, succeeding on a two-point conversion afterwards.

After a short return by Hutch, they went three-and-out and punted out of bounds, leaving the Lions with excellent field position. Jerry Lane hit Wildemont on a slant. He shook off Lyle Whitney and raced fifty yards for a score. Allen Pierce extended his arms before his belly collided with turf, and the tip of the ball barely broke the plane, tacking on another two, making the score 24 to 23 with forty seconds left before halftime.

On the ensuing kickoff Dearl got tackled at the Sleeping Bear 41. Coach signaled for a spot pass where Holt would throw to an area that Cooper was supposed to run to. As if knowing the play as well as the Kodiaks, the free safety got there before Coo and made an easy interception. A cornerback hit Cooper behind the knees, sending him somersaulting onto his back. Racing towards his own end zone, Dearl dove and caught an ankle, tripping up the thieving Lion at the 24, preventing a sure touchdown.

Langton ran Pierce three times up the middle, milking the clock on third down after exhausting the Kodiak's remaining timeouts before kicking a chip-shot field goal to take the lead as the half ended.

♦♦♦

Running a hand over his sweat-soaked hair, Dearl sat down in front of the Pirate locker holding his clothes, awaiting Coach Rainey's halftime adjustments.

Coach looked extremely perturbed, as if they were behind several touchdowns rather than only two points. Dearl knew something really troubled Rainey when he called them fellas instead of girls after telling them to listen up.

"I didn't want to believe it, but after watching Langston's defense through a whole half, I'm afraid what I was told is true. They know our plays."

"Yeah," said Abel Norris, "they really studied our game films well."

"What am I going to do with you, Norris, you don't interrupt me while I'm talking!"

The big junior lowered his head. "Sorry, Coach, won't happen again."

"It damn well better not. When two-a-days start this summer you'll be giving me a hundred yards of bear crawls after each practice." Rainey turned his attention back to the team. "I know Truman Jette can't be involved, but somebody on that team somehow got their hands on a copy of our playbook."

A collective gasp filled the air, and Dearl knew everybody had to be feeling the same fiery rage of injustice that burned in him. Hutch hollered "Shit!" and obviously wanted to say more, but apologized to Coach instead for speaking without permission.

"I don't know how they got it," Rainey continued, "but there's nothing we can do about it at the moment. According to what I was told, this apparently happened last week, so other than the three plays we installed for this game, their defense knows them all.

"You girls remember drawing up plays in the sand when you were little squirts? Well, the only thing we can do to fool the Lions is something similar, but you've got to keep your thinking caps on. Holt, when I hold my thumb down instead of signaling the play that'll mean it's up to you to improvise. Don't get too creative, I don't want any illegal formation or delay of game penalties. Meanwhile here's the plan for every first down if I don't signal a play. We're going to run a wishbone power sweep with Tipps at fullback, Hutch and Pond as running backs. Whitney, you'll replace Cooper at tight end. Hutch, you'll line up left and Pond will take the right side. Tipps, you'll get the ball every time, and wait till Hutch and Pond are both in front of you before going full speed, they'll be your lead blockers. If the ball's spotted on the right hash, run left, and do the opposite when it's placed on the left hash. When the ball's in the middle of the field, take it up the gut. When that happens, Hutch and Pond, you guys charge through the zero hole, pop the first Lion you see, and try to clear a path for Tipps. When Langton starts catching on do just the opposite—left hash, sweep left, right hash run right—and when the ball's spotted in between the hashes, you decide whether to take it right, left, or over center, Holt."

Dearl raised his hand.

"Tipps?"

"Have you heard anything about Kenny Higgins?"

Coach's face dropped. "I was hoping you wouldn't find out until after the game, but they had to take him to the hospital. He's got a ruptured spleen."

Dearl leaned forward and moaned into his hands, feeling hot tears dripping through his fingers. "I'm not going back out there, Coach—I'm done with football forever."

Pandemonium ensued. Rainey had to reprimand several of his teammates for cussing him out and telling him to quit being a pussy. When he got everybody quiet, Coach said, "I sympathize, Dearl, but injuries are a fact of life in football. If you want to give up a brilliant career in the National Football League, an opportunity I'd have given anything to have had, that's up to you. But you've got way too much in here—" Rainey banged his chest "—to quit before finishing this game. However bad you feel right now about sending Higgins to the hospital, it'll pass. But it won't begin to compare to how lousy you'll feel the rest of your life, knowing you let your team down. That was a clean hit you put on Higgins, not a cheap shot, and he'll recover just fine. But you won't if you quit."

Dearl wanted to snidely ask if he'd be getting the same pep talk if he wasn't such a vital part of the team, but didn't. He felt disgusted—the way he had over the big turnout at his mother's funeral because of his gridiron exploits rather than respect for her.

Cooper—who'd been as pissed at him as everyone else—came over, popped him on the shoulder pads a couple of times, and rested his hands on them while leaning forward. "I'm sorry for mouthing off, Dearl. I'd probably feel just like you if I'd hurt Higgins, but let me ask you something, bro. What would Higgins do if he'd knocked your ass out of the game? Would he quit?"

That startled him, Coo really hit a nerve. "No way."

"Is he a better football player than you, have a bigger set

than you—is he more of a man than you?"

He sneered at him. "Of course not."

"Then why the fuck are you talking such nonsense then? We can take these motherfuckers down and you know it. Hell, they're cheating and we can still do it. What say, poor boy? Let's finish this deal, and do what we swore we'd do since junior high."

Crying again, but with the fury emotion of the Kodiak spirit stoked by his half brother, Dearl stood up and faced his teammates. "Guys, I don't know who that was talking through my mouth awhile ago, but that pussy's gone—Dearl Tipps is back."

Grinning, Coach Rainey ran a finger across his throat to stop the cheering, and folded his arms across his chest. "We've only got a few minutes left before half's over, girls, so let's go over the adlibs again . . . ."

♦♦♦

He'd reached for the Maalox when Dearl Tipps creamed Higgins, sending his best player to the hospital, but Dick had taken a serious chug of it when his ulcer flared after Sleeping Bear scored on their first offensive play. Having never seen that one before, he feared he'd been double-crossed and someone had alerted Rainey. But on the Kodiak's second possession, he'd relaxed, knowing he hadn't sold his boat and camping trailer in vain after all. That sly fox Rainey had come up with some trick plays just for this game and his youngsters had scored on both of them. Expecting to see a few more in the second half, he'd alerted the defense to be slow to react against anything they didn't recognize and kick it into high gear only when the Kodiaks' intentions became obvious.

"Giving up a first down is a hell of a lot better than giving up six points," he'd told them.

Truman had instructed the return team to watch for an onside kick, but Dick knew Rainey wouldn't try anything so risky with the game this close. However, he'd agreed with the head coach in warning the defense to expect Sleeping Bear to start the second half the same way they had the first, with that double-lateral pass. Dick had made adjustments for it, and Cooper Pond would have a safety as well as a cornerback on his ass any time the Kodiaks appeared to be running an option sweep.

Unlike Rainey, Truman had reserved all his trick plays for the second half. One of them, a flea-flicker, was sure to go for six if the Kodiaks bit on the run, which he fully expected them to do.

♦♦♦

Zechariah had listened closely as Luther enlightened him about what was going on during the first half of play. The sport would have seemed little more than senseless violence to him otherwise. One of the Langton players had gotten injured at the start of the contest and he'd been amazed that both teams had left the field without suffering several other casualties, the way those young men so fiercely rammed into each other.

Al had sought out the coach as soon as they'd arrived, warning him of Luther's suspicion that Langton had obtained a copy of the playbook. Luther had become more convinced of its certainty as the game progressed, angrily claiming the Lion defense might as well have been in the

Kodiaks' huddle.

The big Cherokee had practically gone berserk when Dearl got penalized at the onset. Al hadn't been very happy about it either. Zechariah hoped the Kodiaks could somehow manage a victory despite being at such a disadvantage—he dreaded the reaction of his present company if they didn't. If Luther's interpretation of the dream was correct, he didn't know how much good warning the coach so close to the start of the game had done, since the guy told Al he had to be mistaken. Perhaps the coach now thought otherwise, but he wondered if the short break in the action could possibly be enough time to develop a counter strategy.

Enjoying a third hotdog, he watched the pretty cheerleaders waving their pompoms as the teams returned to the field. Along with the refreshments, he found the energetic girls the most appealing aspect of the game by far. Too bad look was all he'd ever be able to do with any female. He again found himself wishing he'd accepted Emma's offer to feel her breasts.

# 27

EXCEPT FOR COOPER'S TOUCHDOWN CINDY had appeared resentful every time Sleeping Bear scored during the first half. Jetti kept thinking about Zechariah's concern, and wondered if he'd been warned Cindy was a duplicitous bitch that wanted Langton to win, though she couldn't imagine how that would cause physical harm to anyone.

Watching Dearl on the sidelines as halftime ticked to an end, she smiled inside as her man squirted Gatorade into his mouth from a squeeze bottle. He seemed happy again. She'd so wanted to run onto the field to comfort him when catching a glimpse of his face as Kenny Higgins got carried off. Tears had been pouring from Dearl's eyes and that had made her cry too.

Cindy was cheering for Cooper, who stood with his back to them in front of the Kodiak bench. Her feelings for the tight end made the notion of wanting his team to lose seem absurd, yet she couldn't shake the feeling that Cindy did.

A clap of thunder roared through the stadium. It had been a clear day with little wind and the temperature hovering in the mid fifties, making for perfect football weather. But before the first half ended a bank of dark clouds floated over from the west, threatening rain. She loved seeing Dearl all grass-stained and muddy at Kodiak Field when having to play in the rain because he looked so macho and tough, but this game was being played on artificial turf. Rain would only make for slippery footing, and she certainly didn't want that.

The players took the field and a few moments later the Kodiaks kicked off. Allen Pierce caught the ball near the end zone and returned it to the Lions' 25 before Abel Norris and Delbert Hutch forced him out of bounds.

As the Lions got set she could hear Dearl scream "Door!" several times. Making a mental note as the play unfolded to ask him what that signal meant, she quickly jumped to her feet and started cheering her heart out.

"Oh yeah! Oh yeah! Come on, Dearl, run! Take it all the way—all the way, baby! Yay . . .!" she threw her arms up like the referee, signaling a touchdown. Dearl had stripped the ball from Allen Pierce as Lyle Whitney and Cooper were trying to tackle the Langton star. Her sweetheart had stiff-armed his way past two Lions and glided in for the TD.

From the corner of her eye she saw Cindy frowning.

Soon Jetti started cheering again as Dearl fought his way through a pile of Lions and scored two more points.

◆◆◆

Coach Rainey had made one last adjustment before they'd left the locker room for the second half. "Pearl," he'd said, "you've got a strong set of paws, and we're going to need all the help we can get. Every time Allen Pierce gets the rock, lay back and let your teammates go after him before closing in. When you do, forget trying to tackle him, just go for the ball."

Dearl had made a lot of touchdowns but none seemed sweeter than the one he'd just scored after stealing the ball from Allen Pierce. Those cheating bastards weren't going to beat them this time. He swore to himself the Sleeping Bear Kodiaks were going to leave this field as State Champs even if he had to carry the whole team on his back to do it.

He still felt bad for hurting Kenny Higgins but it didn't dampen the rage burning within him that this championship battle wasn't being fought on a level playing field. Sucking in a chest-full of air, made humid by thunderheads, he grabbed the mouthpiece dangling from his chinstrap, popped it over his lips, and bit down on the rubber between his teeth. Fellow senior Mark York kicked off and Dearl tore downfield.

They were ahead 32 to 26. He'd have been ecstatic to win by the skinniest of margins at the start of this gridiron war, but now Dearl refused to settle for anything less than a blowout.

He wanted to humiliate the devious Langton Lions.

Number 30, the speedy half-pint that had scored after Pierce lateraled to him during a punt return in the first half, caught the ball at the 10 and bolted towards the sideline in a diagonal path.

Hutch forced the returner inside towards him. Dearl thrust his right arm between thirty's ribs and the ball, easily dislodging the pigskin. Abel Norris dove on it and Sleeping Bear took possession at midfield.

Dearl glanced at Coach Rainey and saw he wasn't signaling a play to Holt, who hollered for everyone to huddle up. "Okay, we're on the left hash, so it's a wishbone power sweep to the right on three. Break!"

Lining up directly behind Rick Holt, Dearl grinned when he saw the confusion on the defense's faces as Hutch and Cooper set as the 'bone running backs.

It started raining as Holt barked out, "Green forty-three! Green forty-three! Hut! Hut-Hut!"

Cooper took out the cornerback and Hutch buried Higgins' replacement as Dearl turned the right corner, clutching the slippery ball with all his might. The strong safety dove at his legs and Dearl hurdled him, colliding with number 48, the free safety, in the process. He drug 48 for several yards before more Lions caught up to him and finally brought him to the wet turf at the Langton 38.

Hutch spit out his mouthpiece and shouted with his horse's smile, "Fuckin' A! Twelve yards, most of it on your own, Tipps," while slapping him on the ass.

With the ball placed on the right hash mark and Coach again not signaling a play, Dearl waited until Cooper sped by him before charging left, accepting Holt's toss along the way. He reeled off fifteen yards before being gang tackled at the Lions' 23.

The rain was really pouring down now, so it shocked Dearl to hear Holt say Coach signaled for a pass.

"Shit, is he crazy?! Let's run another sweep, I promise I'll take it to the house."

Holt grinned at him behind his dripping facemask. "What, you've got a death wish all of a sudden, Tipps? Rainey would kill us both—you for suggesting it and me for going along with it. Okay, listen up . . .!"

◆◆◆

Due to the thunderstorm they'd been forced to retreat to the press box, high above the field. Rex had been amazed to see Coach Rainey bring back his version of the wishbone he'd abandoned after his first year of coaching in Sleeping Bear.

Dearl Tipps, then a varsity rookie, had been awesome running from that formation, but Rainey had blamed himself for losing Bi-District against Langton that year because of it, feeling it had been too easy for Truman Jette to counter. The salty marine vet hadn't used it again until now. He wondered if Kenny Higgins not being in the game had spawned the coach's change of heart. It seemed likely since Higgins had certainly held his own against it.

Emma tossed him a smile. "Our Kodiaks looked unstoppable on that drive, eh?"

"They sure did."

Whispering, she said, "Wish we were alone so we could celebrate Cooper Pond's touchdown properly."

A nerve twitched in his groin. "Me too, believe me. It didn't make any sense to me that Rainey wanted to pass after Dearl was chewing up such big chunks of yardage running on that drive, but that's why he's a coach and I'm not. Langton never expected a pass either, and Cooper made an easy six points catching that slant."

Langton had called timeout before the Kodiaks could try for another two-point conversion. Being early in the third quarter, Rex figured Truman Jette had to be chewing out the player that'd burned one of their allotted three. True, Langton had twelve men on the field, but that penalty wouldn't have mattered because Sleeping Bear would most likely succeed on the conversion anyway, as they had all day regardless of what the Lions did.

The referee signaled for play to start and the Kodiaks lined up in an I-formation with Tipps at tailback. Rex winced when he saw Holt fake to Dearl and drop back to pass again in the heavy downpour. A moment later he grabbed Emma for a celebratory hug when Lyle Whitney caught the two-pointer in back of the end zone.

"Can't wait to get you home," she whispered in his ear.

"Yeah," he whispered back, "then I can return the favor. I only hope I can make you feel half as wonderful as you did me."

She smiled, knowingly.

He glanced at the scoreboard and sighed with satisfaction. It looked almost as sweet as the way he felt having Emma in his arms:

Home: 40      Visitors: 26

♦♦♦

Dick lowered the Maalox bottle and motioned for Roy Sanchez to come over when he trotted off the field after the damn return team finally managed to hold onto the fucking ball for once and give the offense a chance. Along with his defensive duties, Dick co-coached special teams with a talented second-year coach still a tad green behind the ears.

Something had to be done.

The small-fry Sanchez had moved to Langton last spring and when Dick saw him run track, he'd talked him into giving football a try despite his size because of his incredible speed. The gullible Mexican only played on the return team, but he'd gotten himself a touchdown today and Dick hoped that taste of glory had put enough stars in the boy's eyes to make him so greedy for more he'd be malleable enough to accept his plan. He waved a come-here to him as he walked a ways from the bench so they wouldn't be overheard.

"Yeah, Coach?"

"How bad do you want to win this game?"

The kid looked excited, obviously thinking he was planning on having Pierce lateral to him again. "Real bad, Coach."

"Bad enough to do something . . . unorthodox?"

He frowned with confusion. "Like what?"

"Listen, we're not going to win as long as Dearl Tipps is on the field. I want you to take him out. You might get ejected but I'll make it worth your while by making you the primary return man next year."

Eyes popping, Sanchez took a step back. "I ain't gonna do nothing illegal, Coach Parsons."

Dick grinned at him. "Naw, nothing like that. When a knee gets bent sideways ligaments pop loose, but they can be refastened easy as pie, and they heal real quick. All I'm asking you to do is wait until Tipps tries to tackle Pierce, and hit his knee from the side while his leg's planted. Just tell Truman you were only trying to block Tipps if he reams you over it."

Sanchez shook his head. "Uh-uh—no way, nope, don't want to hurt nobody. Count me out, Coach."

"All right. If winning State doesn't mean that much to you, you don't deserve to be on this team. Don't plan on playing next year."

The ungrateful punk looked towards the field and shouted, "Motherfucker!"

Dearl Tipps breezed past with the football. The son of a bitch had gotten another turnover. Dick tore the wet cap from his head and threw it to the ground as 20 scored yet another six points on defense."Fuck, it's too late now anyway, Sanchez. Just forget I said anything. Damn what a cold, dark day . . . ."

♦♦♦

She'd screamed herself hoarse, and Kelly had damn near done the same. A moment ago Dearl Tipps broke through the Langton offensive line, took the ball away from the quarterback, and ran seventy yards for another Kodiak touchdown. Now he'd just scored another two points, running up the middle, somehow managing to plow through all the white jerseys suffocating the goal line.

Anita watched the points go up on the scoreboard: 48 to 26. Then she looked at Jetti—several rows above, jumping up and down, screaming for her boyfriend. It felt so right that Jetti was here watching Sleeping Bear playing for State with her mommy and most likely her daddy. If only they were all three sitting together everything would be perfect. She promised herself she'd find a way to win Jetti over.

Tears streamed down Kelly's cheeks, mingling with the raindrops. "Damn it, woman, we're gonna do it—we're finally gonna whip those fucking Lions!"

Anita gave him a quick kiss. "Damn right we are!"

Kelly had gallantly tried to give her his hat when it started raining, but she'd refused. Her hair was a tangled mess now but she didn't care—let the goddamned rain fall. Sitting with her fiancé, watching her beloved Kodiaks stomp their foes en route to a state championship, witnessing her beautiful daughter rooting for her future son-in-law, she had to be the happiest woman on earth. The fact that Jetti's beau was the catalyst in this blowout made it all the sweeter.

Suddenly she thought of Maureen. If only she could be here to see her son making Kodiak and possibly high school football history. The woman had given birth to an amazing athletic prodigy.

When she got through cheering, she turned to Kelly. "How many offensive plays has Langton ran this half?"

Kelly grinned at her. "Not very damn many, that's for sure."

Anita wished she hadn't asked the question. Langton was moving the ball now instead of coughing it up. The Lions' brutal running back was making four yards here, three yards there, just enough for a first down on the third carry, and kept right on doing it no matter how many Kodiaks tried to stop him. They'd gone from their own seven yard line to the Kodiak 4.

"Hell I'm not believing this!" Kelly bellowed as Dearl yanked the ball away from the Langton quarterback. Delbert Hutch tried to pick it up but it slipped from his hands. Dearl blocked a Lion trying to grab it and Abel Norris scooped it up with one hand. A Lion knocked it to the ground, and Cooper Pond dove on top of it, giving Sleeping Bear possession at the 10.

Kelly cupped his hands around his mouth and yelled, "Run the wishbone sweep again!"

♦♦♦

"That's right, pump those legs, Dearl!" screamed Luther.

Zechariah got caught up in the excitement and also cheered as the boy made another touchdown.

Al clapped his hands and turned to the Cherokee. "Can you believe out of all the times he's scored today, that was Dearl's first rushing touchdown on offense?"

"Well it won't be his last, I promise you," Luther vowed. "He chewed up the clock on that drive, getting the ball every time. Eleven plays, ninety yards."

"That boy's playing like a man possessed," said Al.

He thought about Al's statement for a moment and glanced at his employer. "Perhaps he is. Possessed by the Holy Spirit to even out the scales for Langton cheating. I'm confused as to why the second touchdown only counts for two points instead of six."

"What second touchdown are you talking about?" Al asked, frowning.

"They're trying for one right now."

Luther chuckled. "No, Zechariah, that's a two point conversion. Remember when I explained how Langton got one point for kicking the ball through the uprights after scoring a touchdown? Well, if you run or pass for it you get twice as many points. When a team scores they get a chance for extra points. A successful kick counts for one, a successful run or pass counts for two."

Once again Al clapped his hands. "Attaboy, Hutch!"

"See," said Luther, "we just scored on a two-point try."

"Why are the players swapping sides?"

"Because the third quarter just expired. We're twelve minutes away from being State Champions."

Zechariah scratched his head. That seemed very confusing. "Why switch sides?"

"So one team won't have an advantage over the other because of weather. I'm sure even you can understand that you can kick or pass a lot further with the wind than against it."

"Oh, that makes sense. I wonder why they decided to make each quarter last twelve minutes instead of rounding it off to ten or fifteen."

"In college and pro ball, quarters *are* rounded off to fifteen and kickoffs take place from the thirty-five yard line instead of the forty like high school. It used to be from the thirty in the NFL."

# 28

CINDY'S EMOTIONS WERE A TANGLED mess. Seeing how impressive the Kodiaks were instead of just hearing about it was somehow eroding her contempt of Sleeping Bear. They were *stomping* Langton. A flurry of erotic chills had engulfed her when Cooper made his two touchdowns, but she'd resented any other player in blue scoring. Sensing Jetti had grown suspicious that she secretly rooted for Langton, she'd stood and cheered alongside her when Dearl got the ball back after the Kodiaks kicked off. Now the boys in blue were huddled up, about to run their first offensive play in the fourth quarter. Soaked to the bone, she wished the game was over even though Sleeping Bear would win. With Langton behind thirty points it appeared inevitable anyway.

She couldn't help admiring Jetti's school spirit—even envied it a little—but not enough to wish she'd grown up in Hicksville. How else could it be acquired? Gwendolyn obviously worshipped the Kodiaks as well, the way she screamed and carried on each time they scored. Whichever coach had forked over his cash for the playbook could kiss her ass if he was even dreaming about getting his money back. Her low-life cousin could refund his if he wanted to, but she'd be hanging on to hers in order to buy Cooper a beautiful wedding ring. He'd told her, "Cindy, if you stay true to me next year while I'm away at college, you're going to be my wife."

Her clitoris tingled, and this time she in no way faked her enthusiasm. Cooper caught a pass from Delbert Hutch and scored another touchdown.

"That's the play Dearl taught me, Grandma!" Jetti screamed. "It's called eighty-nine black motion red sweep double lateral!"

Lyle Whitney caught a pass for the two point conversion. With the score 64 to 26 the game was obviously out of reach even if Langton *could* manage to put together a whole drive.

But they weren't able to, and Cindy found herself cheering with genuine elation when Dearl sacked Langton's quarterback on fourth down. The importance of this game had completely eluded her until now. The Sleeping Bear Kodiaks were going to be crowned State Champions and Cooper would forever be a part of that monumental accomplishment.

A stark realization came to her: she'd betrayed the man she loved in her effort to get even with the town she hated. Cooper and his teammates not only represented Sleeping Bear, but the very high school she attended—and the whole student body, herself included, shared in this awesome occasion. Why hadn't she seen that before?

"Go, baby, go—take it all the way!" Jetti hollered as Dearl crashed through the Langton defensive line, stiff-arming players left and right. A pile of Lions finally took him down, but he lateraled the ball to Cooper before hitting the turf.

Now Cindy was screaming for *her* baby as he made his way down the field. She almost came when he crossed the goal line, and had to hold her breath to keep from doing so—how embarrassing it would have been to have an orgasm in front of Jetti and Gwendolyn. When the volatile sensation finally passed, guilt over what she'd done overwhelmed her. *My god, what if Cooper had lost this game because of me?!*

"That shows Coach Rainey's class," said Jetti when the Kodiaks kicked an extra point instead of going for two. "He doesn't want to pile on points."

She began to sob and Jetti turned to her with a frown.

"All right, what gives, Cindy—why are you rooting for the fucking Lions?"

Gwendolyn leaned over and slapped Jetti. "I'd better not ever hear that word come out of your mouth again, young lady! I raised you better than that!"

Rubbing her cheek, Jetti apologized to Gwendolyn and glared at her. "Answer my question, girl!"

"I'm not," she insisted, wiping her eyes. *At least not anymore.*

"Then why are you crying?"

"Because I'm so happy for Cooper . . . ."

◆◆◆

Myles high-fived Bart Newly. "Seventy-one to twenty-six! What a heads up play, Tipps tossing the ball to Pond instead of eating it. Turn out the lights, Langton, the party's over!"

Bart laughed. "Sing it like Dandy Don."

"Nobody can sing it like Dandy Don Meredith, you know that."

"I can. *Turn out the lights, the party's over.*"

"Not even close, Bart," he razzed. "Nothing to shoot for now except a second half shutout. The Lions haven't put up a solitary point this half."

"Don't say that out loud, Myles, you might jinx us!"

"Nah, this is our day. See, what did I tell you?" His chest swelled with pride as Allen Pierce got taken down hard at his own twenty yard line on the kickoff return. Langton had assigned too many blockers to keep Dearl Tipps off him and hadn't taken into account how good Delbert Hutch, Abel

Norris, Lyle Whitney, and Cooper Pond were on special teams.

Myles rose to his feet with alarm when Pierce tossed the ball back to Jerry Lane on a flea-flicker after appearing to run up the middle. The Kodiaks bit on it, and Lane fired deep. Hugo Wildemont caught the son of a bitch but dropped the slippery football after taking a few steps. "That's a live ball, somebody get down there before he picks it back up!"

Lyle Whitney and Dearl Tipps were racing towards it but Wildemont retrieved the damn thing and sped towards the end zone.

"Holy shit, guess I did jinx us, Bart." He anxiously stroked his wet moustache as Wildemont crossed the Kodiak 30 with Tipps and Whitney both nearly five yards behind the speedy receiver. They'd never catch him.

Wildemont flew over the 20, the 15, the 10, the 5, then Myles' chin practically hit his chest. Dearl Tipps made an unbelievable dive, swatted the ball from 84, and Lyle Whitney fell on it at the 1.

Grabbing Bart in an ecstatic bear hug he screamed, "What'd I tell ya?! This is our fucking day, dammit!"

◆◆◆

Burly had two emotions boiling inside as he watched the Kodiaks, who'd started on the one yard line, reel off a string of running plays to wind the clock down: ecstatic joy over a surefire victory, tormenting sorrow that he'd never have the beautiful Anita Fury in his bed again.

The exhausted Lion defense had given up over five yards each play this drive, and barely stopped Delbert Hutch from breaking away for a touchdown on a simple run up the middle. That one went for 15 and Sleeping Bear had a first and ten at the Lions' 35.

After two more runs, each netting a first down, Rick Holt fumbled the snap and the Lions recovered. Jerry Lane hit his tight end for a gain of five, then garnered seven yards himself on a quarterback draw. He'd have lost yardage if Dearl Tipps hadn't gotten his legs cut out from under him by Allen Pierce, after bulldogging his way through the offensive line. They ran a pro-like reverse that went for twenty-five yards, and it began to look like Langton might finally get on the scoreboard in the second half.

But the Kodiak defense stiffened and once again the Lions turned it over on downs deep in Kodiak territory. Again running from the wishbone formation, Sleeping Bear marched downfield and went for it on fourth and six rather than kick for an easy three points from the Langton 11. Dearl Tipps ran a sweep for a touchdown but a holding penalty nullified the play. A pass to Cooper Pond got batted away and the Lions took over.

Running some fancy trick plays, the Lions again threatened to score but Delbert Hutch intercepted a pass intended for Allen Pierce coming out of the backfield and got brought down at the Kodiak 20 with just under three minutes left on the clock.

Holt kept feeding Tipps the ball and the quarterback took a knee at Langton's five yard line to let time expire.

Burly shot to his feet, screaming his lungs out—maniacally waving his hands in the air like his fellow citizens, savoring the sweet taste of victory. Sleeping Bear had blown out the mighty Langton Lions 71 to 26 and were State Champions.

# 29

THEY'D BARELY BEEN ABLE TO board the bus. The males of Sleeping Bear, young and old, congratulated them with hard slaps on the back, bone-breaking handshakes, and rib-crunching bear-hugs, while the cheering females couldn't keep from kissing them. Most of the players looked like they'd been in a make-out orgy with all the lipstick smears on their cheeks. Coach Rainey and his assistants had been similarly mauled as well. Only one girl had kissed Dearl on the lips and he'd kissed her back, hard and deep. This time when Jetti declared her love for him, he'd involuntarily said, "I love you too." Realizing what he'd done, he repeated the words, amazed at how effortlessly they'd rolled off his tongue. Her eyes had flashed with surprise and she'd broken down with sentimental tears.

Tonight after the celebration party he'd tell her his secret, and once she knew he had no experience and wouldn't be expecting a super stud, he'd make love to her. At least he hoped to.

Sitting beside Cooper, staring through the rain pelting the window, Dearl pondered his future as they neared Sleeping Bear. Tornado Hill really looked like an actual twister in the whirling storm. Kenny Higgins had changed his life's direction. While taking off his pads in Woodrow Dearl had made up his mind it would be the last time he'd ever wear any. If Al didn't want to pay his tuition to attend Texas he'd work for his father on the ranch. Either way, a career other than football awaited him.

He hadn't told anyone, and felt nervous about what Jetti's reaction would be. The three seniors he'd dated wouldn't have given him the time of day if he hadn't been a gridiron hero, and he'd known that at the time, but the prestige of being seen with popular upper-class chicks, knowing most of his peers thought he was boning them, had been compensation enough. None of those girls ever appealed to him beyond a superficial level, but Jetti was different. He'd been painfully aware she'd devastate him—totally and permanently—if he discovered her attraction was only for his gridiron exploits.

Tonight he'd find out once and for all.

◆◆◆

The van reeked with the smell of wet hair. Other than Mrs. Rainey, Pat was the only one that hadn't dozed off. For over half an hour they'd all been jabbering nonstop over winning State with high-pitched overly excited voices made hoarse from cheering. After they all simmered down Darlene dropped first, then Bibi, now Delores, Joie, and Marybeth were also fast asleep. It seemed so surreal, as if too good to be true, but the Sleeping Bear Kodiaks were 2A Division-I State Champions.

Mrs. Rainey had been right. The moment Langton kicked off nervousness flew out the window and she'd felt nothing until time expired in the fourth quarter but an influx of the mighty Kodiak spirit and hometown pride. From that point on everything seemed like a dream. She couldn't imagine why the other girls were sleepy—if someone had shot her up with speed she couldn't have been more wide awake.

The poor players had literally gotten assaulted by every

cheerleader, band member, student who'd only watched from the stands, and the rest of the townsfolk before reaching safety on the chartered bus. She'd gone on a kissing frenzy and smooched off all her lipstick—most of it on the lips of Abel Norris and Lyle Whitney. Dreamboat Dearl escaped her. Jetti Fury had captured the boy like everybody in high school knew she someday would, and they'd sucked face the whole time he got pounded on the back by the men and smacked on the cheeks by the ladies.

◆◆◆

"You have to tell him, Al," Luther insisted as they came to a halt at the ranch house.

Al killed the engine and got out. Zechariah eagerly did the same after Luther climbed out the door, grateful the drive back from Lubbock was finally over.

Luther grabbed Al by the arm. "Did you hear me?"

"Yeah, I heard you, but nobody's saying anything to Cooper until we get to the bottom of this. Don't forget we're basing the accusation on Zechariah's dream. What if that's not what it means?"

Zechariah nodded. "Al's right, Luther. And I seem to be misfiring here lately anyway. Kelly told us he's going to marry Anita Fury, yet I could have sworn the Lord gave me that message for him so he could work things out with Emma."

"See," said Al, "even Zechariah agrees we may not have the correct interpretation. Anyway, we need to get everything ready for the party. We've got less than an hour before the caterers get here."

*I've set one before you to anoint in your stead here, for I have need of you elsewhere.* Zechariah frowned and mentally asked the Lord how he would know him.

*You will know.*

He entered the house grimacing with irritation. It chapped his hide when God spoke in riddles.

A man wearing a Budweiser uniform walked in while he was helping Luther set up tables for the food and guests.

"Same place?"

Luther nodded. "You did remember we ordered four kegs this time, right?"

The beer man grinned. "Expecting a big turn out since you won State, huh? Congratulations, by the way."

"Thanks. Yeah, Al figures the whole town's liable to show up."

"Sleeping Bear's a small town," said Bud, "but four kegs won't begin to suffice for that many people. Want me to bring some more?"

"Nah, if the well goes dry they can just do without. Besides, Al bought a shit-load of wine coolers."

"Who's your new compadre?"

Luther winked at him. "Zechariah, meet the Bud Man, I call him Bud."

"He calls me that because it's my name. Good to meet you."

"Same here," said Zechariah.

Bud left to take care of his business and Zechariah unfolded the legs of another table before turning it upright. During the action he received a word about Emma that tugged at his heart, further depressing him that he couldn't be the man in her life.

◆◆◆

Will Amarod wouldn't answer his calls so Dick drove to the motherfucker's house. Banging on the door, he yelled, "I know you're in there, goddammit! Open the door, Will, or I'll break it in!"

The scrawny bastard finally obeyed and Dick pushed past him. "Who the fuck copied that playbook? Were you in on the double cross?"

Shaking with fear, Will squeaked out, "What double cross?"

Dick sneered at the weasel, trying to look so innocently bewildered. "Most of the second half plays weren't in the son of a bitch—I was set up. Now tell me who you got that fucking playbook from, because I'm gonna make them pay big time. You two better not have spent my fucking money because I want that back too."

Will turned up his palms. "Look, all I know is my cousin called me and said she'd copied her boyfriend's playbook and wanted me to find out what she could get for it. I thought you'd be interested but I never mentioned your name, I swear. She hates living in Sleeping Bear and can't stand the Kodiaks so I know she didn't double cross you. Our deal didn't guarantee a Lions victory today so you don't have the right to demand your money back."

"The hell I don't!"

◆◆◆

They'd made love on the living room floor, neither wanting to waste a minute after they got inside. Emma had practically ripped her clothes off and Rex hadn't been able to get out of his fast enough. Now they were leaning against the couch, ankles crossed on the carpet. Her shapely legs radically contrasted with his narrow thighs and bony knees.

He savored Emma's nakedness as she smoked her cigarette.

"Rex, you were wonderful, I've never had a stronger orgasm in me life."

Reaching for a cherry nipple he said, "Same here."

She giggled. "Men always come the same way, you liar."

"No, that's not true. Semen may come out every time, but the sensation does vary. The orgasm you gave me on the highway runs a close second."

Her pretty lips spread with a sated smile. "That was fun. I don't want to go to the victory party. Let's stay home and make love all night after we get tomorrow's edition done."

He pulled her to him for a kiss. Her mouth tasted of nicotine but the pungent flavor in no way hampered the thrill he felt as their tongues intertwined. After finally pulling away, he grinned at her. "People will talk."

"Let them. I don't care if the whole town knows."

"Nether do I . . ." he kissed her again and slid his hand between her legs.

◆◆◆

Myles wished he could go out to the Pond Ranch and get tanked with everybody else, but since a goodly portion of the populace was out there, leaving rows of empty houses to tempt a burglar, he'd have to celebrate the state championship a good while after midnight when most of the partiers would be back home, making it unnecessary to keep cruising all the neighborhoods. A highway patrolman owed him a favor and Myles had called it in, having him baby sit the town through the afternoon so he and Bart could both attend the big game.

Bart had threatened to close his joint down for the night since business would be so slow, but not wanting to piss off the few patrons who weren't football fanatics, he'd decided against it. Myles would have gladly let his deputy spell him if he had.

He pulled into The Kodiak Cave's drive-through. There were only two cars in the parking lot and it surprised him when Burly Swain slid the window open.

"The usual?"

"Yeah, and toss in a couple of glazed doughnuts with the coffee."

A couple of minutes later Burly held out a bag.

He took it from him, pulled out the coffee, and set the doughnuts on the passenger side floorboard. "Figured you'd be at Al's celebrating."

"I'd planned to until I found out about Anita Fury and Kelly Newly."

Myles rubbed his moustache. "Yeah, saw them sitting together at the game. What about them?"

"They're getting married."

"Shit, you say!" Seeing Kelly with Anita at Woodrow had shocked him enough since that cowboy had always hated her, but to hear they were getting married threw him for a hell of a loop. "Well I'll be a son of a gun. I always had a feeling Anita would eventually come to her senses and give up whoring. She has, right—Kelly hasn't decided to become a pimp has he?"

"No, she told me I was her last customer." Burly said it like the world was coming to an end.

"Watch that kind of talk, don't forget I'm a lawman. I'm going to ignore that remark this time, but don't let it happen again."

Burly shot him a sarcastic frown. "You know damn well I

was always one of her steadiest customers. Who's kidding who here?"

"Watch it now, Burly."

"The way I feel right now, I really don't give a fuck. You wanna arrest me, go right ahead."

"What'd you do, fall in love with her?"

"No . . . but she was the closest thing to a wife I'm ever gonna find. Other than a few trips to Juarez, I spent the ten years she was gone jacking off."

He pealed the lid off his coffee and took a sip, reflecting on his barren ex wife for a moment. She'd left him for another man, but far from being tore up about it, he'd celebrated. They hadn't been married three months before he'd discovered tying the knot with her had been the biggest mistake of his life. But he'd sworn till death do us part and never would have broken the vow. He'd been enjoying his freedom ever since she'd made a mockery of hers.

A car pulled up behind him. "Guess I better git. Cheer up, Burly, remember we won State. It's ungodly for you to be down on such an occasion."

That yanked a smile out of Burly. "Stomped the hell out of those Lions, didn't we?"

"Damn sure did. Be seeing ya." Continuing through the drive-through, Myles took note of the Cadillac stopping at the window.

He'd never seen it before.

◆◆◆

"What'll you have?" Burly asked the well-attired stranger sitting behind the steering wheel of a red Cadillac.

"I'd like some information please. I met someone at a

convention in Houston and haven't been able to locate her. She told me she went to high school here, so I was hoping someone might be able to tell me where she lives now. Have you resided in Sleeping Bear long?"

"All my life."

The man smiled. "Great, then you probably know her."

"If she ever lived in Sleeping Bear I guarantee you I know her. What's her name?"

"Anita Fury."

The dude had to be one of her johns. "Well if you're looking for her for the reason I think you are, you're out of luck."

"Why's that?"

"She's not hooking anymore. Told me earlier today she's getting married."

"Oh no!" the man gasped like he'd just been shot.

"Yeah . . ." Burly gave him a sympathetic smile. "I know how you feel, believe me."

"So she lives here now?"

"Well she will before long, that's for sure. Right now she's at a party celebrating the fact our football team won State today. Just follow the road signs like you're going to Amarillo, and when you get a few miles out of town you'll see a big sign over a cattle guard that says Pond Ranch. It'll be on your right. That road'll take you to a great big house where the party is."

The guy blew out a sigh. "Oh I couldn't do that."

"Why not?"

"I wasn't invited."

"It's an open party, everybody's welcome. This is a real friendly place and everybody knows everybody here. Just tell the first person you see you're looking for Anita Fury and they'll show you where to find her. Tell them Burly Swain sent you."

♦♦♦

Anita stood beside her man in the back of the room as Al signaled for everyone's attention from the fireplace. Dearl Tipps had his arm around Jetti and they were facing the crowd on one side of Al. Cooper and a pretty girl with light-brown hair were on the other.

The victory speeches had already been made by the head coach and several players. She couldn't imagine why Al wanted to be the anchorman since he had nothing to do with today's game other than cheering the team on like all the other Kodiaks in the stands.

"Friends, I have some great news to share with you all tonight. The details will be published in The Hibernator so I won't go into all of them here. These two boys and I have kept it under wraps until now so as not to distract the team from football, but now that we're State Champions it's time to spill the beans.

"You all know Cooper's my son. Well, several days ago I learned he's my number one son, meaning he was the first born. Ladies and gentlemen, I'm very proud to say that I also have another son—a great guy who you're all familiar with, and most of you watched his heroic efforts in Woodrow today in leading us to victory. My number two son is none other than State Most Valuable Player, Dearl Tipps."

Cheers, applause, and gasps of wonderment filled the air. Jetti obviously didn't know about Al siring Dearl until now, she looked as dumbfounded as everyone else, as did the girl with light-brown hair.

Anita winked at Kelly. "Our suspicions were correct."

"So they were. Let's go tell our daughter who her father is."

They couldn't do that because she wasn't one hundred

percent sure, and besides, Jetti couldn't stand her. "She doesn't like me, Kelly, but I'm going to do my best to win her over. We'll tell her then."

He took a big swig of beer and grinned. "Well she don't know me well enough to feel one way or the other, so I'm gonna tell her. Wait here."

She tried to stop him but Kelly pulled away and made his way through the crowd. "Oh, Kelly, please don't!"

"It's all right, Anita."

Whirling around, she saw the words had been spoken by Zechariah.

"Forgive me for eavesdropping, but I couldn't help overhearing. I know you don't believe I hear God but I do. However, once in a while I forget a piece of a message, misunderstand a word or two, or think The Almighty's saying something when He ain't. I'm afraid I goofed about you being eight days with child."

"Boy did you ever."

A knowing look followed a short laugh. "Oh I had the eight right but not the second part. I got the word here on the ranch and by the time I relayed it to you my memory had mixed it up a mite. I was pretty emotional over something at the time, so I guess that's why it happened."

She rolled her eyes and took a sip of beer. "I've never come across such a fruitcake as you. You need help, fella."

"Nah, I ain't no fruitcake," he sternly asserted. "A few minutes ago the Lord informed me He'd said *hours* rather than days, and what I was supposed to have told you at the Simmons place was you *would be* with child within eight hours. He had more to say after that—told me enough to convince you that He really does speak to me, so here goes. A man you babysat for as a teenager is responsible for the temptation of harlotry you yielded to. Last night you unintentionally caused Kelly and Emma Riley to be at odds with each other at a bar. Some time later you and Kelly wound up together in a motel room. You slept with each other and now you're betrothed."

"My god! How—"

"How did I know? You said it at the first, 'My God' . . . and your God, the one you don't believe in. You are indeed now with child. You and Kelly are going to have a son."

The Budweiser cup slipped from her hand.

Zechariah grabbed it and foamed sloshed over the edge. He handed it back and dried his wet hand on his jeans. "Are you okay?"

"Yeah, you just shocked the daylights out of me that's all. How long have you had this amazing psychic ability?"

He shook his head. "I'm no psychic, it's just the way God uses me. Say you believe in Him or I won't tell you who got you pregnant with Jetti."

She gasped. "You mean know?!"

"Mm hmm, but you're not going to hear who until you say you believe in Him. Say it, Anita, even though you don't mean it, and He'll impart the faith you need."

"Look, I've been a whore most of my life but I do have principles, and saying I believe something when I don't goes totally against them."

Zechariah shrugged and turned to walk away.

"Don't go! I believe . . . I believe in God, now tell me, please."

A warm smile greeted her when he turned around. "Kelly is Jetti's father, not the man who raped you, and the Lord will heal the hurt between you and her. God's blessing on the three of you and your son. If I were you, I'd go easy on the booze. You know what they say about drinking while you're pregnant."

The strangest feeling came over her as she watched Zechariah walk out the door. "Jesus Christ was crucified for your sins," she'd heard all her life. To her, Jesus was nothing but a religious fanatic who'd managed to fuck up the minds of billions of people throughout history. Until now.

Her bladder began to complain, so she left in search of a bathroom. It seemed odd to her that Al's dad hadn't put one in this huge room, obviously designed to entertain a herd of people.

♦♦♦

Jetti was greatly disappointed over Dearl not being a virgin after all—his big secret turned out to be he'd found out who his father was—and though she felt happy for him, it hurt that he hadn't trusted her to keep his confidence. Then, Kelly Newly had asked to speak with her alone, saying he had something very important to tell her, adding confusion to her mixed emotions. He guided her to the hall and continued past the glass wall of the game room.

Zechariah waved them over.

"I know what you want to tell her, Kelly, but maybe I should do it."

"Reckon I need to, Zechariah."

Now extremely baffled, Jetti asked what they were talking about.

"Suit yourself," Zechariah said to Kelly, ignoring her question. "Just trying to help smooth things over. I'll leave you two alone."

That made her nervous. Surely this half-lit cowpuncher wasn't trying to hit on her. "Please stay, Zechariah!"

Kelly cleared his throat and took a drink of beer. "After thinking on it, he's probably right. I'll let him tell you."

Zechariah wrapped an arm around her shoulders and

positioned her so she stood less than two feet from Kelly, then released her. "Jetti, the Lord told me this man is your father."

She'd never been directly face to face with Kelly Newly before. His squinting eyes, now filling with tears, were the exact color of hers. She pictured the cowboy on top of her mother in some seedy motel room, the cash he'd laid out for sex lying on a night stand beside the immoral bed. "So you're the—they're called johns, right? So you're the john that sired me. How much did you pay dear ol' Mom?"

Kelly tightened his jaw.

She couldn't tell if he was reacting in anger or shame. Perhaps both, she thought idly, not caring which. "Have you known all along, or did Zechariah inform you?"

He took a deep breath and blew it out through puckered lips. "Your mama told me today that she knew it was either me or one other guy, but was pretty sure it was me. I always had a hunch Al Pond was Dearl's real father, so when he announced it awhile ago I had a sudden urge to tell you that your mother thought I was yours. I didn't know for certain until just now, when Zechariah said the Lord told him."

She folded her arms beneath her breasts. "You believe he's a prophet then?"

"Yep, sure do."

"So what did it cost to conceive me?"

"I didn't *pay* anything, Jetti, I was never one of Anita's clients. It's a long story but the short and tall of it is we only had sex that one time . . . until last night that is. Your mother used to be a whore, that's true, but she's not anymore and we're going to get married. She's a good woman who got sidetracked and I love her. Anita loves you, and I want you to give her a chance to make you love her back. She made a big mistake, she knows that, but all she can do is go forward from here—not a damn thing can be done about the past.

Myself, I'm prouder'n a peacock to know I'm your daddy."

Dearl walked up, looking concerned. "Is everything okay, Jetti?"

She took his hand and clutched it tightly. "Well tonight must be forever dubbed Father's Night. I no sooner find out Al is yours when I get informed that mine is Kelly Newly here. Dearl, I'm hurt you didn't tell me—I'd have kept your secret."

"That's not the secret, Jetti."

"Huh?"

"Zechariah and Al came to my house and told me Al was my father, but I didn't believe them until Zechariah told me the very secret that I told you I had. Like Al said, we all agreed to keep it to ourselves until after the championship for the good of the team."

She glowered at him. "Well then you should have told me earlier tonight instead of me hearing it from Al."

"Sorry, I didn't know it would offend you or I would have."

"Humph," she grumbled. "Men."

Zechariah laughed and said, "Never underestimate the stupidity of one where sensitivity's concerned, Jetti."

The statement forced a grin and she lightened up. "Isn't that the truth."

"Forgive me?" Dearl asked with pleading eyes.

She pecked him on the lips. "You're forgiven."

"Um, I was going to make an announcement but I guess I should tell you first so you won't be mad at me again. That hit I put on Kenny Higgins ruptured his spleen, and if they hadn't gotten him to the hospital in time he could have bled to death internally. I'm giving up football, Jetti."

Dumbfounded, but not all that shocked to hear it because she'd seen how Higgins' injury devastated him, she just gawked at Dearl, wanting to tell him he was crazy to make such a decision, but unable to. Only he knew the anguish he'd felt injuring another human being. And what if Higgins had done that to Dearl and they hadn't been able to keep him from bleeding to death? The thought terrified her. From the corner of her eye she saw Anita enter the hall from the house and hurry into the game room as if she didn't want any of them to see her.

Dearl took a sip of beer and gave her a nervous smile. "You're taking it a whole lot better than I thought you would. Figured you'd be cussing me out about now."

She noticed the news apparently hit Kelly the way Dearl thought it would her.

"Son," he said, "take some time and think this over real careful-like before you give up on the idea of playing football. There's thirty-two teams in the NFL that'll be chomping at the bit to get their hands on you when your collegiate career's over. Before you guys took us all the way this year I played on the squad that advanced further in the playoffs than any other Kodiak team in history. We lost Regional to Seagraves by one point and that loss tore me up so bad inside I turned down several scholarships to play college ball. Well look at me now—a plain old ordinary ranch boss is as far as I'm ever gonna get in life. I'd give anything to have that chance again, because I would have gotten a college education and a whole world of opportunities would have been available to me."

Dearl smiled appreciatively. "Well I'm hoping to still go to Texas."

Kelly shook his head. "No, son. I don't just regret not going to college, what I really regret is not finding out how far I could have gone in football. I wasn't a shoe-in for the pros like you, but I was one damn mean fullback and probably could have landed a spot on somebody's roster as a free agent. It'll always haunt me that I didn't find out. Dearl, whatever you do don't let it haunt you. One damn game changed my attitude, just like that one play today changed yours, and by the time I realized what a mistake I'd made it was too late—I'd lost a step in speed and wasn't near as quick anymore."

Jetti felt a tear slip from her eye. "My gosh, Mister Newly, how horrible for you. Don't you like working here on the ranch?"

"I wish you'd call me Daddy, but if you won't then call me Kelly." He turned up his cup, swallowed hard, and sighed. "I like being a cowpoke all right, but what I'm trying to get Dearl to see is that had I accepted one of those scholarships and made it in the pros, I'd have my own ranch and all those glorious gridiron memories to cherish while branding my own cattle instead of another man's."

She could tell Dearl was seriously considering Kelly's advice. His eyes were narrowed in thought and his lips were firm. At length he said, "Did you ever hurt anybody?"

"Yeah, twice," Kelly answered, a soulful expression portraying it still bothered him. "A kid broke his arm when he stuck it behind his back to break his fall as I was running over him. And I got blocked into a guy whose foot was locked up in the pile and his knee got bent backwards. Tore it all to hell. I felt like you feel about Higgins—real bad—but that's football, son. Myself, I never got hurt on the field but I've got plenty of scars from ranching. Accidents happen in every walk of life, not just sports. I watched you plow into Higgins, and there was nary a damn thing wrong with it. I've seen that same type of hit a million times and watched the player get up and keep playing. Who knows, maybe Higgins' has a glass stomach, or maybe his innards are arranged funny and his spleen was bound to get ruptured through playing football anyhow. Not everyone's cut out for the sport like you and me."

Jetti's pulse quickened. Kelly really seemed to be getting through to Dearl but she wasn't sure she wanted him to play anymore. What if he got paralyzed?

# PART 4

# Goodbye Stranger

# 30

COOPER HADN'T TOLD HER ABOUT Dearl being his half brother when he'd picked her up to take her to the party, only that his dad was going to make a surprise announcement. And *surprised* she'd been. Now she had a surprise for him. Her parents agreed to let her spend the night on the ranch, unaware of course that she'd be sneaking into Cooper's bedroom after everyone went to sleep.

Luther hadn't returned her hello when they'd arrived and appeared offended as if she reeked with body odor every time she'd been near him since. Cindy was glad she preferred wine coolers because she had the feeling he wouldn't fill a beer cup for her. Cooper's dad was rather cool towards her as well, but hadn't refused her request for strawberry flavored alcohol. Dearl had gone to check on Jetti, who'd left with Kelly Newly, and she noticed the woman who looked so much like her had come back to the game room. She nervously stood alone, wringing her hands, looking very anxious about something.

A few minutes before the lady returned Delbert Hutch spilt beer on Cooper and he'd gone to his room to change clothes, so she decided to introduce herself. She cut through the crowd and gave her a friendly grin. "Hi, I'm Cindy Shane."

"Anita Fury," the woman replied with a forced smile.

"Ah, no wonder you look so much like Jetti, you guys have to be related."

The smile seemed to turn genuine. "I'm her mother."

Jetti hadn't spoken to her at the game so she guessed they must be estranged. Small wonder, since she'd let the Simmons raise her. "Well it's a pleasure to meet you, I just love Jetti."

"Thank you."

"I saw you at the game sitting with Kelly Newly. You must not live in Sleeping Bear or I'd have seen you around before."

"Moved away years ago."

Cooper came back and she waved to get his attention. "Over here!"

He walked up wearing one of his killer smiles. "I know you, you're Anita Fury and as beautiful as ever."

Anita donned an incredulous grin and said, "You remember me after all these years, Cooper?"

"Sure do."

"Gosh, you were just an eight year old kid when I left Sleeping Bear. I'm flattered."

"Oh I never forget a pretty woman."

A light blush colored Anita's cheeks. "You inherited Al's charm I see. It was like a dream seeing you little shavers all grown up and playing for State. I'm so proud of you boys."

"Thanks. We were very inspired when Coach told us at halftime the Lions had a copy of our playbook."

"You're kidding me—" Anita brought a hand to the base of her throat.

"Nope, but it worked in our favor. The game might have gone either way if we hadn't been so pissed off the second half. We wanted to rub those cheaters noses in the dirt."

Cindy felt like her soul was being sucked from her body. No wonder Luther and Al were acting so strangely—they knew. But how? Cooper obviously didn't suspect she had anything to do with it. Why hadn't Al and Luther told him, and what were they planning to do about it?

"Well it serves those low-life's right that you did," Anita angrily avowed. "How did they manage to do it?"

Cooper shrugged. "Don't know. Cindy, are you okay?"

Trying to keep from crying, she turned her back to Cooper, hands covering her face.

"Cindy . . .?"

♦♦♦

Abel Norris nervously slipped her a note and stood with hands in pockets as she unfolded it. Pat read the five word question over and over, feeling her smile grow bigger each time.

*Will you go with me?* it read.

She finally answered with a vigorous nod and he kissed her.

♦♦♦

A few years ago an awful rumor started floating around about Kelly Newly being homosexual. Like Cooper, Al, and Luther, he'd known it was pure bullshit, and couldn't imagine who'd started it or why. Dearl had always admired Kelly. Rock-solid, a man of his word, never afraid to speak his mind, the cowboy had always been a role model for him—the kind of man he aspired to be. Midway through the season he'd broken the Kodiak record for total varsity rushing yards set by Kelly, and it would always stand as a special milestone for him. To hear his fellow Kodiak had deep regrets about not playing college ball made him realize he'd better let all the emotions over Higgins' injury run their course before making a final decision.

"I'd made up my mind but you've given me a lot to chew on, so I won't be announcing anything tonight after all. I'm going to let some time pass and see how I feel about everything then."

"Attaboy!" Kelly slapped him on the back.

Having stuck with Dr Pepper Jetti still had her car keys. He turned to her and grinned. "I've had enough of crowds today. What say you take me for a drive in the rain?"

She gave him a knowing smile. "I'd love to."

"Oh, just remembered something. Zechariah, I had a weird dream last night that I told Cooper about, and he said it meant God has a call on my life."

"Cooper's now an expert on such things, is he?" joked the prophet. "Well let's hear it."

"I was in my algebra two class . . ." he recounted the dream.

Zechariah scratched at his chin, frowning with thought. "Earlier today I got a word to anoint someone to take my place here because the Lord is about to send me somewhere else. Excuse me a minute."

Jetti's mouth fell open. "You can't leave us, Zechariah, you belong here in Sleeping Bear! Why do you have your eyes closed?"

"Shush!" Kelly put a finger to his lips. "He's listening to the Lord."

The prophet's mouth curled into a smile when his lids finally parted. "Indeed I was. Dearl, you've been called all right, and blessed with an intuition that's probably confused you more than enlightened you up till now, but it's not time for you to accept my mantle—you're nowhere near ready yet. God has other plans for you in the meanwhile and will gradually groom you along the way.

"Give up any notions about abandoning football. The Lord just told me that a long, very successful professional career awaits you, and when you retire, I'm to anoint you to take my place. I asked the Lord if that meant I'd get to stay on this ranch until then. He didn't answer me but I sure hope that's what He intends."

"Oh, Dearl, how exciting!" Jetti shouted. "And to think I was going to try to talk you out of playing for fear you might get seriously injured."

Those were the most beautiful words he'd ever heard in his life. It *wasn't* just the football star she loved. He gave her a big hug and turned to Zechariah with a grin. "God didn't happen to mention which team I'll be playing for and what my final stats will be, did He?"

"I'm afraid not."

Kelly pounded him on the back. "Congratulations, Dearl. Say, Zechariah, what's the deal with that word on Emma and me? What happened there?"

"Funny you should ask," Zechariah replied, looking a little bewildered. "The Lord informed me earlier today that she and Rex are no longer just friends, and awhile ago said they conceived a son tonight. You and Anita did the same on that motel bed y'all slept in last night."

"Are you telling me I've got a son on the way?!" Kelly belted.

"Yeah."

Kelly beamed like a lighthouse. "Hot diggity dog, a little cowboy to carry on my name!"

Jetti whirled around and shouted, "I'm going to have a baby brother!"

"You are at that." Kelly handed his beer to Zechariah and pulled her to him.

Jetti held her arms in the air, as though Kelly might give her cooties if she touched his back.

Dearl set his cup on a nearby hall chest, shoved his hands in his pockets, and cleared his throat. "Congratulations, you two. Guess that means I've got a brother-in-law on the way."

"Is that a proposal, Mister Tipps?" Jetti asked, grinning at him over Kelly's shoulder.

"Yep. Will you marry me, Miss Fury?"

She suddenly dropped her arms and squeezed Kelly tight, still smiling at him. "Until I become Jetti Tipps I'm going by Newly like my daddy and baby brother, and like my mother will be doing shortly. In fact I'm going to have my maiden name legally changed to Newly when I turn eighteen. So propose to me again by my real surname."

He chuckled. "Okay. Will you marry me, Jetti Newly?"

She pulled out of Kelly's arms and stepped to the side. "I'm sorry, didn't quite hear you. Maybe if you got down on one knee my hearing would improve."

Sore from the game, he gingerly lowered his left leg, rested his forearms on his right thigh, and leaned forward to ease the stress on the small of his back. "I said, will you marry me, Jetti Newly?!"

"Oh yes!"

"Great, then help me up. I don't have a muscle that doesn't hurt and my butt's cramping."

"Oh, I'm so sorry, Dearl—" Jetti pulled him to his feet.

"Thanks. I'm ready for that drive now."

Kelly grabbed her hand. "Don't leave until your mama hears the good news that she's carrying your brother."

"I've already told her," Zechariah said, handing Kelly his beer back.

◆◆◆

Anita had heard of twisted love before but nothing like this. The girl that professed to be madly in love with Cooper was the culprit that betrayed the Kodiaks by copying his playbook. Cindy Shane had been crying uncontrollably since confessing it.

Cooper was furious and clearly heart broken.

The three of them were in his bedroom, where Cindy had asked to go after saying she needed to tell him something. Anita could only surmise the girl invited her along to help fend off her boyfriend should he lose his head and beat her over it.

Indeed Cooper *had* thrown a punch, but it put a hole in the wall rather than a bruise on Cindy's face. One of his knuckles was bleeding but he refused to bandage it despite he's girlfriend's pleading. He'd quit screaming at her, and stood with arms hanging limp, blood dripping on the carpet, the pain of being starkly betrayed engraved on his face.

Convinced the girl really did love Cooper and truly regretted what she'd done, Anita tried to help her. "Look, I agree what Cindy did was despicable, but she didn't have to tell you, and you'd never have known otherwise. You said yourself the game could have gone either way if you boys weren't so fired up over Langton cheating. So in a way, she did us all a favor."

Cindy gave her a tearful smile of gratitude and turned to her boyfriend. "Cooper, I hated the Kodiaks because I resented being forced to move to Sleeping Bear. And until today I honestly didn't realize how important this game was to you. I cheered for you every time you scored but hated it when anyone else on the team did. But you have to believe me, at some point during the fourth quarter I was cheering for the whole team—the whole town—because I realized that I'm now a Sleeping Bear Kodiak and will be until the day I die no matter where I live. Jetti's school spirit rubbed off on me I guess, I don't know. I wish I'd felt like a Kodiak the night of the last party because I wouldn't have done such a horrible thing. I was going to use the money for your wedding ring, but I can see now I'll have to give it back."

Cooper glared at her, eyes burning with anger and utter disbelief. "Damn right you will, and you can forget about us ever getting married. I thought I knew you, Cindy, thought you were the one . . . but I don't, and you're not."

Head turned down, tears hitting the carpet near Cooper's blood splatters, Cindy muttered, "I can't blame you. It's impossible to explain, but I really didn't know me either until that point in the game when it hit home what a shitty thing I'd done. I'll call my dad and have him come get me."

She started for the door but Cooper spun her around. "Who'd your cousin sell it to?"

"Someone on the coaching staff. He wouldn't tell me the name."

He released her and coldly said, "Okay, you can go."

♦♦♦

Jetti gave her daddy a final hug and turned to leave with Dearl, but the sound of someone bawling made her turn around. Cindy Shane ran down the hall, head tilted back, features contorted with such pain she looked like her whole world had just crumbled to ashes. "What's the matter, Cindy?"

"Oh, Jetti," she wailed, "I've ruined my life!"

"What happened?"

Cindy stopped in front of her and Jetti saw she'd been crying for a long time. Her large brown eyes were totally bloodshot.

"Can we please go somewhere and talk, Jetti, just the two of us? I was going to call my dad to come get me, but maybe you can help me."

She glanced at Dearl and refocused on Cindy. "Um, Dearl and I were about to go for a drive and uh, kind of wanted to be alone."

Embarrassment made the agony on her face look even more severe. "Oh, sorry. I'll go ahead and call my dad. You guys have fun."

"Where's Cooper?" Dearl asked.

"I left him in his room."

"We'll go for that drive after you take care of Cindy, Jetti. I wanna talk to Cooper."

A man wearing an expensive suit came out of the entryway. "Can anyone tell me where I might find Anita Fury?"

Kelly frowned at him. "Who's asking?"

"Eli Adams."

That seem to surprise Zechariah, who said, "You look awfully familiar. You wouldn't happen to be Eli Adams the computer whiz Noah told me about, would you?"

"Noah Adams the theologian?"

"Yeah. I'm Zechariah."

"Noah's protégé?"

"Uh huh." He extended his hand and Eli Adams shook it, vigorously.

"So we meet at last, Zechariah. What a small world."

"Why didn't you come to Noah's funeral? You were the main member of his family I was anxious to meet. He kept up with your career and had some pictures of you, taken when you were in high school."

"I was in Israel at the time, demonstrating a program I'd developed. The army sent me over there and I couldn't get away."

"What do you want with Anita?" Kelly demanded to know, still frowning.

"I have something to discuss with her. Burly Swain told me I'd find her here."

"Burly Swain?" Kelly started towards him. "Anita ain't whoring no more, and if you go anywhere near her I'll bust you up so bad you'll wish you were dead. In fact why don't I take a piece of you right now so you know I mean business?"

The man's face turned ghostly with fear as Kelly drew back his right hand, making a fist.

"Kelly, no!"

Jetti turned to see Anita, who'd screamed the words, running towards them.

"This man is a friend of mine!" She grabbed Kelly's fist with both hands. "Eli, I'd like you to meet my fiancé, Kelly Newly. Kelly, this is my good friend Eli Adams."

"I know what his damn name is," Kelly growled.

Looking more petrified, Eli Adams took several steps back and nervously smoothed his lapels. "Uh, congratulations. I spoke to a man at a restaurant in town who said you'd be here and gave me directions. He said his name was Burly Swain."

Still squeezing Kelly's hand, Anita whispered something in his ear.

He grinned but didn't lower his fist. "Zechariah done told me. Jetti knows too and is plum excited to be getting a baby brother. He also told her I'm her daddy. Now I've got some business to tend to."

Jetti grabbed Kelly's wrist, helping her mother restrain him. She hoped he wouldn't decide to drop his beer and use his left hand on the poor man. Despite their efforts his arm started in motion. His fist was moving very slowly but they were both losing their grip as he stepped forward, pulling them with him. "Don't hit him, Kelly, Anita said they're just friends! Dearl, Zechariah, wanna give us a hand here?!"

"Leave me out of this," said Dearl. "I'd do the same to anyone that tried to hit on you."

Zechariah frantically waved his arms back and forth as if signaling a driver to stop. "Kelly, please! Eli's like kin to me."

Kelly froze and cut his eyes to him. "That right?"

"It is."

"Listen," said the frightened man, "I only wanted to talk to her—that's all, I swear. I can see now I obviously shouldn't have come here, and I apologize for causing a scene. I'll be leaving now. Congratulations again, Anita."

"Hold up a minute." Kelly lowered his arm but she didn't let go. Neither did her mother. "If you didn't come here trying to screw my woman, it's me that owes the apology."

Relief poured over the man's face. "No, I didn't come here for that."

"What did you want to talk to her about?"

Nervously backing up another step, he cleared his throat and said, "I was going to ask her to marry me."

Jetti clamped down on Kelly's wrist with all her might, certain he'd go berserk. But to her amazement he bit into the rim of his cup, held it with his teeth, and freed his arm from their grasping fingers with a swoop of his strong left hand. He then grabbed the cup again, took a swig, and smiled. "You've got good taste, Eli. She's quite a woman ain't she."

Anita gawked at her with astonishment. "Can you believe this cowboy, Jetti?"

Feeling every bit as flabbergasted, she merely shook her head, grinning.

Kelly set his beer on one of the many cabinets adorning the walls of the spacious corridor and pulled a bag of Beechnut from his hip pocket. He shoved tobacco in his mouth, then pointed at her. "Eli, this pretty filly here is Jetti, our daughter. And that handsome buck over yonder is our soon to be son-in-law Dearl. Miss weepy over there, her name's Cindy. She apparently had a spat with her boyfriend, Dearl's half brother. Come on with Anita and me and we'll get you a beer, then we'll have some barbecue."

Jetti giggled over the incredulous look on Anita's face as Kelly led her away with one arm around her waist, the other draped over Eli Adams' shoulders. She watched Kelly take them into the game room, then turned to Cindy. "Okay, let's go somewhere so you can tell me what happened."

# 31

DEARL WAS FURIOUS OVER THE shocking news Cooper
had laid on him. For the last five minutes poor Coo had been
sitting on the edge of his bed, looking up at him with teary
eyes brimming with frustration, repeatedly asking, "How
could she do this to me?"

Each time Dearl merely shook his head for an answer.

"Anita said she did us a favor by doing it."

That went all over him. "Holy fuck, Coo, how does she
figure that?!"

"Because I'd told her about us all thinking the game
might have gone either way if we hadn't been so mad after
Rainey told us they had our playbook."

"You're still gonna dump her I hope."

"Oh, not to worry, I already have."

"Good."

"Problem is . . . I still love her."

He tried to imagine how he'd feel about Jetti if she'd
pulled such a shitty stunt. Unable to picture her betraying
him in any way, he soon gave up. "There's a world of pretty
girls out there, Cooper. In a few months you'll be having to
fight 'em off at Texas. Austin's the pussy capitol of the state,
you know."

"No, it's known as the party capitol, Dearl." Cooper sniffed
and ran a finger under his nose. "Ever since she started
giving you the eye our freshman year I knew you and Jetti
would wind up together. You're a lucky dude, Dearl. I really
thought Cindy was the one for me, I really did. Fuck, I just

can't believe she did this."

"Me either, bro."

"Remember how tore up I was when Darlene Fox dumped me?"

Dearl nodded.

"I feel a thousand times worse than that now. Man, you got all the way through school without ever getting your heart broke. Three years running those seniors broke it off when they left for college and it didn't faze you at all. How come?"

He shrugged. "Because I knew they were just using me, and in a way I was using them. Jetti's the only girl I've ever fallen in love with."

A smile contradicted Cooper's mood. "Just using them for that sweet piece of ass, huh?"

At first he started to lie and say that was exactly right, but opted for honesty with an ulterior motive. Cooper had a reputation as a real lady killer in bed. "I wanted everybody to think that, but the truth is I've never done it."

"Never done what?"

"Screwed a girl."

Face blazing with skepticism, Cooper rose to his feet. "Are you shittin' me?"

"Nope, I'm a virgin, and get this—so is Jetti. That's the secret I had that made me believe Zechariah was really a prophet when he knew about it."

Cooper let go a humorless laugh. "You've never fucked anybody, not one time?"

"That's right."

"Wow."

Dearl cleared his throat. "And now that you know, how about some advice, big brother?"

"Big brother? Dearl, I'm only three weeks older than you."

"I know that, but technically that makes you my big

brother. Now, about that advice."

"All right. What all have you done with a girl?"

"Never got any further than feeling one up."

"Good grief, Dearl, you've never even fingered anybody?"
He shook his head.

"What all has a girl done to you?"

"Nothing, other than kissing."

"So you've never gotten a hand job or blowjob?"

"Nope. Jetti's the only girl that's ever touched my dick
and you were there when it happened, taking pictures of us.
And she hasn't touched it since because I told her I didn't
want to make love until the time was right."

"So you've never gotten naked with Jetti or seen her
naked?"

"Uh-uh."

"Well, you've felt her up at least."

"Only that one time when she pulled my hand over her tit
while you were taking those pictures."

Cooper guffawed and squinted at him like he was an idiot.
"Man, I never dreamed you were a prude. What, were you
scared to try it? Screwing, I mean."

"Yeah, and if you buck-buck me, Stupor-Cooper, I'm
gonna kick your ass."

"Nah, I know you're not a chicken shit where Jetti's
concerned anymore. Let me get a beer and then I'll learn
you the facts of life, baby brother."

"I need another one too. Stay here, I'll be back with two
brewskis in a minute."

◆◆◆

They were sitting in Jetti's car at the base of Tornado Hill.

She'd confessed her atrocity when they'd driven away from the Pond Ranch and Jetti had been livid, screaming she deserved to be dumped by Cooper. But by the time they got here—whether through real sympathy or merely wanting her to quit bawling, Jetti claimed to believe her, even said she felt sorry for her.

"So now you're a real Kodiak, huh?"

"Absolutely," she answered, despising herself for what she'd done. "And will be for life. Like I said, somehow during the fourth quarter I wasn't faking it anymore, and I think I owe most of it to your school spirit rubbing off on me. You do believe me, right?"

"Mm hmm. What we need to figure out is how to get Cooper to believe you."

Joyful relief washed over her—Jetti really seemed to mean it. "I've admired you ever since I moved to Sleeping Bear, and I'm so glad you're not writing me off over what I did. I'd give anything if I could go back in time and undo it."

Jetti gave her a firm look. "If I didn't believe that we wouldn't be here. By the way, I don't want you to give the money back to that sorry-ass cheating coach. He deserves to be burned. You say you wanted to buy Cooper a ring with it? Well do it."

"Oh I have to give it back, Jetti, I couldn't live with myself otherwise. I'll have to trust my cousin to do it though, because only he knows who bought it."

Jetti smiled. "I was only testing you, Cindy. Now I'm even more convinced you're truly repentant. When we get back to the party I'll pull Cooper aside and do my best to convince him to give you another chance."

A horrid thought occurred to her. "What if Dearl won't let you after he finds out, which he probably already has by now."

"Oh I know he has. He was going to talk to Cooper when

we left, remember?"

She buried her face in her hands. "I am *so* fucked."

"Well, I'm not going to defy Dearl, Cindy. If he doesn't want me to try to fix things between you and Cooper, I'll try my best to talk him into letting me—but if I can't convince him, you're on your own. Sorry."

"I understand."

"Wow!" Jetti brought her hands together in a single clap. "It just dawned on me what Zechariah's dream means."

"Zechariah's dream?"

"Yeah. He dreamed about Dearl, a bear, a lion, and you. He was afraid you wanted to harm someone but I just now realized God was warning him about Langton having the playbook."

She squinted at her. "Are you serious?"

"Oh yeah. Like I told you, he's a prophet."

"So that's what he was talking to you about in the parking lot this morning?"

"Mm hmm."

"Come on, Jetti, there aren't any prophets anymore."

"You won't think that much longer, girl. We're going back to the party and confer with him about your problem."

◆◆◆

"Emma Winters . . . my, I like the sound of that."

Rex leaned over on his elbow and smiled. "So you'll marry me then?"

"Does an Irishman like whiskey? Of course I will."

They'd gone to his bedroom after returning from the newspaper. Other than occasional trips to the bathroom they hadn't left his bed since.

"Oh man, just remembered something."

"What, Rex?"

"Al Pond said after we won State he was going to reveal what convinced him Zechariah was a prophet and let us print it. I guess we'd better go to the party after all and find out what he's been sitting on."

Emma stretched and yawned. "Well I'm a bit hungry anyway and not in the mood to cook us a late supper, so let's go out there and enjoy some barbecue."

He grinned at her. "Mind if I tell everyone what *we're* sitting on?"

"You mean us getting married?"

"Yeah."

"Of course not, silly."

◆◆◆

Anita was very impressed with Al Pond's cavernous meeting room where the catered food had been laid out. Kelly said the school board often gathered here. She couldn't believe the shine he'd taken to Eli Adams. Eli had been ill at ease at first, but loosened up after his first cup of Budweiser and at least appeared to enjoy Kelly's company as well.

"Anita," said the rich widower, lowering his third beer to the table, "though I'll always be sorry I wasn't able to win your hand, I'm genuinely happy for you. It looks to me like you're marrying a fine man."

Kelly grinned. "Why thanks for saying that, Eli. Mighty nice of you."

"I'd like to show you something, and you'll understand why I was so attracted to Anita when I saw her in Houston." Eli pulled out his wallet and handed Kelly the picture she'd seen. "That wonderful woman was my wife. I lost her three years ago."

Kelly's brows shot up. "Well I'll be. Dang she looks an awful lot like Anita, don't she?"

"She sure does."

He gave the picture back. "What happened between you two?"

Eli's eyes moistened. "She died."

"Oh . . . sorry to hear that. She was sure a pretty lady."

"Thank you. So what do you do for a living, Kelly?"

He turned up his beer and burped while plopping the cup back on the table. "I'm the foreman of this here ranch you're sitting on."

"That must be a wonderful job. I always wished I could be a cowboy, but the only talent I have is a flair for mathematics. Will you two be living in this house?"

Kelly frowned with thought for a moment, then cut his eyes to her. "Hell, Anita, where *are* we gonna live? We can't shack up in the bunkhouse with the boys."

"Well hell no we can't," she laughed. "You'll just have to commute to the ranch. Let's buy one of those empty lots on the north side of town and hire Burly's uncle to build us a nice home. If he still has his construction company, that is."

"He does, but you know? I was always partial to that house you and your dad lived in."

"I sold it ten years ago."

"I know, to the Moss's—but maybe they'd sell it to us."

She made a sour face and shook her head. "Forget it, Kelly. Living there would constantly remind me of my hooker days."

"Do you own a house in Houston," Eli asked, "or live in an apartment?"

"An apartment."

Eli drummed his fingers on the table with his left hand

while taking a swig of beer with his right. He lowered the cup and said, "Do you suppose the owner of this ranch would sell you an acre so you could build a house on it?"

Kelly let out a dry laugh. "The Ponds have owned this land for eight generations, and when Al passes on his two boys will make it nine. There's a stipulation in the original deed that forbids it being subdivided in any form or fashion."

"I see . . ." Eli took another pull from his cup. "What about the land next to the ranch, can any of it be purchased?"

"The only available country land lies on the other side of Sleeping Bear," said Kelly. "This ranch starts where you passed the city limits sign on your way out here, Eli, and runs way past the county border on the other three sides. I'm used to living where I work and would hate having to drive out here from the other side of town."

"Oh my, what a burden, Kelly," she sarcastically ribbed. "I think Eli has a great idea. Let's buy a few acres and have a little ranch of our own. We could raise miniature horses. They're so cute."

He shot her a facetious grin. "Well if you've got the money, honey, I've got the time."

"I do."

"Oh do you now? How much you got?"

"Two hundred thousand in savings and a stock portfolio worth almost twice that."

Kelly blew out a long whistle. "Woman, you just got prettier than ever."

"Actually—" Eli started laughing before he could get out whatever he intended to say.

"Actually what?" she queried.

"The reason I was asking is because I'd like to fund it as a wedding present. I've got more money than I know what to do with and no one to share it with."

"Oh we couldn't let you do that," Kelly stated, firmly

shaking his head.

"I promise there'd be no strings attached, other than you guys allowing me to come visit every now and then. And I give you my word I won't try to coax Anita into trifling on you behind your back."

She reached over and patted Eli's cheek. "You wouldn't be able to no matter how hard you tried. But Kelly's right. Thanks for offering, but we'll have to say no."

He leaned back in his chair and sighed. "Okay, what *will* you allow me to give the two of you? I insist on buying you a wedding present."

"Hmm, I could sure use a new pickup."

"Kelly!" She slapped his back, giggling in the process.

"A new pickup it is. And what kind of vehicle would you enjoy, Anita?

"I was only jokin', Eli," Kelly said as if he should have known it without being told.

"Well what would you like?"

Kelly leaned forward and folded his hands on the table, seriously thinking it over, judging by his expression. "You can get me a good pocketknife. That's what I'd like."

"Are you being serious this time?"

"Mm hmm."

Eli looked disappointed.

Anita feared Eli was trying to finance his way into her life so he could visit a living replica of his departed wife from time to time, foolishly thinking the more expensive the gift, the more time he'd be allotted. Kelly liked him and so did she—he didn't have to pay for the right to visit them, and wouldn't have been able to no matter how generous the offer if they weren't fond of him.

"Okay, a pocketknife for Kelly. What am I getting you, Anita?"

She winked at him and turned to Kelly. "Does Al still

throw the goat cook-off shebang every year?"

"Oh yeah."

"Eli, what I want for a wedding present is your promise that you'll come to Sleeping Bear every fourth of July and be our guest for two days. The goat cook-off is always a lot of fun."

"I'd like that," Eli said with a grateful smile. "Tell you what, when you two get your house built, let me offer the first housewarming present and I'll quit badgering you about it."

"You've got a deal . . ." she gave him another pat on the cheek.

"Well lookie what the cat dragged in," said Kelly, glancing over his shoulder. "Over here, Rex! You and Emma come sit with us. I want you to meet my new pal."

◆◆◆

Luther tried to show him how to squirt beer into a cup without filling it with pure foam but Zechariah couldn't get the hang of it. As a result he'd been relegated to picking up empty wine cooler bottles, paper plates, and abandoned beer cups as the party continued. He went to the kitchen to fetch a trash bag.

He'd been in the meeting room when Rex Winters announced he and Emma were engaged. Kelly had applauded like everyone else, and then Emma congratulated him over his engagement to Anita. Zechariah figured when Eli confessed he'd come to ask Anita to marry him, his honesty in the face of almost certain adversity had drawn Kelly's respect and also showed the quick-tempered cowboy he didn't view Anita as a mere sex object. He couldn't imagine why Eli wanted to marry a prostitute, and hadn't been able to ask him about that or anything else due to Kelly monopolizing his time. Zechariah hoped to talk with him some more before he left because Noah's relatives were the closest thing to family he had.

Jetti strolled into the kitchen with Cindy Shane. "Zechariah, I've been looking all over for you. I know what your dream means, at least I'm pretty sure I do."

She proceeded to tell him and he figured her interpretation to be right. The Lord used the most important Kodiak player to represent the whole team, therefore Dearl turning into the bear and the lion turning into Cindy was symbolic of her desire to make them lose.

Most of the Lord's motives on the matter made sense to him now. If he hadn't relayed his dream Langton would've defeated Sleeping Bear just as the lion transforming into the girl had vanquished the grizzly. But God knew he'd tell Al, who'd inform the coach. The coach wouldn't believe it until seeing how well the Lions defensed his players in the first half, and would alter his strategy for the second, assuring victory. But the final act of the prophetic drama had yet to be played out: the fate of Cindy Shane.

He studied the pretty girl as she tearfully recounted her transgression at his request, careful not to let his gaze drift to her breasts, vividly recalling how tempting they'd looked uncovered in his mind's eye.

Now the drum major part of the dream made sense. If she wasn't lying. "Cindy, are you being totally honest about changing your mind and really wanting Sleeping Bear to win?"

"Absolutely."

"At the end of my dream I saw you marching in place, knowing you were victorious. I assumed that meant the bear lost the fight, but I had it backwards. You *were* victorious in the end, but you'd changed sides, something I couldn't have known in my dream."

"Will you help me convince Cooper she's truly sorry and he should take her back?" Jetti asked.

He hesitated, the Lord was speaking to him. When the message ended he said, "Cindy, I sense you're skeptical about me hearing the Lord, but fortunately for you Cooper knows I do. Now let me convince you. Your cousin's name is Will, a fact you've neither told Jetti nor Cooper."

Cindy gasped and took a step back, looking as if she might faint.

"You didn't tell me how much you were paid for the copy of Cooper's playbook, only that you sold it, so how come I know that you and Will divided ten thousand dollars between you?"

Her mouth flew open and she gawked at him as if he was a ghost.

"And I know something you don't—the name of the coach he sold it to."

"Omigod, you really are a prophet like Jetti said!" Cindy's hands were pressed against the sides of her awestruck face.

"I don't call myself such, I'm merely a messenger."

Jetti grinned at her and winked. "Told you so."

"So you'll help me with Cooper?"

"Yes, Cindy, I'll speak to him on your behalf, but it's up to you to earn his trust back, if you can. Jetti, he and Dearl are in his room. I think it would be wise for Cindy to stay with me while you tell Dearl you're ready to take that drive, because he's most likely pretty hostile towards her at the moment. I'll take Cindy to my room and peak out the door. When I see you two leave, we'll go talk to Cooper."

# 32

REX, WHO'D GORGED HIMSELF WITH brisket and potato salad, grinned when Emma abandoned a leg quarter of barbecued chicken with most of the drumstick still intact, resting beside a pile of macaroni and cheese.

"Eyes were bigger than me stomach," she moaned.

He'd dreaded telling Kelly, so to see his old friend happy for him when he announced their engagement had really made this magical day perfect. Kelly couldn't hide his emotions at all, and clearly no longer felt any animosity towards Emma. She was friendly to him as well. They'd been introduced to Eli Adams, a friend of Anita's. Rex had read about the computer-programming genius. Eli didn't appear to be much of a football fan so the four of them had probably bored him to tears as they'd animatedly relived today's championship almost play by play.

Earlier, Kelly followed him to the bathroom and said God told Zechariah he was Jetti's father and he'd conceived a son with Anita. The part about Jetti had floored Rex. He would always have a difficult time believing Kelly screwed Anita back in those days—that *whore* the cowboy had so despised.

"Who'd have ever imagined this scenario," said Emma, "Kelly and I sitting here drinking beer together after the bloody row we had last night? And it was over him being rude to you, Anita. Now the two of you are going to tie the knot. My, but life is strange."

Anita nodded. "After he left you he cornered me in the motel parking lot, and I was afraid he might pound me into the pavement for awhile there."

Kelly shot her an incredulous scowl. "Were you really?"

"Oh yeah."

"Anita, I'd never hit a woman, you know that—at least you damn well should have. Shit," he snarled.

"Well I didn't think you would, but you were *some* mad, and I didn't know how much whiskey you'd drank and was afraid you might not be in your right mind." She kissed the frown off Kelly's face and turned to him. "So when are you two planning to get hitched, Rex?"

"Whenever Emma wants to." He smiled at the gorgeous redhead sitting beside him.

"Answer me a question—" Kelly tapped his forehead with the rim of his beer cup. "You two knew soon after you met you'd never be more than friends, yet something happened today that changed all that. What the hell was it?"

Emma tossed Kelly a sly grin. "It happened last night actually, not long after you left. Let's just say Rex suddenly saw me in a new light, and I did likewise."

On the way out here she'd confessed what that 'new light' had been concerning him. "Oh go ahead and tell him, Emma, I can handle it—though I still can't believe it. You're going to get a real kick out of this, Kelly."

"All right I will," she said. "After you left, I ran upstairs heading for my room, all upset as you can imagine. We'd woke Rex with our shouting, and when he stepped into the hall to find out what was wrong with me the bugger didn't realize he was only in his underwear. Well, he wears boxers and the pee-slit was gaping open, allowing a glimpse of his willy, and it turned me on."

Kelly guffawed. "And here I thought you were going to say it was his He-Man physique."

It had been twenty years since Kelly last poked fun of his build. They'd snuck over the fence at the fairgrounds one

Saturday night to go skinny dipping in the lake, manmade and only a quarter of a mile in diameter. It had bothered him then, but not now. Emma loved him in spite of his lack of machismo in the muscular sense. Nonetheless he said, "You could have gone all night without saying that, Kelly."

"Aw, Rex, you know I didn't mean nothing by it. Okay, Emma fell in love with you because of your dick. What made you fall for her, partner?"

"Me body," Emma answered for him, very matter-of-factly.

"Why hell, he's seen your figure every day since you moved here, what made him shift gears last night?"

"Because he saw it naked."

"Oh . . ." Kelly's mouth formed a circle, accentuated by his elevated brows.

"Okay, now it's your turn, bloke. What turned your opinion about Anita?"

Kelly drew a deep breath and sighed. "I'll let your fiancé help me answer that, Emma. Rex, you remember that day back in high school when you told me you'd just found out Anita was a hooker?"

"I remember it all too well."

"What was my reaction?"

"You pitched a conniption fit and called me a liar. Threatened to kick my ass if I didn't take it back. It took the testimony of Burly Swain and that new kid, whose name escapes me at the moment, to convince you."

Emma frowned. "Why'd you believe them and not Rex, Kelly?"

"I'll tell you why," said Anita, a hurt look on her face showing it was still a painful memory. "Because those two paid me to pose naked, and they showed him the pictures."

"I didn't know you knew about that?" Kelly half shouted, gawking at Anita as if she was sitting there in the nude now.

She looked down at her plate. "That *new kid* told me about showing them to you."

Rex noticed Eli's eyes watering. The man looked like he was about to cry. He raised his beer and said, "Hey, those days are gone forever, Anita, and you're not a hooker anymore. Here's to your new life, darlin' friend."

Kelly also toasted. "Anyway, Emma, finding out Anita was a pro flat out killed me, because I was hoping to marry her after we graduated. But now she's done with that shit for good."

Emma turned to Anita. "So when did you quit?"

"Oh . . . last night, actually."

Rex was glad to see Anita smiling again. Her good spirits had waned when the topic turned to her past. He glanced at Eli who appeared to be feeling like a fifth wheel. "I've read several articles about your work and was very impressed. Sooner or later I'm going to have to come out of the dark ages and join the high-tech community myself."

"What do you mean?"

"Abandoned my old linotype. I'm well versed with offset print but just love jostling hot lead around."

"So you're a printer?"

"Yeah, newspaper man. I'm the editor of The Hibernator."

Eli perked right up. "My grandfather had a print shop when I was a kid and used to let me work the Ludlow on occasion."

"Yeah, I love my Ludlow."

"Turns out Zechariah and Eli here are old acquaintances," Kelly said to him, then eyed the programming wizard. "You have Zechariah to thank for me not kickin' your ass, Eli. When he said you were like kin I held back out of respect for him. Then when you said you'd come out here to propose to Anita, I could tell by the look in your eye you weren't lying so I invited you to hang around with us so I could check out

Anita's reaction to you. And damn if I didn't find out you're a good ol' boy even if you ain't a Texan."

"You were checking *me* out?!" Anita huffed, gaping at her fiancé.

"Sure was," Kelly answered with his lazy grin. "And it didn't take long for me to see you feel sisterly towards him. Anyway, Eli, any friend of Zechariah's is damn sure a friend of mine."

"When did you meet the amazing Zechariah, Eli?" Rex asked.

"Actually, though we both knew about each other while growing up, we met for the first time tonight."

"Did you know he was a prophet?" said Emma.

Eli frowned. "A prophet?"

"Yes indeed."

"Well I knew my Uncle Noah had raised him to be a theologian but didn't know about that. Noah was a very brilliant man who turned sour against the world and went into seclusion. He bought a farm somewhere in Arkansas and wouldn't tell any of the family where it was because he didn't want visitors. He communicated with us through the mail. All any of us knew was his post office box number in Little Rock, he wouldn't give out his unlisted phone number."

"Zechariah told me a bit about him," Emma said, fiddling with her plastic fork. "Noah found him in a cornfield when he was a baby."

"That's the way family rumor has it. Noah wrote my grandmother about it and asked her not to tell anyone else in the family, but she did anyway. So Zechariah claims to be a prophet?"

Emma winced. "No claim to it, he is one. Everyone here excepting Anita knows that because he's proved it to us, though he doesn't call himself that. Says he's a messenger."

"Oh he proved it to me too, Emma." Anita shifted her eyes to Eli. "He's the real deal. I was an atheist until this very night, but not anymore. And it's all because of Zechariah."

Kelly billowed a sigh, shifted in his seat, and winked at Emma. "Funny how he got everything mixed up about you and me, ain't it?"

"Not really . . ." she started fidgeting with the fork again.

Rex knew she wanted a cigarette but was politely refraining because no one else in the room was smoking.

"All he actually received from God was the explanation of what caused the problem that pushed us apart, Kelly. The notion that we'd work everything out was Zechariah's. He never claimed it was from the Lord."

Anita giggled.

"What's so funny?" Emma asked.

"He definitely got mixed up over something he told me last night, but God straightened him out on it. See, when he gets a message he doesn't always deliver it exactly right. Zechariah told me he misunderstands God on occasion, sometimes forgets a word or two, and at times thinks God's speaking to him when He isn't."

"Well that may be," said Emma, "but I think The Almighty intended for Kelly and I to misunderstand on purpose so we'd try to have another go at it and wind up having that fight which led to the correct two matches: you and Kelly, Rex and me. Look at how strange it is the four of us coupled-up the same day. Call me barmy, but that can't be coincidence. It's the hand of God, I tell ya."

Kelly slapped the table. "You nailed it, that's exactly what it is! Way to go, Emma."

Rex agreed it seemed a logical explanation, but Eli was looking at all of them like they were a few bricks shy of a load.

An odd grin popped up on Kelly's face. "Rex, did you and

Emma talk to Zechariah before y'all came in here to chow down?"

"No. Why?"

"Because he's got some news for the two of you."

"Such as?"

"Oh, far be it from me to take it upon myself to speak for the Lord."

Emma squinted at him. "You saying he has a word for us, Kelly?"

"Man, *does* he."

♦♦♦

Cooper had already made her come during foreplay, throttling her G-spot with his finger—concentrating on it as if he had radar flashing out her pleasure points. Now, laying beneath him, he was transporting her to another orgasm with his penis. Locking her legs around the back of Cooper's thighs, she hissed his name and begged him to come too.

♦♦♦

Cooper's dad and Luther believed her because of Zechariah. The prophet had told them who'd bought the playbook, and she'd agreed to give Al the five thousand. He in turn would give it to Mister Rainey who'd confront the defensive coordinator in the presence of the Lion's head coach before handing over the money.

Zechariah had tried hard to convince Cooper of her sincerity but he'd refused to take her back, saying he'd never be able to trust her again.

Cindy stood beside Delbert Hutch and Rick Holt, guzzling beer, trying to numb the pain with Budweiser since wine coolers weren't helping much. The game room had thinned out a little due to alcohol-induced munchies. Neither of them knew about her wicked deed, so they were both quite friendly.

Rick had shown up at the party going stag, and Darlene Fox arrived much later. Throughout the night neither had seemed hostile to the other but they'd obviously broke up. Darlene must have gone home, she hadn't seen the head cheerleader among her clique in the game room for at least an hour.

"How come you and Cooper called it quits?" Delbert asked.

Cindy looked at the foam nestled near the rim of her cup. "Because I did something stupid . . . really, really stupid."

"So he broke it off, huh?"

She sank her lips into the floating suds and reared her head back. Wiping her mouth while swallowing, trying not to cry, she nodded.

"Man, tough day for cupid huh, Rick? First you and Darlene mutually decide to go your separate ways, and now he's pulled his arrows out of Cooper and Cindy here."

"Yeah, guess so," Rick replied while turning to her with a sexy smile. "Wanna know something, Cindy? If I hadn't been going with Darlene at the time, I would have asked you to be my date for the homecoming dance."

Despite her grief, she felt very flattered to hear him say that. Rick Holt was *totally* hot. "Would you really have?"

"Mm hmm—" he turned up his beer and smiled at her again. "And if I had, what would your answer have been?"

"Oh I'd have said yes." Like any other girl in school except Jetti.

"And if you'd been seeing Cooper at the time, what would you have said then?"

"I'd have said no. I'm in love with him."

Delbert sported a wide grin. "Ah, so cupid hasn't totally bailed after all."

Rick appeared taken aback by her statement which didn't surprise her. A stud like that obviously didn't hear the word often. Perhaps he'd never heard it before in his life. She gazed around the room, quickly passing over the happy couples to keep from crying. If only she could go back in time and leave that fucking playbook alone.

Darlene Fox hadn't gone home after all. She ran past the glass wall, hands on face, extremely upset. Her direction would take her to the front door, so she was apparently leaving. A moment later Cooper entered the game room and she couldn't hold back the tears any longer.

He walked up to Delbert, put an arm around him, and winked at Rick. "You guys remember when Darlene dumped me back in eighth grade?"

They both nodded.

"Well, gentlemen, I just got even . . . ."

# 33

BURLY HEARD A DING AND crossed the empty dining room. Stepping behind the pay counter, he slid open the drive-through window.

A big hombre with a flat top said, "Can I get a coffee to go?"

"Sure can, stranger."

The guy frowned. "Why'd you call me that?"

"No offense intended, just never seen you before."

"Yeah . . . just passing through."

He noticed a bolt action rifle leaning against the passenger door of the dude's beautifully restored '68 El Camino. "How about some pie to go with that coffee? I always carry plenty of snacks when I go deer huntin', and looks like that's what you're up to. We've got fresh baked apple, cherry, coconut cream, and chocolate."

"I'm done hunting for the day, got rained out. A piece of pie sure sounds tempting but I better not, damned ulcer's acting up. Which reminds me, I'll need a lot of extra cream for that coffee. No sugar though."

Spotting a Langton Lions' cap sitting on the guy's lap when he handed him the order, Burly grinned. The dude was apparently afraid to wear his colors in Sleeping Bear. "Where you headed?"

"Amarillo."

"Well be careful driving in this rain, we're under a flash-flood watch."

"Will do, thanks . . . ."

He watched the El Camino disappear down the drive-through and reemerge in his vision after winding back to Main Street. *You just turned the wrong way for Amarillo, mister.*

♦♦♦

An old timey car-pickup combo passed her shortly after she turned onto Ribbon Lane, so named because it weaved left and right like a roll of Christmas trimming coming unwound. The vehicle turned onto Tucker Drive. When Darlene drove past the intersection, noting the cheery yuletide lights shimmering through the rain on the decorated houses along that sparsely populated avenue, she almost started crying again. Cindy Shane lived on that road.

Cooper had been so cruel. After they made love she hadn't been able to stop jabbering about what a magnificent lover he was and how she'd never experienced anything like the thrills he'd given her. Leaning on his elbow, resting his head in his hand, he'd smiled and said, "Well thank you. I'd rate you at . . . hmm, about the fifth best I've ever had, I guess."

"Fifth!" she'd shouted, angrily climbing out of his bed.

"Well who's first?"

"Oh, Cindy Shane without doubt."

"Then why'd you break up with her?"

He'd eased over on his back and sighed. "I've got my reasons, but it wasn't over that. Get on along now, I can see you'll never be able to replace her so I'll have to look elsewhere."

Overwhelmingly humiliated, she'd thanked God for forgetting to give Luther the spare car key in her purse when surrendering her key ring.

Her parents hadn't gone to the party because they'd left for Woodrow at dawn in order to get good seats, and the game had exhausted them emotionally, adding to their fatigue. Knowing Rick and she had decided to part ways, they wouldn't be all that shocked she'd opted to come home early.

She'd been going with Rick almost a year and it had become awkwardly evident they'd never fall in love. The sex had been good but their mutual physical attraction never grew any deeper. When Cooper started catching her eye again, as he had in junior high, she'd known it was time to move on.

Last Sunday night they'd gone parking for the last time. While buttoning her blouse she'd told Rick, "I don't think our relationship is going anywhere."

Completely unaffected by the statement, he'd confessed, "I've been thinking we should probably call it quits since homecoming. Let's make it official now, but wait until after the championship game before telling anybody else—it might distract the team. Meanwhile let's act like we're still going together at school and all. What say?"

She'd agreed and they hadn't done anything more than hold hands to keep up appearances since.

Aiming her remote at the garage door while pulling into the drive, she thought about how ironic it was she'd broken up with Cooper in eighth grade because she hadn't liked the way he kissed. Not only did the boy have a smooch on him now, he could fuck like nobody she'd ever been with. As she'd suspected, Bibi, Marybeth, Delores, and Joie hadn't exaggerated a bit.

Staring through the raindrops without pushing the button, she debated the idea of going back to the party. Before long she shoved her Cobra into reverse and backed out of the drive.

♦♦♦

Rex noticed Coach Rainey and Annabel searching for a place to sit after serving themselves at one of the buffets. "Come join us, Coach!"

Rainey set a platter-size paper plate piled high with hot wings and ribs on the table. A smoked sausage link, petite portions of beans, potato salad, and coleslaw, rested on Annabel's divided plate. Both were drinking iced tea.

They'd spoken briefly in the game room earlier when Rex had gone for a beer refill, and Rainey said he had something that would be very newsworthy once he got to the bottom of it.

"No beer tonight, Coach?" Emma inquired.

"Watching the old belt line, you know how it is." He patted his flat stomach.

She grinned and pointed at his food. "Oh, by all means one shouldn't drink beer with that low calorie fare."

The coach glanced down at his two mountains of meat and chuckled. Then he looked around. "Hey, Cocker, come here!"

Jimmy Cocker shoved the last chunk of a burger in his mouth while hurrying over. "Yeah, Coach?"

"Fetch Annabel and me a beer, will you?"

Still chewing, the lineman gave an eager nod and quickly departed. Rainey winked at Emma. "Feel better now?"

"Much," she answered with a satisfied smirk.

"Well you can drink mine too, dear," said Annabel, "because I really am watching my weight."

"Kind of what I had in mind, sugar, but I can't have

Cocker thinking his coach is a lush, now can I?"

Everyone laughed and Rex gave Rainey a smile of admiration. "You finally took down Truman Jette, Coach."

Anita loudly cleared her throat. "Is anyone going to introduce Eli and me to this coaching genius and his lovely wife?"

Rex made the introductions and let Rainey polish off a rib and a couple of wings before asking what he was planning to get to the bottom of. Jimmy Cocker set two cups of beer on the table and made for the dessert carts before the coach answered.

"Dick Parsons, the Langton defensive coordinator, got his hands on a copy of our playbook but we don't have any proof yet. I know Truman wasn't involved—he'd never pull a stunt like that. Al Pond told me about it before the game started but I didn't believe it until I saw how abnormally well the Lions defense was sniffing us out throughout the first half. Al only strongly suspected someone on the Lions squad had gotten hold of it at the time."

Rex couldn't believe his ears. "So *that's why* you went to the wishbone so much in the second half."

Rainey nodded and took a swig of beer.

"Some high class organization they run over there in Langton ain't it," Kelly groused with his tough-guy scowl. "I'd like to get my hands on that sorry son of a bitch."

Anita sighed and massaged her temples. "I heard all about the conspiracy straight from the horse's mouth."

"Why didn't you tell me?!" Kelly barked.

She dropped her hands and sighed again. "Because I didn't want to get your dander up again tonight. I was going to tell you about it tomorrow."

"Al told me just a little while ago that Cindy Shane owned up to it." Rainey picked up another rib as he spoke. "She made a copy of Cooper's playbook, faxed it to a cousin, he sold it for ten grand, and they split the loot. Her cousin brokered the deal and would only tell her it was someone on the coaching staff. Al wouldn't say how he found out Parsons was the culprit but he's dead sure of it."

Rex smelled Zechariah as Al's source. Nothing like having an employee with a direct connection to heaven. "That idiot has no business coaching high school football. But enough about that, this is a victory celebration. Sorry I didn't get to hear your speech, Coach, and very sad we're going to lose you. No telling how many offers you'll be getting after nailing down this championship."

Rainey washed down a chunk of rib and said, "Losing my four All Stars to graduation, it would sure be the smart thing to move on wouldn't it. But Lyle Whitney, Mike Vaughn, and Jimmy Cocker will still be on the team next year along with Abel Norris, an incredibly gifted linebacker. And even though Seth Jones didn't get much playing time backing up Holt, he hit another level during the season and I've got a hunch he's ready to come into his own. Besides, Annabel and I just flat out don't wanna leave Sleeping Bear."

Rex felt giddy over the possibility of making the playoffs again next year. It would have been a reach to even consider it without Rainey at the helm. "Coach, you'll never know how glad I am to hear that."

"I think Langton knowing our plays was a blessing in disguise," Anita opined. "Cooper told me we might not have won if all the players hadn't been so angry after you told them about it at halftime."

Rainey chuckled. "Well that's something we'll never know, but I'm confidant we'd have still beat the Lions without that added motivation."

"Do you two have kids?" Anita asked.

"Yeah, three daughters in the marines," Rainey answered with a broad grin.

"One's in Okinawa the other two are stationed at Hawaii," Annabel added. Then she winked and said, "Not only did they join the corps like their father, they're all football fanatics too."

♦♦♦

A handsome forty-ish woman opened the front door only wide enough to see who'd come to call.

*Bound to be the girl's mother.*

"Yes?"

"Where's Cindy?"

She frowned. "At a party. Why is a man your age looking for her?"

"Where's your husband?"

The frowned deepened, sprouting wrinkles at the corners of her eyes. "I think you'd better leave."

Dick shoved her and stepped into the house. "Your daughter owes me money and I'm here to collect it—now where the hell is she?"

"Frank! Frank, we have an intruder, help!"

He backhanded her across the face and slammed a fist into her stomach. As she bent over with pain, clutching at her gut, he hammered the back of her neck with his hands locked together, sending her to the floor. Hurrying across the threshold, Dick grabbed the rifle he'd leaned against the house before ringing the doorbell, rushed back inside, and kicked the door closed with his boot heel. When her husband came running into the living room Dick put a bullet in his forehead. He cocked the gun and blew a hole in back of the woman's skull, soaking the carpet with her brains. Leaving that empty brass in the rifle, he retrieved the ejected one and exchanged it for a pair of rubber gloves in his coat pocket. Slipping them on, he went to find the girl's bedroom, hoping like hell she'd stashed his five grand somewhere in there.

He'd have never been able to find out who'd copied the playbook if he hadn't beaten it, and this address, out of Will Amarod before putting an end to the miserable bastard's existence. The house was located in an isolated location down a street that connected to a winding road he'd taken to get here. No one could have heard the shots, so he had plenty of time to search for his cash. Soon locating the girl's room, he spied a large jewelry box and decided to search it first.

He hadn't killed anyone in thirty years, and thought the cure had taken. But the monster within had only been lying dormant in the recesses of his psyche, awaiting something to push it back to that region of his mind where rage overrode all reason. Dick remained lucid now as he had when he'd killed that boy and his family in Tennessee: the bastard had stolen his bicycle and none of them would admit it. The law hadn't been able to try him as an adult and he'd been released from the asylum when he turned eighteen. His records were sealed and no one knew that Dick Parsons, who'd worked his way through college where he discovered a talent for coaching football, was really Richard Cook.

"Hot damn, it's here!" He rolled up the cash, stashed it in his coat, and closed the jewelry box. Cindy Shane had a lot of nice jewelry but he left it behind, reminding himself he wasn't a thief.

♦♦♦

"Don't let this shit ruin *your* night, Dearl," Cooper had

said. "You and Jetti need to get off by yourselves and celebrate the championship and you being named MVP proper-like, if you know what I mean."

Dearl had then finally agreed to leave with her and they'd spent over an hour making out in the car before he told her to start the engine.

Darlene Fox passed them, returning to the party. Jetti had noticed her leave and wondered how she'd talked Luther into giving back her car keys.

They were almost at the highway, and Jetti's hopes were escalating with each passing second—surely they'd wind up making love tonight. "Any place in particular you'd like me to drive to, Dearl? Wanna go to Tornado Hill?"

He took a sip of beer and gave her a smile that turned her all shivery inside. "Drive to my house. Remember when I told you when the time was right we'd both know it? Well tonight's the night, Jetti. And now it's time to tell you my big secret."

Her heart palpitated as he caressed her cheek.

"There are two virgins riding in this car, Jetti. You and me."

God had never seemed so real! He'd destined them to deflower each other as she'd felt in her heart since Dearl's unfinished declaration made her suspect he was a virgin. "I thought that was your secret. Isn't this just too romantic and special?"

"Why'd you think that? Thought I had everybody fooled."

"Because of what you started to tell me and backed off that night I first came to your house. Plus those seniors you dated seemed too prim and proper to go all the way."

He hissed an angry sigh. "Not like Cindy Shane, huh? I can't believe that bitch, using Cooper just so she could copy his playbook. Man what a sleazy thing to do."

Knowing she had to tread very lightly Jetti thought about

not responding at all. But she now considered Cindy a true friend, and as such, felt compelled to defend her. "That's not the way it was, Dearl. She's madly in love with Cooper."

"No she's not! If Cindy really loved ol' Coo she'd never have done it. Thank God he found out what she is before they wound up married."

She waited a moment to let him cool off a little and said, "Zechariah believes she loves Cooper. He and Cindy went to talk to him right after we left Cooper's room. She was just being a typical nosy girlfriend, going through Cooper's things the night we won Bi-District. When she came across his playbook she didn't think a thing about it at the time. Then when we reached State she thought she'd found a way to get even with the whole town of Sleeping Bear. Cindy hated having to live here until today when she suddenly got baptized blue and white. I mean it, Dearl—now she's as much of a Kodiak as you and I."

He laughed, sarcastically, and scowled at her. "How gullible can you be, Jetti?"

"All right, smarty pants, if she doesn't love him why'd she confess, hmm?"

"Because she knew she was going to get caught when Cooper told Anita about Langton getting a copy of our playbook."

"No, Dearl. Something happened to her during the fourth quarter today. For the first time since she copied it she realized what she'd done to Cooper. To her, football was just a game, and she had no idea how much this championship meant to him. But she'd known all along it meant everything to the town and wanted revenge."

Dearl took a big swig of beer and wiped his mouth. "That's bullshit all the way. If she managed to fool Zechariah then she's even more of a conniving bitch than I thought. I won't let Cooper fall for it, I'll snap him right out of her spell."

Realizing she'd never be able to persuade him, she decided to leave that chore up to the prophet and changed the subject. "Enough about Cindy Shane. Let's talk about us. I've looked forward to making love with you for so long, and now the time has come at last."

"Yeah well, you just took me right out of the mood. I can't believe you're defending her, Jetti."

◆◆◆

Tears streamed down Dick's face. "What the fuck have I done?!"

Rage had dwindled away, leaving his conscience to relentlessly torment him as it had when he'd come to his senses after slaughtering those people in Tennessee.

"Hell, I can't take another battle with this shit!"

A car was coming towards him, headlights flickering through the pouring rain as it sped down the two lane highway. He had no way of knowing how many people were riding in the vehicle but hoped there was only one more life to be taken in order to end his own.

He gripped the wheel tightly. "I'm really sorry, whoever you are, but I fucking just can't take this wretched despair a second longer!"

◆◆◆

Dearl yelled for Jetti to pull off the road but she swerved to the other lane instead. As if intending to hit them head-on all along, the vehicle mirrored her movements and Dearl heard her chilling scream go silent when a loud boom exploded in his ears.

# 34

CINDY WONDERED WHY COOPER HADN'T exposed her to all the players yet, leaving her no choice but to leave the party in total humiliation. She supposed it might have been because he seemed to relish ignoring her as he chatted with Delbert and Rick. Deciding not to press her luck any further since the beer wasn't helping much, she pulled out her cell to call her dad and have him come get her.

"Who're you calling?" Rick asked.

"My dad."

"Why?"

"I need a ride home."

"It's still early, Cindy. Why do you want to go home?"

"Oh she has her reasons, believe me," Cooper sourly retorted. "She started to leave earlier but was able to snow Jetti into siding with her."

Delbert furrowed his ebony brow. "Side with her over what?"

"The reason I broke up with her, Hutch."

When Cooper began to relay her cardinal sin she slunk away from the game room and waited in the hall as the damn phone endlessly rang.

*C'mon, Mom and Dad, somebody pick up the goddamn phone!*

They'd had no desire to attend the party and there was nowhere else to go in Sleeping Bear this time of night except the bar or café. They were both teetotalers so she figured they must have decided to have a Saturday night snack at

The Kodiak Cave.

She tried their cell phones. Neither answered. Finding it hard to believe both of them had left their cells at home, she called the restaurant.

*"Kodiak Cave, Burly speaking."*

"Hi, Burly, this is Cindy Shane. Are my parents there by chance?"

*"Nope."*

"Are you sure?" she asked, frowning with concern.

Burly laughed. *"Yeah, the place is completely empty at the moment."*

"Did they drop by earlier?"

*"No. Haven't seen them all night."*

They wouldn't have gone to bed this early—and even if they had, the house phone would have woke them.

Something was wrong.

Darlene Fox, looking as if nothing had happened earlier when she'd left so upset, faked a smile at her while stepping out of the foyer and into the hall.

"What are you doing loitering out here, Cindy—why aren't you with the gang celebrating?"

She breezed past without waiting for an answer.

Cindy watched the snotty bitch enter the game room, then speed-dialed her home phone a fourth time. Still no answer. She called The Kodiak Cave again and asked Burly for the sheriff's number.

◆◆◆

"Take it easy, kids, you're going to be fine." Myles gave the MVP a wink and closed the ambulance door.

Watching it drive away through the rain, he felt a huge

sense of relief that neither of them were lying down in back and the emergency lights weren't on. They'd been sitting in a patrol car when he arrived on the scene. According to his statement, Dearl had climbed out of Rutherford Simmons' smashed up Acura ILX through the shattered passenger window, jimmied the driver's door open with a crowbar he'd found among the debris thrown from the El Camino, and rescued Jetti. Neither appeared to have suffered any injuries other than bloody noses from the airbags, but the paramedics wanted to take them to the hospital in Amarillo to be certain they hadn't cracked any bones or gotten something jarred loose on their insides.

"He came at us like a kamikaze," Dearl had said, disbelief radiating from his bloody rain-drenched face. "He rammed us on purpose."

Jetti had emphatically agreed.

It could have been suicide all right, since the dead man's vehicle was manufactured long before air bags came out and he hadn't worn the seatbelt. According to his driver's license he was Dick Parsons of Langton, Texas. Parsons' wallet had less than thirty dollars in it but Myles found a cash-roll worth five grand in his coat, along with a pair of rubber gloves and a spent shell casing. His thirty-ought-six rifle, that somehow survived the crash, had an empty cartridge in the chamber.

The towing crew headed back to Amarillo with the wreckage, and Myles got in his cruiser. A northerner was blowing in and sleet began to mix with the now-freezing rain. He hoped there weren't going to be more car wrecks when people started migrating back to town after the party wound down at the ranch.

His cell phone rang.

♦♦♦

Standing on the Shane's front porch, Myles called Cindy back.

*"Hello?"*

"Hey, Cindy. The front door's locked, the porch light's on, the house is dark, and no one's answering the bell. Your mama's car is sitting next to yours, behind your daddy's pickup, so they must have left with someone."

*"No, I don't think so, Sheriff—Mom never goes anywhere without her phone. Something's wrong, I can feel it."*

"Well what do you want me to do, kick the door in?"

*"There's a spare key in a magnet holder beneath the mailbox by the door. Please let yourself in and check to make sure they're not there."*

He felt around under the wall mounted box and found it. Cradling the phone between his chin and shoulder, he removed the key and unlocked the door. Light from the porch spilled into the entryway as he groped for the switch. Finally locating it, he flipped it on.

*Holy shit from hell!!!* He'd almost yelled the words aloud as he took in the bodies of Cindy's parents. Her mother lay facedown with a bullet wound on the back of her head. The gooey mass of brain and blood that had pooled from the front of her stilled features revealed she'd been killed by a high caliber hollow-point bullet which causes far greater damage on exit that it does on impact. The poor woman's husband lay sprawled out on his back several feet beyond her. A tidy crimson sphere in his forehead contrasted with the messy puddle of blood surrounding his crown.

He grimaced at the contradictory scene before him. With Christmas only six days away the Shane's tinsel-laden tree had a slew of pretty packages tucked beneath its natural boughs. The sweet holiday smell of pine shouldn't have been diluted with the early scents of death anywhere, but especially not in Sleeping Bear.

"Cindy, let me call you back." He hung up on her despite her protests and phoned the highway patrol. After demanding emergency assistance and a medical examiner he told the dispatcher the murders appeared to have just happened so every vehicle leaving Sleeping Bear should be pulled over and sight-searched.

". . . We're looking for a high-caliber weapon. Anyone with a pistol or rifle bigger than a twenty-two should be brought in for questioning . . . Yes, I'm aware it's still whitetail season and a deer hunter or two might be inconvenienced but that's their tough luck."

Myles hung up, sucked in a harried breath, and hit Cindy's number.

*"Sheriff Grange, what's wrong? Are my parents there or not?"*

"Are you still at the Pond Ranch?"

*"Yes, sir."*

"Bart Newly will be out to get you shortly. Stay there until he arrives."

Again he had to hang up on her, not able to make out half of what she was saying because her voice had raised an octave and she'd started screaming so fast her words were slurred together. He called Bart and broke the shocking news.

"If you don't have anyone to watch the bar you'll have to close down because I need your help, Bart. I want you to pick up Cindy at the party and take her to my office. Don't tell her what happened until you're positive you can keep her away from here because she sure as hell doesn't need to see this. Wait there until I call you. Meanwhile, call Al Pond and tell him to make sure she doesn't leave the ranch with anybody else."

*"He'll wanna know why, should I tell him?"*

"Yeah, but tell him to keep it to himself until I let him know otherwise. He's not to tell Cindy a goddamn thing. Get on it, Bart."

Myles switched off his cell phone and went through the house. Nothing looked like it had been disturbed, but only Cindy would know if anything had been taken. Once the bodies were removed he'd have Bart bring her over. Meanwhile, all he could do was wait for the DPS to arrive.

♦♦♦

Cindy had screamed, tore at her hair, and wailed as if being gutted by the sword of an avenging angel, sent by God to chastise her for the sinful deed of selling the playbook. This whole night had become an apocalyptic nightmare. First she lost Cooper, then some cold-blooded wacko, for reasons she couldn't begin to fathom, shot her parents—killing the two sweetest people that ever existed.

Bart Newly told her their bodies had been taken to the morgue in Amarillo and would remain there until a medical examiner released them. While driving her home he'd said the sheriff wanted her to go through everything in the house to see if anything had been taken.

Numbness set in along the way and she'd quit bawling, but the tears immediately returned upon seeing the taped outlines of her parents' bodies. Sheriff Grange introduced two men as officers with the Department of Public Safety. Another patrolman entered the room and called the sheriff aside.

Cindy couldn't make out what the man was whispering to

Myles but the sheriff's jaw dropped midway through the one-sided conversation. He turned to her when it ended.

"Something's come up and I have to leave, Cindy. I know this is hard, but please check the entire house and see if anything's missing. I'll be back as soon as I can."

Myles seemed to know something he didn't want to tell her. She didn't ask about it, scared shitless the information would also be hurtful to her, and she couldn't handle any more pain. Watching him walk out the door, Cindy wiped her eyes and tried to ignore the tape on the carpet, marking the spot where her mother drew her last breath. The patrolman who'd delivered the message stepped to the hall and waited with arms folded as she examined the living room.

"Anything missing?" he asked.

She shook her head and went to the kitchen. The killer hadn't taken anything from there either.

Except for the two horrible bloody sections of living room carpet everything on the first floor looked normal and nothing was missing. The patrolman followed her upstairs. She checked her parents' bedroom, the guestroom, the closets and bathrooms in each. Nothing amiss. The half bath and storage closet in the hallway appeared undisturbed as well. Lastly, she entered her room.

Cindy's jewelry box mocked her, for it contained the ill-gotten lucre that had destroyed her life. She didn't even want to touch it, much less look inside, so she'd put it off till last. Everything in her chest of drawers, vanity, hope chest, and closet was accounted for. Dreading having to lay eyes on that cursed cash, she begrudgingly crossed the room. The moment she opened the lid Cindy knew someone had rifled through it because she kept her jewelry in meticulous order. It took her a while to go through the disheveled mess the killer had made, but everything was still there. Heart pounding, she lifted the layered tray out of the box to check the bottom compartment, and screamed.

The killer took the five thousand dollars.

She threw the jewelry box against the wall—sending a combination of real and fake precious stones sprawling everywhere—and fell to her knees. "They were killed because of me! . . . I killed my parents, *I fucking killed my parents!!!* . . . Oh God, what have I done?!"

# 35

"WOW!" DARLENE'S HEAD SPUN WITH happiness. She could have kissed Delbert Hutch on his big ugly mouth for sharing such wonderful news with her. Cindy Shane had copied Cooper's playbook and sold it to the enemy. He'd never take that skank back in a million years.

Studying Cooper, she sipped beer while wondering if he'd lied about her being so many notches from the top of his totem pole in order to get even for her breaking up with him. It seemed a likely possibility since Cindy Shane didn't have anything on her. Cindy's boobs were a little bigger than hers but she was definitely prettier and after all, gentlemen preferred blondes.

Rex Winters said hello as he headed for the kegs, carrying two empty cups. He and most of the other older alumni had chosen to hang out where the food was. Rick had paired off with Delores Kaye, and they were dancing to a slow song emanating from the juke box. She found it ironic that it was Ricky Nelson singing *Lonesome Town*. Most of the tunes on there were classics from the late fifties and early sixties, the days Cooper's grandfather had grown up in. Al hadn't added many to the original collection. She'd like to hear some Nickelback or Cold Play.

Lyle Whitney asked her to dance but the song ended before they got to the cleared out area that served as the dance floor. The popular junior shrugged his shoulders and grinned apologetically.

She grabbed his hand as he started to walk off. "Let's

dance to the next one."

When the first chords of *Jailhouse Rock* blared out she shook her head. "Never mind, I'm not going to dance to that."

Laughing, he left in search of another partner to cut the rug with, and she made her way to Luther for a refill. The big Indian had busted her when she'd returned to the party, and forced her to hand over her spare car key because he'd been told she'd driven away. Now she had no choice but to spend the night on the ranch.

But that was all right, because she planned to entice Cooper into a second trip to his bedroom.

♦♦♦

The man driving the ambulance had cleaned his nose, a lady paramedic riding in back with them took care of Jetti's. Dearl feared the airbag might have broken hers, but with all the blood gone it looked good as new. They were sitting across from each other on gurneys with towels beneath their damp jeans. The paramedic—a robust blonde with a heart-shaped face—sat next to Jetti.

"I had such big plans for us tonight, Dearl, and they sure didn't include an ambulance ride to Amarillo."

"This wasn't exactly on my agenda either."

"A car wreck is no way to celebrate winning State," the paramedic sympathized, adjusting her smock.

Jetti turned to her and made a face. "It sure isn't."

"My alma mater has certainly had its share of championships."

"Where'd you go to school?" Dearl asked.

"Promise you'll still speak to me after I tell you?"

He grinned. "Don't tell me you went to Langton."

"Yep. I grew up there."

"Damn, Jetti, and we're trusting her with our lives?"

The paramedic laughed, along with Jetti.

"Actually, Langton and Sleeping Bear didn't have much of a rivalry back when I was in high school. Our mortal enemy was the Hitchcock Hogs and you guys hated Seagraves in those days. Back then they were all classified as One-A rather than Two-A schools. That was long before six man football was named One-A."

Dearl recalled Kelly saying how bad that loss to them hurt. "Jetti's father played Seagraves for regional and lost by a point. Until this year, it was the furthest Sleeping Bear had ever gotten in the playoffs."

"How wild," said the paramedic, grinning with astonishment. "I was at that game, believe it or not—my cousin was Seagraves' starting center. The Kodiaks had an amazing fullback, and everybody rooting for the Eagles was afraid he was going to beat them all by himself."

"Wow, that was my daddy!" Jetti gushed.

"You don't say? Well he was something, let me tell ya." She winked at him. "Just like you were today."

"You were at the game?"

"I sure was, Mister MVP."

"How'd you know that was me?"

"Anyone associated with Langton that gives a hang about football knows who Dearl Tipps is, believe me."

Jetti frowned at her. "You drive all the way from Langton to Amarillo to work each day?"

"Oh heavens no, it's a three and a half hour drive. I live in Amarillo now, but I never miss a Lions playoff game. That's why I'm working the late shift tonight, so I could watch the championship. I'm normally part of the morning crew."

Dearl's nose started itching. He stood up and turned

around so the girls couldn't see him pick it—dug a crust of dried blood from his right nostril—wiped it off on an edge of the towel, and sat back down. "Sheriff Grange said that deranged driver that tried to kill us was from Langton."

"How well I know. That was Dick Parsons, the Lions' defensive coordinator."

Jetti's face turned pale. "He must have known you were in the car and tried to kill you, Dearl."

"There's no way he could have known who was in the car. Something made his mind snap and he wanted to do himself in. Why he wanted to take someone else down with him, I don't know."

"Don't be so quick to judge," the paramedic admonished. "He probably had a heart attack. This type of thing happens more than people realize."

"No, he swerved into our lane and drove steady as a rock, heading straight for us, and when Jetti took the other lane he did the exact same thing. He was suicidal, I'd bet any amount of money on it."

"Me too," Jetti testified, nodding.

"Well the main thing is you two are okay. What does your father do, Jetti?"

"He's the foreman of the Pond Ranch."

"Al Pond's top dog? Well I'm impressed, he must be quite a cowboy."

Dearl resisted the urge to tell her he was Al's son, fearing it would come off braggadocios. Jetti's wet blouse clung to her boobs, making them look more enticing than ever, and they'd held his attention so much he hadn't bothered reading the paramedic's name tag until now. "I see you're Lucy Higgins. You wouldn't happen to be related to—"

"Kenny's my nephew," she knowingly interrupted. "I married his Uncle Weldon right out of high school."

The sick feeling over what he'd done to the linebacker

overwhelmed him again.

"Oh wipe that sad look off your face," she demanded. "I know dirty football when I see it, and you're no dirty player."

Dearl swallowed hard and cleared his throat. "How is he?"

"He'll be holed up in a Lubbock hospital for several days but otherwise he'll be fine. The kid's tougher than nails."

"Tell me about it," he said with a weak grin. "Where's Kenny planning to go to college?"

"Texas."

That blew his mind and thoroughly excited him. "Did you hear that, Jetti?! Me and Kenny Higgins are both going to be Longhorns. Can you believe it?"

Jetti turned pale again. "That means you'll be practicing against each other, Dearl. What if he tries to get even?"

"Kenny's no dirty player either," Lucy informed Jetti. "With him and your boyfriend on the same team, I don't see how a national championship is avoidable."

"National championship," he muttered. "Wouldn't that be something, Jetti?"

"Oh I've already got my heart set on a super bowl ring, Dearl."

A shiver of elation ran through him. He'd been so focused on winning State he hadn't given any thought to college or professional goals other than fighting for the first string tailback slot. Football had just became his whole life again, other than the beautiful girl beaming at him of course.

◆◆◆

Kelly reached for Eli's Budweiser cup to take with his own for a refill but got waved off.

"No more beer for me tonight, I have to drive."

Rex figured he'd better let this one be his last as well for the same reason. The Raineys left twenty minutes ago and the crowd of older Kodiaks had grown sparse. He looked across the table at Anita, who'd switched to coffee. "Where are you and Kelly staying tonight?"

"At the motel I guess."

"You're welcome to spend the night at my place if you'd like."

"No they're not!" Emma belted, winking at Anita. "You understand I'm sure."

"Of course I do."

He scratched his head. "Well would you please explain it to me?"

"Emma doesn't want anyone in her love nest tonight except you, dummy. Kelly and I will be fine, but thanks for the offer."

Zechariah came into the room and headed for their table, looking depressed. A glance at Emma made his countenance fall even further. He sat down in Kelly's empty chair and heaved a sigh. "Rex, I have good news for you and Emma."

"Well you're sure not acting like it."

"I'd be lying if I said I was in good spirits but I'm not down because of the message the Lord wants me to pass on. He wants the two of you to know that your son will be here in about nine months time."

"Say what?!" Emma's sculpted brows were arcing like two crimson rainbows.

Anita giggled. "That's the news Kelly told you about earlier."

Rex nearly keeled over. He'd never wanted kids, but to hear he was going to have a son sent a different type of thrill through him than he'd ever known. "Imagine that . . . Kelly and I are going to raise two little Kodiaks the same age."

"No son of mine is playing football, Rex Winters—no way.

Zechariah, am I to gather I'm already pregnant?"

"A fertilized ovum is journeying to your uterus as we speak, Emma."

"Oh gawd!"

"What's the matter, don't you want to bear my son?"

"Of course I do, Rex."

"Then what's wrong?"

"What's wrong?!" she incredulously snapped as if only an idiot wouldn't know. "I'll have to give up me bloody fags, that's what."

♦♦♦

Zechariah had meant to tell Emma and Rex earlier but got sidetracked by Cindy Shane's murky situation. Then he'd caught up on the chore Luther gave him to do, wanting to get that out of the way first, hoping for a chance to visit with Eli after fulfilling his commission from the Lord to inform the newly betrothed couple they'd soon be parents.

He'd get that opportunity all right, just not the way he wanted. His heart had grown heavier with each passing minute after receiving the latest message from God.

# 36

THE EMERGENCY ROOM DOCTOR DIDN'T find any internal damage so they were released from the hospital. Lucy Higgins offered to drive them back to Sleeping Bear when her shift ended.

"Thanks," said Jetti, "but that won't be necessary."

Dearl started to protest but Jetti winked at him to convey she had something up her sleeve, so he kept his mouth shut.

Once they were alone she explained her plan and he agreed, wholeheartedly. Jetti paid the cab driver cash but covered the motel expense with a credit card.

When they got to their room he said, "How are you going to explain this to Gwendolyn when she gets the bill?"

Grinning, she set her purse on the chest of drawers and pulled out her cell phone. "You'll see."

She told Gwendolyn about the accident, listened to her grandma's response, and said, "The paramedics took us to Amarillo for x-rays. We're both fine but they won't be able to drive us back to Sleeping Bear for several hours. It's too dangerous for you to come pick us up with the rain and all, Grandma, so I think I should get us a motel room for the night."

He winced, certain Jetti was about to get reamed.

"Why rent two rooms, it's a waste of money and I'd be scared all by myself, Grandma. I'll just get one with two beds . . . Look, being alone with Dearl in a motel room is no different than being alone with him at his house—can't you see that? . . . Good. I think it's the best thing to do under the circumstances too . . . We'll get Cooper to come get us tomorrow after the storm passes or stay another night if it doesn't . . . We will, love you too."

"We will what?" he asked as she stashed her phone.

Jetti gave him a sexy smile and started unbuttoning her blouse. "Behave . . . ."

Dearl stood in a surreal daze as she pulled off her bra, exposing the large breasts that had tantalized yet frightened him for so long. Her pretty pink nipples jiggled as she undid her jeans and stepped out of them. When she slid her panties down, the sight of her dark bush ignited a fire inside that compelled him to also get naked—as fast as possible.

His hard on embarrassed him so he refused to look down, but Jetti's eyes were glued to it. The blaze in them, and slackness of her mouth, turned him on all the more.

At length she started eyeing him from shoulders to toes, over and over, as if appraising the worth of statue. "Oh, Dearl . . . your body is *so* beautiful."

Hers intoxicated him.

"I love you with all my heart and every fiber of my being, Dearl Virgil."

"I love you more, Jetti. You're the most gorgeous woman I've ever seen." He swept her off her feet and cradled her in his arms while stepping to the bed. Still holding her, he said, "I've been scared of you since our freshman year—afraid you'd bust me up inside if I gave you half a chance. Promise you'll never leave me."

Her magnetic eyes burned through him like laser beams. "I'm yours for life, baby. Now lay me down and make love to me."

She begged him not to put the condom on but he didn't want to risk getting her pregnant until he could provide for his family properly, so he rolled it down his penis per Cooper's instructions. He'd taken eight of them from Coo's stash, not knowing how many encores they might want to have, sticking two in each front and back pocket of his jeans.

Jetti lay before him with legs spread, arms reaching, lips parted. Cooper warned him to be gentle as possible the first time because it would hurt her initially, then added: "But you won't be able to hold out anyway so that'll all be over with in a flash, then you can regroup and really start to have fun."

Slowly he lowered himself over his fiancé and penetrated. He'd never felt anything so pleasurable and ejaculated immediately, but Jetti yelped with pain. Carefully easing himself out of her, he rolled over on his back. "Promise I'll do better next time."

She snuggled against him. "Oh Dearl, we finally made love."

"Yeah . . . man that felt wonderful."

"Well it felt awful to me, just like Grandma said it would."

He frowned at her. "You told Gwendolyn we were going to do it?"

Giggling, she pulled his face to hers. "No, silly. She told me that when she gave me my sex talk after I had my first period."

Reaching for a boob, he squeezed it tenderly and gave her a quick kiss. "Well Cooper gave me my sex talk tonight. According to him, I'll find a spot with my finger somewhere inside you that'll really make you feel good."

Jetti grabbed his hand and shoved it between her legs. "Well get to searching, baby . . . ."

Her vaginal canal clamped down on his finger when he began rotating it round and round like Cooper told him to.

"Oh you found it! Finger me upwards, Dearl—hard! Oh yeah, baby . . . oh yeah, don't stop, don't stop . . . yes, yes . . . *oh Dearl!*"

Arching her back, fiercely grimacing—she kept gasping,

sharp and loud. Then suddenly she grabbed his hand again, this time to make him stop, and went limp all over as her face relaxed with a sluggish smile. "My first orgasm . . . Oh what a special night this is, Dearl."

♦♦♦

Myles had left the Shane residence when the patrolman whispered that a man in Langton had just been found murdered in the same manner as Cindy's parents. He'd driven to his office and faxed the Langton sheriff pictures of everything he'd found on Parsons, including the rifle.

Now he was back, and wanted to slap the shit out of the bitch despite the fact she seemed to be mentally whipping herself severely enough for the two of them. Cindy's eyes were two watery pools of hopelessness and regret. The tale she'd told him boggled his mind but there was no doubt Will Amarod and her parents had been murdered because of what she'd done. He'd told the Langton sheriff about Dick Parsons' apparent suicide, and learned Parsons was the Lions' defensive coordinator. The Amarillo police department would have to confirm him as the killer through ballistics, but that was a mere formality at this point.

Dick Parsons murdered the man who'd sold him the playbook, and the parents of the teenage scum that set the wheels in motion. Then Parsons attempted to commit vehicular homicide at the cost of his own life. Myles wondered if the bastard had tried to get even with Dearl for being the spearhead that thwarted a fourth straight championship for Langton, but couldn't figure out how Parsons could possibly know Dearl was in Rutherford Simmons' car.

He looked across the bedroom at Cindy, sitting slump-shouldered on the floor amidst her scattered jewelry, repeatedly moaning she wanted to kill herself. A part of him was tempted to help her accomplish that.

"Let's go, Cindy. I'm putting you in jail for your own protection. We'll get a psychiatrist to check you out and take it from there."

♦♦♦

"Where's Dearl and Jetti?" Darlene asked, trying to make small talk with Cooper rather than really wondering about the lovebirds. She figured they'd slipped away to Dearl's house and were bopping each other's brains out.

"They went for a romantic drive in the rain," he answered, wearing his magic smile.

She snickered. "Yeah, right."

"Oh ye of dirty mindedness."

"Takes one to know one."

The smile vanished. "Don't think you're getting anywhere with this, Darlene. Like I told you, you're just not quite the woman I'm looking for."

His jab hurt but she tried to hide it behind a flirtatious grin. "I lied about the reason I broke up with you. Wanna hear what really made me do it?"

He took a sip of beer instead of answering but she could tell he wanted to know.

"Fine, I won't tell you then . . ." she raised her own cup to her mouth.

"Suit yourself." He turned to Delbert. "Say Hutch, you still planning on OU?"

Delbert nodded.

"Man it'll sure feel weird when Dearl and I have to kick some Sooner butt with you on the enemy's side."

"Got it backwards there, Pond—it'll be me kicking your butts."

Cooper winked at him. "Let not he that puts on his armor boast as he who removes it."

"What, you talking Bible to me, man?"

"Sure am. Been learning it from Zechariah."

Rick grinned at Cooper. "The only Bible I know is that piece in the Song of Solomon where the gal claims her tits are like towers."

Delbert cackled. "Just like you to recall only a dirty part of the good book, Holt. Typical of a lowlife Red Raider."

"It's been quite a ride, hasn't it, guys?" Rick guzzled some Budweiser.

"Sure has," Delbert agreed. "Now we'll be going our separate ways after graduation."

"Except for the brothers Pond," said Rick. "Is Dearl going to change his last name?"

"Nah, he's sticking with Tipps. Sure wish you guys were going to Austin with us."

"It would be nice," Delbert said, "but I want the ball more and they plan to use me as a tailback instead of a fullback. The best I could hope for at Texas is being Tipps' backup. I've got a much better chance of starting at Oklahoma just like Rick has a better shot at getting on the field at Tech."

Cooper sighed. "Dearl will be starting right off, no doubt, but it'll be an uphill battle all the way for me to get on the first string offense. Figure I'll be wearing a sweat-free game uniform for some time."

Rick raised his cup. "Well here's to us all making first string our freshman year in college like we did in high school."

Darlene felt tears coming. It had been such a pleasure

cheering for the four stars, the thought of them never playing together again broke her heart. If her plan didn't succeed she'd be off to Waco at summer's end to become a Baylor Bear, but she hoped to lasso Cooper and continue rooting for him and Dearl as a Longhorn. The competition would be stiff but she'd try out for cheerleader either way.

Delbert asked where she planned to earn her degree.

"My dad wants me to go to Baylor like he did, but I'm undecided about whether to go there or another school I have in mind."

Cooper narrowed his eyes. "Let me guess, the other's Texas."

"Yep."

"Why not Tech instead?" the love machine asked. "It's much closer to home."

Rick grinned at her. "Because that's where I'm going, and Darlene's had enough of me."

"You know that's not true. You and I will always be friends as far as I'm concerned."

"Here, here," Rick replied, tapping her cup with his.

Pretending to listen as the guys talked football, she began formulating a plan to lure Cooper to his bedroom.

◆◆◆

They were engaged and Dearl had deflowered her, making her dreams finally come true. They'd made love two more times afterwards and he'd improved with each performance. Their last go-round hadn't hurt at all, and almost felt pleasant to her. After that he'd brought her to a second orgasm using his tongue. She'd wanted to catapult him to the same oral heaven but he'd fallen asleep.

Jetti wondered if she could possibly ever feel this happy again. Not only did she have Dearl all to herself, at long last she knew who her father was and he'd soon be marrying her mother who'd given up prostitution. A baby brother had been conceived and the Sleeping Bear Kodiaks were State Champs.

If only Dearl and Cooper would forgive Cindy, everything would be perfect. She hadn't brought up the subject again because it had almost spoiled the night, and most likely would have if the wreck hadn't happened. They'd been heading for town when Dick Parsons rammed them.

Pissed at her for taking Cindy's side, Dearl had demanded she turn around and head back to the ranch. The side of the highway had been too muddy to attempt it without getting stuck, so she'd told him he'd have to wait until they got to the outskirts of Sleeping Bear. Ironically, if she'd been able to make that u-turn they'd have been on the ranch road by the time Parsons got that far down the highway—the wreck wouldn't have happened and she wouldn't be lying beside her man in an Amarillo motel room.

Gazing at him as he lay sleeping, she had but one regret about their lovemaking, those despicable condoms. "How many damn rubbers did you bring?" she'd asked when he'd pulled a third one from his pants despite her begging him not to.

He had five left. Jetti wanted to flush them down the toilet so he'd have no choice but to allow her the pleasure of feeling his penis inside her flesh-to-flesh, and the gush of his hot semen. But she dared not do it because he might refuse to make love in the morning without one.

◆◆◆

She'd been introduced to Luther's new helper Zechariah and laughed over Cooper saying he was a prophet. When Luther swore he was too, she'd flipped. Now she lay on her side in Cooper's bed, naked and staring into darkness. The evenness of the state champ's breathing revealed he'd fallen asleep.

Delores had never been in this room before tonight, and her thoughts were tortured over the possibility of being a mere rebound. "Yes," she'd answered immediately when he'd asked her to go with him in the game room as they danced to a slow song sang by some guy named Slim Whitman. Luther had informed her of that when they'd refilled their Budweiser cups afterwards. Fifteen minutes later they were in here, quickly undressing.

He'd made her promise to be true to him while he was away at college next year. After swearing she would, he made love to her, and she'd been disappointed to discover that Rick Holt, who'd gotten the love machine's permission to use his room, was no Cooper Pond.

♦♦♦

Myles drove to the Pond Ranch and asked to speak with Al alone.

Al made sure all the ice chests were locked and took him to his study.

"Did you keep all this shit to yourself like Bart damn well have better told you to?" he said after filling Al in on Dick Parsons being the killer.

"Yeah, Myles."

"Good. I don't see any reason we should spoil the night for everybody so I plan to sit on it until tomorrow."

"Good idea," said Al. "I especially don't want Cooper to know. Where's Cindy?"

"Locked up in a cell. She was threatening to kill herself over being the reason her parents got murdered. I'm not letting her go until a psychiatrist assures me she won't go through with it."

"Oh boy . . ." Al shook his head, eyes weary and downcast. "This is all too unbelievable."

"I know. Well I'm gonna help myself to some of your party grub and get back on patrol . . . ."

After making his rounds in town he drove to the jailhouse to check on Cindy. The frantic sobs he'd heard until closing the front door of the jailhouse behind him when leaving forty minutes ago had stopped. He'd left the lights on in lockup but hoped she'd fallen asleep despite the glare.

Quietly he opened the access door and entered the cell area.

"Shit, Cindy!" He ran to her and put a hand on her neck.

No pulse.

She'd rolled up her bra like a rope, tied it around the lock of the cell door, and hung herself.

Five people were now dead because of a fucking stolen playbook—the asshole who'd bought it, the man who'd handed it to him, the parents of the one who'd set the wheels in motion, and the girl herself.

With hands behind her back, she'd forced them through one of the sleeves of her t-shirt past her wrists to keep instinct from forcing her arms to thwart her grim pursuit—apparently after she'd gotten the lethal brassiere situated in front of her throat—then she'd kicked her legs straight back.

Cindy Shane died with only the top of her shoes touching the cement floor, the nipples of her big tits pointing directly at it.

"Not tonight," Myles bleakly muttered, "not tonight,

goddammit. Nobody in Sleeping Bear is going to hear about this until tomorrow either, not even Bart or Al."

He called the medical examiner, who'd given him his card at the Shane residence, and told him to get his butt to the Sleeping Bear jail pronto.

# 37

AL HAD TOLD ELI TO pull under the carport jutting out from the kitchen so they wouldn't get soaked while loading. Al, Cooper, Luther, Kelly, Anita, Rex, and Emma all wore the same sad look on their faces. Goodbyes had been said and it was time to depart.

Looking down at his knapsack, holster belt, canteen, and a suitcase containing the clothes Al had bought him, Zechariah closed the trunk and got in the Cadillac.

The celebration party hadn't ended but his time on the Pond Ranch had. His surmising that he'd get to stay on it until Dearl retired from the NFL had turned out to be wishful thinking. The word he'd received before telling Rex and Emma about their baby was that his mission in Sleeping Bear had been fulfilled and he had to leave with Eli. He wouldn't be returning to these parts again until the time came to anoint Dearl to take his place.

God had lured Eli here through Anita for this very purpose. *I have need of you elsewhere,* the Lord had said. The *elsewhere* turned out to mean many places. He'd been commissioned to convince all the important people Eli knew that the Great Falling Away from revealed truth was no longer a future dread but a present reality, and without wholesale repentance the end times would surely occur before this generation passed.

When the day came for him to lay hands on Dearl and pour the olive oil on him, the Lord would be requiring his spirit. His earthly sojourn, that began with Noah Adams, would end in the presence of Eli Adams.

Tears filled his eyes as he waved. The two women were crying and so was Cooper. He hated not getting to say farewell to Dearl and Jetti but they never came back after going for that drive.

Eli pulled into the rain and Zechariah forced his eyes forward. Lightning flashed and he spotted Tornado Hill in the distance. When darkness reacquired the red marvel, he sighed and turned to his chauffeur. "So you don't believe God speaks to me, huh? Well, Eli, how is it I know . . .?"

# About the Author

Arley Owens, Jr. is a musician, vocalist, composer, poet, author, editor, producer, and rancher. A native Texan, he resides on his ranch in Midland County with his lovely wife Cristi, also born and raised in Texas. He's a member of the musical group TORN PAGE.

Website:
http://www.tornpageband.com

## Other books by Arley Owens, Jr.
A Tale of the Mojave
The Cyrus Syndrome
A Texas Ghost Story
Incident in Baltimore
Death Ranch
20 Miles to Justified
The Genocide Directive

**READ ARLEY OWENS, JR. ON YOUR KINDLE:**
http://www.amazon.com/author/arleyowens

SHORTY MAE PRODUCTIONS
P.O. BOX 81102
MIDLAND, TEXAS 79708